BAD BLOOD

Mark Sennen was born in Epsom, Surrey and later spent his teenage years on a smallholding in Shropshire. He attended the University of Birmingham and read Cultural Studies at CCCS. Mark has had a number of occupations, being variously a farmer, drummer and programmer. Now his hi-tech web developer's suite, otherwise known as a shed in the garden, has been converted to a writer's den and he writes almost full-time.

Please visit www.marksennen.com for information on the DI Charlotte Savage series.

Also by Mark Sennen

Touch

MARK SENNEN

Bad Blood

AVON

AVON

A division of HarperCollins*Publishers*
77–85 Fulham Palace Road,
London W6 8JB

www.harpercollins.co.uk

A Paperback Original 2013

1

Copyright © Mark Sennen 2013

Mark Sennen asserts the moral right to
be identified as the author of this work

A catalogue record for this book is
available from the British Library

ISBN-13: 978-0-00-751816-6

Set in Minion by Palimpsest Book Production Limited,
Falkirk, Stirlingshire

Printed and bound in Great Britain by
Clays Ltd, St Ives plc

MIX
Paper from
responsible sources
FSC **FSC® C007454**
www.fsc.org

Acknowledgements:

A number of people helped me navigate to this point. To everyone involved, I'm very grateful.

Special thanks to: my agent, Claire Roberts. She's unfailingly cheerful and does what all agents should do – laugh at an author's jokes; to my editors at HarperCollins/Avon, Caroline Hogg and Lydia Newhouse. To use a footballing analogy, Caroline provided a perfectly weighted pass into the box and Lydia slotted the ball home for the winning goal; to the rest of the hard-working team at Avon, especially Claire Bord who has left to do something much more exciting and demanding (twins, in case you are wondering). Without Claire, DI Savage might never have made it into print.

Friends from worlds both real and virtual provided help and distraction in equal measure (without you lot I'd probably have written the book in half the time!). And, as always, my wife and daughters were supportive and my parents encouraging. Thank you all.

Finally, the biggest shout-out must go to you, the reader. Without the complimentary reviews, emails and tweets, and the knowledge so many people enjoy reading about Charlotte and want more, *Bad Blood* may never have seen the light of day.

For Gitte. Thank you!

Prologue

The pain always came when Ricky Budgeon least expected it. Right now a wave swept from within and hit him between the eyes like a needle pushing hard into the bridge of his nose. He put his hands up and gripped his scalp, pulling and clawing at the burning sensation which spread across his forehead to his temples. The last attack had had him writhing on the floor, but this time the jabbing ceased after a few seconds and he merely needed to steady himself. He moved his hands from his head, clasped them tight around the cool metal bar of the gate, and stared across the field into the night.

A scan had showed nothing but the old scarring, afterwards the doctor muttering reassuring words about migraine and mentioning therapy, maybe acupuncture.

Crap.

The idiots must have missed whatever was in there that was causing him such misery. Some sort of mutation of the cells, a cancer or a tumour, the latter growing fat on bad memories, enmity and bitterness.

When the doctor disagreed with his self-diagnosis and said surgery was out of the question he'd thought of taking a drill to his own skull, imagined placing the bit against his head and pressing the trigger. The whine of the motor would come first, followed by agony as the drill ripped into skin and bone. Then the spinning metal would seek out the tumour and chew it to a pulp. The pain would be gone forever. He had even gone so far as to go to his workshop and set up the equipment. With the drill in its stand all he had to do was press the switch, put his head beneath the bit and pull down on the lever. Eventually he had decided against it. Whatever the thing was inside his head frightened him, but it motivated him too. Remove the pain, and what would drive him forwards?

Budgeon stood in the darkness, gulping air and then biting his lip until he tasted blood. The throbbing in his head subsided and ebbed away. He bent and picked up his fag: a half-smoked roll-up, dropped as the agony had come on. Drawing on the cigarette, he looked out again and took in the landscape spread before him.

Close at hand, the hedges and trees appeared black against the sky. In a nearby field, the occasional sheep bleated, and from a copse off to his right the hoot of an owl rang out. But beyond the empty countryside lay the city, a corona of brightness where a thousand glittering lights promised excitement and danger, their individual pinpricks of heat coalescing like a mass of stars at the centre of a distant galaxy. Moving outward from the core, white dots crawled between avenues of static orange; cars heading for the soft radiance of the suburbs and home.

A twinge in his forehead caused him to screw his eyes shut.

Home.

He opened his eyes again and took another drag from the roll-up, pinching the end between the tips of his thumb and forefinger so he could extract every last piece of worth without burning himself. The way he had smoked in prison.

Years ago, before he had gone down, he'd had friends in the city. Friends who'd grown up on the same street as him. As kids they'd pinched sweets from the same shop and sworn at the same old ladies whose flowerbeds they trampled across. Later on, as young men, they'd thrown bricks at the same police cars, shared the same prison cells and sworn vengeance on the same enemies. They'd been like brothers, the three of them. Blood brothers.

Those days seemed so long ago now. As if someone else had lived the time for him.

Budgeon took a final drag from his fag and then dropped the butt to the floor, stamping the orange glow into the mud.

Everything had been fine until *she* came along.

Why did it always come down to a woman? Almost biblical. Garden of fucking Eden and all that shit.

In the end, he had been the lucky one, sliding around on silk sheets, relishing how sweet she tasted, promising her everything. But afterwards, as they shared a cigarette, he realised things weren't going to be the same. Not with the others wanting her too.

He shook his head and took one last look at the distant lights, before moving back to the van and clambering in. The thin, pale man in the driver's seat grunted and asked him if he was ready to go.

Was he? Peering down on the city and reminiscing about his childhood, thinking about the group of them as little boys, without a care in the world, had made him reconsider for a moment. Now, as the warmth of the van slipped around him, he felt cocooned and cut off from everything but those memories. He could easily get misty-eyed again. Half a lifetime later perhaps it was time to forgive and forget, move on.

An ache flickered across his brow.

No, life didn't reward that kind of thinking. He'd gone soft over the girl and when his guard had been down he'd been betrayed. There were rules, unwritten maybe, but rules all the same. If you broke them, you paid; and some debts took more than money to settle.

Much more.

Of course he was ready to go. And the sooner they got the show on the road, the better.

Chapter One

The noise carried through to Savage in the kitchen. Laughter. Samantha and Jamie's high-pitched squeals layered over her husband's voice as he sang an inane song in a mock-Swedish accent. The cause of the frivolity was Stefan, the family's unofficial au pair, who had just returned from his home country laden with chocolates for the kids and two matching sets of stupid-looking knitted gloves and hats for Savage and Pete. Pete had shoved the hat down on his head, pointed out the window at the daffodils in the garden, and teased Stefan about being a little late with the winter gear. Stefan responded in kind, putting on a thick West Country drawl, muttering something about pilchards.

Savage had retreated to the kitchen to make a pot of tea, thinking Pete was right about the change of season. Mid-January, Christmas not much more than a few weeks ago, and already the east side of their garden a swath of gold, ochre and lemon. Other changes too: Pete returning from deployment at the back end of November, after nearly nine months away.

The celebrations had run on into the Christmas period, resulting in one long spell of parties, relatives, more parties

5

and more relatives. Now the holiday season was over Savage was pleased for life to settle down a little. Pleased too that spring had arrived early in Devon. The forecasters had spoken of a hard winter, but despite some snow in November, so far they had got it wrong. Out of the kitchen window the sun hung low in the sky, a cool yellow rather than the deep red of a summer sunset. Below the sun the Sound lay placid, only a hint of a swell disturbing the surface. A yacht, black against the light, motored in past the eastern end of the breakwater. The crew on the yacht waved to a trio of dinghy sailors struggling to catch a zephyr to take them home before the chill of nightfall. Last night the frost had returned, but the first two weeks of January had been unseasonably warm, pushing the temperatures close to the mid-teens. Weather more suited to t-shirts than to a gift of hats and gloves.

A couple of days earlier Savage had received an altogether different type of Christmas present. One of the best ever, although Pete hadn't seen it that way. He told her in the kitchen, as she prepared a pizza, her hands floured with dough. The news stunned her and she could hardly take his words in.

'Scrapped?' she asked.

'Yes,' Pete said. 'Decommissioned. Mothballed. Sold off. Cut up and made into ploughshares for all I know. Seems as if I'm to be based ashore now. For good. Bloody stupid cuts.' Pete's face looked ashen and his eyes brimmed with emotion.

'I'm sorry.' Even as she said the words she knew she wasn't. Pete might be losing his ship but for the past fifteen years and more she had lost her husband – and the kids their dad – for months and months on end. It wasn't as if she hadn't known what she was getting herself into when they got married, but back then heart very definitely ruled head, and the day-to-day practicalities of juggling a job and young children appeared to be years off. Pretty soon though, the twins, Samantha and Clarissa, had come along, unplanned, and in her mid-twenties she'd found herself with two babies and an absent father. Later she'd had Jamie and then the tragedy of Clarissa's death to cope with, Pete around for what seemed like mere fleeting moments.

'You're not,' Pete said.

'No.' Savage moved over and hugged him, pressing her face into his neck and kissing him, aware of her floury hands making prints on his jumper. 'I'm sad for you, of course, sad for your crew too, but I'm not sorry. Have you known long?'

'Before the last voyage I got an inkling of what might happen. At least the old girl went on a grand final trip.'

Pete had taken the frigate on a circumnavigation of South America, cruising down to the Falklands, through the Straits of Magellan and up the Pacific coast of Chile, using the Panama Canal to get back to the Atlantic. Before that the ship had been on patrol in the Gulf and seen action in Pirate Alley. As with every warship returning to Devonport after active service, she had steamed into the Sound to a hero's welcome, although one unnoticed by anyone living outside the city.

Now, as Savage poured water into the big blue teapot, she felt a warmth from knowing Pete would be in Plymouth and bound to a desk for the foreseeable future. With a more normal job perhaps they could have some sort of existence like a normal family. For years she'd coped on her own, but combining her job and home life was almost impossible. Having her and Pete's parents living close by helped, and more recently they'd employed Stefan. It still wasn't easy though, and with Jamie being six and Samantha thirteen, there was hardly ever a time when she could relax.

The steam from the pot curled upwards and she chinked the lid in place, watching the final wisp of vapour dissipate, along with her thoughts, as the phone rang. DC Patrick Enders calling from Major Crimes.

'Don't you ever have days off, Patrick?' Savage said.

'It's the overtime, ma'am. Worth its weight. If there's any available I snap it up. I can always take a day off in the week when the kids are at school. So much more peaceful.'

Enders was late twenties, already with three children and a mortgage and designs on a four-bedroomed place in Mannamead where his family could spread out. But then, Savage thought, when she'd been that age she'd had the same aspirations. When the twins were born, she and Pete had been lucky enough to find a large wreck of a house on the coast, before prices sky rocketed and such properties became unaffordable to all but the very few.

'Well, what can I do for you?' Savage said. 'I'm just about to sit down with my own kids and have cake and tea so you had better not have something for me.'

'No, just a reminder, ma'am. The DSupt says not to forget about the *Sternway* meeting tomorrow. He's sending you a bunch of stuff, so check your email.'

'Great,' Savage said, without much enthusiasm. She already had a mountain of papers to read concerning Operation *Sternway* – the force's long-term drugs operation – but she promised Enders she would check her email, hung up, and gave a silent 'thank you' that she didn't have to rush out. The irony, given her recent talk to Pete about how much his job had taken over his life, wouldn't be welcomed.

The call from Enders reminded her there was other paperwork to complete too: notes for an upcoming PSD inquiry.

The Professional Standards Department wanted to know why she had left the scene of a car accident in which a man had been killed. No matter that the man had been a serial killer who had tried to abduct her own daughter Samantha, Standards wanted answers. Over Christmas and New Year she had pushed all thoughts of the inquiry to the back of her mind, but now, with the interview looming, she knew she needed to spend time preparing.

Savage sighed and then went back to the living room, to find Stefan teaching the kids some toilet humour. The scatological references sounded twice as funny in Swedish and soon all five of them were conversing in a mixture of languages, interspersed with prolonged periods of giggling. Savage turned from the mayhem and looked out through the big window. Shadows crept across the lawn, painting black shapes on the grass which glistened with silver moisture in the fading light. Beyond the garden, the cliff fell away to a mirror which stretched to the horizon where the sun was just kissing the sea, somewhere out past Edison Rocks. Sunday afternoon bliss.

Chapter Two

On any other Monday, the three builders cradling mugs of steaming tea and sitting on the low brick wall outside seventy-five Lester Close might well have been discussing the weekend's footie. Plymouth had gone down three-nil at home and the handful of points the team had collected in their last ten games wasn't enough to appease the fans. A demo had been arranged and there were calls to sack the manager, the players, the board, the boot boy, anyone who could conceivably be to blame for the team's recent abject performance.

On any other Monday.

Jed Rammel was the oldest of the three – twenty years the oldest – and he'd never seen anything like it. Except, of course, when he'd been over in Iraq, but that was different. You expected things like that there. Not here, not on a Monday morning when all you'd come to do was dig up somebody's back yard to put some concrete footings in, preparatory work for a new conservatory. Jed guessed the owner would be cancelling the work now. Nobody in their right mind would want to be sitting out the back any more. Lying bathed in sunlight, relaxing, dreaming, and sipping a beer. Thinking about what had once been buried there. Give over.

Jed scratched his head, slurped another gulp of tea, tried to forget the toothy smile showing from behind the dried-up lips, and those empty eye sockets which seemed to be staring right out at him.

They'd started that morning at seven-thirty, with barely enough light to work by. Carted picks, crowbars, sledgehammers and shovels round the back. Jed had checked the instructions and marked out the limits of where they were to dig with lines of chalk powder and a couple of stakes. Young Ryan had first dibs, lifting the broken paving slabs with the edge of his pickaxe and then going ten-to-the-dozen with the crowbar on the old concrete beneath.

Youth, Jed had thought, all now-now-now, no care for the future. And so it proved. Ten minutes later and Ryan was knackered, so Jed and Barry took over, breaking the concrete while Ryan shovelled the residue out the way.

They'd found the bones of a small dog soon after. Nothing to get excited about, Jed said, even as Ryan began to lark around. The larking ended when they found the box nearby. Plastic, buried in the soil under the layer of concrete about two feet from the dog. Jed wondered if the thing wasn't some sort of drainage sump, but when they took off the lid and saw the contents they realised it wasn't. They'd thought the thing inside was a doll at first. A big doll, sure, but a doll nonetheless. Jed's granddaughter had one, a large, lifelike thing he and the wife had bought the kid the Christmas before last. But no, it wasn't a doll. They'd realised that when Ryan's spade pierced a hole in the chest where he poked it. Crackled like parchment the skin had, and through the split the three of them had seen the bones of the ribcage.

Definitely not a doll.

Jed sipped his tea again. Thought about Iraq. About things he'd never told his workmates, nor his wife. Things he'd only

11

shared with the men he'd served with. The type of horror he'd thought belonged thousands of miles away, in another country.

'Losing three-nil,' Ryan said. 'At home. You can hardly fucking believe it, can you?'

No, Jed thought, you couldn't.

Savage drove into the car park at Crownhill Police Station a little after eight fifty-five to see DC Jane Calter jogging over, her breath steaming out in the cold air. She pulled the passenger door open and collapsed in the front seat.

'Off to a property in Efford, ma'am. Right next to the cemetery. Handy, because there's a body under the patio. And I'm not joking. Wish I was.'

'Who's in charge?' Savage said.

'DCI Garrett.' Calter raised a hand and thumbed in the direction of the station. 'He's inside sorting things. We're to get over to the scene right away.'

'Right,' Savage said. 'You sure you're OK? You don't look so good.'

'Bad weekend, ma'am.'

'Oh?'

'Brilliant, I mean.' Calter pulled the sun visor down to shield her eyes from the glare as they headed back towards town, the sun still low in the south-east. 'Too much booze, not enough sleep. I never learn.'

The DC leant back in her seat and ran both hands through her blonde bob, pulling at a couple of tangles and squinting at the vanity mirror on the back of the visor.

'I barely managed a shower this morning, let alone a hair wash, and these clothes are the first ones that fell out of the wardrobe.' Calter indicated her rather crumpled grey skirt and jacket.

12

'I hope you didn't get into too much trouble.'

'No,' Calter grinned, 'unfortunately not. But I am seeing him again next week.'

As they drove to Efford Calter sat quietly, fumbling once in a pocket for some painkillers, dry-swallowing them and then closing her eyes. Only a dozen years or so difference in their respective ages, Savage thought, but Calter's lifestyle was a world away from her own. Not that she was beyond getting drunk herself, having a good time, partying – Christmas being a case in point. But there was always the knowledge that the next morning any hangover would be punctuated by a seven o'clock visit from Jamie wanting to be up and at the world, Samantha needing a lift somewhere, and Pete feigning his own hangover as near life-threatening.

Efford was an innocuous part of Plymouth sandwiched between the A38 and the Plym estuary. A mixture of older social housing, now mostly owner-occupied, and some newer but smaller properties, made the place out to be working class. Really though, Savage thought as they negotiated streets still busy with school-run traffic, you couldn't tell any more.

The web of crescents and avenues which made up the area was interspersed with plenty of green space, the largest being the twenty-acre cemetery which Lester Close backed on to. The close itself had been cordoned off, already a number of people hanging round the junction with the main road. Heads turned as Savage was waved through and drove into the close. The road rose in a gentle slope, the houses on each side post-war semi-detached, pebble-dashed, and featuring uPVC windows with net curtains. The front gardens, neat little patches of lawn, with a shrub or two for good measure.

'Pleasant,' Calter said, opening her eyes, 'but I'm more of a penthouse flat type of girl myself.'

13

'Rich, is he?'

'Forces.'

'Don't go there,' Savage said, smiling. 'And as you know I speak from experience.'

Calter laughed as they reached the far end of the narrow cul-de-sac, where a patrol car on the left hand side marked the property; a house in need of some TLC, the front garden full of clutter stripped from inside. Behind the patrol car a Volvo estate straddled the kerb, the rear door up, a jumble of plastic containers and toolboxes crammed in the back.

'Layton,' Savage said. 'The sooner he gets to a scene the happier he is.'

John Layton was their senior CSI and where crime scenes were concerned he could be labelled a misanthrope, believing only himself and his team had any right to be present and hating all other invaders. Especially interfering detectives. Savage got out and retrieved her protective clothing from the boot.

'You might as well start with them, Jane,' Savage said, pointing to the builders sitting on the front garden wall as she suited up. 'I'll risk Layton's wrath.'

At the house, the youngest of the builders nodded a greeting as Savage went down the passage to the side. The other two stared into their mugs, one of them shaking his head and muttering something under his breath.

Round the back, a patio stretched the width of the plot. Or rather, it once had, because one end was now a mass of broken slabs and concrete, the spoil from a large hole creeping across the postage-stamp-sized lawn beyond. Beside the hole, Layton and Andrew Nesbit, the pathologist, knelt, peering down into the mud. Layton stood up as Savage neared, tipped his battered Tilley back with the finger of a blue-gloved hand and pointed at the brown goo.

'Bloody mess.' Layton scratched his roman nose with the back of his hand and shook his head. 'Builders don't wear ballet shoes, do they?'

Nesbit glanced round and smiled, his eyes sparkling behind his half-round glasses. He raised his bushy eyebrows, looked at Layton and then turned back to the hole.

'Mondays, Charlotte,' he said. 'What is it about Mondays?'

Savage walked over and peered at the puddle forming down in the excavation, a grey sludge-like liquid which oozed from the surrounding soil.

'The thing on the right is a dog,' Layton said. 'The builders found the animal first. But that wasn't why they called us.'

Savage could see a set of tiny bones and a pointed skull. A leather collar had rotted to almost nothing but the buckle and a little brass name tag. Next to the skeleton, a large translucent plastic storage box, the kind you shoved under the bed or stacked up in the garage full of junk, lay close to the concrete foundations for the boundary wall. A snap-on lid concealed the contents, something pale and indistinct pushing up against one side, promising nightmares for weeks to come.

'According to the ID disc the dog's name is Florence,' Layton said. 'Don't know if she is named after the place or the character from the *Magic Roundabout*. Whatever, I'd say the animal was buried a good few years ago. The crate was probably only buried within the last few months.'

'The lid?' Savage asked.

'The builders removed the top of the box. I put it back so the photographer could take some pictures. Andrew?'

Nesbit reached down, long fingers inside his nitrile gloves feeling around the edge of the lid, clicking the plastic back, lifting it off.

Savage gasped at the tangle of flesh and bones inside, the

tiny hands clutching at a red house-brick, the torso curled round in the box, foetal-like. The child's skull had plenty of skin left on, hair twisted in long, curly strands, teeth bared in a mocking grin. The flesh on the limbs and body hung loose, looking stiff and like starched clothing or light brown paper. The child was naked, but there was a bundle of rags up one end of the box. That fact alone spoke volumes to Savage. It was unlikely this was a terrible accident, somebody trying to cover up an RTC for instance; not when the infant had been stripped. She considered the skin again, which was the colour and consistency of filo pastry. The corpse reminded her of mummies she had seen in a museum and she said as much.

'Desiccated,' Nesbit said. 'The body was kept somewhere hot and dry after death and that caused the effect you are looking at.'

'So how long?'

'Very difficult to know at this stage. Maybe we will find some entomology or something else organic to help us establish the time of death. All I can tell you for sure is that she was buried here a good while later.'

'She?' Nesbit's confirmation of the gender chilled Savage; not that 'he' would have been any less horrific. It was the fact an identity was now beginning to take form, a life created from the sad heap of skin and bone. Something solid to mourn over. Something solid to try and seek justice for. If possible.

'The hair looks like a girl's, and then there's that,' Nesbit pointed down to one side of the plastic box next to the rags. A patch of pink flashed out, vivid and incongruous alongside the bone and flesh. 'It's a trainer. I didn't want to disturb anything too much, but I managed to note the size. Twelve. Children's that is.'

Twelve. Which would mean the child would be half that:

five, six or seven. Savage peered down again at the body in its makeshift plastic coffin. Once the girl would have snuggled up to her mummy or daddy, perhaps clutched a teddy to her for comfort as she fell to dreaming. Now she only had a brick to cuddle.

'We'll move the box and all to Derriford,' Nesbit said, standing and nodding to the two mortuary technicians who had come round the corner of the house. 'It will save disturbing her. Better that way.'

'Yes, better,' Savage said, wondering how anything could be much worse.

When Savage went back round to the front of the house, she found Calter doing her best to intervene in an argument between one of the builders and a young man in a smart suit.

'Mr Evershed, ma'am,' Calter said, and then nodded to a little way down the road, where a heavily-pregnant woman was leaning against a big BMW with a high-end paint job and a massive spoiler on the rear. 'And his wife.'

Evershed couldn't have been more than early twenties. He had close-cropped dark hair and a brash suit with lapels which were too wide. His wrist bore a chunky watch, gold like his cufflinks. He gave little more than a flick of the head to acknowledge Savage as Calter introduced her.

Calter explained that Mr and Mrs Evershed were the owners of number seventy-five. They had bought the property only a month ago with the intention of renovating, but hadn't yet moved in.

'Waiting until the sprog is born,' Evershed said, turning to Savage now. 'Once that's out the way I'll be free to deal with this. We'll do the place up, add fifty K to the value, sell it on and move up. Easy money.'

'So you were getting some work done before you moved in?' Savage asked.

'That's just the point.' Evershed raised an accusing finger at the builder. Bared his teeth like a dog. 'I don't know what the hell these cowboys are doing here. I never asked them to do any work. First thing I know about it is when I get a call from our new next-door neighbour saying there's a police car parked out front. As far as I am concerned these idiots are bloody trespassing on private property and you should arrest them for criminal damage.'

'And?' Savage turned to the builder, a man in his fifties, weary, as if he'd seen it all.

'Don't blame me.' The man held one hand up and then reached into the breast pocket of his donkey jacket, pulled out a little spiral-bound notepad and showed the booklet to Savage. 'Job's down on my worksheet. Number seventy-five Lester Close. Pull up old patio slabs and remove soil and rubble. Dig holes for footings and lay concrete in preparation for new conservatory. Boss fixed us up with it Friday. Short notice, like, but he said it was an urgent job. We had to be in and out by the end of today.'

'Well you've got the wrong address, haven't you?' Evershed said, jabbing his finger again. 'So I suggest you call your boss and tell him he's cocked up. Then you can go round the back and clear up whatever mess you've made.'

'That won't be possible, I'm afraid,' Savage said. 'Not for a day or two at least. The whole of this property is now a crime scene.'

'*What*? You're joking, right?'

'Sorry, no.' Savage closed her eyes for a second and wondered how to explain about the little girl. She decided something approaching the truth was best. 'We've found the body of a child beneath the patio.'

Evershed's wife had walked up from the car and now she reached out for her husband, grasping for his arm with one hand, the other moving to her swollen belly.

'Nightmare,' Evershed said, shaking his head and wondering aloud about the resale value of the place.

Ten minutes later he was still talking figures as he ducked into his car. His wife stood on the other side of the vehicle for a moment, looking first at the house, then Savage, and then staring far into the distance at something beyond the rooftops at the end of the street. She got in, the door clunking shut with a noise which had a finality about it, Savage thinking about endings in her own life too.

Chapter Three

'Ready to say goodbye to Martin Kemp then?' DS Darius Riley said, leaning against the railings and gazing across the river Tamar. Drake's Island and Plymouth Sound lay to the right, the Torpoint chain ferries and the dockyards to the left. Just behind the two men, a black flag with a white cross hung limply from a flagpole next to the Edgcumbe Arms. The flag was there to remind anyone, should they need reminding, that they were standing on Cornish soil, another county from that which lay across the water. For some, it was another country.

For a moment Riley's companion said nothing, his eyes focusing on a patch of water midstream where a buoy, stationary against the tidal flow, had created a downstream eddy. Small pieces of flotsam swirled into the centre of the eddy and disappeared beneath the surface.

'Yes. Just a little joke that. Something to add a bit of flavour, a name to hang a conversation around, should I ever need to. But you can still call me Marty. If it helps.'

The man pulled a packet of cigarettes from his leather jacket and offered Riley one.

'No thanks . . . Marty.' Riley shook his head and smiled

as the man lit up. Since their last meeting just before Christmas, Kemp's hair had changed somehow, losing the greasy blackness and taking on a cleaner sheen. The clothing was more subtle now as well; no longer the flashy suit, the bracelet on the wrist, the rings on his fingers, instead just a plain leather jacket worn over a sweatshirt and jeans. Riley had been there, done it himself, knew about the little details which made for a convincing act. And Kemp's act was good. Very good. It had to be, because one slip and not only would the whole of Operation *Sternway* be jeopardised, but the man's life would be in danger as well. Riley was all too aware of that aspect of undercover work, having been on the wrong side of a beating when he'd been in London.

He had handled Kemp for the past couple of months, always meeting the man well away from Plymouth, usually at an anonymous pub or roadside café, but now Kemp's time was over and the officer could let the mask slip a little before returning to his own force. Riley knew Kemp was based in the North West, but he didn't know the name of the force, nor did he have any idea of the man's real identity. 'Better that way,' Kemp had said when they first met, and Riley agreed. If he'd been half as cautious as Kemp then maybe he'd still have been on the Met, still ducking and diving in his old haunts, playing the game. Instead he'd been transferred away.

'Best for you, Riley. We can't be too careful,' his boss had said, placing a little too much emphasis on the word 'careful'. And 'best for you' meant best for the rest of them, the team he'd let down. It had been tough at first, moving to what his old friends would have described as the back of beyond. Now though, after more than a year down in Devon, he'd settled in. And getting the chance to put his old skills to use on a case like the one he was working on with Kemp was a real bonus.

Riley watched as a light wind began to ruffle the ebbing tide, throwing up little wavelets as the water slipped out of the river and eased its way past the Mayflower Marina, the surface roughing up in the narrows between Royal William Yard and Mount Edgcumbe. He had come across on the Cremyll ferry, Kemp arriving in his car from the Cornish side. The ferry was mid stream now, heading back across the quarter-mile stretch of water to Devon, the steep landing ramp Riley had jumped down onto lengthening by the minute as the tide fell away, swathes of mud either side exposed to the attentions of numerous gulls.

'There, it's up the top of the creek.' Riley pointed across the river to a sliver of water which snaked between the marina and the stone quays of Royal William Yard. 'Beyond the Princess Yachts' hangar. Tamar Yachts is the one with the green roof. Considering what they do the business couldn't be better positioned.'

'Nice to put a face to a name,' Kemp said. 'During my trips down here I stayed away from the place deliberately.'

Riley had been over at Tamar Yachts back in the autumn and had interviewed the owner and a number of employees. The visit had been unrelated to Operation *Sternway*, at the time Riley not even realising the place was under surveillance. He had been impressed with the set-up, the way Tamar retro fitted kit to luxury motor yachts, exactly the kind of boats which the Princess factory produced. Given a tour of a huge gin palace – now to be equipped with the latest radar, communications hardware and security systems – Riley had calculated how long he'd have to save to afford such a beast, shaking his head when he realised retirement would loom long before he reached the sum required. To his uneducated eye the business seemed on a sound footing, with half a dozen craft in for anti-fouling or engine maintenance and a number of charter boats bobbing alongside a pontoon, prepped and ready for corporate days out.

'Bizarre,' Riley said, thinking aloud. 'I still can't get my head around it. When I was there everything seemed above board.'

'They always do. That's the point.'

It turned out that Gavin Redmond, the managing director of Tamar Yachts, was anything but above board. Discrepancies in his financial affairs had led to the tax authorities alerting police to the possibility that the business might be washing drugs money through its books. The economic crime section of Major Crimes soon realised what Her Majesty's Revenue and Customs had not: Tamar Yachts not only provided a means for money laundering, it was also the perfect cover for a smuggling operation. Proving it was another matter entirely. Which was where Kemp came in.

Kemp had spent the previous eighteen months inveigling his way into the Plymouth underworld, playing a Scouse drug dealer keen to find new supplies. He'd spent tens of thousands of pounds of taxpayers' money convincing local middlemen he was genuine, all the time waiting for the big fish to take the bait. The big fish being a villain named Kenny Fallon, who just happened to own fifty per cent of Redmond's business.

Depending on how you viewed him, Fallon was either a visionary property developer, entrepreneur and investor with a knack of always being in phase with the market, or a lowlife scum who funded his legitimate businesses with a web of illegal activities ranging from protection rackets to scams to drugs. Every city had a Kenny Fallon, a piece of dirt that somehow managed to climb from the gutter and establish itself as the kingpin. The skill they all shared was to stay one step removed from the dodgy activities and hold the shit they dealt with at arm's length. Fallon achieved that through a mixture of shrewd decision-making and creative accounting. So far neither the police nor HMRC had managed to make the necessary connections to trap him.

'We'll get him,' Kemp said, almost as if he'd read Riley's mind. 'The delivery is due soon. A big one, according to my contact. He'll text me, we swoop, Fallon goes down. Fairytale ending.'

'Can we trust your contact though? When push comes to shove will he come good?'

'He wants out, doesn't he? He either helps us . . .' Kemp scuffed his foot on the ground, kicking a small stone out through the railings. The stone hit the mud, sending little splatters of liquid out around it. 'Or he's a dead man.'

An hour later and the owner of the building company turned up at Lester Close. Peter Serling drove an immaculate bright red Audi TT with plastic covers on the seats, the material crackling as he eased his bulky frame out of the vehicle to speak to Savage. If the car was an unusual choice of transport for a builder, the man's attire wasn't; he wore a lumberjack shirt, a dusty fleece, jeans and tan boots. Specks of sawdust clung to scraggy brown hair and white paint flecks on the back of his hands contrasted with a healthy tan. Serling apologised for not arriving sooner, explaining he'd been up on a roof without his phone.

'Susie from the office had to drive round and get me.

24

Right state she were in. Can't say I blame her, if what she told me is true. I nearly fell off the roof when she shouted the news up. I'm hoping she got the wrong end of the stick and there's another explanation.'

Savage said there wasn't and asked about the mix-up. Had his men got the wrong address?

'No, love.' Serling looked over to the house where two CSIs were carrying a large box of equipment round to the rear. 'I was here last week speaking to Mr Evershed. Went into the back garden and he explained exactly what he wanted doing. He'd been let down by another builder, apparently, and needed some groundwork done quick in preparation for a conservatory. The company were coming to erect it later this week and he'd told them the patio would be cleared and the area readied in time.'

'Mr Evershed denies that,' Savage said. 'He says he never asked you to do any work. In fact he denies even knowing you.'

'Well, he would, wouldn't he? Considering what my lads have found.'

'And you're positive there couldn't have been some mistake?'

'Yes.' Serling closed his eyes and kept them shut. 'There's a patio round the back. Stretches the width of the plot. Kitchen door's pale green with a glass panel, in need of a paint. I noticed some rising damp to the right of the kitchen window, probably caused by the downpipe from the guttering not discharging into the drain properly. I asked Mr Evershed if he wanted me to fix it. He said "no", he was quite capable of doing that himself. He said he would have lifted the patio slabs, but at his age he needed to start to take it easy. I said "me too" and we had a laugh about that.'

'At his age? What sort of age would that be?' Savage replied.

'Hey?' Serling opened his eyes. 'About mine. Mid-forties. Looked pretty fit to me. Short and stocky, not much hair, but plenty of muscles, not running to fat like most of the rest of the world.'

'What about payment? Contact details?'

'He gave me a mobile number and he paid cash, upfront.'

'Isn't that unusual these days?'

'Yeah,' Serling smiled. 'But not without some advantages.'

'Tax?'

'Yes. Forget I told you.' Serling raised a hand and brushed his hair. A few pieces of sawdust fell on to his shoulder like flakes of oversized dandruff. 'Mr Evershed said he was going to be away for a while and thought it best to settle up beforehand. Seven fifty in an envelope. He said he was trusting me and that I wasn't to mess him around. The job had to be done Monday, come rain or shine. Well, I thought, for seven fifty you could add in hell or high water too.'

'Wasn't it over the odds? Seven hundred and fifty?'

'Yes. Although to be fair it was going to take my lads all day to lift the slabs and dig out to the required depth.'

'Have you still got the envelope or the money?'

'What? You want it back?'

'For fingerprints. You'll get a receipt.'

'Yes. It's at home.' Serling smiled again. 'I wasn't going to bank it, was I?'

Savage thanked Serling and directed Calter to go with him, retrieve the money and take a full statement. Then she went back to the rear of the house where the entire panoply of police resources were now in evidence. Three of Layton's team of CSIs were working on excavating the rest of the patio, carting barrow-loads of soil round to the front of the house where they were sieved into a skip. A photographer recorded any item recovered as it was removed and an exhibits officer bagged and catalogued those of interest. Away from the patio a woman pushed what looked like a small grass mower back and forth over the lawn.

'Ground-penetrating radar,' Layton said when Savage asked. 'Should tell us if anything else is buried there. Let's hope she's wasting her time.'

'And inside?'

'We'll see.' Layton turned to look at the house. 'The place is due for a refurb which means, luckily, the decor hasn't been touched for years. We should be able to ascertain if anything has been disturbed recently. And before you ask, no, nothing in the loft. Thank God.'

DCI Mike Garrett turned up an hour later, looking, as always, as if he had arrived direct from an upmarket tailor. Not so much as a piece of fluff on the dark surface of his suit, his shirt brilliant white, the collar starched, tie perfect, Garrett's hair not far off the colour of the shirt. Unblemished was a moniker which could be applied to the older detective's career too. He had taken a while to climb to the rank of Chief Inspector but had done so without stepping on toes, without getting his fingers dirty. Colleagues respected him and he was well-liked among all ranks. Sometimes though, Savage found him a little too stuffy.

Once Garret had clambered into his protective clothing, he came round to the back armed with a friendly greeting and a name for the operation.

'*Brougham*,' he said, as he stood over the hole, gazing

down at the rubble. The plastic crate and its contents had gone, accompanied to the morgue by Nesbit and Layton, but several numbered markers lay scattered around, and Garrett's eyes moved from one to another as if he was playing a perverse game of join the dots. 'I'm Senior Investigating Officer,' he said to Savage, 'you're my deputy. As you can imagine, Hardin wants a quick result on this one. Have you seen the *Herald*'s special on their website?'

'No.' Savage shook her head. She hadn't seen the local paper's website but she guessed the media would be one reason Hardin had made Garrett Senior Investigating Officer. Garrett wasn't exactly media-savvy, but he played with a straight bat and had the appropriate gravitas. And then there were those suits he wore: black with no colour. The murder of a child – if that was what this was – had to be handled differently. A soft tone, but serious, determined and with a get-the-bastard-whatever-it-takes attitude.

'Cromwell Street is what they are saying. House of Horrors. That sort of thing. Someone spotted the plastic box being loaded into the mortuary van. Body parts being the inference.'

'Layton doesn't think there are any more.'

'Really?' Garrett looked up to the lawn where the GPR operative was packing away her equipment, then turned to Savage and arched an eyebrow. 'I hope he's bloody right. If he is we might just keep the national media away from this one. Have you traced the previous occupier yet?'

Savage told Garrett what she knew from Mr Evershed and his wife. Prior to their purchase the house had been a rental property. The landlord, fed up with ongoing repairs, had been wanting to get the house off his hands. The couple had no idea who the last tenant was, but they knew the name of the letting agency.

'Dream Lets,' Savage said. 'It's just round the corner, top of Efford Road. I've been leaving messages on their phone for the last couple of hours. Nobody has got back to me yet. I'm going up there now.'

'Dream Lets?' Garrett said, glancing up at the brown pebble-dash house and then back to the hole where the bones of the dog poked out of the sludge. 'Do you think we should do them under the Trade Descriptions Act?'

Dream Lets sat above a bookmakers' at the top of Efford Road. The location didn't do much to lend any credence to the salubrious name, nor did the young woman smoking a cigarette next to the agency's entrance. Short skirt, big tattoo on a bare calf above a gold ankle chain and blonde hair from a bottle, with four weeks' worth of dark roots showing. She glanced over as Savage and Calter approached, hacked out a globule of phlegm and then flicked the cigarette butt to the floor before opening the door and going inside.

Savage caught the door before it closed and she and Calter followed the woman up some stairs to a small office, where a handwritten notice on one wall announced what was obviously the agency motto: 'We Let, No Sweat.' The woman didn't seem to be surprised to be followed and she manoeuvred her large frame in past a filing cabinet and a bookshelf. She plonked herself down at a desk, scrabbling amongst a mess of papers and folders until she found a biro.

'Alright?' she said. 'What can I do for you ladies?'

The voice, low and coarse, came from a forty-a-day habit. Savage reflected sadly that the woman wasn't much more than a girl and probably no older than Calter.

'Seventy-five Lester Close,' Savage said, pulling out her

warrant card. 'We know the property was one of yours until recently and we'd like a list of the previous tenants.'

'Is there a problem?' The woman ruffled the mess on the desk again before retrieving a folder from an ocean of manila. She lifted the flap and extracted a single sheet.

'You could say that.'

'Right. A problem.' The woman paused, but when Savage didn't fill in the dead air she peered down at the piece of paper for a moment before continuing. The way she scrutinised the few lines of type on the page it almost seemed as if she was translating the text from ancient Egyptian. After half a minute she continued. 'Mr Franklin Owers was the last tenant before the property was sold. He'd been there for a number of years. I remember he wasn't best pleased to be leaving, but the owner was looking to make a few quid before the market tumbled again.'

'Do you have a forwarding address?'

'Mr Owers is still one of ours. Unfortunately.' The woman grimaced, and then realising Savage didn't get her joke she added: 'He rents a property over in Stonehouse, on Durnford Street. One twenty-one B.'

The woman scribbled on a piece of scrap paper and handed it to Savage. Savage passed the slip across to Calter, who took out her phone and left the room.

'Is there a problem?' The same words, but this time a quiver in amongst the gruffness. 'Only maybe I should inform my boss. If you could just tell me what this is all about?'

'Your tenant did some building work at the property in Lester Close. In the garden.'

'Did he? They're not supposed to you know, not without permission. Anything like that has to be authorised, otherwise we can get into all sorts of legal difficulties. The tenant can create a right mess and eventually their DIY efforts come back to haunt us. Is that what has happened?'

'Haunt you?' Savage said. 'Yes, you could say so.'

'Well, are you going to tell me the details?'

'No. Do you have a sparc kcy for the Durnford Street property by any chance?'

'Would it help? You know, keep things quiet?'

'It might,' Savage said, knowing nothing would keep what she had seen at Lester Close quiet.

The woman reached across to a cupboard, and opened the door to reveal a pegboard with dozens of keys hanging on numbered hooks. She thought for a moment and then grabbed a set and handed them over, her eyes still asking for more.

'Watch the news tonight.' Savage turned and opened the door to leave. '*Spotlight* if you're lucky. *News at Ten* if not. Thanks for your help.'

Downstairs Calter stood talking into her phone, nodding every so often as she paced back and forth in front of the bookies. She ended the call and then told Savage what she knew.

'Franklin Owers has got previous, ma'am. He did seven years for sexual activity with a child. A six-year-old. Spent time up at Full Sutton. You know, where they keep the real nutters. It was a while ago though, he was out a few years back. On the sex offenders' register for life, of course. Apparently his MAPPA status was downgraded to level one several years ago.'

Savage nodded. MAPPA stood for Multi-Agency Public Protection Arrangements. Any sex offender had a long list of people involved in their life on the outside, with everyone from probation officers and social workers to housing and health professionals having a say in managing the offender's activities. The idea was to share resources and information across agencies. Savage suspected a by-product was the ease with which the buck could be passed along the line.

'We'd better get over to his place now,' Savage said, glancing up at the window of Dream Lets. The agent stood gazing down at them, a sliver of black pressed against one ear and an unlit cigarette in her other hand. 'Before anyone else gets wind of the story.'

Chapter Four

Later, Riley and Kemp went into the Edgcumbe Arms and ordered lunch, Kemp going for a beef stew, Riley choosing the Thai sweet chilli chicken. Two beers as well, Kemp laughing at Riley's lager top as he supped his bitter.

'How did you come to be down here then?' Kemp said, polishing off the mushroom sauce with the last of his new potatoes. 'I mean . . .'

'You mean because I'm black?'

'Well, not exactly wall-to-wall diversity in this part of the world, is it? And your accent, posh, educated, but London in there somewhere. South of the river?'

'Good, Marty. Postcode?'

'Given enough time I can come up with the colour of your first fuck's knickers. Still thinking about my original question though. Why?'

'Nosey, aren't you?' Riley said, taking a mouthful of noodles before considering his answer. 'Let's just say circumstances.'

'Oh, those. Plenty of the buggers around. Work related?'

'Yeah, work related.'

'Enough said. I'll not intrude on your misery any further.' Kemp took a drink of his beer. 'You settled down here? Got a girlfriend? Plans?'

'Yes,' Riley said, thinking of Julie Meadows, the woman he'd met a couple of months ago and had been seeing ever since. Julie worked for NeatStreet, a charity dealing with deprived youngsters on some of Plymouth's worst estates, and at the tail end of last year she'd wangled him into taking a group of boys from North Prospect up to London to watch his beloved Chelsea play. From that day on he'd been smitten. Now he was unable to prevent a smile forming and, embarrassed, he looked away and out through the pub window. On the far bank of the river Plymouth shone gold in the light from the low winter sun. He turned back to Kemp. 'For the first time in a long time I suppose I do feel settled. I guess it's not having to do what you do any more. You know, undercover. I'm not sure I could deal with the crap any more, the fear. Getting settled is easier now I'm away from all that.'

'Here,' Kemp reached into his jacket, pulled out his wallet and slipped it across to Riley. 'My little girl.'

'Thought you were offering to pay for a moment there.' Riley opened the wallet, saw the smile before anything else, then the blonde hair and the blue eyes.

'Elsie. She's eight. Keeps me grounded. Her and her mother. Trouble, both of them. Trouble you get to love.'

'Elsie. That in real life?'

'Not the name, but the picture, yes. Makes it easier to play the part, doesn't it?'

Easier to play the part, Riley thought, his mind slipping back to his time in London again. Sometimes playing the part was all too easy. You forgot who you were in real life, you went native. And when that happened the inevitable followed:

circumstances. He shook his head as he passed the wallet back to Kemp, and bent to his food again.

After the meal they went back outside so Kemp could have another smoke. They watched as a tiny sailing yacht nosed its way out from the Mayflower Marina and into the main channel, one of thousands of boats of all sizes that used Plymouth Sound as a base.

'If Gavin Redmond had kept a low profile, stuck to something like that, we might never have known.' Kemp waved his cigarette at the boat. 'It's those bloody gin palaces. You can smell the illegality in the fumes whenever one passes. From Russian oligarchs to small-time dodgy car ringers, they all want the same thing: a tanned blonde and a penis substitute.'

As if in response to Kemp's statement, a loud parp from an airhorn caused them both to look to their right. The sailing boat was drifting in the channel as the skipper fought with a line which trailed behind the boat. Blue language drifted across the water and Riley guessed the rope may have fouled the prop. The horn came from a large motor boat, forty foot or more, moving up the main river and into the pool. On the flybridge a man gestured at the little boat and it wasn't the friendly greeting of one seafarer to another.

'Talk of the devil.' Kemp turned away from the water and leant on the railings, his back to the action. 'That's Redmond.'

'He's got other things to worry about than spotting us,' Riley said as the motor boat spurted forward, lifting its nose and sweeping round the sailing boat. A large bow wave washed across and rocked the little yacht and the man hung onto the backstay for balance. He returned Redmond's gesture with interest, the single finger held aloft followed by a string of obscenities.

A rigid inflatable boat appeared from between the pontoons with two Mayflower staff on board. They nosed up to the yacht and began to guide the disabled vessel back to the marina.

'Cocky fucker, isn't he?' Riley said.

'All on the surface,' Kemp said, watching as the white hulk of Redmond's boat glided up the pool to the Tamar Yacht pontoons, leaving behind a swirling vortex of water. 'Underneath he can barely hold it together. The business is on the rocks – excuse the pun – and Kenny Fallon has him by the bollocks.'

With the boat gone, Kemp turned to Riley, hand outstretched.

'Well, I'm off, back up the motorway. Pity I won't be here for the bust, but Mr Kemp needs to stay low in case he's needed again. I'll be seeing you. In court, I hope. When it's all over we'll have some more beers and you can introduce me to your girl. She must be sweet if she can make you smile like you did just now.'

He shook Riley's hand and walked away without looking back, disappearing round the corner of the pub and into another life.

'Cocky fucker,' Riley said again.

Durnford Street was in the Stonehouse area of the city, on an odd-shaped piece of land reached by an isthmus running between the ferry terminal and the Royal Marine Barracks on one side and a creek on the other. Surrounded by water on three sides, and accessible only across the isthmus, the location had risen in affluence relative to the rest of Stonehouse. The latter had acquired a reputation for vice, hardly helped by the presence of Union Street and its array of nightclubs at its centre.

'We're too late,' Savage said to Calter as they parked up.

They got out of the car and approached the imposing terrace of four-storey houses. At number one twenty-three a young woman stood holding a baby. She was talking to Dan Phillips, the *Herald*'s crime reporter, while a photographer took shots of the next door property, where someone had spray-painted the immaculate gloss-white door with the vivid red words 'Paedos rot in hell'.

'Detective Inspector?' Phillips turned and came down the steps, blocking her way along the pavement to one twenty-one. Pinprick eyes scanned her face trying to read her mind from her expression. 'A child's body is found under a patio and next, the police are visiting the house of a certain Mr Franklin Owers. According to my sources he's a known paedophile. Anything to say on the matter?'

'Give us a chance, Dan.' Savage wanted to ask him how the hell he had got here before them, but instead she pointed to the graffiti. 'I can tell you the idiots who did that have got the wrong address. Or maybe I should say *you* have got the wrong address.'

'Hey!' Phillips said. 'You don't think I would do such a thing, surely?'

Savage pushed past the smiling reporter, knowing that spraying the door himself just to get a good picture was exactly the sort of thing he would do. She opened the little iron gate to one side of one twenty-one and descended a narrow set of steps, leading down to a basement flat which lay below the level of the road. At the bottom, the small concrete area had flooded at one end and a plastic bin had fallen on its side, disgorging its contents to float on the grimy liquid. A distinct odour of dog shit hung in the air, overpowering the whiff of the rubbish, and Savage spotted little piles of the stuff half-submerged in the water.

'Ma'am?' Calter had joined Savage at the bottom of the

steps and now she crouched in front of the frosted-glass door, peering through the letter box. 'Doesn't smell too nice inside either.'

Savage rapped on the glass and waited. Nothing. She tried again, and when a third lot of knocks failed to produce an answer she pulled out the set of keys.

'Let's try these, shall we?'

She snapped on a pair of latex gloves before inserting the key into the lock.

The door opened into a hallway, a sheet of pale blue lino leading towards the rear of the property, the edges torn and cracked. Three piles of dog shit lay near to a doorway to the right where a pool of yellow liquid flowed across the lino and off the edge. The urine had seeped into the pine floorboards, turning the wood dark.

'Police, Mr Owers,' Savage said. 'We'd like a word.'

Nothing.

Then they heard a yapping and a noise halfway between a purr and a growl.

'You don't like dogs, do you, ma'am?' Calter said, moving past Savage and into the flat. 'Better let me deal with this.'

At that moment something the size of a large cat came shooting at them from the rear of the hallway. A pink tongue lolled from jaws surrounded by a black face, atop a fat and stocky tan body. The thing stopped a couple of metres away and horrid little round eyes stared at Savage for a moment before she stepped aside to let the dog run through the front door. The animal scampered by, splashing through the flood and up the stairs to the street.

'Pug, ma'am. Poor little thing. Must have been shut in here all the time. Lovely breed of—' Calter stopped as Savage glared at her. 'Anyway, now we know about the dog shit.'

Thank you, Jane.' Savage said, closing the door. 'Let's stop the bloody creature getting back inside at least.'

'Three piles of poop. I'd say that means the dog has been shut in here for a while.'

'Feel free to investigate further. Personally I am going to leave that to John Layton. I am sure he is an expert in canine faecal deposits.'

Savage negotiated a way between the piles of poo and the pool of urine and went into the room to the right, a living room with thin, moth-eaten curtains and a raffia rug. One corner of the rug had been chewed and bits of palm leaf lay scattered around. A television stood in the corner on a triangular pine video cabinet which was trying its best to look antique. Judging from the age of the television it wasn't far off. The only other piece of furniture in the room was a sofa covered with a tatty blanket. A Freemans clothing catalogue lay open on the sofa, faces of little girls smiling, happy. The coloured tab at the top of the page said 'Ages 5-7'.

'Bloody pervert,' Calter said, coming into the room and wrinkling her nose as she peered at the glossy pictures. 'Still up to his games, I reckon. So much for that downgrade to MAPPA level one.'

'Have a look through those, would you?' Savage pointed at the row of DVDs stacked on a rack beside the TV and DVD player. She left Calter and went down the hallway. At the rear of the property, a doorway to the right had a ribboned fly curtain and no door. Behind the curtain a minuscule kitchenette contained a grubby and dangerous-looking gas cooker and a little fridge sitting on a stained worktop. To the left was the bedroom. A single duvet, out of place on the double mattress lying on the floor, wore a Barbie cover. Savage's stomach churned; until a few years ago her own daughter had had exactly the same one. In the centre of the duvet a small depression had been formed right on Barbie's impossibly thin waist and a few black and tan hairs were visible on the cotton.

To one side of the bed a tea chest appeared to function as a linen bin and was full to the brim with jogging bottoms, jeans, shirts and underwear. The stench from the unwashed clothes invaded Savage's nostrils and she tried to breathe through her mouth, but that just meant she gagged on the smell instead.

Apart from the bed and tea chest the bedroom was bare like the living room. Either Franklin Owers hadn't believed in having possessions or else he couldn't afford them. All in all it seemed a depressing existence, and for a moment Savage sensed the man's need for the uncritical type of companionship which perhaps might only come from a dog. Or a child. But then, for a man like Owers, mere companionship with a child wouldn't be enough. Savage turned from the room and shook her head. Haunting wasn't the half of it.

Ricky Budgeon stared out of the window to where a patch of late afternoon sunlight painted a nearby field, the warm glow in stark contrast to the dark patterns cast by the clouds. He guessed the harsh light presaged a bout of heavy rain. The stream which ran past the rear of the house would fill, bank-full, and gurgle through the night. If he left the window open the noise might help him sleep. Assuming the pain stayed away, that was.

The headaches had got worse in recent weeks and moments when he was free of worry were like the brush-strokes of gold on the field, either side of which were black shadows. One day those shadows would close in for good.

He reached out for the rough wall to the side of the

window and touched the lacquered stonework. The barn conversion had been nicely done, the place luxurious. A rich man's pad. Not home though. Never that.

From another room he could hear the sounds of the boy, gurgling like the stream, his mother clucking to him in Spanish as she prepared a meal. He should be in there with them, playing with the boy, pulling him close with one hand, the other reaching out for the girl. They were family after all, living with him, and Budgeon knew he should be trying to make the place more of a home. Somehow he couldn't bring himself to do that. They meant something to him, sure, but he knew the woman only hung around because of the money. An ugly mug like him with a pretty girl on his arm? He'd seen it often enough in his line of work. When she was on her knees in front of him, head bobbing, he didn't kid himself that her actions were anything to do with love or attraction.

And the boy?

The boy was cute. Dark hair, dark skin, a real punchy little kid with an iron grip and eyes that promised an intelligence which Budgeon knew he himself lacked. The boy would be someone, wouldn't spend half his life inside. Not if Budgeon had anything to do with it.

He wasn't sure if the feeling he felt for the little lad was love or some kind of vicarious ambition. Still, the next week or so, if things went well, would see the kid sorted, the boy and his mother set up for life. One worry gone, one ache salved.

Budgeon sighed and then reached forward and picked up the local paper from the windowsill. The lead story was of a dead girl beneath a suburban patio, a paedophile missing, police doing all they could to find the man, confident they would be making an arrest soon.

Fat Frankie.

Budgeon had never liked him. He remembered an argument with Big K one night way back, must have been twenty years ago. The three of them in the little room Big K had above the offy. Handy for free takeouts. Round the corner from the massage parlour too, often a couple of girls spreading themselves over one of the sofas, lips pouting like fish in a tank wanting a mouthful of food.

'It's the figures.' Big K looks up from the table, chucks his cards in. Folding. Nodding across to the third guy in the game. 'Lexi, he's canny with the politicos, you and me, we know the streets, and Frankie does the numbers.'

'He'll be on the numbers before long. Frankie Fiddler – and I ain't talking an Irish jig.'

'You're right there, Ricky.' Lexi this time. All too friendly. Collecting up the chips in the centre. 'Trouser dance while watching the kiddies is the only rhythm he's beating out. We still need him though.'

'Look at it this way.' Big K points to the pile of chips next to Lexi. 'Tonight, you and me lost. Lexi's taken me for a oner, you the same twice over. Tomorrow he'll let us win it back because he knows if he doesn't we'll beat the shit out of him. But real life doesn't work like that. The house never loses unless you've got an edge. Frankie is the edge.'

'Still don't like him.'

'I'm not asking you to eat grapes from between his arse cheeks. All you've got to do is tolerate him.'

'Think you can do that, Ricky?' Lexi again. Smiling. Big K as well. Like they are sharing the punchline to some joke you don't understand.

Lexi and Big K. Too close sometimes. All that talking and planning. Lexi in particular has a face with two sides. Trying to work him out is like trying to catch hold of a fart; for a *moment there's a stink but then comes a quick burst of air freshener and nobody is any the wiser.*

'The amount of money Frankie has saved us,' Big K says, starting to laugh, 'he's worth his weight.'

'Even if he is particular to kiddies?'

'It's a fuck or be fucked world, Ricky. You told me that.'

From the kitchen a clatter of pans brought Budgeon back to the present, the noise jarring through his head. He raised a hand and squeezed his temples to try and relieve the building pressure, then looked through the window where he could see the sun had been swallowed up by a mass of cloud which brooded on the horizon, far to the west.

Frankie should have stayed in Plymouth and not come west last summer. Once he'd been given a tour of the area, shown the tourist hotspots, he'd been gagging for it. Let loose for a few hours, the pervert had been in little-girl heaven.

'Urges, Ricky,' Frankie said afterwards, eyes downcast, knowing he'd walked into a trap. 'They're prick-teasers. All of them. She was cute, so very cute. I couldn't help myself.'

So Frankie had helped himself.

The pans clattered again and Budgeon closed his eyes. This time the noise caused white light to crackle across a grey background, and he balled his fists as needles of agony pierced his temples. He clenched his teeth and swallowed. He wanted to go into the kitchen and hit the woman. Slap her for being so clumsy. Instead he opened his eyes and lashed out with his arm, sweeping a vase of daffodils from a nearby table. The flowers fell in slow motion and then the vase exploded on the slate floor.

A second later and the girl was at the door with the child on her hips. A hand went to her mouth, lips quivering, tears forming at the corners of her eyes. The kid smiled across, for a split second his expression reminding Budgeon of someone from his past. He creased his forehead, willed the kid to repeat the smile, tried to recall the face again but the moment was gone. Then the boy sensed the tension and began to cry.

Budgeon nodded at the girl. Remembered to breathe. Said it was OK and then waved her away. He stepped from the window, crunched over the remains of the vase and eased himself down into the creaking leather of the big sofa. Tucked down behind a cushion he found his bottle of Scotch. He pulled the bottle out and fumbled with the screw top, necked a draught straight from the bottle. A burning sensation caressed the back of his throat and he felt the tension fall away. He cradled the bottle in his lap like a newborn and closed his eyes again.

Big K's face floated in the grey mist, mouthing the words from all those years ago: fuck or be fucked. Well, what goes around comes around, Budgeon thought. Payback time; the stuff with Frankie only the start, an illustration that he was serious and a prelude to something much grander. Something to take away his final worry and which would bring his old pals a whole symphony of pain and misery and suffering.

Chapter Five

Crownhill Police Station, Plymouth. Monday 14th January. 2.10 p.m.

Early afternoon, and Savage headed back to Crownhill. Inside the Major Crimes suite Operation *Brougham* was in full swing, the information discovered earlier in the day entered into the system by the indexers, actions already mounting up as each incoming lead generated numerous tasks for the inquiry teams. Three pairs of DCs had begun working the area around Lester Close. So far they had nothing but gossip. The story coming out of the neighbourhood was that Franklin Owers was a loner, frequented local playgrounds and by common consent, deserved castration. People were glad he'd moved away. The tale was similar over Stonehouse way, in the maze of streets surrounding his flat. Owers had only moved in a couple of months back, but already someone had noticed him hanging around outside the local primary school. Nobody questioned in either area had any idea where he might be and his MAPPA team were equally clueless. So much for monitoring sex offenders, Savage thought.

'Naughty, Charlotte, naughty,' Garrett said, entering the Crime Suite a few minutes later. 'I should slap your wrist. More, according to John Layton.'

'Sorry?'

'Owers' flat. Scene of crime. Layton has gone ballistic.'

'Shit.'

'Kept on talking about first dibs for him and his team. Muttered something about cross-contamination too. I told him to calm down but he stormed off.'

'So John's gone over there now?'

'Going to "rip the fucker apart" were his exact words. I hope Owers is our man or else we are going to face one hell of a repair bill.'

'And Lester Close?'

'Clean. Nothing else there, he reckons. At least nothing we can find without bringing in the bulldozers, and I'm not ready to do that. Not until we've got something more on Mr Owers.'

'It's beyond reasonable doubt though, sir. The fact he's offended before, the stuff we found at the flat, local people saying he acted suspiciously.'

'Depends *whose* reasonable doubt we're talking about.' Garrett raised a finger and tapped his nose. 'Everything so far is circumstantial.'

Savage disagreed, thinking a body beneath a patio was way more than circumstantial. She said nothing, guessing the real reason for Layton's anger was the lack of anything incriminating from Lester Close. Now he'd be hoping to find something in Owers' current residence, hoping Savage hadn't mucked things up. She was sorry she had pissed him off. They were on the same side, after all.

Garrett was still talking, moving around the room and raising his voice to include everyone in the conversation. There were three main questions, he said. Who was the little girl in the box, who was the man that Peter Serling, the builder, had met at Lester Close, and where was Mr Franklin

46

Owers? Answer any one of those and they'd be well on their way to cracking the case.

Early days, but so far the inquiry teams had nothing on Owers. Where he was remained a mystery.

Peter Serling would be coming in to give a more detailed statement and to work with the team's e-Fit specialist to compile a likeness of the man who had impersonated Mr Evershed. The mobile number the man had given him was being traced, but likely as not would turn out to be a pay as you go and worthless.

That left the girl.

Garrett was off to the post-mortem, saying he hoped to return with information which would aid the identification. They already knew she was aged around six, had brown curly hair and a gap in her front teeth where two milk teeth had fallen out. There were so few missing persons of that age that establishing the girl's identity should have been easy. However, the missing persons' list didn't contain any young children.

It wasn't until Garrett had been gone for half an hour that Savage remembered a news story from last summer.

'Missing, presumed dead,' she said to herself. 'Not on the misper list.'

'Huh?' DC Enders looked up from his screen and ruffled his brown hair with one hand. 'Not following you, ma'am.'

'Last summer. Pete was away but I'd persuaded Stefan to accompany me for a week-long cruise with the kids. We went down in convoy with another family boat and ended up getting stuck down in Newlyn. A big depression had cleared through, but the sea state kept us in harbour for a couple of days.'

'Sorry, ma'am. I don't get it.'

'I remember the local newspaper headlines. A young girl

had gone missing a few miles to the east at the Lizard. The lifeboat, coastguard and an army of volunteers searched the sea, cliffs and coast path, but she was never found. The conclusion was that she must have slipped over the cliff edge while her parents were having a picnic. There was something else too which I can't quite—'

'It's here, ma'am,' Enders said, pointing to his screen where he had brought up the local police file on the incident. 'Simza Ellis was her name. Her parents were travellers, down in Cornwall for seasonal work. Ditto everything you said, but apparently the parents claimed there was somebody taking photographs of children, a "weirdo" in their words. There was also the fact that her sun hat was found in a car park set back from the coast. It says here investigating officers concluded the hat had been dropped by a dog or a gull or maybe had been carried there by an updraught from the cliffs, the hat coming off as the girl fell. The facts were considered at the inquest, but the overwhelming evidence pointed to Simza falling into the sea . . . shit!'

'Patrick?'

'. . . including the discovery of a pink trainer-type shoe by the lifeboat crew.' Enders shook his head, an expression of distaste spreading across his face. 'Because they were travellers nobody fucking believed them, did they? If they had then maybe she would be alive today.'

'It's easy to be wise after the fact,' Savage said, moving over to Enders and patting him on the back.

'Sorry, ma'am, but look at her.' Enders pointed to a picture of the girl on the screen and clicked to make it bigger. 'Didn't she deserve a bit more?'

Brown curls cascaded to the edges of the image and a red tongue poked out from a pretty, playful face intent on mischief or fun, or both.

'She'll get the attention now, of course,' Enders said, clicking the image shut.

Savage turned away, thinking that the young DC was right. Traveller or not, cute or not – and she was very cute – the girl had deserved more. But now was too late. Way too late.

Later, Savage climbed the stairs to Detective Superintendent Conrad Hardin's office to give him the news on the situation at Lester Close. Hardin resembled a beached whale as he tipped his office chair backwards, interlocking his hands around his stomach and groaning.

'Went to an afternoon buffet at the Guildhall. Bloody councillors, wasting public money on pointless functions.' Hardin's eyes roved to the jar of liquorice sticks he kept on his desk as part of his diet regime. He shook his head and huffed out a gallon of air. 'Good food though.'

Being in Hardin's office alone with the DSupt always made Savage feel uncomfortable. The sheer physical bulk of the man led to the illusion of him filling the room entirely, and in any prolonged silence the stark walls offered few distractions. At least the out-of-date calendar of Greek islands Hardin had had on the wall for the past two years had been replaced. The new one was of Dartmoor landscapes and January's picture showed a suitably wintery scene with two children and a pony in the snow, the dark rocks of Haytor brooding in the background.

'The girl in the box,' Hardin said, following her gaze. 'Where are we at?'

Savage filled Hardin in on the details, noting his eyes narrowing with anger when she told him about the pink training shoe, as if somehow the physical object made the horror more real.

'Any ideas who she is?' Hardin gritted his teeth and

reached for his mouse. 'And more importantly, who put her there?'

'We've got a hunch she could be a girl who was thought missing after supposedly falling from a cliff down in Cornwall. As for a suspect, a previous tenant at the property turns out to be on the register. Committed a serious sexual offence a few years back. Layton and his team are all over the man's place now, but there is no sign of him as of yet.'

Savage continued talking as there was a knock and DCI Garrett entered. Garrett, despite having spent the day tramping around a muddy patio and attending the post-mortem, looked immaculate as ever. Savage went on to outline the steps the inquiry was taking, Garrett nodding every now and then but seeing no need to interject. At the end of Savage's summation Hardin looked at Garrett for his opinion.

'A tragedy,' Garrett said, 'but no accident. Preliminary findings from the PM suggest the girl was strangled. Nesbit couldn't say if she was sexually assaulted or not, but if we assume she was I don't think we'd be going out on a limb. Could well be this Franklin Owers is our man, but first we've got to find him.'

'To which end,' Hardin said, 'the media is not bloody helping.'

Hardin reached to one side of his desk where a folded newspaper stuck out of his wastepaper bin. He pulled the paper out and laid it on the desk. Dan Phillips' headline had done the *Herald* proud. 'Get Him!' Below the headline was a picture of Franklin Owers' grafittied front door, with an inset thumbnail of Owers himself. Hardin thumped the desk and then pointed to a subheading beneath the pictures: 'Police Clueless in Hunt for Paedophile Killer.'

'That,' Hardin said, looking at Savage and Garrett in turn, his face beginning to redden, 'is nonsense, isn't it?'

Savage said nothing.

The *Sternway* meeting went ahead at six-thirty in Briefing Room A, the acronym for which never failed to raise a smile from the more infantile of the Crownhill officers. Darius Riley liked to think he was above such things.

He'd spent the afternoon summarising Kemp's final report and dotting the I's and crossing the T's on a longer document which pulled together a whole mass of intelligence from numerous sources. Now he slid copies of the document across the table to DSupt Hardin, DCI Garrett, DI Phil Davies and DI Savage. Savage smiled at him and Riley thought she looked happier than she had for a while. Her husband had returned from a long stint away so maybe that was the reason. It could certainly explain the sheen of her red hair and the smartness of her attire; Riley couldn't remember seeing her appearing quite so attractive before.

He leant back in his seat and wondered if he might be considered infantile himself for thinking his boss was looking sexy. Davies sat opposite and he glanced at Savage and then looked across at Riley and winked. There was no chance of anyone thinking Davies was sexy, Riley thought. He slumped down in his chair in a crumpled brown number which Riley wouldn't have been surprised to learn had come from a charity shop running a discount promotion for items they couldn't clear. Even from across the table Riley could smell several nights' worth of beer and fags in the clothing.

Mike Garrett's clothing had, literally, been cut from a different cloth. Riley didn't think much of the older detective's abilities – the man was too cautious, too rule-bound – but he'd always admired his suits.

Hardin was Hardin. Bursting out of his shirt, almost knocking over the pot of coffee when it arrived, and then grabbing a couple of biscuits with one hand while typing on his laptop with the other.

'OK, *Sternway*.' Hardin turned to his laptop and clicked again. He reached out and adjusted the angle of the screen, and for a moment Riley feared he was going to swing the computer towards them and show one of his dreary PowerPoint presentations. Instead he leant back in his chair and ran his tongue over his lips before continuing.

'So, Darius had his final meeting with our undercover officer earlier, nom de plume Mr Martin Kemp. Mr Kemp is returning to his force and Darius,' Hardin nodded over at Riley, 'is off on holiday in a couple of days. Now we're just waiting on the intel. As soon as Kemp gets the word he'll let us know. I'm pleased to say *Sternway* is finally drawing to a close and there will be no happy ending for Mr Kenny Fallon. Not this time.'

Riley switched off as Hardin began to map out the final stages of the operation. He knew the details back to front, had worked on them with Kemp and Hardin. As the DSupt elaborated on the endgame Riley hoped his words wouldn't come back to haunt them, since Hardin had been placed in charge of *Sternway* precisely because of the failure of previous investigations. Usually an operation focusing on somebody such as Fallon would have been dealt with by SOCIT – the Serious and Organised Crime Investigations Team – however, rumours had been spreading of one or two bad apples within the police, someone even going so far as to distribute flyers around city car parks which accused the team of corruption. The allegations were without any evidence or reason, but the brass over at force HQ in Exeter had panicked and decreed the next major operation dealing with organised crime would be run independently of SOCIT and by someone with an unimpeachable record. Enter DSupt Conrad Hardin, mates with Simon Fox – the Chief Constable, friends in the local military and bogey golfer who could cheerfully lose to the worst. With Mr Clipboard, checkbox, do it-by-the-book Hardin in charge, what could possibly go wrong?

Riley blinked as he heard Hardin mutter his 'bloody good policing' catchphrase and peer over at him for an answer. He had no idea what he was talking about but he managed a 'yes, sir', and Hardin continued.

'If our intelligence is correct, the cargo vessel we are interested in may even now be loading in Rotterdam. At some point in the next few days the vessel will be passing approximately ten miles south of Plymouth, where it will drop a package overboard. Once the vessel is well clear, Gavin Redmond will head out in one of those f-off yachts of his and pick up the goods.'

When Riley had first come onto *Sternway* and heard of the arrangement he'd had to concede it was clever. The pickup boat never had to go more than a few miles offshore and never anywhere near the ship which dropped the drugs. All it required was knowledge of the tidal streams and a short-range tracking device. Plus a little faith from the crew on the cargo vessel that the millions of pounds worth of drugs they were heaving overboard were going to end up in the right hands. All Customs and Excise's fancy plotting equipment – which mapped out the closest point of approach of suspect vessels and watched for small boats making regular trips across channel – proved useless against such a tactic.

The ploy might have gone unnoticed if Fallon hadn't made the mistake of using Tamas Yachts and Redmond as a way of washing money too. Tamar owned a subsidiary charter company in Nassau, out in the Bahamas. A swish website showed a number of top-end crewed yachts costing tens of thousands of dollars a week to hire and every month a payment appeared in Tamar's bank account, the funds originating from a Bahamian bank. Twice a year Tamar Yachts paid Fallon a hefty dividend from his shares, the sums involved matching the supposed income from the charter business. An HMRC investigator, risking the wrath of her boss, decided to take an unauthorised trip to the Bahamas. She discovered nothing. Literally. The charter company didn't exist, other than as a managed office sharing an address with hundreds of other companies. It was then that HMRC had contacted the police, realising the income flowing in from the dummy charter operation was most likely drugs money.

'You all know your roles,' Hardin said, leaning forward and jabbing a finger at each officer in turn. 'Phil will liaise on additional evidence, Mike will run the interviews, Charlotte will manage the post-arrest local inquiry teams, and Darius, when you return from your jaunt, you'll be collating the threads and working with the team to turn what we have into something the CPS will wet their knickers over. Finally the Tactical Aid Group will be carrying out the raids and you can bet I want you guys there as well to prevent the trigger-happy cowboys messing everything up. Apart from that it is just a waiting game. Questions?'

There were dozens. Operational, technical, legal, Hardin dealing with each in turn in his methodical manner. An hour later and he wrapped the meeting up with a final pep talk.

'The objective is to shut down the city's drug supply network and catch Fallon red-handed. Once we have Fallon we will be able to round up everyone from him down. It's been tried before and we've always made a hash of the endgame; Fallon has always evaded us.' Hardin paused, looking gloomy, before smiling and adding with a whisper: 'Until now.'

Riley glanced across at his fellow officers. Garrett wore a serious expression whereas Davies grinned, eager to be up and at them, kicking down doors and smashing heads. DI Savage smiled at him again.

Afterwards, as they left the room, Savage came across to them.

'If, Darius – God forbid – this all goes wrong, you'll be glad to be on a beach four thousand miles from here.'

'If this goes wrong, ma'am,' Riley said, 'I think a million miles might be a safer distance.'

Alec Jackman lay back on the bed in a state of post-orgasmic exhaustion. The girl beside him slept, almost silent, the only noise the faint sound of her shallow breathing. Jackman traced the line of the sheet as the material rose along her legs to her hips and fell down to her waist. She had pushed the sheet down from the top half of her body and Jackman let his eyes rest on her breasts. Round, but small and pert. Tiny goosebumps marked the mesmerising curves and her nipples stood erect.

As Jackman pulled the sheet up to cover her, the girl stirred and yawned, but she didn't wake. She would be tired. Worn out. Sometimes the young ones were shocked at what he could do. What he could *still* do. Most men of his age weren't as fit as him, most were heading downhill toward a six-foot hole in the ground and oblivion. At times like this Jackman almost believed he would live forever. Rubbish, of course, but there was no reason he shouldn't go on enjoying himself as long as possible. And he usually went on a long while. The coke helped, although he hadn't done much. The drug was mostly for the girl's benefit. A little inducement to keep her sweet.

Jackman glanced at the bedside clock. He ought to be out of here, he had an important meeting to get to and then home to his wife, Gill. He had promised he wouldn't be too late and he didn't want to push things, even though he realised she probably had an inkling of what was going on. She knew the score. Understood the price to pay. All those shoes, handbags, the hired help, the nice house. The goodies cost money and the girl was payback. One squeak from Gill and she could say goodbye to the little treats and the lifestyle as well. Glamour, parties, trips abroad, local recognition. Without him she had nothing.

Then there was his brother-in-law, Gavin Redmond. Gill owed Jackman for him too. The idiot should have been rolling in dough with the yacht business he ran, but he seemed to piss away the stuff. A few years back Jackman had helped him get the company back on a sound footing by finding a new investor and an extra revenue stream. The sideline was far from legal, but nobody got rich keeping to the rules. The bankers proved that.

He sighed and got out of the bed, found his jacket and rummaged in a pocket for his pack of cigarettes. Like the cocaine, he knew he shouldn't, but this would be the first of the day. Self-control. Like with the girl. He'd come as the gasp from her own orgasm spread a smile across her face. Now Jackman smiled too. A real cutie, this one.

The lighter flared and he drew on the cigarette. Redmond was pissed off about the girl. As he would be, the girl being his own daughter, Jackman's niece. Not blood related of course, but still, the frisson was there. Something to do with some of his wife's genes being in the girl, Jackman suspected.

He thought about Redmond again. In truth the idiot worried him. Lately he'd looked tired and nervous. Jackman had told him to get a grip. He only had to hold himself together for a few days and then they'd be quids in. All of them. On the other hand, one wrong move and everybody was going to get screwed.

Unless . . .

The meeting could change things and swing the possibility of success their way. Jackman went to the bathroom and then quickly got dressed.

Thirty minutes later he pulled into the car park at Jennycliff, a parkland area to the south of the city which sat above cliffs on the eastern edge of Plymouth Sound. Over the sea the light had long gone from the sky. The daylight, anyway; a swathe of orange off to his right painted the underside of the clouds and below, the city glowed.

Jackman sat in his car, tapped his watch, waited. He shivered as the air in the car cooled. Early evening dog-walkers returned from the park and loaded their charges into the back of cars. A couple of hardy runners headed home.

The minutes ticked by and the legitimate visitors all left. A car cruised in, followed by another, and then another. They parked up one end, the interior light in one car flicking on, a woman and a man visible inside, while a couple of men climbed from the other cars and skirted the vehicle, cameras in hand.

Usually the proximity of sex would have aroused Jackman, but not tonight. He turned his attention away from the free show and towards the car park entrance where a pair of headlights announced a new arrival. This time the vehicle didn't head up the slope to the top but pulled alongside Jackman's car. Even in silhouette the pickup looked like it had seen better days. Patches of white filler adorned the dark bodywork and one wing had a large dent. When the interior light went on it illuminated a bulky man with a beard. A woolly hat perched on his head struggled to cover large ears.

The man nodded across at Jackman and then reached over and opened the passenger door. Jackman got out of his car and ducked down into the passenger seat, closing the door. The light went off and Jackman heard the man sniff and cough, a waft of bad air coming Jackman's way a few moments later.

'Well?' Jackman said. 'This isn't the sort of place I usually come for a meeting so let's get on with it.'

'It?' the man said.

'Kenny Fallon said you had something for me. You hand it over and he lets you go about your business.'

'Cash. Up front. He promised.'

'Look, you're a poacher, a petty housebreaker when you get the chance. Some pheasants, a rabbit or two, a laptop or phone if you spot an opportunity when you're out and about. I can't see what you can have come up with that's got Kenny so excited, but if it's good you'll get your money.'

The man stirred, shifted in his seat as he retrieved something from a pocket. A little screen popped into life in the gloom.

'A phone? I hope you're not winding us up. Where did you nick it from?'

'I didn't, it's mine.' Fingers swept over the surface of the phone and a movie clip started to play. 'I want five thousand for this.'

'Five thousand? You're crazy.'

'When you've watched it, you'll pay.'

'Let me see then.' Jackman leant over, trying not to inhale the mixture of bad breath and sweat.

Poor quality video played on the screen. Black and grey

chunks of pixels swirling. Static on the audio track. That, and the sound of heavy breathing. Jackman was about to ask the man what the hell he was playing at when a bloom of light grew and danced in the centre of the picture as the camera zoomed and struggled to focus. Then the image steadied and Jackman was able to resolve the jumble of light and shadow. As the film ran on he realised this was dynamite, and a minute or so later when the clip finished he had to struggle to contain his excitement.

'Good, eh?' A finger touched the screen and the man pocketed the phone. 'Five thousand.'

'How the hell did you get that?' Jackman felt his heart beating, but tried to remain calm. 'I mean, were you waiting there or what?'

'I was in the area on business. There's a holiday home, couple from London. They're down here every weekend and they've got careless. They started to leave a few things around the place and I spied them through the window. There's a key under the flowerpot for the cleaner. They've got the brains to earn all that money but really they're as thick as they come. I—'

'Alright, I understand. Get on with it.'

'I heard an almighty smash as I was going through their stuff. When I rush out I see the car upside down. I recognised her immediately. I was about to make a run back into the woods when something made me stop. I whipped out the phone and started to film. Twenty minutes later the place was crawling with police, the fire brigade, ambos, everything. That's when I legged it.'

'Give me the phone.' Jackman reached into his back pocket and extracted his wallet. Pulled out all the cash he had. Two fifties and a bunch of tens. 'Here.'

'A couple of long'uns? You must be fucking joking.'

'I don't carry five K around. You'll get the rest once Kenny's seen it.'

'But I need my phone. Anyway, how do I know I can trust you?'

'It's not me, it's Kenny. He plays fair. And when he doesn't play fair he sends someone round to kick your head in. You don't have a choice. You'll get your phone back tomorrow.'

'Alright.' The man grunted, retrieved his phone and dumped it in Jackman's hand, in exchange for the money. 'Five thousand. Remember?'

'Sure,' Jackman said pushing the door open and gulping fresh air. 'I'll be in touch.'

The engine started up as Jackman slammed the door and the car jerked forwards and then slewed out of the car park.

Jackman stood still for a moment. Let out a breath. Felt in his pocket for the phone. The smooth surface tingled the ends of his fingers, almost as if there was something magical about the object. He smiled, glanced up to the doggers at the top of the hill and then thought of the girl waiting for him back at his flat.

'You lucky, lucky boy,' he said to himself as he climbed back into his car.

Chapter Six

Tuesday morning, Savage was roused early by Jamie snuggling into the bed and wanting to know when Father Christmas was coming again. Pete muttered something along the lines of 'never, if you don't let him get some more shut-eye', but by then Savage was wide awake, all chance of further sleep gone.

Down in the kitchen for breakfast Pete stifled a yawn, let it slip into a smile and then put his arm around her when she came over. He was finding it difficult, she knew. Adapting to a permanent life ashore was always going to be tricky after the routine of his previous existence. He loved Samantha and Jamie as much as she did, but often he'd only seen them at their best. Day-to-day was a totally different experience for him.

As Savage drove in to the Stonehouse area of the city to catch up with the inquiry teams, she let her thoughts mill around. Concluded that although things could be better, they could be a whole lot worse too.

By the time she arrived the sun had crawled up over the horizon into a clear sky, a smudge of cloud off to the south-west and a change in the wind direction hinting at an end to the cold conditions of the last couple of days. A call to DCI Garrett informed her that yesterday's door-to-door trawl hadn't produced anything fresh, so she made her way back to Owers' flat at one twenty-one Durnford Street. John Layton's Volvo stood alongside a resident's parking sign, an 'On Police Business' sticker on the inside of the windscreen. Layton sat in the front passenger seat, spooning something from a pot into his mouth.

'Yogurt and muesli,' he said as the window slipped down. 'A bit nineteen eighties but still as good for you now as it was back then.'

'Sorry,' said Savage. 'I messed up. Too eager I suppose.'

'And I apologise for getting angry,' Layton said, finishing the last of the yogurt and stuffing the plastic pot and spoon in a paper evidence bag. He took his Tilley from the dash-board, got out of the car and plonked the hat on his head. 'I blame it on my daughter. Ever since she was born . . . well, you know, don't you?'

Savage did know. When her own daughters, the twins, Samantha and Clarissa, had been born, something had changed in the way she approached police work. Cases involving violence towards the innocent or powerless became magnified in their importance. The crimes became personal, as if they had been committed against her own family, and the anger and despair could only be ameliorated by catching the perpetrators. Or, as in the case of the man who'd tried to abduct her daughter Samantha – the serial killer Matthew Harrison – seeing that he received a fiery retribution.

'Can I go in?' Savage asked, swallowing a lump of emotion.

'Yes, of course. I've nearly finished so there's no need to worry about suiting up this time. Just about to check the U-bends in the bathroom and then I'm done.'

'U-bends?' Savage said. 'As in plumbing?'

'Yes. You get hair and nail clippings and all sorts in them. You should have a gander at yours sometime, you'd be surprised how much gets stuck down in amongst the sludge and gunge.'

'Yuck,' Savage wrinkled her nose. 'I don't want to think about it. If I want to get them cleaned I'll call a plumber.'

'If you can find one.'

They went down the steps and into the basement flat where Layton disappeared to his plumbing duties. Savage went into the living room, where a set of floodlights on a stand illuminated several boxes of papers and files stacked ready for dispatch to the station.

She wandered out of the living room and down the corridor. Floorboards had been pulled up in places and a section of plasterboard cut away from a wall where a patch of paint appeared fresher than the rest of the flat. In the bathroom the white floor tiles gleamed under the glare of another set of lights. Layton's legs sprawled across the tiles, scrabbling for purchase on the shiny surface. His body was wedged under the bath where he'd removed a panel from the side. Banging, huffing and the occasional swear word came floating out. Savage left him to it and moved onto the bedroom. The bed had been stripped of the Barbie cover and sheets and the tea chest Owers used as a linen bin contained nothing but air. Savage wasn't sure what she was looking for; Layton and his team usually went through a crime scene like locusts through a field of crops and it was unlikely they would miss anything.

She stood in the centre of the bare room, thinking how Owers' life was being taken apart. He'd probably killed Simza Ellis so he deserved all that was coming to him, but it looked as if he had been living a bleak, empty existence for years.

He may have gained some perverse pleasure from his paedophilia, but was the pleasure so great it was worth sacrificing everything for?

She went back into the living room again. The blanket covering the sofa had gone, however the Freemans catalogue remained. The catalogue no longer lay open but sat placed on one arm of the sofa, as if someone had forgotten to pack it away in one of the boxes. Savage went over, picked it up and began to flick through the first few pages. As she perused the dresses she looked at the models – teens and early twenties most of them – and thought about herself at a younger age. Back then, when she'd first got together with Pete, she remembered he'd often teased her about her scruffy attire, but then conceded he preferred her without clothes anyway.

Savage smiled to herself at the memory and then shook her head. For too long her life had been on autopilot, her relationship with Pete the same. Passion had been fuelled by distance, love by his absence. Now he was back for good they'd have to work on things, make an effort. She wondered if that might include needing a change of wardrobe.

She moved on through the various sections, but nothing grabbed her. Then she reached the children's clothes, spotting the page which had been open the first time she had seen the catalogue. She flicked on, and a few pages later the catalogue opened at a slip of paper wedged deep in the seam. At the top of the page two girls dressed in vests and knickers stood against a pastel background. Savage removed the paper. Nothing on either side. She looked back at the catalogue. Near the seam there was a hollow space, a recess cut away, inside which was the distinctive shape of a USB memory stick.

*   *   *

After handing Layton the catalogue with the cut-out and the USB stick, Savage left the property, strolled down Durnford Street and then up to Admiralty Street, looking to see where the inquiry teams had got to. At St George's Primary the shrieks of children floated out from the playground at the rear. They were out of view, safe from the prying eyes of a pervert like Owers, but a minor inconvenience like that wouldn't stop someone like him. He'd find a way. The question was, had he gone down to the Lizard in Cornwall for just that reason?

Up the street she could see two members of the inquiry team talking to Enders. Enders waved and then jogged towards her, a wide grin on his face. He reached her, breathless, words pouring out. Savage told him to calm down. Take it slowly. Enders explained the two officers he'd been talking to had scored big time.

'We've got a reliable sighting of Mr Owers. He was seen scuttling up the cut at the back of Admiralty Street early Sunday evening, something about a confrontation with two other men. Then a white van drives off at speed.'

'Have we got anything else on the van?'

'Of course.' The grin widened and Enders nodded over at a small sign attached to a nearby lamp post. 'Neighbourhood Watch. The van was double-parked near the school and somebody snapped a pic with their phone. We've got the index.'

'And?'

'Registered owner is a Stuart Chaffe. Turns out he has form. Major. Went down for assaulting a police officer after being stopped on the motorway during a drugs bust. The assault was a knifing. Sliced the officer open and pulled the man's guts out with his bare hands. Chaffe spent five years in Broadmoor before being moved to an ordinary prison to complete his sentence. He was only released last year after an eighteen-year stretch inside.'

'Sounds like he could be old enough to be our mystery man, the one who impersonated Mr Evershed. Do we have an address?'

'Southway, ma'am. Kinnaird Crescent. Since he's only just out of the nick he'll have a probation officer. Shall I try to make contact and get some sort of lowdown before we head out there?'

Savage thought back to an incident a couple of years ago. In a similar situation she'd gone by the book and had a quiet word with somebody on the offender management side of things. When she'd turned up at the suspect's house – a youth wanted for attacking a mum-to-be with a hammer – the door had been opened by a local solicitor, the lad already briefed to keep his mouth shut.

'No,' Savage said. 'Better if our visit comes as a complete surprise to Mr Chaffe, don't you think?'

Kinnaird Crescent lay on the northern edge of the city in the maze of Drives, Closes, Walks and Gardens which made up the district of Southway. Stuart Chaffe lived in a block of flats on the north side of the crescent, one of a number of five-storey blocks dotted every fifty metres or so. The road traversed a slope and the flats had been built on the lower side, meaning the ground floor – which consisted of garages – and the first floor lay below street level. Each block had a concrete bridge which led across to the entrance door. Net curtains adorned the lower windows of the flats, hiding away whatever grimness lay within. Depressing, Savage thought, as Enders drove along the crescent, past block after block of identical buildings.

Halfway along they came to the correct block. They

parked up and strolled across the strange little bridge to the glass-fronted lobby area, where a list of names ran down a column of bell-pushes to the right of the locked door. 'Chaffe' had been scribbled in pencil alongside the number '324'. Three presses of the bell later, the third with Enders keeping his finger held down for a good thirty seconds, and a lanky figure shuffled down into the foyer from a stairwell to the right. Stuart Chaffe wore ill-fitting jeans and a denim jacket, his wrists and ankles protruding from the sleeves and the bottom of the trousers, as if he was a kid growing too fast for his parents to keep him in clothes. In his early forties, he appeared older, with greying hair and bloodshot eyes, his skin bearing an unhealthy pallor, as if he had returned from a long sea voyage where fruit and vegetables were in short supply. He gazed through the glass before leaning against the wall next to a bare noticeboard.

'If you are from the good Lord Jehovah you can fuck off.' Chaffe rubbed his eyes and yawned.

'I have heard my boss called many things, Mr Chaffe,' Savage said, 'but God isn't one of them.'

'Pigs then? These days only pigs and religious folk dress like you two twats.'

'Let us in, Stuart,' Enders said, pressing his warrant card up to the glass. 'We want a word. Or two.'

'I was right then. All that time inside and I've still got a good sense of smell for crap.' Chaffe made no move to open the door, instead he straightened and gestured around the hall. 'Talk away. No one around to hear, just a few deaf old coots. The rest are out at work.'

'And you, Stuart?' Savage said. 'Have you got a job?'

'The name's Stuey, not Stuart, and "Had" is the word. Gutting chickens in a factory wasn't my idea of fun. Not

67

after having spent the last eighteen years in a battery farm myself. Jacked it. You should have seen my proby's face when I said I'd had enough, you'd have thought I'd knocked one out over her.'

'Let's talk about this inside, Stuart. You can make us a nice cup of tea and we can ask you a few questions.'

'Tea? You're joking, right? Believe me, sweetheart, when you've done a stretch like I have the last thing you are going to be drinking on the outside is tea. So, if you'll excuse me, I think I'll go back and fix myself something a little stronger before you guys bore me back to sleep.'

Chaffe turned and began to move towards the stairs. Enders grabbed the door handle and rattled the door, the noise echoing around the bare hallway.

'You own a white van,' Savage said. 'Were you out and about in it on Sunday evening? Maybe around the Stonehouse area?'

'So what if I was? Got to make a living somehow.'

'Do you have any friends who live over that way, Stuart? On the gross side, the type who like to play with kiddies?'

'Hey?'

'A man known as Franklin Owers. You'll likely as not have seen his picture in the *Herald*. I don't suppose you've heard of him, have you?'

Chaffe stood for a moment, a smirk creeping across his lips. Then he turned and walked across the hallway, his beanpole-like frame disappearing as he went down the stairs.

'Ma'am?' Enders had stepped back from the door and pointed to a white plate on the outside wall of the flat. 'Says numbers two ninety-four to three twenty-four. Which means Chaffe's flat is on the top floor, and if you remember he came *down* the steps.'

'Shit.' Savage moved back onto the bridge and peered over. A row of windows marked the first floor flats and then, below, the grass slope led down to rendered wall with a couple of smaller windows and some pipes. Somewhere out the back of the flats an engine coughed into life, followed by a squeal of tyres.

Enders was already running for their car, key fob in an outstretched hand. A white transit van came from behind the flats, shooting up the access road and sweeping round and up to join Kinnaird Crescent proper. The vehicle skidded into the road, turning sharp left and roared back towards where Enders was crossing over. He dashed across, diving for the pavement as the van sped past, Chaffe leaning forwards in the front seat, mouth hanging open, eyes wide. Enders picked himself up as Savage arrived at the car and jumped in the passenger side. Enders was in the car and starting the engine as Savage reached for the radio.

They had parked facing the direction they had come so Enders floored the accelerator and spun the wheel. The back end of the car slid round but not quite enough to prevent him from having to engage reverse gear and back up. Then they were going forwards again, Savage spotting the van disappearing over a rise a couple of hundred metres away. The crescent curled up to the right, meeting the larger Clittaford Road at a mini-roundabout. Chaffe went left, screeching across the roundabout and clipping a car parked a short distance up the road. Enders had the headlights on and the grille-mounted blue strobe flashed in response to the warble of the siren. A motorcyclist came from the right and Enders had to thump the horn to prevent the rider from venturing into their path.

'Idiot!'

69

Savage had control on the radio and swore when the dispatcher said the nearest unit was at the Crownhill station. It would be at least a couple of minutes before back up would arrive.

Clittaford Road had speed bumps for the first quarter of a mile, but Enders took them at full pelt, the car's suspension bottoming with a jar each time they hit one. Another mini-roundabout marked the end of the residential area and the start of an industrial complex on the right, a number of vast warehouses standing like sad monoliths. The road continued to bend to the right, looping in a great circle until houses once again appeared on the left and the road came to the much busier Southway Drive where a queue of cars waited at a red light.

Up ahead, Chaffe swung over to the wrong side of the carriageway and steamed by the queue, hanging a right and speeding onto the main road. Enders followed and they joined the road just in time to see Chaffe slow down and take a sneaky left up a side street.

'Got him,' Enders said, flooring the accelerator once again. They shot along the main road and Enders took the left turn at speed, careering round and bumping the curb. Out of the corner of her eye Savage spotted a sign: two figures holding hands – one taller than the other – inside a red triangle.

'No!' she screamed.

The dad in the middle of the road grabbed his three-year-old and leapt for the pavement, but an older child stood rigid with fright. Enders wrenched the wheel and stamped on the brake pedal. The ABS juddered as the car began to turn and then the whole of the vehicle was sliding sideways, the back end swinging round so when they stopped they were pointing back the way they had come.

Savage looked over her shoulder but couldn't see the child. She jumped out and ran to the rear of the car. The girl knelt on the ground crying, pointing down into the road where a little black cat lay squashed under a wheel, a mass of polystyrene beads escaping from the soft toy's stomach.

By the time they had waited for a Traffic unit to arrive so the incident could be logged and assessed – the attending officers taking photographs and measuring the marks on the road as well as interviewing the available witnesses – the day was fast disappearing.

When Savage had seen the little girl standing there she had been transported back through the years to when her daughter Clarissa – Samantha's twin – had been killed in a hit and run up on Dartmoor. The accident had been altogether different, of course: Clarissa had been on her bike and the driver hadn't been a skilled officer who had completed several pursuit courses but a maniac handling his car with no respect for other road users. The investigation had been much more involved too, but despite numerous leads the driver had never been traced, Clarissa's death – or murder, as Savage saw it – unattributed and unavenged.

Savage took the wheel for the short drive back to Crownhill and as they drove away from the scene, Enders stared down at his lap. She knew Enders understood about Clarissa and he also had young children of his own.

'It's OK, Patrick. She didn't have a mark on her. The only thing damaged is your pride.'

'Inches, ma'am, inches.' Enders shook his head. 'I should have made a judgement of the risk. Time of day, the weather, danger to other road users, the seriousness of the offence the suspect we were pursuing may have committed . . .'

'Textbook rubbish. Impossible for us to do if we were to have any chance of catching up with Chaffe. Anyway, I think murder is serious enough for a high-speed pursuit, and Chaffe is mixed up in this somehow.'

'You think Chaffe is a paedophile like Owers? Maybe involved in killing Simza Ellis?'

'No idea. Call me old-fashioned, but I don't think the fact he's done eighteen years makes him a reformed character. He doesn't exactly look like a complete innocent either, does he? And if he is, then why on earth did he do a runner?'

The call had come from a policeman in Plymouth. Unexpected.

'Simza,' the voice said; Tony Ellis listening but not needing to know, not wanting to know either.

'Back then,' the policeman continued. 'Well, it turns out you might have been right all along.'

Ellis opened the front door and stepped on to the veranda of his little park home, out of earshot of Lisa, his wife. A cold dampness touched his face and he heard the roar of the traffic on the M5. A blur of cars and lorries sped by on the embankment above, the monotonous whooshing like waves pounding a beach.

Back then. Last summer. No beach, but a series of jagged rocks at the bottom of the steep cliffs of the Lizard. A huge swell from a distant storm way off in the Atlantic crashing into the shore, the spray misting his face but the water warmer than today's drizzle. Rainbows dancing in the morning sun, and Simza laughing as he had thrown sandwiches out into the void where gulls swooped and caught them.

Then she was gone. Just like that, when their backs had been turned for one moment.

Within minutes the Lizard lifeboat had been launched, the orange craft rising and falling on the waves as it searched the water below the cliffs. Fifteen minutes later and a rescue helicopter roared overhead, the tourists gawping at the free airshow. Within an hour a coastguard cliff-rescue team and half a dozen police officers were scouring the clifftops too, guys in harnesses abseiling down to check unseen ledges, voices crackling in radios.

'*That's a negative down here, repeat, negative.*'

'What about the fat guy with the camera?' Lisa had whispered to him. The one with the strange smile, all-too friendly as he patted Simza on the head as he passed by on the coast path.

A word to the officer in charge had brought a shake of the head. That sort of thing didn't happen down here. Not in Cornwall. He promised to organise a search of the nearby car parks and maybe station a patrol car up the lane. However, when Simza's pink trainer was plucked from the sea by the lifeboat crew all efforts were once again concentrated on the water.

'But he'd been taking pictures,' Lisa said. She remembered him leering from behind a white van parked down by the gift shop.

'No, love,' the officer said. 'I can understand why you'd want to think that, to cling onto some glimmer of hope, but no, she's gone over the edge. Happens every so often. It's why we have the fence. People don't realise how dangerous the coastline is.'

'Mr Ellis?' The voice was still on the line as Ellis collapsed onto the white plastic chair on the veranda. Now the officer was asking Ellis some questions, mentioning a name or two, did they sound familiar?

You might have been right all along.

'Do they sound familiar, Mr Ellis?'

Ellis could barely hear the voice above the traffic roaring past on the motorway, the noise of waves pounding a beach. His fists pounding to a bloody pulp the face of some pervert who'd taken his little girl.

Chapter Seven

Nr Bovisand, Plymouth. Wednesday 16th January. 8.27 a.m.

Wednesday morning, and Savage stood outside with Pete waiting for the kids to emerge from the hallway for the trip to school. Pete was shaking his head, pointing at various bits of the house which needed attention. Roof, guttering, windowsills, the damp-proof course, they all needed work. He took Savage's hand and smiled at her. Lucky he was going to be around for a bit, he said.

Peregrines was a sprawling structure, hardly beautiful except in its oddity. The original open-plan single-storey building had been added to over the years, growing various appendages until it had a number of different levels and wings and more resembled a bodged-up Greek island villa than a house. The previous occupant had been an admiral and at first Savage and Pete had rented the property from him while he embarked on a round-the-world sailing trip with his second, and somewhat younger, wife. Three years in, still not having fully explored the Caribbean, he decided he was never coming back and sold them the house. Over the years they'd reached the conclusion that the place hadn't been so much a bargain as a gift horse, but short of doing what the admiral himself had done, Savage didn't think they'd be leaving anytime soon.

The position, high on the eastern side of the Sound near Bovisand, was incredible. Surrounded by fields on three sides, and on the fourth, the sea. Cliffs plunged to the surf line, and were home to numerous birds, including the occasional marauder, the eponymous peregrine. The only downside to the position was the westerly wind which battered the house in bad weather.

Right now the air was still, the sky clear and cold. Pete went to start the car and Savage shouted in at Jamie not to forget his scarf and gloves. Jamie came running out of the front door whirling the scarf around his head and then skidded on the lawn, landing on top of a molehill.

'I'll get some diesel,' Pete said, climbing back out of the car. 'That will teach the little blighter. Half a litre and he'll think twice about doing it again.'

'Diesel?' Stefan came out onto the porch, raised his eyebrows and held the front door open for Jamie as he trooped in to get a fresh pair of trousers. 'Is that the British way? Wouldn't be allowed in Sweden.'

'The mole, you daft turnip. You pour it down the hole and they bugger off.' Pete grinned. 'Although now you mention it perhaps I could spare a bit for Jamie. Might have the same effect.'

'Cool,' Samantha said emerging from inside, fingers pressing keys on her phone as she spoke. 'I'm going to post that right now.'

Savage stood on the doorstep, shaking her head at her family's antics, reaching for her own phone as it trilled out.

'DC Enders, ma'am,' the voice said. 'We've found Franklin Owers.'

'Great. Are they taking him to Charles Cross? Tell DC

Calter I'll meet her there and we can work out an interview strategy together. Make sure DCI Garrett is informed too. Better get onto his MAPPA contact as well.'

'He's not going to the custody centre. He'll be going to Derriford,' Enders said.

'Resist arrest did he? Get hurt in the struggle?' Savage followed Jamie upstairs to help him get changed. 'Well make sure somebody stays with him at the hospital, we don't want him slipping away.'

'Not A and E, ma'am, the mortuary,' Enders said. 'He's dead.'

In a tower block in Plymouth city centre, Jackman glanced at the bedside clock. He groaned. Despite his intentions of the previous night he'd stayed over, phoning his wife and telling her he'd met an old colleague and they needed to catch up. After his meeting at Jennycliffe he'd returned to his flat, woken the girl and entered her, fucking her slowly for a good thirty minutes. Afterwards he had done a few hours' work while the girl slept and then they'd ordered some food in, fucked again, slept.

Fantastic, last night. And not just the stuff with the girl.

He couldn't resist viewing the material once more, so he heaved himself out of the bed and, naked, padded across to the desk next to the window where his laptop sat. He glanced out for a moment, taking in the grey morning, before he flipped up the lid on the machine and logged in. Last night he'd transferred the movie from the poacher's phone to his computer and deleted the original file. Now he navigated to the folder he wanted and opened the new copy.

Full screen on the laptop the quality of the video was worse than ever, but after a few seconds the image was unmistakable: a woman stood next to the wreckage of an upside down car, bathed in a headlight beam coming from somewhere off-camera. Her bright red hair nicely foretold what was about to happen, Jackman thought, as he heard a man's voice echoing out, pleading for help. The woman ignored the pleas and turned and walked away. A little later the car exploded in a fireball which overloaded the camera's sensor in a white flare, before the exposure compensated and the raw beauty of the yellow and orange flames became visible. For a few seconds an awful screaming rent the air, but the noise didn't last long. Jackman knew from the newspaper reports that there hadn't been much left by the time the fire brigade had arrived; only a set of charred bones, the flesh and fat having burned and bubbled away.

Even though he had watched the film several times the footage was still causing Jackman's heart to thump. Not that he was concerned about the man in the car. No, he'd been a murderer and burning was almost too good for him. What raised Jackman's pulse, what made him think life might be about to get even sweeter, was the woman. She shouldn't have walked away and she shouldn't have lied about doing so either. Not when she was a Detective Inspector with Plymouth CID.

Jackman closed the movie file, flipped the lid on the laptop down and smiled. Power and control was what the movie gave him. Given the situation with Redmond, the poacher's night-time encounter had brought some timely good fortune.

Thinking of Redmond, his mind turned to the girl. He looked over to the bed and feasted his eyes on her body. Curves not yet fully developed, face angelic, mind uncorrupted. He liked them that way. She was seventeen and legal, of course. He was no pervert and it was best to keep things above board, even if the affair with the girl – his niece – would be an unforgivable misdemeanour. Especially for a married man who was the deputy leader of Plymouth City Council, and a member of the Devon and Cornwall Police and Crime Panel.

Two words were all the directions Savage needed from Enders to reach the crime scene: 'The Hoe.' Fifteen minutes later and she drove up Hoe Road, swung past the army fort and turned right up the narrow access ramp onto the Hoe. A row of flagpoles bordered a huge expanse of tarmac, the flags hanging down, sad and unmoving. In summer the place thronged with pedestrians, kids on bikes, roller skaters, skate-boarders and dog walkers. A grassy slope to one side of the tarmac was a fine place for picnicking and offered fantastic views over the Sound. Right now the area was deserted apart from a BBC outside broadcast car, a cameraman taking some establishing shots, and a pretty young female reporter in a hideous purple coat. Behind them stood the iconic red and white lighthouse. Whether it acted as a beacon or a warning probably depended upon your view of the city.

Savage parked alongside a patrol car, a van and Layton's Volvo. Layton stood next to the car, phone pressed to ear, his free hand agitated, the crime scene manager doing most of the talking. As Savage got out he looked across at her, nodded and pointed over towards the public toilets. The toilets lay at the eastern end of the Hoe, not far from the Hoe Lodge Restaurant, which, notwithstanding the grand name, was in reality nothing much more than a snack bar. Despite the weather a number of people were sitting outside, DC Enders and a uniformed PC weaving between the tables, taking statements.

Savage retrieved her PPE kit from the boot and struggled into a white coverall before crossing the tarmac to the path which led round to the toilet block, a low, brick building which had a number of roof lanterns poking up from a flat roof. One of Layton's CSIs stood next to a couple of poles with blue and white tape and he proffered a log, which Savage signed, before pointing down the path to the male toilets. DC Carl Denton was waiting at the entrance, a couple of strands of his hair falling loose from the hood on the white suit.

'Ma'am, shall we?' Denton rubbed his hands and stamped his feet as Savage approached. 'Only I've been here for ages and I'm dying for a cup of coffee.' He nodded in the direction of the Lodge. 'I hear the cafe is giving out free ones to our lads.'

'Is it Mr Owers?' she asked as she led the way in, padding across the damp floor of the entrance and into the toilets proper.

'I think so. The body matches the description anyway. Take a look. Third one along,' Denton said. 'Not that you need telling.'

'So somebody caught up with him before we did,' Savage said. 'Rough justice.'

'Not really rough. All things considered.'

'No.' Savage thought of Simza Ellis. Missing, presumed drowned. Never, until Monday morning, assumed sexually assaulted and murdered by some pervert. 'You're right. Simply justice.'

The man's body almost filled the cubicle, a mass of flesh the colour of lard prostrate before the toilet. On the seat a dusting of white powder contrasted with the black plastic, but the man's head was bent forwards, away from the powder, his face down in the bowl, as if he had been trying to get a drink of water, like a cat lapping up milk. His faded blue jeans and grey boxer shorts had been pulled down to his ankles, exposing a brown mess which had exploded from the deep cleavage of his bottom and been smeared all over the buttocks. The left arm hung down and brushed the wet floor while the right one lay at a funny angle up by the head, as if trying to grope for something. Impossible, since the forearm ended with two sticks of bone surrounded by ripped and bloodied flesh.

Jesus, Savage thought, life or death didn't get much more appalling than this. Or if it did, she really didn't want to know about it.

'Glad I'm not doing the recovery, ma'am,' Denton said. 'They'll need a bloody crane to get him out.'

Denton was right, Savage thought. The man must weigh thirty stone at least. Extracting him from the toilet would be tricky. If they were to use any sense of decorum in retrieving the corpse the team would need to dismantle the cubicle. The alternative would be to dismember the body.

Savage moved closer, not wanting to, but needing to see more. She held onto the door for support as she leant in. Franklin Owers, definitely. The mugshot which had been distributed hadn't been a good one, but there was no mistaking the round face, the receding hairline and the little goatee beard. Now she was closer she spotted a short piece of black cardboard, rolled in a tube, protruding from the man's left nostril. Gold print ran across the glossy surface, but Savage couldn't make out the words.

'He's got a business card shoved up his nose.' Savage pointed to the powder on the seat. 'Do you think that's cocaine?'

'Forgive me, ma'am. Given the circumstances, I didn't want to taste it to find out. However, down in the bowl there's a bag floating in the water and it's stuffed with white powder too. I'd say the bag contains four ounces or so.'

'A hundred grams? That's several thousand pounds street

value. Tends to suggest whoever killed this guy didn't care for drugs.'

'*If* it's coke. Anyway, the stuff has gone in the bowl. Would you want to use it?'

'Not really. Besides, red wine and caffeine are my drugs of choice.' Savage moved back from the corpse to where Denton stood next to a row of urinals, her nose detecting a sweet smell of citrus lemon mingled with piss. 'Who found him?'

'The attendant. Came to unlock the toilets at eight-thirty this morning and found they were already open. He noticed water overflowing from inside one of the cubicles and went to investigate. He swears the body wasn't in the loos last night when he closed up after the place had been cleaned. He's sure the door was locked properly too.'

'Well the victim didn't squeeze in through a window, did he?' Savage glanced up at the narrow slits above the urinals and at the overhead roof lanterns. 'But then again he didn't walk in here either. You saw the hand?'

'I saw *one* hand.'

'Exactly. I wonder what the pathologist will make of that.'

Minutes later and the white-suited figure of Dr Andrew Nesbit shuffled in, displaying his characteristic stoop and offering a little homily by way of a greeting as he glanced over the top of his glasses.

'Wednesdays are all very well, Charlotte, but they are only two better than Mondays. Whether you like them depends if you are a glass half full person or not.' Nesbit edged round a large puddle of water and peered into the cubicle at the body. 'What have we here? A suicide?'

'That's what the toilet attendant thought when he phoned triple nine. But us amateurs guess not.'

'Let's see then, shall we?' Nesbit put his black bag down in a dry patch and shuffled closer. He spotted the white powder. 'Drugs OD?'

'I don't think so.'

'Ah, no!' Nesbit had seen the arm. 'Silly me. Not a suicide either. I don't think anyone would choose to kill themselves by cutting their hand off and if they did, my hunch is they would find it impossible to walk very far once they'd done so.'

'Doc?'

'He didn't die here.' Nesbit moved the left arm. 'He's in rigor, but he must have been brought here before the stiffness set in. And there is no blood, or very little. With both the ulnar and radial arteries in the arm severed, blood would be gushing everywhere. I can see some splatter marks on the man's right leg but not much on the floor. The hand was removed somewhere else.'

'How long before rigor sets in?'

'A few hours, but look at the lividity in the lower legs and the left arm. Some blood has oozed from the right too. I'd say the body was moved shortly after death. One to two hours at the most. To sum up, before rigor mortis but prior to livor mortis.'

'And the severing of the hand caused death?' Savage asked.

'Too early to say that, Charlotte, but it is possible.' Nesbit stared at the body for a moment and then reached forward and pulled the man's right sleeve up. 'There's something else here. Strange.'

Savage moved closer and Nesbit pointed at the forearm. There was a rectangle of skin marked with black and white stripes in a crude pattern resembling a zebra crossing.

'Appears to be paint,' Nesbit said touching the arm with a gloved finger. 'Dry too. Never seen anything quite like it.'

'Not a tattoo?'

'No, this is on the surface of the skin.'

'Can you get that thing out of his nose? The business card?'

'Let's see . . .' Nesbit reached for the black tube and teased it from the nostril and then flattened the card and showed it to Savage.

'Fastwerk Bookkeeping,' Savage said. 'Notte Street. That's close to here, back down Hoe Road.'

Nesbit turned to Savage. 'Can you pass me my thermometer and some wipes from my case please. An evidence bag too. I am going to take a rectal temperature reading, but I'll need to clean up a bit first.'

Savage opened the bag and found the thermometer unit with its remote probe and a packet of wipes. She handed them to Nesbit. Denton grimaced as the pathologist began to wipe the excrement from between the man's buttocks.

'And I used to think nappies were bad,' Savage said.

'How's Pete, Charlotte?' Nesbit said in an upbeat tone, the question sounding the sort which might be posed at a dinner party. 'I completely forgot to ask you on Monday. Rude of me, I know. I read in the paper he'd returned. Hero's welcome, razzmatazz and all.'

The switch from professional to personal matters caught Savage off guard, but she knew Nesbit was prone to small talk in an effort to distract from the task in hand.

'Fine. Getting cabin fever from being ashore, but the kids love him being back. I am trying to persuade him to swallow the hook.'

'Hey?'

'Meaning to give up his command. A desk job would be better for the children and my stress levels.'

'Come on, Charlotte,' Nesbit stopped wiping and turned

to give her a quizzical look. 'Pete giving up the sea would be like you giving up all this.'

Nesbit returned his attention to the body and shoved the white probe of the thermometer between the man's buttocks.

Savage burst out laughing.

Budgeon played the pressure-washer jet across the concrete floor of the barn. Full power, red water sluicing away in rivulets, specks of white bone gliding along them until they disappeared down the drain. As he worked, a distant ache inched its way across his forehead, all the time diminishing until the feeling became not much more than a mild irritation.

It felt good. Fucking good.

At last, things were in motion and he'd made a start. Wheels were turning, the freight train on the move. Nothing was going to stop him now. Nothing.

The last of the fat bastard's blood swirled around the drain cover, a gurgling echoing Frankie's last sounds.

Please, Ricky, please!

He'd screamed plenty before the final words, blood spurting everywhere as he thrashed around like a fat, sloppy fish flapping on the riverbank. He'd talked too. Plenty. Facts and figures. Everything Budgeon needed to know about Big K's business, from turnover to throughput. Budgeon had been impressed. Big K had quite an operation running and Budgeon's South American friends would be keen to get some of the action.

Payday.

Budgeon tidied away the pressure washer and went inside. He'd recorded the local lunchtime news bulletin, and now, back in the house, he played the programme back on the big screen above the fireplace. He sat down on the sofa, cradled a glass of Scotch in his hand and sat back to watch the show.

An establishing shot panned across the scene before the girlie reporter did her piece to camera. Behind her a sign read 'Public Conveniences' and the viewer's eye was drawn over her shoulder, following in the sign's direction to alight on the dank building in the background. You could almost smell the piss.

Nice camerawork, he thought. The guy should win an award. Nice use of the words 'toilets' and 'paedophile' by the reporter too. And when they cut away to Lester Close and pictures of the little girl flashed up, Budgeon knew the stuff with Frankie had been genius. The message was clear, and there were those out there who would understand it all too well.

You shall not steal; you shall not deal falsely; you shall not lie to one another.

Lexi, Big K. They knew the code. And they knew the consequences if you broke it. The thief would lose his hand, the betrayer his life.

He rubbed his forehead, aware of a slight discomfort, then he touched the remote, pausing the playback as the reporter began to hand back to the studio.

He took another swig of his drink and swirled the liquid across his teeth before swallowing. The reporter stared out from the TV, smile frozen. She was a pretty one, for sure. A local girl made good, but she wouldn't be around here for long. London calling and all that.

London.

Another home, and more memories.

After prison, London had seemed the best place to start again. You were anonymous up there, nobody nosing into your affairs, no history to worry about. He'd done fine, made a lot of money. Enough to buy some investment property out in Spain and start to think about retiring to the sun. But then he'd been well and truly screwed and that was what this was all about too.

Why him? It was a question Budgeon had asked himself before. Did he look like the type of guy who enjoyed taking it up the arse? Did he look like a pushover? Of course not. Just the opposite. The only explanation could be that those who'd wronged him were stupid or mean, or both.

Tossers.

The discomfort had turned into a soreness now, a prickly feeling he knew presaged another attack. A few more gulps of Scotch eased the tension and then he pushed himself up from the sofa. He went over to the fireplace, picked a log from the basket and placed it on the fire. A shower of orange sparks flared for a moment before being sucked up the chimney. He glanced up from the fire to the screen just a few inches from his head. This close the pixels on the display were distinct, like thousands of coloured crystals on some sort of collage, each one a part of a bigger picture. If he pressed 'play' on the remote, the scene would spring into action again, people would move, speak, smile. Life would go on.

But that wasn't going to happen. Not for those who'd crossed him.

Budgeon reached across for a phone on a nearby table. Punched out a number, and when someone answered, he spoke.

'The cop. We set him up next.'

He hung up and put the phone down. Then he took up his glass and gulped the rest of the Scotch, unable to suppress a smile at the serendipity of the situation. He supposed he ought to thank the *Herald* for printing the picture. A minibus full of kids from North Prospect, Chelsea scarves waving, the pig standing there smiling, along with a couple of PCSOs. Who would have thought he would turn up right on the doorstep like a meek lamb walking to the slaughterhouse?

He returned to the sofa, pointed the remote at the screen and pressed 'standby'. The reporter's frozen smile beamed down for a moment before the screen went black.

Chapter Eight

Outside the toilet block, the pathway had been cordoned off for fifty metres in both directions and Hoe Road had been closed. A team of half a dozen white-suited officers were working their way along the path and the grassy bank adjoining the road. John Layton was standing by some steps which led down to the road, talking into his phone again. Whoever was on the other end this time was getting a right earful. Layton ended the call and came across to Savage and Denton.

'Bloody jokers. The head honcho at the council in charge of toilets says he wants his crew to dismantle the cubicle. If we take the thing apart he says he'll bill us for any damage. Tosser.'

'So?' Savage said. 'Let them do the job.'

'He won't call the crew out here until late afternoon because he'll miss his overtime targets if they abandon the job they started this morning. What are we supposed to do, twiddle our thumbs while fatso decomposes in there? Jobsworth.'

'You and the mortuary recovery lads do it. If they send us a bill then we will bung one back for removing the body.'

'Good idea,' Layton nodded his assent and then began to fill Savage in on his team's progress. 'You've seen the victim, he's bloody massive. To get him into the toilets must have been a horrendous task. I reckon you would need two or more people, unless someone could have driven a vehicle along this access path.'

'And could they?'

'Look, the route leads back to the Hoe.' Layton pointed along the thread of black tarmac. The path curled to the right and joined the wide expanse of pavement which covered the top of the Hoe. 'There are any number of access points, but they all have either locked barriers or bollards.'

'I'll get the local inquiry team to check if they are all secure.'

'The other alternative is bringing the body up these steps. Two people might manage that. Two *strong* people.'

'CCTV?' Savage glanced up at the nearby lamp posts, hoping she would spot a white box with a lens pointing in their direction.

'Nope. None near here.'

'Too much to expect.'

'Don't worry, Charlotte. When Nesbit has finished I'll get my lot inside. We'll find something. We always do. Mind you, life would be easier if *he* was the killer.' Layton pointed along the path to where DC Enders was returning from the cafe, two hands clamped around three cups of steaming coffee. At every step a sprinkle of liquid splashed over the rims, leaving a trail on the ground.

'Hey, what are you lot laughing at?' Enders said, holding the cups out for Savage to take one. Layton went to grab a cup, but Enders grunted that it was for Nesbit, nodding to where the pathologist was hopping on one foot as he tried to get out of his protective suit.

When Nesbit came over, Enders gave him the cup. Nesbit took a sip and Savage asked for his conclusions.

'Coffee's not bad, not bad at all,' Nesbit said, winking at her. 'As for our friend back in the toilets, I can tell you he didn't expire in such an undignified position. However, he must have been moved soon after death otherwise he could never have been arranged in that pose.'

'Because of rigor?'

'Yes. The body would have become so stiff after a few hours it could never have been placed in the kneeling position.'

'And wherever he was killed there would have been a lot of blood?'

'I'd say the place would have resembled an abattoir after the task had been done. Unless he was dead before the hand was cut off, but we won't know that until the post-mortem.' Nesbit took a gulp of coffee and then poured the rest into the hedge. 'Now, one of the CSIs told me they do a fine bacon roll at the cafe so if you'll excuse me, I am going to ascertain if he was correct.'

'I hope he's washed his hands, ma'am,' Denton shook his head as Nesbit strolled off. 'I mean, you saw the state of the man's arse.'

'Thanks for reminding me of that delightful vision, Carl,' Savage said. She nodded at Enders. 'Patrick, Carl, you continue working with the local team here. I'm going back to the station to report to DSupt Hardin and DCI Garrett that we have found Mr Owers. Arse and all.'

The DSupt's greeting as she entered his office was hardly welcoming.

'Fuck it, Charlotte. This is the last thing we bloody need.' He swivelled his chair away from the computer and leant forwards, hands clasped together. On the desk in front of him was an array of Post-it notes, lines of Hardin's careful block writing across each.

Savage nodded and took a seat as Hardin continued. Trying to find Owers' killer would be a nightmare, he explained. They'd be up against a wall of silence, nobody wanting to shop someone who in many people's eyes would be a hero. Unearthing the story behind the girl in the crate would lead to misery all round, what with the grieving parents, disgruntled social workers, outraged local residents and the wrath of the press. No good could come of the investigation into either death. Hardin paused.

'Where's the bugger been?' Hardin reached out and tapped the calendar on the wall. 'You were round his place Monday and he was killed Tuesday night. Whoever made the connection made it pretty quickly.'

'No, sir. I think it was the other way around. Owers was seen near his place with two men on Sunday night, one suspected of being Stuart Chaffe. The body of Simza wasn't dug up until the following morning.'

'Hey?' Hardin glanced at the calendar again and then back to Savage. 'Tell me.'

'The builders weren't supposed to be there. The whole thing was a set-up.'

'So somebody already knew the girl was under the patio?'

'That's my guess. Peter Serling was contacted last week and he scheduled his men to do the job at Lester Close on Monday. It looks like Owers went missing Sunday night.'

'So why now?'

'Maybe some new information came to light, maybe Owers told somebody, maybe there was more than one person involved in the girl's abduction.'

'That is one possibility I don't want to consider,' Hardin said. He stared down at his desk at the Post-its and selected one, peeling the yellow paper off the surface and scrumpling it up. 'Now, DCI Garrett will continue to handle the case of the little one. We will spin off the investigation into Franklin Owers' death into a separate operation and you'll be the SIO. You are to cooperate fully with *Brougham* at all times. The death of a child must take precedence over that of an adult, especially when the adult concerned is in all probability the murderer.'

'Senior Investigating Officer,' Savage said, thinking she should be grateful to be offered the lead role in the inquiry but casting her mind back to the toilets on the Hoe, the stench of piss and shit and Owers' trousers round his ankles. She wondered if it was time for a career change to Traffic. 'Yes. Thank you, sir.'

Hardin lobbed the little ball of paper across the room towards the wastepaper bin where it hit the rim and bounced out. He appeared not to have noticed as he turned back to his computer and began typing.

'Good,' he said. 'Job done.'

Budgeon sat next to Stuey in the white transit parked halfway along Maxwell Road, in the Cattedown area of the city. The place was basically a huge industrial estate, with the emphasis very much on the industrial, evidenced by the huge BOC gases plant just to their left. Its towering white storage containers and rows of bottled oxygen hinted at one almighty explosion should anyone ignore the numerous 'No Smoking' signs plastered on every surface.

Stuey flicked the remains of his fag out of the window and then grinned across at Budgeon, the skin on his gaunt face resembling tissue paper stretched over chicken wire.

'Fucking hell, Stuey. You trying to get us killed?' Budgeon pointed at a sign on the wire fence a couple of car lengths away.

'Shit.' Stuey peered out the window down at the road surface where the glowing end smouldered on the tarmac. 'S'alright. Not going anywhere.'

'At this rate, neither are we. You sure about this?'

'Sure I'm sure.' Stuey's bony fingers grasped the steering wheel as he leant forwards to peer along Maxwell Road towards a small brownfield site where a Portakabin stood next to an open-sided corrugated shed. 'Dowdney works mornings until one and then knocks off. Takes this route home for lunch every day. Clockwork.'

Dave Dowdney. In his fifties now. Running a crappy taxi company – when he wasn't chucking away his profits down the bookies or pissing them away at his local. Once he'd been right up there as Big K's muscle-boy. The same sort of relationship Budgeon had had with Stuey. Only Dowdney was a bit brighter than Stuey. Maybe a bit too bright for his own good.

When Frankie had been screaming, he'd blurted out something about Dowdney.

'What?' Budgeon had said, moving in close and sliding a hand around Frankie's throat.

'Way back, Ricky, way back!' Frankie slobbered and slithered, wobbling like a pink blancmange on a butcher's block. 'I tell you, it was Dowdney!'

Dowdney? Budgeon had thought. Didn't seem right. Dowdney was bright, but not that bright. Not that stupid either. Then again, maybe he had the information Budgeon wanted. The confirmation. Thinking about Dowdney had also given Budgeon an idea concerning the man's taxi company. Good ol' Davy could do him a little favour.

'Here we go,' Stuey said, tapping the windscreen as a hunched man came down the steps from the Portakabin and trudged across the waste-ground in front of it. 'That's Dowdney.'

Budgeon waited until Dowdney had crossed the road and was nearing them before clicking the door open and stepping down from the van. Dowdney looked wasted, a shell of the man who had boxed down the gym three decades ago. Sparred with a world champ, rumour had it. Now the only rounds would be those at the bar, supplemented with cheap take-out cider.

'Dave,' Budgeon said, as if it had been days rather than decades. 'How's things?'

'Hey?' Dowdney stopped trudging along and looked up. Diverted his gaze from Budgeon to Stuey and then back again. 'Ricky? It can't be, not old Ricky Budgeon.'

'You're the old one, Dave,' Budgeon said. 'Down on your luck too. If you get my drift.'

Dowdney shifted his stance and for a moment Budgeon thought he'd raise his fists too, but the arms stayed by his sides, drooping like the man's expression.

'Ricky . . . I didn't, I mean she—'

'Just a word, Dave. Somewhere quiet.' Budgeon gestured to the rear of the van where Stuey was opening the doors. 'I've come back to sort a few things out and I think you might be able to lend a hand.'

Budgeon swung a punch at Dowdney's abdomen and Dowdney groaned and collapsed to the ground. Didn't even change his stance or offer any resistance.

'Pathetic,' Budgeon said as Dowdney scrabbled at the pavement with one hand, trying to find purchase to push himself up.

Then Budgeon stamped on his fingers.

* * *

Savage went back downstairs in search of DS Gareth Collier. She found him outside in the car park, smoking.

'*Corulus*,' he said as she came over. 'The name for the Franklin Owers investigation.'

The office manager was in shirtsleeves, as if the month was June, not January. Military discipline, thought Savage. Impervious to discomfort, opprobrium or pressure, Savage knew that he would ensure the inquiry would run as if on rails.

'You've confirmed the initial ID then?' Savage asked.

'One of the DCs has forsaken Twitter for long enough to pull up some stuff and he's found some better pictures. Mr Owers is not licking piss from a toilet rim, but you can tell it's him alright. Turns out he's got no close family, so I'm not sure who's going to officially identify him.'

'Has Hardin given you everything you want?'

'We've got a fair few bodies up there. Considering.' Collier waved a hand up at the grey concrete building, coughed and stubbed his cigarette out on the side of a bin. His sense of discipline didn't extend to quitting smoking, something he'd been trying to do for years. 'Although I wouldn't exactly say they are raring to go.'

Collier was right; when Savage returned to Major Crimes she found that a Friday afternoon atmosphere had set in. And it was only Wednesday.

People had scattered themselves around the room in ones or twos, some holding steaming cups of tea or coffee, Enders back from the scene and munching on a jumbo-sized Mars Bar as he typed an email one-handed. Nobody looked in any way eager to get stuck into the case, apart from Calter who sat at a chair near the whiteboard taking notes.

Over in a corner, DS Riley was sorting his things. On his desk a number of paper clips had been arranged to spell out the words 'bye bye' and he was shuffling a pile of documents, sliding the sheets one by one into a nearby recycling bin. Unusually for him, several buttons on his shirt were undone and his jacket and tie hung over the back of his chair. Enders sat staring at his screen, but every now and then casting a glare at the DS.

'Ma'am?' Enders turned his head and called across the room. 'I can well understand these cuts the Government are bringing in. From where I am sitting there is a hell of a lot of slack in the system.'

A paper dart flew past Enders' head and Riley began to first hum and then sing a song in a language which sounded a little like French.

'Darius,' Savage said. 'Can I infer from your behaviour that you don't have a lot on at the moment?'

'Everything done, ma'am. The *Sternway* final report filed, all my paperwork up to date and every last email answered. Just waiting for the little hand to move down to the five and then I am off. Spending tomorrow packing and then first thing Friday morning . . . whoosh!' Riley held his hand out flat and then moved it diagonally upwards and began to sing again, this time in English but with a strong Caribbean accent. Savage recognised the song as 'Jamaican Farewell'.

'Have you summarised those notes from the PACT meeting we attended last week?'

'No, ma'am. I thought they didn't need to be done until the end of—'

'Well?'

'Sure, yes.' Riley leant forwards to his keyboard as the dart skimmed back and landed on his desk, sliding into the paper clips and disturbing the neat pattern of letters.

'Members of the *Corulus* team, listen up,' Savage said. She strolled up to the whiteboard where a photo of Owers had star billing. In the picture Owers stood by the side of an outdoor swimming pool, bloated, pink and sneering at the camera. Behind him, three young girls played in the shallow end. Little bikinis, smiles and an innocence which came from not knowing about the predilections of the man standing a few paces away.

'Franklin Owers was a paedophile,' she continued. 'He was convicted a good number of years ago for a vicious assault on a six-year-old girl, so let's not pretend any of us are crying into our school milk over his death. Certainly not me.'

'Too true,' someone said from the back of the room.

'But whoever killed him was prone to extreme and sadistic violence themselves. I doubt Mr Owers is the only person to have suffered at the hands of the perpetrator. Which means catching him, her, or them is top priority. Now, DC Enders has got more on our victim. Patrick?'

'Aged forty-four,' Enders said, picking a sheaf of papers up from his desk and moving across to the whiteboard. 'An accountant by training, but after a minor, non-custodial conviction he was kicked out of the ACCA.'

'Which is?' asked Calter.

'Um . . .' Enders peered down at his papers and ran his finger across the page. 'The Association of Chartered Certified Accountants. Apparently the offence was something to do with a dodgy submission of a tax return for a bogus travel agency. After that he seems to have been happy enough with straight bookkeeping, but it looks like he wasn't able to get a proper job so he set up on his own. Convicted ten years ago for assaulting a six-year-old girl. He got twelve years, out in seven.'

'That's what passes for justice these days,' Denton said. 'Bloody disgrace.'

'Anyway,' Enders continued, pointing at a photocopy of the black business card stuck on the board. 'After he was released he still couldn't get a job so continued in self-employment. He called the new business Fastwerks. The office on Notte Street specified on his card proved to be phony. Nothing there but a little lobby area with a pigeonhole his mail was left in. We've found some paperwork which shows he did accounts for a number of small businesses in the Stonehouse area: the newsagent just round the corner from his flat, a small boatyard, a couple of the local pubs, several other firms too. I guess that's why he decided to move over there.'

'Could there be anything in that, ma'am?' Calter said.

'What?' Enders said. 'Someone gets mad because Owers gets a few decimal points in the wrong place? Not what I'd call a motive.'

'Jane, you can follow up on that,' Savage said. 'Make sure actions are in place for all the people and businesses he was working for. Patrick will help you. Carl, I want you to try and find out about Owers' social life. Who he mixed with, if he had any friends. As part of his licence terms he wasn't allowed access to the internet, but he may have got round the restriction somehow so don't leave the web out of your search. There's a USB stick which Hi-Tech Crimes are looking at too and I am going to be speaking to a member of his MAPPA team tomorrow.'

Savage glanced around at the rest of the team. They still didn't look enthused. To be fair, she still didn't *feel* enthused either.

'So, what do we think?' she said.

'A vigilante killing?' Calter said, looking up from her note, taking.

'You mean the parents of the little girl he assaulted?' Denton said. 'A traveller family. I reckon they might have connections.'

'Here we go,' Enders said, shaking his head and muttering something under his breath. 'Need a crimo? I've got loads. Paddies, gyppos, blacks, Pakis, long-haired hippies, anyone with a "funny" accent, anyone who doesn't—'

'Are you calling me prejudiced?' Denton said, pushing his chair back as he began to get up. 'Because if you are, then I'm going to—'

'DC Enders, Denton. Enough!' Savage said. 'For God's sake grow up the pair of you. This is a murder investigation, not a playground.'

Thirty minutes later, after designating actions to the other officers on the team, Savage wound the meeting up. Despite the earlier tension, nobody jumped out of their seats and ran from the room, nobody seemed excited or motivated. Calter came across as Savage was about to leave. She nodded over to where three DCs were chatting about last night's telly.

'Tough, ma'am. I don't think you could get this lot moving even if you offered a ten thousand pound reward.'

'I'm going to ask you again,' Budgeon said, feeling the thumping pressure build in his forehead, trying to ignore it and stay calm. 'Was she the one?'

'No, Ricky. Never. I told you. Not Lynn.'

Dave Dowdney tippy-toed back and forth across the barn floor, on pointe like a prima ballerina. His hands were above him, reaching for the ceiling, pulled upwards by the rope around his wrists. Two of the fingers on his right hand pointed off in an impossible angle, the skin around the joints black and swollen from where Budgeon had stamped on his hand. The rope went from his wrists up to a beam and then down to a hook in the wall. Beside Budgeon, Stuey grinned like the Cheshire Cat on acid. Inflicting pain was what Stuey got off on and right now he bounced around, eager to get down to business.

'I know you told me,' Budgeon said, 'but I don't believe you, because you ain't giving me any other names.'

'I can't, Ricky. I don't know. Must've been some bloke. One of the lads who worked for you and Big K.'

'But they did it on the orders of Big K himself. Him or Lexy. Does that sound right?'

'Honestly, Ricky, I don't know. It was way back.'

Budgeon stepped away from Dowdney, turned into the shadows. He spat on the back of his hand and rubbed the spit into his brow where it cooled, easing the tension. Not Lynn. Not the woman he'd once loved. That was good to hear. Anything else would have been too much to bear.

A couple of weeks ago he'd heard it from her own lips. They'd met up in one of the car parks at the Eden Project. The vast domes looked like they were from a science-fiction movie, sitting alien in the Cornish landscape. Lynn had wanted to go in, but Budgeon hadn't. Not after he'd seen the way she looked. He needed a drink. 'My place,' he'd said, climbing back into his Porsche and giving her the address, remembering that the girl had gone out for the day, taking the kid with her. Back home, he'd asked Lynn the same questions he was asking Dowdney. Only, hearing her answers, he'd believed her. Or rather, he'd believed the woman she'd once been. The pathetic lump sitting in his living room, drinking his Scotch, didn't resemble anyone he'd ever known. And yet in her eyes there was a glint of something, maybe just a memory. Everything else had gone, wiped out by Big K, a failed marriage, and a string of men ending with Dowdney. Nothing much left but regret and resentment.

Dowdney. If he was telling the truth about Lynn, then what about the rest of it? For a moment Budgeon wondered if he'd got the other stuff wrong too and perhaps the words Big K sent to him in prison all those years ago were true?

We don't know who split on us, Ricky, but we're going to find them, sort them. Pay them back.

Bollocks.

He hadn't believed it back then and he didn't now. 'Some bloke' was Dowdney's attempt at self-preservation. There was no one else. He knew that. Stuey knew it. Fucking Dave Dowdney knew it too. The coolness had gone and the pulse in his head made him clench his teeth and then ball his fists so his nails could dig into his palms.

'Bloody liar!' Budgeon whirled round and rushed at Dowdney. He raised his hands and grabbed Dowdney's ears, then jerked the man's head at the same time as he pushed his own forward and smashed the top of it into Dowdney's nose. There was a crunch like a walnut cracking and Dowdney screamed.

'Oh God!' Dowdney snorted and then a fine spray of blood spurted out. Budgeon dodged to one side.

'Nice one, Ricky,' Stuey said, bouncing on his feet, hands held up in a southpaw stance. 'Can I have at him, can I?'

'You and Lynn,' Budgeon said, waving Stuey away. 'I hear you're an item. That right?'

''S'pose so,' Dowdney sobbed. ''S'only recent. Never knew you was coming back.'

'Told you, Ricky,' Stuey said. 'He's been porking her. Every night in that office.'

'Leave it, Stuey.' Budgeon moved across to the workbench. 'Get his trousers off, keks too.'

'No!' Dowdney wailed and then snivelled. Blood ran down from his nose and dribbled off the end of his chin. 'Ricky, please, listen. The police got lucky, heard a rumour, nobody snitched on you.'

Budgeon retrieved something which resembled a pair of pliers from the bench and returned to Dowdney. He moved up close, spittle oozing from his mouth.

'You fucking loser, Dave. You think you can fool me? Stupid Ricky. The dumb one. The ugly fucking duckling. You think you can screw my girl and get away with it?'

'No, Ricky. It wasn't like that. You've been gone for years. I never knew you were coming back.' Dowdney swung to the left as Stuey pulled his jeans down, bunched them at his ankles and then grinned as he reached for the off-white boxers.

Budgeon shook his head. Felt something like a cigarette burning behind his right eye. Dowdney's face blurred and then distorted into a mass of white dots. Budgeon closed his eyes. His usual defence mechanism. The grey descended. Calm. Focus. Lynn was as old as Dowdney. Her body sagged in the same way and her sparkle had faded. The allure of the beautiful woman from back then had gone. She worked for Dowdney now as a taxi driver and gave her fares blowjobs for an extra twenty. Ten if that was all they had. Budgeon reminded himself that this wasn't supposed to be about her. Not any more. This was about the others.

'Forget about Lynn,' Budgeon said, opening his eyes. 'Just tell me whose fucking idea it was? Big K's, Lexy's, or are you telling me it was a coincidence? Five thousand cars up that motorway every bloody hour and they decide to stop me an' Stuey? Rotten luck, Ricky old boy, mustn't have liked the colour of your motor.'

'You ask him, Ricky,' Stuey said. 'Ask him which fucker decided to shaft us.'

'This is an elastrator.' Budgeon said, ignoring Stuey and instead holding up the tool he'd retrieved from the workbench. He slipped a tiny but thick rubber ring over the end. 'As the name suggests it's a tool used for castration. Lambs, calves, kids. There's no blood or anything because it uses an elastic band. You snap the band on and in a couple of days the bollocks just shrivel up and drop off. Only you wouldn't really call this thing an elastic band. It's a bit too powerful for that.'

Budgeon gripped the handles and the rubber ring flexed open. He let go and the band snapped shut, the internal diameter of the ring no bigger than a pencil.

'Jesus, Ricky! I'll tell you, I'll tell you! For God's sake there's no need to go any further.'

'Too late for that, Dave. This is going on. Whether we take you to hospital afterwards depends on whether you can give me any names. Whether for once in your pathetic little life you can tell the truth. Whether you promise to help me sort things out.'

'Yes! Anything!'

'Can I do it, Ricky?' Stuey said, eyes like a dog wanting a treat.

'Go on then.' Budgeon handed Stuey the Elastrator and stepped back. Watched Stuey kneel in front of Dowdney. Dowdney swirled and pirouetted again, swinging back and forth as he tried to escape the inevitable. Stuey's thin fingers reached out and clutched at Dowdney's testicles, cupping them as he brought the tool up to meet them. Stuey muttered in frustration as he struggled to slip the tool on. Budgeon looked away for a moment. Wondered if the pain was going to be as bad as the one boiling over inside his head.

Then Dowdney screamed long and loud, and Budgeon reckoned it might just be.

Chapter Nine

Thursday morning and an early post-mortem; Savage waking at five, rising at six-thirty, leaving Pete in the bed, Jamie snuggled in beside him, both man and boy snoring lightly. The sleep of the righteous, Savage thought, wondering what that made her.

She picked DC Calter up from the station and they drove to Derriford to discover that Owers' post-mortem had been delayed. Calter wanted to go to the hospital cafe for a coffee, but Savage declined, so they spent half an hour waiting in the car with the engine running and the heater on. Ever since Clarissa – Samantha's twin – had died here after the accident on the moor, Savage had tried to avoid Derriford altogether. Since the hospital was the location for post-mortems that was impossible, but at least she didn't have to spend any more time inside than necessary.

A little after nine Nesbit called Savage to inform them he was ready. When they entered the mortuary, he was as philosophical as ever.

'I blame it on portion sizes, Charlotte. Go large. Fifty per cent extra. Buy one get one free. That and Nintendos, cinema-sized TV screens and the two-car family.'

'What?' Savage stared at Nesbit as he put on his green coat and snapped on a pair of gloves.

'Obesity. The reason this post-mortem is thirty minutes late. Although I suppose you could as easily blame health and safety. Needed three technicians to get the bugger in position.'

Out of the corner of her eye, Savage caught Calter grinning. She smiled herself and let Nesbit continue his little lecture.

'Clothing makers, aircraft seat manufacturers and crematoria. All having to make adjustments due to the gluttony of our once-noble race.' Nesbit fiddled with his gloves and then looked at Savage and Calter in turn. 'Present company excepted, of course. Shall we?'

Nesbit's spidery frame could do with a few extra pounds on it, Savage thought, as he gestured from the anteroom into the mortuary proper and the three of them walked in. A technician was standing next to the body making some notes, and he nodded a greeting at Savage and Calter.

Savage didn't think Owers had been an attractive man in life and in death his appearance had not improved. He lay face up on the stainless steel table, a mass of sodden clothing, white fatty flesh and shit. His trousers were down by his ankles, the underwear smeared with brown. Huge rolls of fat on the man's thighs and stomach bulged out, concealing his genitals and making him look asexual. In fact, the thing on the table didn't even look human. Not with the black and purple bruises on the face and the bones sticking out of the man's right shirtsleeve. Usually Savage tried to muster some sympathy for the deceased, to allow a measure of dignity to exist in the cold, clinical room. Looking at Owers brought on only disgust and a queasiness in her stomach. And they hadn't even begun slicing him open yet.

Nesbit got the preliminaries out the way and examined the body. He started at the head, where he pointed out some specks of white around the nostrils, explaining that the routine toxicology tests would determine if Owers had been using cocaine. Next he made a pass over each limb and the torso, but even when he reached the right arm he made no comment about the missing hand, although his lips curled up at the sides in an approximation of a smile. Savage realised he was waiting for her to bring up the subject.

'Spare us the misery, Andrew. What was used to cut it off?' Savage pointed to the right side of the body. 'And no "armless" jokes while you're telling us.'

'Really, Charlotte. You should know me better than that.'

Nesbit moved back to the arm with the missing hand and the rectangle of black and white stripes. A pulp of muscle and shirtsleeve surrounded the two brilliant white bones in the forearm and Nesbit probed with his forceps, then took a magnifier and peered closer.

'Not so much cut off as rasped off. I can see little splinters of bone, but some white dust too. The dust is not consistent with a knife, a saw or an axe or similar chopper. The particles wouldn't be so fine.'

'So? What's your best guess?'

'I don't guess, Charlotte, I hypothesise. In this case, I would say something like an angle grinder was used. I can also see some specks of greyish material in amongst the mess, which I suspect come from the machine's disc.'

'Bloody hell.' Calter. Gone white as the bone. 'Was he alive at the time?'

'That we will ascertain when I come to establish the cause of death.' Nesbit smiled at Calter. 'But I suspect exsanguination.'

'Ex-what?'

'He bled to death. Which means yes, he was conscious.

Anyway, what would be the point of chopping off the hand with an angle grinder if he wasn't alive?'

Calter glanced over at Savage and the two of them shared the horror. Nesbit was matter of fact about the whole thing, but then he eviscerated bodies for a living and had acquired a method of distancing himself from the awful reality he found lying on the autopsy table in front of him every day. For Savage, professional detachment was much harder. She drew in a breath of air, tasting the disinfectant and the other things: sweat, piss, shit, the metallic odour of blood. Despair didn't have a smell, but maybe the invisible concoction swirling in the draught created by the extraction fans should be bottled and put on sale. One sniff every month or so would be enough to remind people of the thin line they walked. And of the inevitable lying at the end of that line.

Nesbit bent close to the arm again, poked at the black and white markings and used a pair of tweezers to peel back a piece of the substance which he dropped into a test tube.

'I am going to go against my usual reticence and hazard a guess on this,' he said, holding up the tube. 'Nail varnish. Heaven knows what woman would want to use black or white as a colour of choice, but there you go. The skin around the markings is remarkably free of blood so I'd say the arm was wiped clean before the pattern was applied. In other words, the artistry occurred post-mortem.'

'But why and what do they mean?'

'Absolutely no idea,' Nesbit said, placing the tube on a rack to the side before returning to the body. 'But that's not my job, is it? Now then . . .'

Thirty minutes later and Owers lay naked, the technician having cut away the clothing. Nesbit spent a few minutes going over the body once again, but found nothing of interest.

'Boss?'

Calter came across to Savage and began to make small talk about her plans for the weekend. Savage realised why as Nesbit retrieved a scalpel from a side bench and returned to the body where he began to cut Owers open, slicing him down the centre. The technician stood ready with a pair of shears to cut through the ribcage. Savage said something to Calter about going out for dinner with Pete on Saturday night as Owers' huge belly came apart, Nesbit cutting deeper to reveal the internal organs. Pinks and greys and browns sloshing in fluid.

'I'm going vegetarian,' Savage said.

Hours later, Savage and Calter took coffee from a machine and escaped into the grounds of the hospital. The grey concrete buildings rose to try and touch heaven, but that lay out of reach somewhere up in the blue sky, across which white clouds scudded in packs, racing to the horizon as the weather freshened. Neither detective spoke for a while as they strolled, sipping the scalding coffee. The post-mortem hadn't been pleasant; not that any were, but this had been among the worst Savage had remembered, even though Owers had been no innocent victim. It had something to do with the size of the man, the sheer mass of flesh and bone and guts. Blubber, she had thought at one point, imagining Owers as a whale captured by an old ship, with Nesbit and the technician dressed as whalers and wielding cutting spades.

'Sick,' Calter said.

For a moment Savage thought Calter had read her mind and was censoring her. Then she realised Calter meant whoever had cut Owers' hand off with an angle grinder.

'Or a parent,' Savage said, indicating a nearby bench they might sit on.

'Are you talking personally, ma'am? You could do that?' Calter sat next to Savage and took a gulp of coffee.

'Yes.' Not only *could*, Savage thought, remembering Matthew Harrison screaming as he burned to death in his car. A situation she should have rescued him from. 'If someone hurt my kids, I would want to hurt them. A lot. It's hard to explain, Jane, but having children turns you instantly from a bleeding-heart liberal to a hang 'em and flog 'em Tory. You'll see.'

'Well, I am not exactly a liberal to start with, so God knows where I'll end up. Somewhere to the right of the Klu Klux Klan probably. Although without the racist bits, I hope.' Calter shook her head and smiled. 'But I'm not ready to have children yet. Haven't done with the practice sessions.'

Which took them back to Calter's plans for the weekend again. Savage couldn't help but feel old and past it, thinking about the energy Calter was going to expend on the dance floor and in the bedroom. And the girl was also planning a long run, fitness fanatic as she was. The conversation ran dry when a middle-aged woman walked by, all skin and bones and no hair.

'Christ,' Calter whispered and raised a hand to point. 'Life's little pleasures, hey?'

Savage followed Calter's finger. The woman clutched a fag in her shaking hand and brought it to her lips, drawing in the smoke, her eyes glazing for a moment with relief. Savage could only think of Owers again. Of how she would have killed him if one of her children had been assaulted.

'I'm not sure the person who did Owers was a parent of a victim,' she said.

'Why not?'

'It wouldn't be enough. Not simply chopping off his hand. They would want to do more, to hurt him more.'

'Really?' Calter's eyes widened, still not understanding.

'Yes.' Savage stared after the cancer patient, tried to imagine wielding the angle grinder, bringing the whirring disc down onto Franklin Owers' wrist and watching the bits of flesh and bone fly out. 'This was a message. Those weird black and white lines tell us that. If someone had wanted to punish Owers for what he had done the whole thing would have been over too quick. He wouldn't have suffered enough. Not for me anyway.'

'Glad you are on our side, ma'am.' Calter half-smiled. 'All things considered.'

Alec Jackman had lunch upstairs at the Bridge, the restaurant down at the marina at Mount Batten. His companion was one of Plymouth's three members of parliament. The stupid one who looked like a prick. Nothing wrong with politicians – he was one himself of course – but this idiot hadn't a clue. Jackman had wanted to use the meeting to elaborate on a scheme he had to develop an area of wasteland just upstream from the marina near the Laira Bridge, but the MP didn't know one end of a regeneration strategy from another. Or his arse, most likely. Jackman had talked about cogs needing oiling, grants needing to find their way to the right people, but the man had looked blank, face creasing every time Jackman opened another mussel. It was as if he'd never done anything which required a little courage. Hence the ploughman's, Jackman thought. A bit of lettuce and a hunk of cheese never caused anyone any offence. Probably a focus group thing, like the bottled water the guy had drunk with his meal. Wanker. At least his own food had been good, even if the conversation had been a waste of time.

With the MP gone to a tour of a nearby primary school,

Jackman stepped out onto the balcony of the restaurant to make a call. He leant on the railings, taking in the rows of yachts and gazing across the water to the industrial wasteland of Cattedown. Huge storage tanks, prime waterfront wharves, light industrial units and vast warehouses. Someday it all had to go. That's what the MP didn't understand. Waterfront strategy. Turn the industrial land into a leisure and marine park, stick up some luxury apartments, and the city would reap the benefits. The payoff for Jackman would be handsome too.

He muttered another curse as his call connected and then he was asking the man on the end of the line if he'd heard the news.

'Of course I fucking have,' came the response. 'And before you ask, I never knew he'd been up to his old tricks. If I had, the fat shit would have already been history.'

'That's not what worries me.' Jackman shook his head. His associate always let his temper flare before he shone a light on the situation. Subtle, he didn't do. 'I want to know if he blabbed about anything. Money, quantities, dates.'

'Listen here, mate, if I strapped *you* down and threatened to chop something off, your hand, maybe worse, you'd blab, wouldn't you? But no, I don't think we need to worry, Frankie didn't have any information relating to the delivery.'

A couple emerged from the restaurant, hand-in-hand, to admire the view of the yachts, maybe to dream a little. Jackman paused and then moved away to the end of the balcony out of earshot.

'You still there?' Jackman spoke with a softer tone, aware of the anger his last line contained. 'I need to know if we are still on. Because if we—'

'We're on. Why wouldn't we be? This was some vigilante attack. The slob was killed because he was a paedo, not because he worked up a few spreadsheets for me. I doubt he was worried about my cash flow when he was offed.'

'Just so you're sure. I wouldn't want to take any unnecessary risks. Not in my position.'

'*Life's* a risk, pal. You want out, I can arrange that.'

'No, not out. Just . . .' The couple had returned to the restaurant, the woman sniffing and wrinkling her nose. 'Just be careful, OK?'

'Careful is my middle name. How do you think I got to be so old and ugly?'

Jackman laughed and felt the mood mellow a little. Out in the deep water of the Plym a pilot boat zipped back and forth, shepherding a couple of yachts to the side so a large tanker coming up river could turn around and back up to a wharf.

'You know a couple of days ago I mentioned I might have some good news?' Jackman said.

'You got it? The video?'

'Yes.'

'Well then, why are you worrying so much? We're as good as fucking sorted.'

The call ended and Jackman stood for a moment. The tanker was turning now, great boils frothing around it, the water brown-grey with disturbed silt. He reached into his pocket for a pack of Rennies. The food had been good, but the mussels, mixed with a little too much wine, weren't sitting easy in his stomach. He popped a tablet into his mouth, as he did so catching a whiff of sickly sweetness on the breeze. Something from the fish-processing plant across the water, something gone very bad.

Chapter Ten

Back at Crownhill, Savage and Calter went to the Major Crimes suite, where the gossip was all about some guy who'd been dumped at the doors to A&E.

'Stark naked,' Savage overheard Enders say to Denton. 'With one of those rubber rings round his bollocks. You know, the type of thing they use to castrate lambs?'

'Castrate lambs?' Denton shook his head, mouth opening and his eyes dropping to his crotch. 'You mean—'

'Couple of lads went up there to take a statement, but the fellow wouldn't talk. Personally I'd say it was a waste of time because I already know who did it.'

'You do?'

'All the evidence points to a certain female DC not a million miles from here.' Enders looked across at Calter and winked.

'I'd be careful,' Calter said. 'You'll be giving me ideas.'

'And the best bit,' Enders continued after giving Calter a double take, 'is the man's name. Dewdney or something similar. Like the pasty company.'

'Brilliant!' Calter said. 'How many testicles would it take to fill—'

Savage silenced Calter with a stare and then looked at Enders. 'Update. Now.'

'Simza's parents, ma'am.' Enders pointed at his screen. 'Someone from *Brougham* spoke to them Tuesday and a local officer popped round with some pictures we sent up to the Somerset and Avon force. You said something about a meeting so I've arranged a visit last thing today. They're up the other side of Weston-super-Mare. Bit of a trek I'm afraid.'

'Anything else from the door-to-doors?'

'Zilch. A couple of lads have gone to interview some of his clients but apart from them Owers didn't seem to have contact with anyone except health professionals or members of the criminal justice system.'

'OK,' Savage said. 'His caseworker is coming in later, so we'll see what she says.'

'She?' Enders looked appalled. 'What woman in their right mind would want to have anything to do with him after what he did to his first victim?'

Nicky Green was the woman.

When Savage and Enders arrived in the interview room she was eyeing the plate of digestives on the table in front of her, both hands wrapped around a mug of tea as if for warmth.

'Don't you have heating in this place?' she asked.

'Bloody finance people,' Enders said and went over to the radiator and fiddled with the controls. 'I swear they come round after we've all gone home and turn the heaters down to frost setting.'

If Savage had any preconceptions about social workers they were wiped clean by Nicky Green's appearance and

116

manner. She was neat and well-presented in a business suit, didn't smell of garlic and the paper she'd brought with her to read was the *Daily Telegraph* and not the *Guardian*.

'Ms Green?' Savage said as she sat down, not quite certain they had the right person.

'Yes. Call me Nicky.' Long lashes fluttered over hazel eyes, her shoulder-length hair the same colour to a shade.

'DI Charlotte Savage and DC Patrick Enders. You're one of the registered MAPPA contacts for Franklin Owers?'

'He was a client of mine. Level one. Poor bugger.'

'You feel sorry for him?'

'No, not really. Contrary to what you lot seem to believe, we don't have a lot of sympathy for men who go around abusing young girls. It is simply a question of managing the situation. And I believe in this case we managed things rather well. Franklin was released several years ago and he'd stayed out of trouble ever since. Continual assessments, monitoring, evaluation. Those are not just words from some mission statement, they are part of the action plan prepared specifically for Franklin.'

'We found some catalogues round his place. Young kids in swimwear, that sort of thing.'

'Franklin had urges. Better he satisfied them by looking at a few pictures rather than out on the streets.'

'So you didn't know he had been hanging around the primary school round the corner from his flat?'

'No, I didn't, but if you got that information from the locals you'd do well to consider its veracity. Once people become aware of an offender they load all the evils of the world onto him. The story may be nothing more than local gossip.'

'Maybe, but what isn't local gossip is the body we found beneath the patio at his previous residence. A young girl.

Six years old. If that's "managing the situation rather well" then I think you are going to be looking for another job in the very near future.'

'What? Are you saying . . .' Nicky Green had lost her composure. Her face paled and the hands clasping her mug shook. She placed the mug down on the table, tea slopping out.

'Simza Ellis,' Enders said. 'Went missing middle of last year.'

'But that was . . .' She opened the file in front of her. 'Years after his release. I mean, there was no indication of anything amiss. How could we have been aware of his activities?'

'Oh I don't know,' Savage said. '"Assessment, monitoring, evaluation", something like that?'

'Please, you don't need to be flippant. If all the correct procedures have been followed and everything possible done to manage Owers then it was hardly our fault, and if she is the only one—'

'It's alright then, and nobody is to blame, nobody gets the sack?' Savage shook her head and was about to say something else when she realised she was letting her emotions run away with her. She tried a more conciliatory tone. 'Look, Nicky, I hope you are right, and Simza is the only victim. It might surprise you to discover that isn't my concern. Her case is being dealt with by another team. For my sins I am trying to find out who killed Mr Owers. For that we need your help. We have no idea of his friends, acquaintances – professional or otherwise – nothing.'

'But he didn't know anyone. Apart from his clients, the ones he did accounts for. I assume you have details of those?'

'Yes, thanks. There must be other people though. Are you saying he has lived all these years with no contact with anyone?'

'Pretty much, yes. He sees me or another of my team once every three months and the psychiatrist once a month. There are other health workers too, but apart from those people he keeps himself to himself. Or rather he did. He told me life was better that way. Simpler.'

'And he has never been anywhere in all that time? He's never visited friends or family outside Plymouth?'

'No. He went on holiday a few times. I think the last trip was back in the summer.'

'What, abroad?' Enders said. 'Tiny Tots Tours, paid for with my taxes?'

'No!' Green scowled at Enders. 'Of course not. He isn't allowed to leave the country. He stayed in a caravan down in Cornwall. I think it belonged to his parents or something.'

'On a site?' Savage said.

'Again, no. Do you think we're stupid? The caravan is on a farm. My colleague visited the place to check and found it quite suitable. Remote from beaches, schools and whatever. We stipulated he could only visit if he promised to stay in the vicinity of the caravan, which was fine with him because all he wanted to do down there was paint and let his dog run around.'

'Paint?' Savage asked.

'He learnt in prison. Some sort of art therapy.'

'Bollocks!' Enders was shaking his head, close to losing it. 'The world's gone crazy. And it's not as if the therapy worked, is it?'

Green ignored Enders and fumbled in the file. She pulled out a piece of paper and slid the sheet across the table. At the top, a snapshot of the caravan sat next to an address. The picture showed the caravan standing on the edge of a field against a mature wood. Through the trees a hint of blue sea sparkled with sunlight.

119

'The farm is somewhere down past Falmouth. As I said, the last time he went to Cornwall was in the summer. August, I think.'

'Which, Ms Green,' Savage said, 'is exactly when little Simza went missing from the Lizard, not much more than ten miles from Falmouth.'

Green put her hand back in the file and rifled through several bits of paper, as if searching for some sort of directive or memo which would get her off the hook.

'Well?' Savage said.

Green closed the file and appeared to study the label on the front as if even that might be of some use to her. Then she shook her head, bit her lip and uttered a single word.

'Shit.'

Two hours up the M5 to visit Simza's mum and dad, Enders driving, wasn't Savage's idea of fun. They left mid-afternoon, immediately after concluding their interview with Nicky Green. The sun was already low in the west, the light projecting an elongated patch of dark on the road in front, the car's shadow keen to be there before them.

Somewhere between Weston-super-Mare and Clevedon the traveller site flashed by on the left, a cluster of little chalets pushed up against the motorway like debris swept into a corner by a broom. Enders began muttering about discrimination and ethnic cleansing, but before he could get started they were turning off the motorway and doubling back to find the place amongst a maze of lanes which seemed to lead anywhere but to their destination.

After twenty minutes of dead-ends and U-turns they found the entrance to the site, where they asked directions to the Ellises' place from a bright-eyed, elderly woman with a scarf tied tight around her head. She pointed at a green chalet several rows down. A black pickup truck sat low on its suspension, a dozen rolls of sheep netting and several large fence posts piled up high in the back.

As they drew up outside, the door to the chalet opened to show two people standing there staring out at them, before the woman turned and retreated inside.

'Tony Ellis,' the man said. 'You must be Inspector Savage. Come in.'

Savage went up the steps and into the house, Enders remaining outside, already moving to the neighbouring property, notebook drawn.

Savage wasn't sure what she was expecting inside – maybe something like the interior of a shoddy mobile home – but she scolded herself for being prejudiced when the living area turned out to be little different from a hundred houses she had visited. The usual TV and hi-fi, some art prints on the walls, white carpet and a yellow pastel sofa and armchairs. No toys though, no brothers or sisters to Simza, nobody to ease the loss.

Savage outlined the recent developments, raising her voice a little so Mrs Ellis could hear in the kitchen as she made some tea. Tony Ellises' reaction seemed muted. He'd been told on the phone, but Savage thought there would be something more, some anger directed towards the police. Instead Ellis simply sighed and gave a shrug of resignation. They'd expected nothing else, obviously. Savage moved to the real reason for her visit. She explained that other officers would be coming to take detailed statements relating to Simza's disappearance, but she was here to remove them from the scope of the Franklin Owers murder investigation.

'Purely routine, Mr Ellis,' Savage said. 'Can you account for your movements between Sunday and Wednesday?'

Mrs Ellis entered the room and placed a cup and saucer

down on a little side table, her hand shaking slightly. A chink sounded out in the near silence, the only other noise a background hum from the motorway.

'I was here, wasn't I, love?' Mr Ellis turned to his wife, the look one from a man not used to lying.

'Yes.' Lisa dabbed at a drop of tea on the table with a tissue. 'Here. All night.'

Which night? Savage thought. She hadn't asked about a specific day.

'Do you know what ANPR is, Mr Ellis?' Savage said. Both man and wife shook their heads. 'No? Then I'll elaborate. It stands for Automatic Number Plate Recognition. Now I'm not at liberty to tell you how many or exactly where the cameras are, but there are a number of units between here and Plymouth. If you've driven down our way then we are going to know about it.'

'OK, OK, so I came down on Tuesday.' Ellis held his hands up, palms outward. 'I drove around a bit, bought a couple of local rags and read the stories. I discovered where Mr Owers lived, but he wasn't there was he? You guys were, and the place was cordoned off. Didn't know what to do then. I went over to the house where you found Simza and then . . .' Ellis stopped, shook his head, breathed in and out. 'I came home.'

'Impotent,' Lisa said. 'That was his first word when he arrived back. Wasn't it, Tony?'

'Yeah. Impotent. Nothing I could do.'

'And this was Tuesday?'

'I got the call from your lot in the morning and a local officer comes round, shows me a couple of pictures and takes a statement. Set off midday Tuesday and mooched around the city in the afternoon and evening. Small hours of Wednesday by the time I got back here.'

'Two o'clock,' Lisa said. 'I stayed up waiting.'

'Even allowing for the journey, that was a lot of hours to spend in Plymouth just driving around.'

'I had a few drinks afterwards, didn't I? Probably shouldn't have driven home. Woke with a sore head to the news that the paedophile had been offed. If it hadn't been for the hangover I'd have poured myself a shot in celebration there and then.'

'At the moment, Mr Owers is no more than a suspect for Simza's murder.'

'Do me a fucking favour. I've seen the pictures, remember? Slimy fat git. Recognised him straight away. Guilty. End of.'

'Due process,' Savage said, pushing herself up from the chair, thinking she was on the wrong side of the argument. 'It means respecting legal rights.'

'What about Simza's legal rights? The police laughed at us. Said we were wrong.' Ellis moved to the door and opened it, waving Savage out as if she was a cat which had crapped on the carpet. 'Legal rights? What a joke. My daughter would be alive if your fucking due process had been followed.'

Savage went out on the veranda and turned to say something, but Ellis slammed the door, the entire chalet reverberating in response.

'I have to concede, Mr Ellis,' Savage said to herself as she went down the steps, 'that you may have a point there.'

They drove back westwards at dusk, pushed along by a mass of rush-hour traffic heading towards Exeter, an equal number of cars coming the other way, their headlights blazing against the darkening sky.

Enders, as it turned out, had met with blank stares as he'd roamed the rest of the site.

'Nobody wants to say a word. They've got a natural suspicion of authority, and of the police especially.'

'You can't really blame them for that, but I'm disappointed you didn't get anything.'

'There was the old woman, the one we met at the entrance. She was keen to talk.'

'And?' Savage asked.

'She said something disturbed her, woke her up late at night. Sounded like a car.' Enders began to laugh and glanced across at the oncoming traffic on the opposite carriageway. 'Next she pointed up at the motorway and said that wasn't unusual round here. Then she told me to piss off.'

Chapter Eleven

Central Plymouth. Friday 18th January. 4.30 a.m.

The phone beeped out an alarm at four-thirty Friday morning, not much more than an hour after he had fallen asleep. Riley groaned, threw back the duvet and staggered to the bathroom and had a shower, the last twenty seconds full blast cold. Drying himself, he went to the kitchen and flicked the switch on the kettle. A cup of instant coffee – strong and black – and a round of toast later, and he was beginning to wake up. As he munched the toast and slurped the coffee he stared out the window of his flat. The drone of a large vehicle rattled the glass and moments later a yellow light strobed past. A gritter. Riley allowed himself a smile. In twelve hours' time he would be dipping his feet in the Caribbean Sea, and the only thing sub-zero would be the ice in his drink.

The trip would be his first real holiday since he had arrived in Plymouth a year ago and while he'd miss his new-found friends and colleagues it would be good to blow away some winter blues. Ostensibly the purpose of the trip was to visit a couple of relatives, a great-aunt and some cousins he'd never met. When one of them had invited him to her wedding Riley had thought of the vivid blues and whites of the sea and sand, remembered from an earlier visit many years before. In the end it had been too much to resist after the appalling autumn weather and he accepted the invitation and booked flights and a hotel. But the prospect of two weeks on Martinique wasn't the only reason he was happy to be off.

Julie.

Short hair, funny nose, cute. Riley had fallen for her big time. Too much to resist there as well.

He remembered the minibus trip back from watching the Chelsea game. They'd chatted for a couple of hours before Julie fell asleep. At first her head had rested on his shoulder, but later she nuzzled into his neck and murmured how much she liked him. Usually talk like that would have him running for the exit. Most often the morning after the night before. Somehow this was different.

At first the relationship had been casual, but it quickly developed into something Riley had never expected. Which was how he came to ask Julie if she would like to join him for the second week of his holiday. He would have liked her there for the whole time, but she couldn't get two weeks off so soon after Christmas. Still, she'd arrive for the big wedding and the party.

A horn blared out front for a second and Riley was scrabbling into the rest of his clothes, rushing to open the front door and signal to the taxi to hang on, and then returning to check the place over. The heating was down low, everything electrical off except a light on a time switch. Keys, passport, wallet, phone? Got them. He grabbed his bags and went outside, almost braining himself on the icy pavement. The driver, an older woman with a round, sagging face and a substantial chest, popped the boot and asked if he was going anywhere nice.

'Caribbean,' he said, as he hefted the bags in.

He ducked into the back so he could stretch out, and soon he was half-asleep, listening to the driver's conversation as they drove through deserted streets and then sped along the A38 towards Exeter, where a flight to Paris would connect him to the transatlantic service to Martinique.

The rhythmic cadence of the headlights sweeping the inside of the cab began to loll him into a dream filled with sun, sand and sea. The waves washing up the beach: whoosh, whoosh, whoosh. Making love with Julie in a hotel bedroom, a big fan on the ceiling spinning in time with their gasps, Julie calling his name over and over as she came . . .

'Excuse me?'

'Huh?' Riley blinked awake. The road noise had stopped, through the windscreen nothing but the faint outline of a hedge, beyond trees set against a hint of dawn light.

'Puncture,' the woman said. 'Do you think you could change the wheel for me, only my back has been giving me a bit of gyp recently. Jack and spare are in the boot.'

'Shit,' Riley said and then sat upright. 'Yes, of course. Sorry, must have dropped off.'

'You were talking in your sleep, love. Julie? Sounds a like a nice girl.'

'Yes, she is.' Riley got out of the car, wondering exactly what he'd said, and then opened the boot and retrieved the jack. The driver remained in her seat and Riley tapped the window. 'Where are we?'

'Just beyond Ivybridge, couldn't see a lay-by so I took the first turn-off.' The window had only slid down a couple of inches and the woman raised her hand and flicked her thumb backwards. 'It's the offside rear, my lover. No rush.'

Charming, thought Riley. She couldn't even be bothered to get out of the car and talk to him while he did the dirty work. He moved to the back of the car and knelt to position the jack. Strange, the tyre didn't appear punctured. Riley stood and tapped the window again. The woman glanced out at him for a moment and then looked at her watch. A quick movement of her hand and a buzzing noise came from the door. She had activated the central locking.

'Hey, what are you doing?' Riley grabbed the door handle and wrenched it up, aware of headlights approaching up the lane. Fast. He flattened himself against the car, raising his arm to shield himself from the glare. The vehicle roared past, a screech from the tyres as it braked hard and stopped a few metres down the road. Riley had time to register that the vehicle was a white transit van before the rear doors opened and two guys in ski masks jumped down. One held a long piece of wood, something like a pickaxe handle, and he bounded forwards, swinging the weapon. Riley raised an arm and the wood smashed into his wrist. He recoiled from the pain, stumbling backwards and falling to the floor. The other man ran across and planted a kick in Riley's stomach and then something hit him in the head.

Groggy, he tried to get up, but instead felt himself being grabbed by each arm and dragged towards the van. His body crashed into the rear bumper, before the two men bundled him up and inside.

'Have this 'an all,' one of the men said and the baseball bat smashed down again, catching Riley on the shoulder.

Now the men were up in the van too, pulling the doors shut and shouting 'go, go' to someone in the front. The van lurched backwards and forwards a couple of times, turning in the road, and then accelerated, the engine rough, the noise from the exhaust echoing against the bare interior.

Riley kept his head down near a wooden makeshift seat and reached into his jacket pocket for his phone. Calling wouldn't do much good, they'd have the phone from him before anyone could answer. Instead, he tried to remember the sequence to access the call logs to retrieve the last number he'd dialled. He was pretty sure the number had been Julie's. Menu, down, down, select, right, down, select? Was that the key sequence to bring up the number and open a new text message? He kept his hand in his pocket and pressed the keys. Each key press sounded a small beep, but although one of the men peered down, all Riley saw were teeth grinning in the passing headlights. Now, what message? A name, that's what he needed to send. Seven letters and thank fuck he didn't have predictive text switched on. He thought for a minute or two about the positioning of the keys and the number of times he would need to press each one to get the correct letter. Then he began to type the message: Beep, beep, beep, beep, beep, beep, beep, beep, beep, beep . . .

'What the hell are you playing at?' The man lunged across and grabbed Riley's arm. 'He's got something in his pocket!'

Riley pressed 'send' as the man wrenched his arm out. The phone slipped from his grasp and span across the floor, the green glow an easy target for the guy with the baseball bat. The bat crashed down on the phone, plastic splintering, pieces flying everywhere. Then the other man punched him hard in the face and the lights from passing vehicles seemed to slow, the rhythm winding down, that fan on the hotel ceiling spinning slower and slower. Julie was calling his name again, but this time the words were drawn out as if he was falling away from her: Darius . . . Darius . . . Darius.

Chapter Twelve

Crownhill Police Station, Plymouth. Friday 18th January.
9.05 a.m.

Friday morning and the front lawn sparkled, laced with silver frost, Savage thinking as she stepped out of the front door that she might have been a little presumptuous in heralding the arrival of spring. At the station, she caught Enders as he headed to the canteen for coffee and cake, gave him a ten pound note and told him to buy some sandwiches instead. He didn't understand what she meant until she explained they were going to Cornwall to visit the caravan where Owers had stayed.

'DCI Garrett, ma'am. Shouldn't we let him know?'

'No.' Savage bundled him out of the door and headed across the car park towards their pool car. 'This might be a long shot and I wouldn't want him to squander his resources needlessly. Maybe the trip will turn out to be a waste of time.'

'Right, ma'am,' Enders said, shaking his head again. 'So why are we bothering then?'

Savage held up her right hand, index finger pointing towards Enders, thumb pointing upwards.

'Just get in the car and drive. And don't even think of making a run for it.'

Enders laughed and bleeped the doors to the Ford Focus open, and before long they were cruising along the A38, heading down towards the Tamar Bridge and the crossing into Cornwall.

Savage explained how she wanted first dibs on the caravan because so far the Simza Ellis inquiry, *Brougham*, seemed to be taking precedence over *Corulus*, the inquiry into Owers' death. If they let Garrett get to the caravan first, any evidence would be bagged up and out of their sight before they had a chance to even see it. Likely the place would be sealed off as well and they'd have to wait days to get their hands on anything.

An hour and a half later they were close to Falmouth, the satnav struggling to resolve the final part of their route. Savage peered at the piece of paper Nicky Green had given her and reached for the road atlas. Fifteen minutes and a few wrong turns later, they rolled into a farmyard not far from the village of Constantine.

The farmer turned out to be an old guy by the name of Williams. He walked with a stoop and the lines criss-crossing his weathered face put him at over eighty. Savage thought he should have retired at least a decade ago, but apart from the stoop he seemed fit and healthy enough. The man explained he was a tenant and had nowhere else to go. Besides which there wasn't much left of the farmland now, just under thirty acres. The estate had been divided up when it had been sold off years ago. Most of the land had gone to neighbouring farmers and a nearby barn complex had been developed as a luxury residence. It had changed hands recently for over a million, the new owners, an expat and his Spanish wife, moving from abroad. The farmer rolled his eyes and said that sort of money for a couple of barns was crazy. His eyes glazed as he began to tell them about the days when the farm had been home to his herd of pedigree cows, and how that all came to an end with the foot-and-mouth epidemic back in two thousand and one.

'That's when things all went wrong.' He turned his head towards a small meadow to one side of the farmhouse. 'Piled up over yonder they were. Burning. Every last one of them.'

Savage followed the man's gaze to a mound where the grass struggled to compete with a mass of nettles and thistles. It wasn't hard to picture the scene, one repeated all over the country; the diggers scraping a hole, pushing the bodies in, the corpses smouldering, the smoke drifting.

Savage steered the conversation round to Franklin Owers. Had he visited here?

The farmer nodded, eyes still on the little field.

'Last summer, I reckon. Stayed in the old caravan. Right state the place was in, but he didn't seem to mind.'

'It belonged to his parents, is that right?'

'Parents?' The eyes switched to Savage. 'No, love. You've got that wrong. I used to rent the caravan out in the summers, and in the spring the shepherd who came for lambing lived there. When they rang I told them the accommodation wasn't really suitable any more, but they didn't seem to mind.'

They. Them. Social Services most likely. It sounded like Owers had spun Nicky Green's colleagues a tale about his parents and they'd fallen for the story. In turn, Ms Green hadn't told the truth either: no one had visited to check the place out, the risk assessment had been done on the phone, probably with a glance at a map for good measure. But why had Owers come here? Savage said she would like to inspect the caravan and the farmer pointed to an open gate where a track led away from the farm, disappearing down the curve of a hill.

'Half a mile, but you'll get down if you're careful.' The

man raised a finger to his forehead and scratched. 'Like I said, bit of a mess. If I'd known he was bringing his daughter I'd have tried to fix the bloody thing up.'

Daughter? Savage wanted to know more. She pulled out the picture of Simza. Might that be her?

'Yes. I mean . . . I'm not sure. Is she his daughter? She looks a little like her but this one . . . I've seen her somewhere else. On the telly?'

On the telly sounded about right, Savage thought. Simza might not have got the attention she deserved from the authorities, but she'd have been all over the local media for a day or two. Williams would have been sitting in his parlour with the paper on the table and the TV on. The little girl's face had screamed out 'It's me!' but he hadn't made the connection.

'Quiet little thing she was,' he said. 'Is she coming again? Because if she is I'll need to sort the caravan out. Did I mention it's in a bit of a state?'

'Yes, Mr Williams, you did,' Savage said. 'And no, she isn't going to be coming here again.'

Williams nodded and then stared over at the little pasture once more, eyes gone, something like shell shock.

'Pity,' he said.

Nobody had been down to the caravan in a car for a long time and the centre of the grassy track was raised to such a degree that every bump meant a risk of grounding.

'Easy,' Savage said as a horrid grinding noise came from beneath them.

'Sorry, ma'am,' Enders said, slowing the vehicle to a crawl. 'This track was designed for Ford tractors, not a Ford Focus.'

The twin ruts weaved away down the slope towards a patch of gorse and Savage caught a waft of the sweet, syrupy flowers, well in bloom even though it was mid-winter. Beyond the gorse a straggle of stunted trees formed a small copse, and beyond that another field stretched down to a narrow strip of estuary. The water bristled with mini-whitecaps, whipped up by the same fresh breeze which carried the scent of the gorse to them.

'Remote, ma'am. Nobody's ever going to find the caravan by accident.'

The dark green and white hulk lay down near the gorse, a few metres from a cattle trough where, according to the farmer, Owers had got his water from. The caravan's green sides and ends contrasted with a white band which ran all the way round. If caravans did go-faster stripes then that was what the white strip was. The roof had once been white too, but now appeared black with mould and whatever had fallen from the canopy of trees above. All the windows were intact, but at the rear end a panel of the green aluminium had curled away, spoiling the graceful curve that a designer must have once thought to be so modern. Brambles covered the towing end and only the handle which raised or lowered the dolly wheel stuck above the thorny vegetation. Beneath one of the windows in the side, an orange propane bottle had a dodgy-looking regulator attached to the top. A rubber hose rose from the corroded brass fittings and disappeared through a hole beneath the window frame. The two windows on the side of the caravan and the windows on the front and rear had venetian blinds and they hung down in the closed position.

Close to the caravan the track turned away and continued to the next field. Enders steered off the track and stopped, the car sliding on the grass.

'Do you think we can get back?' Savage turned and glanced up the slope. The hill appeared to be a lot steeper from the bottom.

'Well, the farmer will be able to help if we can't.'

They got out of the car and Savage surveyed the area. It was a long way to the farmyard and the coast path crossed the main estuary a mile or so away; the little tributary had no footpaths. If Simza had been here, no one but Mr Williams would have ever known about the little girl.

'Ma'am?' Enders had trudged across to the door and was fiddling with the handle. 'It's locked, but the metal is so corroded I reckon I can force the catch.'

'Let me see.' Savage walked over, looked at the lock and for a moment considered returning to the farmyard for a key, but then nodded to Enders. 'Go on, do your worst.'

Enders grinned and picked up a large stone. He hefted it against the door handle and the aluminium buckled around the lock, flakes of paint falling off and fluttering to the ground. He dropped the stone and squeezed his fingers into the gap. With a sharp tug, the door came open.

A waft of damp and dank air overpowered the sweet smell from the nearby gorse. Inside, a thick layer of sludge lay on the floor and several strands of ivy had finessed their way past one window frame and were now struggling to gain purchase along the top of the kitchenette. The material on the cushions in the U-shaped dinette had split, revealing yellow foam inside, stained with patches of mould. A kettle stood on the gas stove and on the draining board a spoon poked from the top of a jar of Nescafé.

Enders moved to one side and let Savage clamber up into the caravan. The structure creaked and Enders stepped back and peered underneath.

'You're alright, ma'am. The tyres have gone flat but the thing is on blocks. I don't think it is going to tip over, but I'd watch the floor.'

To her immediate right a concertina-type door stood half

open. Behind the door a small cubicle contained a chemical toilet; the lid was open, but thankfully whatever had been in there had turned to soil. The cupboards beneath the cooker and sink were ajar and seemed to contain nothing but pots and pans. Savage went across to examine the wardrobe over by the dinette and to probe beneath the seat cushions. The bins beneath the seats were empty apart from a stack of newspapers and an ancient Boden For Kids catalogue. The wardrobe had a single item on a hanger, all yellow flowers on a white background, the flimsy material of the dress shimmering in the draught.

Enders gunned the car up the track while Savage followed on foot, Enders stopping the car at the top of the field to open a gate next to an old stone byre. The gable end stood facing her and as she climbed the hill a glint of sun on glass caught her attention. A window. Strange to have a glazed window in a barn, but maybe the farmer had once used the place as a holiday flat or something. The barn stood open on one side and contained some farm machinery: a red hay tedder with yellow spines, an old three-furrow plough and a transport box. At the other end some steps led up to a door which allowed access to the roof space.

She reached Enders and pointed at the steps. Then she climbed up them and tried the door. Locked. She peered in through the frosted glass. The interior seemed to be one huge room and light streamed in through the window at the far end.

Enders got out of the car and she shouted down to him to go and get the key. A few minutes later he returned.

'Mission accomplished,' he said, holding up a loop of string with a key on as he climbed the steps. 'The farmer says he was doing the barn up to be a holiday flat, but he never finished the job. Apparently Owers asked to use the place to paint.'

Savage took the key from Enders and slotted it in the lock. She turned it and pushed the door open. Inside, the large area had been boxed out with chipboard. A couple of Velux windows allowed light to flood in through the sloping ceiling, and the big window in the far gable offered fine views out across the valley and beyond to the estuary. As she stepped into the room Savage tasted the air; hot, dry and dusty.

Down the far end a table stood to the right of the window, a chair pulled back from it. She looked again, shivering when she realised what the piece of furniture actually was. Not a table, a desk; an ancient, wooden desk with a flip-up lid and a hole, top right, for an inkwell.

'School time, ma'am,' Enders said. 'And I don't think it takes much to work out who was taking the register.'

'Jesus. Sick bastard.'

Savage walked across the room, stopped at one of the Velux windows and gazed out. A field covered with scrub lay between the byre and the property next door to the farm, a large barn conversion. Wooden beams and glass panelling, an atrium at one end with a pool inside. Beyond the house was a tennis court. There were two other barns in their original state and a stone-built stable block. A gravel drive curled through acres of grass and, parked in front of the house, a silver sports car gleamed in the sun.

'Think I'll stick with my postage-stamp lawn, ma'am,' Enders said as he looked over her shoulder. 'That would be a little too big for my Flymo.'

'We're on the Helford Estuary. There's a lot of money down here.'

'Didn't Madonna buy a place—'

'Other side of the river Fal from here, I believe.' Savage

137

looked down from the slanting Velux in the ceiling, following the line of the boarding. About a metre from the floor, it changed direction and became vertical. Savage tapped a foot against the wall. 'There's a void.'

'Ma'am?' Enders had shifted his gaze too and now he pointed along the wall to a flash of brass. 'An access panel.'

Savage moved along the wall and lifted the little brass catch. The panel swung open. Behind the panel was a triangular space, easily big enough to crawl into. She crouched down and poked her head in. Inside, the space was pitch black and she could see nothing, but if anything the air in the void seemed hotter and drier than in the room.

'Simza was in here, I know it. Owers brought her down to the caravan, had his fun and killed her. He stashed her body in the void and later, for some reason, he retrieved her corpse and buried it under the patio back at his place.'

'But why? He could have buried her in the wood, chucked her in the sea or even left the body here.'

'No idea.' Savage stood up, strolled over to the desk. On it lay a Dora the Explorer kid's colouring book. The pages were yellowed with exposure to sunlight and the glossy cover curled back. Savage flicked through the book. The first ten or so pages had been coloured in, swirling crayon lines in red, blue and green, but the rest were untouched. The final picture in the book was of Dora and her monkey sidekick, Boots, swinging through jungle trees on vines, big smiles on their faces as they made their way to a little house at the top of the page where Dora's mother could be seen waiting for her daughter.

Little Simza Ellis had never got that far.

By six p.m. Savage was back at Crownhill, the light gone from the day, just a scattering of vehicles left in the car park.

Enders scampered off to his car, home to the wife and kids, while Savage sat for a moment reflecting on the trip down Falmouth way.

In the dark interior of the car the memories of what she'd seen in the caravan came flooding back. It was all too easy to imagine what might have happened down there, tucked away out of view, out of earshot. The little girl had probably played along to start with, scared to do anything else. Until Owers had started on his idea of fun. Savage shuddered and tried to free herself of the image of Simza crying and begging. Then she clenched her fists and pressed them to her forehead, knowing that if Simza had been her daughter, simply slapping a pair of cuffs on Owers and sending him off to a courtroom wouldn't have been enough. She would have wanted to be sure he suffered, sure he didn't escape justice. Had somebody else felt the same way? Justice was rarely clear-cut, she thought, but in this case the line was pretty obvious. She cast her mind back to the night Matthew Harrison had tried to abduct Samantha. In the end he hadn't succeeded and he'd driven off in his car. The car had crashed and Savage had had the chance to save him. Instead she had walked away. Judge, jury and executioner.

Savage shivered, then climbed out of the car and walked across to the station entrance. In the sterile lobby the duty sergeant muttered something about 'trouble', explaining that her impromptu trip had managed to piss off DCI Garrett, John Layton and a couple of detectives down at Truro nick. However, when she caught up with Hardin in the canteen his reprimand was on the light side and he seemed to be surprisingly relaxed about the whole thing.

'Bah! You've stolen Garrett's thunder by wrapping up the case for him before he had even got started, that's all. As for Layton, he's a complete fusspot when it comes to crime scenes. Treats them like my wife treats a new living-room carpet. And I'll get onto the boys in Cornwall and let them know you were only trying to save them time.'

Hardin shepherded his tray along in front of the hot-food counter, opting for a ladle of curry poured over a portion of chips, then picking up a pot of tea and a white iced bun.

'Wife's book club night,' he explained as if he needed to absolve himself of the guilt. 'Now, where do you see us going with the Owers case?'

'Simza's father is one possibility. He admitted to us that he had been down here on Tuesday. Owers was likely as not dead by then, but Mr Ellis is still a suspect in my mind.'

'You really think he did this?'

'Could be, could be some other family member, a friend, somebody else in the community, or it could be nothing to do with travellers at all. Maybe there are other victims we don't know about. Then there is Stuart Chaffe. We are trying to establish a connection between Mr Ellis and Chaffe. Perhaps this was a paid hit.'

'What about the earlier offence Owers was convicted for?'

'From our records it appears as if the family concerned in that case have moved abroad. Italy, I believe.'

'Doesn't put them out of the frame, does it?'

'No sir, it doesn't. Just bumps them down the list a little.'

'Right.' Hardin smiled at the lad on the till and fumbled at the buttons on the card reader. Then he picked up his tray, moved to a nearby table and sat down. 'You not joining me, Charlotte?'

'No, sir. I'll be off home, I need to sort out some material for the Standards interview next week.'

'Nothing to worry about there, everything will be fine. I'll be with you and everyone knows how much the Chief

Constable admired your efforts in catching Matthew Harrison. You'll get a telling off, no more.'

Savage hoped Hardin was right. She thanked him and bid him goodnight, asking as an afterthought what his wife was reading at her book club.

Hardin smiled and used his fork to extract a jumbo-sized chip from beneath the steaming curry. He studied it for a moment before popping the chip in his mouth and mumbling out an answer.

'Ian bloody Rankin,' he said.

Riley came round with a bad head and an ache in his shoulder he couldn't touch because his arms had been secured behind him. He moved his hands, feeling the cold metal around his wrists and hearing the clink as he tried to jerk free. Handcuffs. Ironic that. As he opened his eyes the world seem to tumble. Upside down. The wrong way up. For a moment nothing made sense until he realised he was lying on his side facing a wall. He rolled over, gasping at a jab of pain the movement caused. He looked around.

Straw, dark-stained wooden panelling to head height, stonework above, a door which was full height but somehow cut in two horizontally across the middle, and a window high in one wall, no glass, simply wire mesh. Riley pushed himself upright into a sitting position using his elbows, and tried to understand what he was seeing. In the corner of the room was a galvanised trough with a bright blue PVC pipe running down to a brass fitting and hanging on the back wall, a bundle of hay in a large net.

A stable.

It explained the smell of horse shit, piss and animal sweat, but didn't help much when he tried to work out where the hell he was.

He scrunched his eyes and swallowed, tasting blood from a split lip, the back of his throat as dry as parchment. He shuffled across to the trough on his knees, falling once flat on his face, grateful the floor had such a deep layer of bedding. In the shadows the water appeared black, but the surface seemed clean enough. He took a precautionary sniff and stuck his face down and gulped in several mouthfuls. The cool liquid stung the cut on his lip but eased his thirst.

Better.

Riley moved away from the trough and slumped against one wall, shivering as water ran down his neck. His breath clouded in front of him, rising to meet beams of light which came through an airbrick in one wall. He wasn't dressed for this sort of weather, but then he hadn't been expecting to wake up in a freezing stable. Far from it. He wore a shirt and a light jacket, lightweight trousers too. The coldest thing were his feet: they'd taken his shoes and socks. Real pros, these guys. You didn't get very far, very fast without footwear.

What the hell was this? Something connected to *Sternway*? It seemed unlikely. He wasn't the one undercover, taking the risks. He handled the intelligence, sure, but the information he had was shared amongst the team. A beating and kidnapping didn't seem Kenny Fallon's style either. He wouldn't be stupid enough to stir things up by snatching a police officer. As soon as Riley's disappearance was noticed there'd be massive resources deployed. If so much as a sniff suggested Fallon's involvement, his life would be turned upside down and any chance of the shipment making it in undetected would be gone.

If not Fallon, then who?

London. Had to be.

How anyone had managed to find him down here he didn't know. Then again, his relocation hadn't involved a new identity or anything. It wasn't thought necessary as the risk level had been assessed as minimal, and there were officers who were meant to be keeping tabs on the people involved. Unless they'd got careless.

He dismissed that possibility as unlikely and pushed himself to his feet again, using the wall and the trough to help him get off the ground, and walked over to the air brick. The round dots of light told of a bright sunny day outside. He put an eye to one of the holes and squinted out.

A neat grass lawn, several farm buildings and an expanse of gravel on which sat a left-hand drive silver Porsche Panamera. The bodywork gleamed in the sunlight and Riley could just make out a black and white scarf stretched across the rear parcel shelf. All of a sudden Riley knew exactly who his kidnapper was, remembering the face staring back from the front of the transit, the grin full of gold teeth, the crazy look of the man's eyes.

Yes, London.

And that wasn't good. Not fucking good at all.

Chapter Thirteen

Union Street, Plymouth. Saturday 19th January. 1.05 a.m.

Dixie Lowdon was fourteen and loving it. Hating it too. Weird that, but then everything was so mixed up, on and off, that half the time he didn't even know which day of the week it was. Something to do with his hormones. He'd learnt about that at school in his personal and social development class. The one run by the lush Ms Ferndale. The lesson was basically a chance to have a piss around while the teacher tried to educate them about love, relationships, caring and crap like that. All he knew was if he got Ms Fondle alone some day he'd like to teach *her* a thing or two about *his* personal development.

Right now, hormones had landed him and his mate, Rab, in a heap of trouble.

The whole thing had kicked off when Dixie had sauntered across the dance floor and brushed against the girl's tits. Rab made a move for her arse at the same time, giving it a squeeze and then running his fingers down the thin material of her dress and slipping them between her thighs.

Idiot. Rab should have paid more attention in PSD.

Dixie reckoned the girl had been up for it until Rab had gone too far, too fast. Now she was screaming and the only

144

person up for it was the guy she'd come into the club with. And his mates. All five of them.

Dixie ducked down and dived beneath a table, coming out on the other side amongst a group of older women, part of a hen party. Up ahead he saw Rab sprint across the dance floor and he jumped up and followed. Behind him, a scream caused heads to turn as the girl's boyfriend and his mates shoved their way through the hens, spilling drinks and knocking one of the women to the ground.

Rab slid the last couple of metres across the floor and smacked the bar on the emergency exit. He held the door for Dixie and then they both dashed down the stairs. The two of them flew round and round, down four flights, and crashed through another door at the bottom.

They emerged onto a side road. Several large blue rubbish containers stood to one side of the door, one full with beer bottles. Farther away, up near Union Street, a bouncer had come round the corner from the club entrance on the main road and was having a slash up against a wall. Steam rose around him, yellowing as the vapour caught the glare of a street lamp.

Dixie grabbed Rab by the arm and told him to slow down. The two of them walked towards the bouncer and the main road.

'Alright lads?' the bouncer said. 'Had a good night?'

'No,' Dixie said. 'There's some guys in the stairwell. They tried to sell us some gear.'

'Did they now?' The man fumbled with his zip and bent to the radio clipped to his lapel. He muttered a 'thanks lads' and moved towards the emergency exit.

'Nice one!' Rab said when the bouncer had gone.

Dixie shrugged. He was beginning to regret having gone to the club, but they'd only tried to get in for a laugh. He didn't think they'd had a chance, but Rab was big for his age and the two cute girls they'd queued behind had helped. The older one had knockout tits and she hadn't been shy about showing her cleavage to the guy on the door. He waved the four of them through without a second glance at Dixie and Rab.

Back on Union Street horns blared out as taxis zipped to and fro. The first groups of people were beginning to spill out of the clubs, which meant it must be one o'clock at least. Dixie knew he'd get a clip round the ear from his old man and he wondered if the little adventure had been worth the hassle.

They strolled up Union Street in the opposite direction from Dixie's home in Stoke, Rab saying he would cough for a burger for both of them. As they passed the front of the club Dixie spotted the bastard from inside. He stood with two of his mates. One of them had him by the shoulder and was trying to get him to come back in. A taxi pulled up on the curb beside Dixie and a horn beeped. The guy spotted them.

'Run!' Dixie said, legging it.

The two of them sprinted away from the club, up Union Street and towards the town centre. They dodged traffic and crossed over the road – Rab almost colliding with a night bus – and ran past the Two Trees pub and turned onto Western Approach. On the left was a Toys R Us, and through the windows of the store Dixie glimpsed a massive water pistol with a strap-on backpack water tank. He'd wanted one for Christmas, but Santa hadn't delivered.

Santa? For fuck's sake he was still a kid, this couldn't be happening.

They whizzed by the shop and Dixie risked a glance behind. The bastards were still coming. Up on the left an emergency help point stood at the side of the pavement, but Dixie reckoned he would barely have time to press the button before he got the shit kicked out of him.

They ran past, skirting the Toys R Us car park. Rab ran into King Street, but for some reason Dixie decided to dart into the slip which led into the car park. He realised too late that the gates to the car park would be closed, but up ahead a door to a stairwell was open. He ducked in, hearing someone clump along the slip after him.

Shit.

He moved to the stairs and began to climb, his feet splashing in unseen water or piss, or something sticky like spew.

'Got you now you little wanker!'

The voice echoed up through the stairwell and Dixie went up another flight. A bulkhead light flickered off and he touched the wall, finding a metal handrail leading up into the darkness. Below, he could hear the man was out of breath and puffing hard, but the scrape, scrape, scrape of his feet on the stairs told Dixie he hadn't given up.

Dixie reached a landing, the area black with shadow. Through a barred metal gate the upper level of the car park spread out into the gloom. Deserted, not a car in sight, just concrete pillars dotted amongst yellow lines which appeared to fluoresce in the glow from a light far in the distance. He moved to the gate and rattled the catch. Locked. He moved away, searching out the deepest shadow and then knelt like a cat ready to spring. His hand touched something soft and sticky and at the same time the bulkhead light came on again.

'What the fuck?' The guy stood a couple of metres away, his mouth open. He was staring right past Dixie, at a bundle of clothes lying next to the gate.

147

Dixie turned his head and caught a glimpse of something pink and red. Then the light flashed off and the guy was sprinting back down the stairs. Dixie thinking that getting the fuck out of there was a pretty good idea as well.

The breath steamed out from Savage's mouth, mimicking the cloud of smoke surrounding DI Davies. Davies took another puff on his cigarette, stamped his feet and uttered a string of expletives ending in something about how he could murder a bacon butty. The word 'murder' emphasised. Moronic idiot, Savage thought. Still, in this situation she understood his emotions: 4.30 a.m., cold, dark and not a good time to be about to view a dead body.

If there ever was a good time.

The call had come through an hour earlier, starting her awake from a dreamless sleep so deep that for a moment between the phone's rings she had been unsure what had roused her. She'd struggled out of bed and taken the phone out onto the landing so as not to disturb Pete. She began by lambasting the PC on the end of the line, asking him why the hell he wasn't calling the duty DI instead of her. The PC apologised and said the DI *had* been called and it was him who had suggested Savage should come out because this was something to do with operation *Corulus*.

She cursed and got the details before hanging up and stumbling around looking for clothes, all the while trying not to make a noise but in the end making a good deal.

'Mummy?'

Jamie had come down from his room in the attic and stood on the landing, his eyes mere slits and his head lolling. She propelled him into her bedroom and tucked him up in the bed next to Pete who groaned, but managed to put an arm out to reassure Jamie. By the time she had come out of the bathroom after a quick wash they were both fast asleep again, Jamie's head nuzzled in under his dad's chin.

Now she stood with Davies next to the bottom of a car park stairwell where a uniformed officer unravelled the obligatory blue and white tape from a roll and attached one end to a concrete pillar. Some sort of liquid had run down the stairs and pooled at the foot and the officer tiptoed round the edge, careful not to step in the mess.

The car park sat alongside the Toys R Us store on Western Approach and the bright primary colours of the shop's logo contrasted with the gloom on the manager's face. He had been woken earlier than Savage to come and open the store's own car park so Layton and his crew would have somewhere to park their vans. They hadn't arrived yet and the manager was asking how long the whole process was going to take. If people couldn't park then people wouldn't shop, so could they please get a move on. Savage wanted to tell him the mums and dads would be better off without a trolley full of the type of crap toys consisted of these days, but instead she smiled and said they were doing their best to speed things up.

A car rolled to a stop somewhere out on the street and a door clunked open and a moment later, slammed shut. Footsteps shuffled closer and the stooped figure of Nesbit came through the gloom of the car park entrance.

'They don't pay me enough for this, Charlotte,' Nesbit said, nodding a greeting to Davies as an afterthought.

'More than the likes of us anyway,' Savage said.

Nesbit looked at the mess at the bottom of the stairs, where the light from the orange bulkheads on the stairwell walls glistened in the ooze. His eyes tracked the trickle of liquid upwards, to where it turned a corner.

'I assume someone has already certified death?'

'A paramedic. And I'll bet he was in a better mood than you.'

'Most likely, since he wasn't woken up. Have you been up there?' Nesbit asked.

'No. Only the kid who found the poor guy, the first officer on the scene, the paramedic and a photographer so far. We thought we'd wait for you rather than go trooping up and down.'

'To hold your hand,' Davies said. 'Not for the faint-hearted, according to the photographer.'

'Hand-holding,' Nesbit said with a scowl, seeming to take Davies' joke at face value, 'will not be necessary.'

The three of them stayed silent as they struggled into their PPE items, a ritual Savage found useful in distancing herself from the thought of death. The process of putting on the suit and bootlets, pulling her hair back, tying up the hood and sliding on the gloves removed her identity somehow, made her feel she was simply doing a job.

'Ready?' Nesbit turned to Savage and Davies.

Savage nodded and the three of them ducked under the tape and climbed the stairs, keeping to the right, out of the way of the slick which dribbled down the left-hand side.

'Jesus.' Davies gulped a mouth of air and put his hand to his throat.

Sausage, not bacon. Red and pink and strung out like the blue and white tape, the sausage led up the inside of the stairwell and disappeared into the dazzling glow of a light above.

Nesbit stopped and bent, touching the bloodied tube and shaking his head.

'Ileum. Interesting.'

'His guts?' Davies said.

'Yes. Part of the small intestine.' Nesbit stood and continued up the stairs, following the snake-like object round until it ended in a pile of offal.

'Colon. Among other things.' Nesbit paused only for a moment before walking up another two flights, a faint smear on the concrete steps the only sign something was amiss.

They reached a landing area and another bundle of gut came into view, but this time it was attached to a body sliced open at the abdomen, the mass of pink covering the man's blue jeans, as if the whole lot had flopped out the way shopping tumbles from a split in a grocery bag. One arm lay at an odd angle, twisted behind the man's back; the other hand groped at the stomach area as if it could push the intestines back inside and undo the damage. A puddle of blood and body fluids surrounded the corpse and Nesbit couldn't avoid stepping in the liquid as he moved closer.

'Clever guys, those paramedics.' Davies. Starting on a joke. 'Maybe they should get a pay rise. You wouldn't know he was dead from just looking, would you?'

As well as the exposed guts, the man's face bore signs of severe trauma. The nose appeared flattened and bent to one side, a mass of flesh and blood, and the top and bottom of the jaw didn't line up. A dusting of white clung to the blood, as if icing powder had been sprinkled across the face or the man was an arctic explorer, the white like shards of snow or frost. Whoever he was it was unlikely even his mother would recognise him in his current state.

'When did the call come?' Nesbit asked.

'Around one-thirty,' Savage said. 'Some kid ran in here to escape a beating. After he found the body he went to a nearby help point, blurted something about murder and then scarpered. No idea who he was, but the guys in the CCTV control room confirmed his story about being chased. Any idea how long before that he died?'

'Charlotte, patience please.' Nesbit turned and moved to the side of the stairwell, where he deposited his black bag clear of the bodily fluids. He opened the clasp and rummaged inside the bag for a moment before pulling something out. 'I'll take a rectal temperature reading in a moment which will give us some sort of time frame.'

Nesbit moved back to the body and knelt. He took the man's right arm and lifted it, moving it up and down. Next he placed his fingers on the face and neck, palpating the skin.

'Rigor?' Savage said.

'No, not yet. He's not been dead for more than a few hours.' Nesbit lowered the arm and studied the body for a couple of minutes. 'That powder on the face is reminiscent of the cocaine on the other body.'

'The duty DI called me because he believed there was a connection. If that's it, then I am thinking I might as well have stayed in bed.'

Savage looked away from the body and around the stairwell. The landing they were on led out to the first elevated level of the car park. At street level, a wire mesh door on the stair block was supposed to have been locked the previous evening. The toy store manager didn't know why it hadn't been. For the poor guy lying with his guts all strung out, that had been his undoing. He'd likely as not run in and up the stairs, but when he'd got to the first floor he'd found the door out onto the first level *had* been locked. He had been cornered and the rest of what happened lay spread out on the floor, a Rorschach blot of red, pink and grey for Nesbit and the CSIs to analyse, interpret and argue over.

'Charlotte?' Nesbit had pulled the other arm out from underneath the body. The sleeve of the sweatshirt was ripped at the end and two white sticks poked out from the sodden mess of black cotton. Savage tilted her head, trying to work out what the shiny material was, and then Nesbit mumbled something about radius and ulna. 'Shattered, not cut this time. I'd hazard a guess by something like an axe. A bit of a coincidence though, don't you think?'

'Not exactly the same MO though.'

'No, but here's another connection to the killing in the toilet.' Nesbit tugged at the sleeve and revealed a patch of black and white stripes high on the forearm.

By the time Savage had organised and briefed the local inquiry team, liaised with Layton concerning the release of the crime scene and extracted everything she could from Nesbit it was pushing seven o'clock. A grey dawn began to displace the street-lighting as the city awoke to another murder.

Dan Phillips, the *Herald's* crime reporter, had somehow managed to sniff out the action and stood on Western Approach, begging Savage to be allowed closer. His photographer braced himself against a metal railing, the long lens on the camera pointing in the direction of the goo trickling from the bottom of the stairwell.

'Quiet as church mice,' Phillips said. 'That's what we'll be like. You won't even notice us. Two minutes and we'll be gone.'

'Dan, even if I let you go up the stairs to take pictures you wouldn't be able to print the things anyway.'

'That bad, huh?' The statement came out deadpan and matter of fact, but Phillips' eyes twinkled.

'No comment. You won't trick me like that.'

'Seriously though,' Phillips said, cocking his head to one side, the twinkle gone from his eyes, 'what do you think? Two murders this week. Are they connected?'

'Off the record, let's say there are similarities, but don't print that, OK?'

'Of course not.' Phillips smiled at her and turned away, then walked across to where Davies was talking to a PCSO who'd been given the unenviable job of preventing people from using the car park.

Savage realised she hadn't eaten, so she crossed Western Approach and walked the short distance to Market Avenue, where she found a cafe which was just opening. A cheese and tomato sandwich provided the calories and the coffee tasted better than the stuff available at the station.

When she got back to the scene Nesbit was supervising two mortuary technicians as they loaded a black body bag into the back of a van, the poor victim about to make the same journey as Franklin Owers had. The missing hand and the strange black and white pattern on the forearm meant the two men had something else in common too; quite what remained to be seen.

As one of the men closed the doors to the van, John Layton appeared from the stairwell with a smile on his face and a plastic ziplock bag in one hand. He held up the bag as he came over, the brown leather wallet inside glistening with a coating of blood.

'Three hundred in notes in there, cards and everything. I guess the killing wasn't a robbery gone wrong. Name of Gavin Redmond, according to his driving licence. Any idea who the poor bastard is?'

Savage only half heard the question as she stared past

Layton to where liquid still oozed from the bottom of the stairwell. Gavin Redmond. The MD of Tamar Yachts. *Sternway*.

'Fuck,' she said.

'I'll take that as a "yes" then, shall I?' Layton said.

Chapter Fourteen

A thin light woke him. That and the cold. Riley shivered and pushed himself deeper into the mound of straw he'd rucked up over in one corner of the stable.

Two weeks in the Caribbean? Nah, mate. Decided against it. Too much hassle, too much money. Better to stay here and enjoy the local hospitality. What did they call that type of holiday? Stay-fucking-cation?

The little joke caused a strange sense of calm to come over him for a moment. It took a few seconds before he realised the feeling was probably down to hypothermia. The effects of the cold and a lack of food and sleep were causing his brain to malfunction. There would, he thought, be some sort of weird justice if he died from exposure before his captors could get anything out of him.

The straw didn't seem to have helped much and the cold seeped deep into his body. His head had stopped throbbing, but his chest and shoulder hurt like hell. Broken rib, most likely, collarbone possibly. Riley decided on another tactic, rolled over and struggled to stand, his hands still handcuffed behind his back. He began to pace around the stable, feeling his heart rate quicken and some warmth begin to build beneath his thin clothing.

He'd been walking around for about ten minutes when

somewhere outside a dog began barking, a deep throaty bark which sounded like it belonged to Cerberus or worse. Then there was a clatter from the door. A jangle of a chain and a couple of bolts sliding back top and bottom. Riley stumbled out of the way and fell against the wall as the door swung open. Behind the door a strip light on the ceiling glared white, silhouetting the tall and lanky figure standing there. In his right hand the man held some sort of pistol.

'Turn around. Kneel over there.' The voice was as thin as the man. Nasal. He gestured towards the centre of the stable with the gun. Riley hesitated, but the man nodded down at his left hand. Riley saw a key dangling from a finger.

He did as instructed, facing away from the door and kneeling in the straw. The man shuffled in, and the next thing he knew the gun was up against the back of his head, pushing down hard. Riley bent over, his face down in the muck.

'Fucking pig. Had it my way, we'd blow your brains out now.'

Riley tilted his head a little and caught sight of another man standing in the doorway. This one wore a balaclava. He held a bag of bread in one hand and he muttered something Riley didn't catch. Something in Spanish. The gun pressed harder as the first man fiddled with the cuffs. Riley kept still until they jingled to the ground and the man stepped away. Riley rolled over on his side and then pushed himself into a sitting position. The thin man walked across and took the bag of bread. There was a rustle and then slices were raining down all round.

'Enjoy the meal,' the man said. 'It might be your last.'

The pair retreated and pulled the door shut. The same sound of bolts and chain and then the men retreating.

Riley gathered up the slices of bread and wolfed down a couple of pieces, washing the food down with some water

157

from the trough. He rubbed his wrists and stretched his arms, trying to ease the aching. As he stretched out, the pain shot through his shoulder and he sank to the floor, cursing. He pulled straw over his body and settled down again, munching another slice and thinking on the identities of the fast-food delivery boys.

Who the thin man was, Riley had no idea. He didn't recognise him from the old haunts up in London, nor was he among the known criminal fraternity of Plymouth. The other man was nameless too, but the holes in the ski mask had revealed olive-brown skin and white teeth grinning. Then there was the accent.

A South American.

Which was when he knew was really stuffed.

Before he had time to think on it, a throaty growl from outside had him scrabbling across the straw to peer through the airbrick. The Porsche firing up. The car's wheels spat gravel, the little stones clattering against the stable wall like a hail of machine gun bullets. As the vehicle sped away across the yard Riley could just make out the figure in the front: a short and bulky man with a squashed face. Riley remembered the man's golden grin from the other night and from when he had encountered him back in London. Something like a Halloween pumpkin, only twice as frightening. The last thing Riley saw before he turned away from the airbrick was that black and white scarf on the rear shelf again. The man was crazy about Newcastle United.

Riley slumped back in the straw, his head clearer, things beginning to make sense. This *was* about *Sternway*. Partly, anyway. The South Americans had come for the drugs. Pumpkin head too. Some sort of deal between them. Somehow they'd got wind of the shipment and decided they wanted some of the action. No, Riley thought, they probably wanted *all* of the action. Kenny Fallon might be a big fish in the small pond that was Plymouth, but he was small fry really and they'd find a way to deal with him easily enough. Which could, Riley thought, be one of the reasons they'd snatched him. But only one. He felt the chill creep across his back, the stones cold through his clothing, the fear prickling like icicles too.

Christianity was big in South America, but he guessed these guys weren't much into forgiveness. Neither was Pumpkin head. They'd be wanting to pay him back for what happened up in London and an apology wouldn't be enough. He had little to bargain with either: a name, a bit of inside information, some knowledge of police tactics. He didn't think it would be worth much.

He sighed, remembering his grandfather, a wise old man who'd looked aghast when Riley had told him he was joining the police. Trouble, he reckoned. Yes, Riley thought, there'd been trouble over the years, but nothing like this. The old man had been dead a while now, but Riley recalled with fondness the evenings spent together: cans of Red Stripe and games of liar dice, his grandfather grinning as Riley made some wild bid. 'Darius,' he would say. 'You lying. Washed out. I've got the aces and you ain't got shit under that cup. Nothing, I reckon, but a bag of bones.'

More often than not, Riley thought, his grandfather had been spot on.

Hardin's bulk blocked the window of his office and Savage was tempted to reach for the light switch to supplement the daylight edging round the DSupt. He'd been standing there for a good couple of minutes, not saying anything, just staring down into the car park as if at any moment Kenny Fallon might appear from the back of a police van, head bowed, cuffs on, guilty plea at the ready.

'Bollocks,' Hardin said finally. 'This leaves us up the brown creek without even a teaspoon as a paddle. We'll be using our hands next.' He grimaced at his own metaphor as he turned around, slumped into his chair and reached for his mouse.

Savage often wondered if the mouse and the plethora of spreadsheets, charts and to-do lists which shimmered on Hardin's screen weren't a sort of comfort blanket for the Superintendent. While he clicked and deleted and dragged and dropped he felt he was doing something. His actions were a way of coping with the situation. Right now he clicked once and then pushed the mouse away in disgust.

'Problems, Charlotte, problems.'

'Yes, sir. Redmond.' Savage looked down at her notebook where she had jotted down what the inquiry teams knew so far. 'From what we can tell he was drinking at a bar in town with a work colleague. They parted at around midnight, Redmond saying he was going to walk back to Tamar Yachts where he'd left his car. Someone obviously intercepted him on the way there.'

'Witnesses?'

'None so far, and to be honest I'm not holding out much hope. A little street fracas is not unusual for that area. Must be several every night. Once Redmond had run or been dragged into the stairwell he was out of sight, and there's plenty of traffic noise on Western Approach to conceal the sound of somebody getting a beating.'

'Well the whole thing is a bloody mess. If Redmond is mixed up in this paedophile business with Owers then it's rotten luck for *Sternway*. You think he could be? Killed by the same person or persons who did for Owers?'

'Doesn't make much sense, sir, but we've got to assume the killer is one and the same.'

'I can feel Fallon slipping through our grasp. We're going to have to put people into Tamar Yachts now. Detectives all over the place, rooting around, digging up all sorts of stuff, investigating Redmond's background. Fallon is going to keep a country-mile clear. *Sternway* is sunk.'

'With respect, sir, do we need to go anywhere near Tamar? The weird black and white markings we keep to ourselves, but the media will go with whatever else we feed them. So far they are lapping up the vigilante angle.'

'So Redmond was what . . . in the wrong place at the wrong time?'

'Something like that: "As far as we are aware Mr Redmond had no connection to anything related to paedophilia. He did not know Mr Owers and has no criminal record."'

Hardin chuckled, warming to the task. '"This was a cowardly, unprovoked attack on an innocent man and the public can rest assured we are doing everything in our power to blah, blah, blah."'

'Outstanding, sir. The Chief Constable had better watch his back.'

'Quite.' Hardin smiled for a moment, but the mood dissipated as he made a clucking noise. He shook his head, heaved himself out of his chair and returned to the window, where he tapped on the glass. 'If only it was as easy as a bit of media PR, smoke and mirrors. Unfortunately there are two problems. One, this might be *Sternway* related, on account of the drugs found with Mr Owers and the powder on Redmond's face, although I can't for the life of me see how Owers was involved, unless it's on the accountancy side of things. He's certainly flown beneath our intel radar if that's the case.'

'And the girl, sir. Simza Ellis. She's dug up Monday, Owers is killed a couple of days later and then last night Redmond gets it. There's some connection linking them. Too much of a coincidence.'

'You mean . . .?' Hardin's eyes narrowed, not quite understanding.

'Somebody called the builders in to dig up the patio at Lester Close. Whoever did that knew Simza was buried there. The timing, considering the conclusion of the drugs op, seems planned to me.'

'You're right. *Sternway.*' Hardin reached up to scratch his forehead. 'Which brings me to the second problem. With Redmond gone we have a major issue regarding the coming delivery.'

'You don't think Fallon can find someone else to make the pickup? Can't be that difficult.'

'Yes, possibly.'

'Sorry, sir. I don't see the issue. Fallon sets up alternative arrangements and collects the drugs. The snitch tells us when and where. We nab him. Simple.'

'Life isn't though, is it? Simple. How are we going to know the "when" and "where"?'

'Like I said, the snitch.' Savage paused. 'Sir, are you OK?'

'No.' Hardin turned away from the window, shaking his head again. 'Redmond is dead, isn't he?'

'*Redmond* was our informant?'

'As I said before, Charlotte, shit creek.'

After her meeting with Hardin, Savage returned to the incident room. The clocked ticked up to nine as she entered, but everyone was already at work, despite it being a Saturday. The news that *Corulus* possibly had another body to deal with had brought a new urgency to the investigation, and a number of officers who Savage usually rated as slackers, sat hunched at their desks, fingers clattering over keyboards as if their lives depended on cracking the case.

'Redmond is the owner of Tamar Yachts, ma'am,' Enders said, telling Savage what she already knew. 'Me and DS Riley interviewed him before Christmas. Now he's dead. Strange world.'

'Obviously decided to top himself,' Calter said. 'Most people would after meeting you.'

'Funny girl.' Enders stuck his tongue out of one side of his mouth and continued speaking with it hanging out. 'Not funny ha-ha. Funny peculiar, demented, dribbling.'

'You should know.'

Savage moved away and over to DS Collier. The office manager was trying to organise something from the chaos. He had set up a further three whiteboards: a central board and, on either side, one for each victim.

'Interfaces, ma'am,' Collier said, itching his crew-cut hair with one hand, a big fat marker pen in the other. 'I've split us into two teams initially, one for each killing. Each team will suggest, find and – if possible – eliminate, links between the two victims. They'll be sticking any suggestions they can't eliminate at the edge of the centre board. We can analyse everything on the board and draw connections between various nodes. I've told them I want every node covered, even if the lead is something that at first sight appears innocent. All the information is on the system as well of course, but I think this will help officers to visualise the arcs of probability.'

'Hmm. Yes.' Savage didn't know what on earth Collier was going on about, but she remembered he'd been on a training course a month or two ago. He was probably hoping Hardin would breeze by, note the new set up, and return to his office to tick a couple of boxes. The trouble was, at the moment the centre board was empty apart from three pink Post-its. One had the word 'cocaine' on, the second 'black and white' and the third 'supermarket'.

'Aldi,' Collier said. 'If we confirm the connection we will write it on the board.'

She moved closer and saw the scrawl of pen had a question mark at the end. So much for arcs of probability.

'Owers shopped at his local one,' Collier said, noting the frown on Savage's face. 'We found a stash of carriers at his place and Redmond had some receipts in his wallet. The branch is close to Tamar Yachts so it would only be natural for Redmond to drop in there on the way back from work.'

Savage nodded, wondering what Hardin would say if he *did* breeze by and she had to explain the only new evidence they had to show for their efforts so far was a preference in supermarkets. Correction, a *possible* preference.

'Good effort, Gareth, but a word please. Outside.'

Savage took a concerned-looking Collier into the corridor and they stood next to a poster appealing for players for a charity football match between the local fire station and Crownhill. Several blank spaces on the team sheet suggested officers were reluctant to sign up to yet another drubbing.

'*Sternway*. Know what it is?'

'Long-term drugs op. Organised crime or something. More than that, no.'

Savage told him about Fallon, Redmond, Kemp and the impending pickup. Collier scratched the top of his head, his default reaction when his brain was working overtime.

'So, Mr Owers and the girl . . .?' he said.

'We've no idea at the moment if Owers and Redmond are connected or if Redmond's killing is in any way related to *Sternway*. I simply wanted to let you know we might be getting into something a little more complicated than comparing supermarket carrier bags.' Savage smiled at Collier and then continued. 'Going to be a bit tricky though because of this SOCIT rumour, the "bad apple" stuff.'

'It's malicious, unfounded gossip, ma'am.'

'Undoubtedly. Still, Hardin feels it is best to be on the safe side.' She gestured through the glass panel in the door to the incident room. 'That lot in there can't know what I told you, not yet. Other than simple enquiries into Redmond's movements and the like, we can't be going anywhere near Tamar Yachts until Fallon has picked up the drugs.'

'Oh joy,' Collier said, scratching his head again, both hands up there now. 'Can you tell me where in the manual it tells me how to manage an inquiry when the detectives don't even know what they are bloody investigating?'

Chapter Fifteen

Budgeon glanced through the crack in the barn wall. Police.
Half a dozen of them swarming like flies over the shit in the
farmyard next door. Down at the caravan and in that room
above the byre too. A pair of uniforms had been round
earlier and the girl had been all smiles, the kid hiding behind
her. No, she had told them, she'd seen nothing suspicious,
hadn't even realised anybody had been using the caravan.

They'd asked about her husband and she'd said he was
mostly away in London or abroad. She herself was only around
about half the time. The officers had understood. They were
used to dealing with the rich folk who lived around the Helford
River. Most had second homes in France or Spain, holidays
several times a year, a yacht to cruise with if the English weather
was good. The two men didn't quite touch their forelocks and
mutter 'G'day, ma'am', but the deference was there.

She gave her name, the maiden one on her passport, and
the men left. Budgeon had come out of the shadows and given
her a pat on the bum. Told her she was a good girl.

Now he was watching from the workshop, a little nervous.
The stuff with Frankie had been good but he'd not factored

166

the police turning up. Not here. He'd obviously underestimated the amount the paedo had been monitored. If Frankie had been going to go away for a few days the authorities would no doubt have checked up. Frankie hadn't told him that when Budgeon had worked on him as he lay tied to the table in the workshop. But then he'd had other things to squeal about. Couldn't keep his fat gob shut, all the information about Big K pouring out as if it was really going to make any difference in the end. Perhaps Frankie had kept quiet about the monitoring as some sort of insurance plan in case things went wrong. If that was the case, then so far it hadn't worked.

Budgeon pulled back from the crack. The plain-clothes officers were leaving now, piling into a couple of cars. He recognised two as detectives from Truro, the others were from further away. A couple of forensic guys remained, but from the look of things they'd be packing up soon. The detectives would be wondering how the girl had got from here to Plymouth, how she'd ended up buried under Frankie's patio.

'A little pressie,' Budgeon had said when he'd turned up at Frankie's place with the plastic box and a spade in the autumn. 'Just so I know I can count on you when the time comes. I'll help you bury her, see she gets a decent spot out the back.'

Frankie had almost fainted from shock, but, hands shaking, he'd taken the box and carried it into the house.

Of course, the police didn't know any of that and they had no reason to suspect anyone else but Frankie being involved.

Still, it had been a close call.

Budgeon left the workshop and strode back to the house, glancing across at the stone stable block.

Very close.

This time Jackman took the call instead of making it.

'OK, now you *do* need to be fucking worried,' the voice said.

Jackman was with two other councillors on a Saturday afternoon tour of the Drake Circus shopping centre, the manager explaining the steps they were taking to increase footfall during the hard times. Jackman nodded an apology and stepped away from the group.

He'd been expecting to hear something – *wanted* to hear something – ever since the news had broken. The newsreader said gang violence, the paper claimed vigilantes. Either would have been preferable to the truth.

'Bloody disaster,' he said, walking towards the Cornwall Street exit where a sudden rain shower had begun to streak the huge glass panels. 'Do you think . . .?'

'I don't think, I know.' The voice sounded breathless, panicked. 'Got it wrong with Owers, I thought . . . but now Redmond? Can't be a coincidence, can it? Anyway, I got something in the post. A message.'

'What did it say?'

'*Hands off.*'

'Is that a joke?' Jackman slowed as he reached the exit. Couldn't help but turn and check nobody was following him. 'Because if it is, I'm not laughing.'

'No joke, Alec. He's back and he ain't going to rest until we're well and truly porked.'

Jackman stood to one side of the doors, watching through the glass as people popped umbrellas or ran for cover as the rain came down harder. He struggled to think of something to say and realised that, despite the draught from the doors, beads of sweat were breaking out on his forehead.

'Can we get out of this? Or do we carry on? I mean, all this heat is drawing undue attention to Tamar. Not to mention that Gavin was my brother-in-law for God's sake. I wouldn't be surprised if there's more than just a Family Liaison Officer knocking at my door before long.'

'You ever watch the *Terminator* movies, Alec? Well, it's like that, isn't it? Only worse. But we play this right and we can stay around for the sequel.'

Jackman was only half-listening. He moved forward to the glass, let his head touch the cool material, and shut his eyes. This was always going to happen. Eventually. If you knocked someone down and pissed on them, you bloody well better make sure they didn't get up again. But back then pure logic had won him over. He'd been younger, braver, had less to lose. Things always came around though, didn't they? Full circle. Just like Arnie. To bite you on the arse.

'Do you play cards, Alec? Bridge?' The voice was lower, almost a whisper. 'Complicated game, bridge, but some of my golfing pals persuaded me to learn. Took a while, but I got my head around the rules eventually. You see, when you are defending, your opponent tries to finesse your cards out, tease away at any advantage. But right when he thinks he knows how the cards lie, you know what you do?'

Jackman muttered that he didn't, let his head slide down the glass a little, felt like slumping to the floor, instead waited for the punchline.

'You trump the bastard.' The voice louder, much louder. 'Make that bloody call, Alec, understand? Get the bitch cop Savage onside and we're home and fucking dry.'

Hardin uttered the second 'bloody' in as many minutes and Rob Anshore, the PR guy, winced, stepped forward and concluded the press conference.

'Thank you ladies and gentlemen. Releases are in a pile at the door, please see me if you need any additional information.'

Savage, Hardin and Garrett sat at a table in front of a blue curtain, the force's shield and crest in the centre.

'Walking a tightrope there, weren't we?' Hardin said as the media scrum headed for the exit. 'But I thought we did rather well. Considering what the gutter rat scum were asking. What say you Rob?'

Anshore winced again and reached forward and switched the microphones off.

'A little defensive on the question about Simza's parents, sir. You do know the *Mirror* has signed them? The reporter was just trying to wind you up.'

'Succeeded, the little shit,' Hardin said. 'To suggest we would have handled anything differently had Simza—'

'Not the point, sir. Remember, the message is the thing.' Anshore pointed to the shield and crest on the curtain. '*In Auxilium Omnium.*'

'To the assistance of everybody,' Hardin said. 'Don't we bloody know it, hey?'

'It's an operational thing, the more people are on our side, the more help we get. Media is a tool, not an end in itself.'

'I realise that, but sometimes I wonder whose side these bloody journalists are on.' Hardin huffed and reached up to loosen his tie. 'Come on, Charlotte, let's get out of here, take a walk. I want a word with you and I'm burning up under these lights.'

In the car park a BBC crew were loading their gear into a car, Dan Phillips present, chatting to the presenter. He raised a hand and waved at Savage and Hardin.

'Nice show,' he shouted across, grinning. 'Entertaining. Especially the bit at the end.'

'Bollocks to that,' Hardin said. 'Come on.'

Hardin led Savage out of the station and round to the left where a local road crossed on a flyover, the busy A386 beneath. Halfway across, he stopped and leaned on the railing. Six lanes of traffic rushed by below.

'Can't be too careful these days. No chance of being over-heard here.'

'What is this, sir?' Savage said. 'Tinker, tailor?'

'Soldier, policeman. At least it looks that way, with Redmond dead. Unless his death really is unrelated to *Sternway*, we've got a leak. A mole. Clever too. Make the murder appear similar to that of the paedo and steer everybody in the wrong direction.'

'You mean the Owers and Redmond killings are not related after all?'

'Works for me. Redmond is already lined up for the off when Owers is butchered. Hearing the news gives Redmond's killer an idea of how to throw us off the scent.'

'But . . .' Savage thought about the black and white mark-ings, details of which had not been released. 'You're not suggesting . . . who on the *Sternway* team knew about Redmond?'

'Myself, the Chief Constable, a facilitator at Exeter and Kemp. Plus DI Davies. Considering the risks, it was need-to-know only. Kemp didn't even think Riley needed to know our source was to be Redmond, not at this stage.'

'Davies?' Savage said. 'He didn't appear to recognise Redmond at the scene.'

'Part of the act,' Hardin said. 'He wouldn't be aware that you knew. And you didn't, did you? See what I mean?'

'Yes.' Savage understood what Hardin was getting at. If Davies knew about Redmond he wouldn't want to reveal the fact to her. The DI was good at games and would have enjoyed pulling the wool over her eyes. 'So why Davies?'

'No reflection on you or Garrett. Quite the opposite in fact. Davies swims with the turds, his nose is down in the muck, always sniffing for information. By having him in on the secret we made sure Mr Kemp didn't go too far wrong.

Davies provided intel on Fallon's network and filled us in on every other piece of human crap the guy associated with. We also needed someone outside of SOCIT. Just to be sure.'

'And you think Davies can be trusted?'

'I don't know what to think, but if you have any evidence pointing to a different conclusion, you need to tell me. Now.' Hardin stuck his tongue out over his bottom lip for a moment. 'Well, do you, Charlotte?'

'No, sir.'

'Right then.' Hardin turned and looked back at the traffic again. A squad car on blues and twos joined the main road and headed north, dodged several vehicles and disappeared over the crest of a hill. 'Kemp says he is coming back down Monday, Tuesday at the latest. He'll see if he can keep the deal spinning, but he told me that there's one small piece of hope remaining. Goes by the name of Vanessa Liston.'

'Who's she, sir?'

'Redmond's flesh and blood. His daughter. She's seventeen, lives with the mother we think. Redmond split from the mother a long while ago because she acquired a drug problem. Couldn't make it up, could you?'

'And you think she can help? The girl?'

'Lately, Vanessa has been spending some quality time with her dad. Learning a few things off the old man. She's been seen with him at Tamar Yachts and with Fallon and some of his cronies too.'

'But she's only seventeen.'

'That's a problem, you're right. Legally she is sod all use to us. She'll need all that "appropriate adult" bollocks. Doesn't mean we can't have a quiet word with her though.'

'And say what?'

'Remind the girl her daddy was going the right way about things in helping us. Tell her she should follow his example.'

'You mean get her to become our snitch in Redmond's place? I don't like the idea, sir. I mean, what does she know? And there will be trouble down the line if anyone finds out. Speaking to us wouldn't be in her best interest.'

'We're in trouble now, aren't we? *Sternway* is going to go down the tubes unless we can re-establish some sort of connection. As to what information she has, Kemp reckons little Vanessa knows a lot. Apparently she's been shagging someone connected with Fallon, if not Fallon himself. Seems Redmond wasn't best pleased about that, part of the reason he wanted out. Look, I want you to talk to her. The interview can be under the auspices of the *Corulus* investigation so there will be no problem there. You can see if you can bring her around to the idea of helping us. I wouldn't stand a chance with the girl and neither would Garrett or Davies, but you might. Softly softly mind you. We can't risk anything getting back to Fallon. If it works we might still be able to get him. Once he's in custody we can see about upping the charges to murder.'

'And Davies?'

'Davies?' Hardin raised a hand to his chin, rubbed two fingers up and over his lips and made a sucking sound. 'Just for you, Charlotte, I won't tell him a thing.'

Chapter Sixteen

Sunday morning and Savage was up before the light again. Twenty-four hours until the Standards interview regarding Matthew Harrison's death and she'd still not done more than scribble a few thoughts down on a scrap piece of paper. She spent a couple of hours trying to put those thoughts into some sort of order and by the time the kids came down to breakfast, dragging a weary Pete behind them, she felt a little happier about the trip to force HQ. She had her story off pat and if the panel didn't believe her then there wasn't much she could do.

The rest of the morning went in a blur of homework and household chores. Savage was just about to eat lunch with Pete and the kids when a call came through from the Stonehouse beat manager about Vanessa Liston. The PC said he knew the girl's mother – she had been convicted for soliciting a number of times – and had seen Vanessa around, talked to her once a couple of years ago at a local youth group. Nice girl, but with a mum like that . . . The sentence trailed off midway through and the PC instead gave Savage the address for the mother.

Savage called the station to see who was available, finding – surprise, surprise – Enders there and keen to accompany her. A little over half an hour later and she pulled her car on to the curb alongside a terrace in the maze of roads north of Union Street. Enders stood leaning against the battered Focus pool car. The row of houses looked in a state too, ripe for refurbishment or maybe demolition, judging by the crumbling facade of number thirty-one. The skinny woman who answered the door had some sort of dragon tattoo on her right wrist, a gold chain adorning one ankle and a fag in her mouth which drooped when she muttered an obscenity as the door swung open.

'Yes?' The woman's eyes wandered from Savage to Enders and back again, finally alighting on the card Savage held out.

'Police, Ms Liston.' Savage said. 'We wanted a word with Vanessa if she's around and you wouldn't mind.'

The woman's eyes moved again, a flicker, no more, but enough for Savage to guess Vanessa was around and Ms Liston would very much mind the police having a word.

Enders moved forwards to force the issue and the woman shrugged and stood to one side to let him in, then trekked up the corridor behind him.

Savage entered, taking in the odour of roll-up tobacco and the sweeter, lingering aroma of cannabis, before following Enders through a doorway to the left and into a room where the furniture consisted of a scattering of sofa cushions, two beanbags, an upturned tea chest – which functioned as a table – and a large flat-screen television standing on a pair of nested Tesco home-delivery crates. There was no carpet, but a number of rag-type rugs overlapped each other. Between the gaps Savage noted cardboard had been laid on the floor, presumably for insulation. The window in the room faced south and the sun would have been shining in if it hadn't been for the old woollen blanket hung half across as a curtain and secured with clothes pegs to the curtain rail. Savage realised the purpose was to prevent the light falling on the TV screen, but *Homes and Gardens* styling it wasn't.

'Tea?' the woman said. 'Only the kettle's just boiled.'

Savage glanced at a stained mug standing on the crates next to the TV. The mug overflowed with ash and fag ends.

'That would be great, love.' Enders said, before Savage could say anything. 'And if you've got any biscuits . . .'

'Biscuits?' The woman stared at Enders as if he was mad and turned and left the room.

'We are here to question Vanessa Liston,' Savage said. 'Not have a snack and a tea break.'

'I thought being friendly would get us off on the right foot, ma'am.'

'Not if you eat all the poor woman's biscuits it won't. Besides, have you seen the state of this place?' Savage pointed at the mug. Enders went over and peered in.

'There's some silver foil down in amongst the ash, ma'am. I guess she's a smackhead. Think I just went off the tea. You are right, this place is bloody disgusting.'

'OK, go and tell her to forget the tea and that we need to speak to—' Savage turned to see the woman standing in the doorway to the room, a pot of sugar in one hand and a packet of chocolate biscuits in the other.

'You fucking pigs are all the same,' the woman said and slumped against the doorframe as if the simple expression of emotion had sapped all her energy.

'Sonia, isn't it?' Savage asked, going over and taking the biscuits and sugar and placing them on the tea chest.

176

The woman nodded and came into the room, dropping onto one of the beanbags.

Savage opened the biscuits and handed the woman one, putting the packet back on the chest and ignoring Enders' open mouth.

'We are sorry about Gavin, Sonia.'

'Yeah? Well don't be. Gavin was a tosser. Anyway, we split years ago. He dumped me and then what do you know, he goes and gets rich.'

'So you didn't get a share of the business?'

'There was nothing to share back then.' Sonia glanced across at a patch of damp around the window frame. 'I got this house, or rather the bit of it which wasn't mortgaged. Apart from that he never did anything for me or the kid.'

'Where is Vanessa, Sonia?'

The eyes flickered again, alighting on the door for a second. Savage took another biscuit from the packet and handed it to the woman. Then she gestured for Enders to follow and went out into the corridor. Further down, away from the front and on the right, there was a door to a bathroom. At the end of the corridor, on either side, two doors stood opposite each other. One opened into what must have been Sonia Liston's room; items of women's clothing hung over a wire-frame dryer and on the table by the double bed a box of Durex promised a few minutes of safe fun for somebody.

The other door was locked.

Savage bent to the door. 'Vanessa? Are you in there? This is Detective Inspector Charlotte Savage. I'd like a word.'

Nothing for a moment or two. Then came a scraping, followed by a clatter of something falling over.

'Vanessa?' Savage waited for a few seconds before

motioning at Enders. Enders stepped back and then barged forwards, ramming his shoulder into the door. The lock splintered away from the frame and the door slammed open. Sonia Liston shouted obscenities from the living room.

'Ma'am!' Enders shouted.

On the far side of the room Vanessa Liston stood on a table, trying to get herself through the top part of the window. Enders ran in and grabbed the girl round the waist and pulled her back. She toppled off and fell on top of him, her gangly limbs kicking and punching, blonde hair flying everywhere as she shook her head and screamed. Then she turned her head and sunk her teeth into Enders' arm.

Which was when Savage decided to punch her in the head.

Budgeon flicked up the peephole and looked into the stable. The cop lay in the centre where he'd piled a mass of straw over himself in an attempt to keep warm. Budgeon had a mind to go in and pull the straw off, give the man a good kicking. For old times' sake.

Old Times.

A London club. Steps down to a smoky basement with a ceiling you can touch if you reach above your head. A residue of sweat and nicotine stuck up there, decades in the making. Girls dancing on a tiny stage, men watching and drinking beers in bottles served from a bar in the corner. Deals going down in an alcove to the side.

'Darius Rogere' the man says as he sniffs the sample of coke from the back of his hand, the white powder contrasting with black skin. The accent with a whiff of France about it. A hint of the Caribbean and a couple of streets of South

London thrown into the pot too. The subtle mix marking the guy out as genuine. That and the sharp suits and relaxed attitude.

Not a care for Darius Rogere.

'Ricky B.' He holds out his hand and after Rogere brushes away the specks of coke the handshake is firm, the eyes full of cocky confidence. A young gun on the make, looking for deals, a way up the ladder. 'Maybe we can do business some time.'

'What sort of business would that be then?' Rogere says, glancing towards the little stage where a girl shimmies out of a G-string to a roar of approval from the crowd. Then he looks back, eyes steady and confident.

'We'll see.'

Drinks then, the pair doing a bottle of Scotch, Rogere never asking any questions, just listening, watching and waiting. Hours later and Rogere's standing there saying he's away. Hand outstretched for a parting handshake.

'A few Ks' worth a month,' Rogere says. 'Personal use and parties. Bankers mostly. Rip off the city boys.'

Then he's gone, the stripper with him, not much under the long coat she's wearing but perfume, not much doubt either that Rogere is kosher.

Budgeon dropped the cover on the peephole and, shaking his head, stepped away.

The man had turned out to be a long way from kosher since his real name was not Darius Rogere, it was Darius fucking Riley. Detective Sergeant. The Met. By the time that had come out it was too late. Rogere had managed to get up close and personal, helping in negotiations with the spics, handling the money and the toot, mucking in and getting his hands dirty. And then dumping a heap of shit from a very great height.

The Colombian bigwigs managed to evade arrest, but three foot soldiers were caught. To say the spics hadn't been happy was a bloody understatement.

Nine months in custody for Budgeon as well after that while the CPS built a case. Watertight, until, ironically, the prosecution were forced to disclose that DS Riley had been dipping his wick a little too freely. Not just with the stripper, but with other girls, one young South American lady in particular.

'Corrupting a witness,' the lawyer had said. 'Not so much an undercover cop as an under-the-covers cop. You're home free.'

And so he had been. But that didn't mean the pig was off the hook. He had plans for Riley, but there were other things to do first. Always business before pleasure. And sorting DS Riley was going to be very pleasurable indeed.

Savage stood on the curbside watching the squad car drive off, Vanessa in the back, struggling against the handcuffs. Enders stood rubbing his arm, cursing but refusing to entertain the idea of going to A&E.

'She's a kid, ma'am, not a dog. I'll be fine.'

Savage nodded and then called Hardin.

'I told you softly softly,' he said when she explained what had happened. 'Don't suppose you remember, do you? Undue attention on Vanessa Liston, and we might as well hang a sign around her neck advertising her involvement with us. Now get on and interview her and be circumspect.'

On the drive over to Charles Cross – the station in the centre of town which housed the custody centre – she filled Enders in on certain parts of operation *Sternway*. As they went over the interview strategy, Savage told him they'd need to bring up aspects of the drugs case, but without revealing too much. Enders shrugged his shoulders and, given his lack of surprise, Savage wondered exactly how watertight *Sternway* was.

At the station, Vanessa appeared unimpressed with the hospitality offered by her hosts. When Savage and Enders entered the interview room, Enders carrying a tray holding two coffees and a can of coke, she made no attempt to conceal her feelings.

'I'm pressing charges. You hit me you bitch.'

'Reasonable force,' Savage said. 'You were assaulting DC Enders.'

'Fucking wankers, let me out. I know my rights. You can't keep me here. I need an adult present. A solicitor.'

Enders started to put the tray down on the table but Vanessa banged her hands down on the surface and then tried to lift it, to make it impossible for the DC to finish his task. She swore when she realised the table legs were bolted to the floor.

'Charming,' Enders said, placing the tray on the table well out of reach. 'Didn't your parents teach you any manners? Like not assaulting police officers?'

'Mum's a prossie and Dad's fucking dead. Not exactly role models, are they?'

Savage shook her head. 'That's no way to talk about your mother.'

'What's she ever done for me? If she hadn't shopped me I wouldn't be here.'

'She didn't. She said nothing about you. That's what mothers do. Unconditional love. Do you understand what that means, Vanessa?'

'Fuck off!' The girl turned to Enders who had a smirk on his face. 'And you can fuck off too. Has anyone ever said you look like a right thicko with that grin?' The girl spat across the table, a globule of spit landing close to Enders' coffee. The DC moved his hand over the cup to prevent Vanessa from getting lucky if she was tempted to have a second try.

'Actually, several people have, Vanessa,' Savage said. 'Including me.'

'Hey?' Vanessa's mouth dropped open, the anger replaced by astonishment.

'Not my mum though,' Enders said. 'She always said I was both clever and handsome.'

'The thing is, Patrick,' Savage said, smiling, 'she was wrong. Parents sometimes are. They'll do anything for their kids though. Blood is thicker than water and family ties and friendships are ones which bind. However much you try, they are impossible to break.'

'My mum is dead, Vanessa, like your dad.' Enders said. The girl looked like she was about to begin another outburst, but when she opened her mouth nothing came out. Enders continued. 'But I know she still cares about me because I can feel her love right here.' Enders clenched a fist and punched himself in the chest. Vanessa closed her mouth and her eyes glazed with a watery film.

'Your dad was mixed up with some dodgy people, Vanessa, you know that. But recently he'd started spending time with you, hadn't he? Because he liked you. Loved you.'

Vanessa raised her arm and wiped the back of her hand across her eyes. She sniffed and then looked away and down at the floor. Enders waited a moment and then laid the coke can on its side and rolled it across the table. Vanessa glanced up and caught the can as it fell into her lap. She sniffed again and stood the can upright, popped the ring pull and raised the can to her lips, taking a deep draught.

'Your dad got involved with something illegal,' Savage said. 'We suspect it was his undoing.'

'What?' Vanessa spluttered through a mouthful of coke and then coughed a couple of times. 'You're saying . . .'

'We'd like to know more about what went on at Tamar, what *still* might be going on at Tamar. You hung around there a lot, didn't you? Messed around on the boats, sometimes went out on them? I gather you were learning the ropes, charts and tides and all that stuff. Good idea. Maybe you'll be able to take on the business some day. Only, before you do, you might want to check that everything at Tamar is legal.'

'Are you talking drugs?'

'I don't know, Vanessa, are we?'

'This is a game, isn't it?' Vanessa started to shake her head. Laughed. 'Like on TV. Good cop, bad cop, riddles and you guys talking round and round until you trip me up and I tell you something I didn't mean to.'

'Like what, Vanessa?'

'No, no fucking way! Here,' Vanessa stood up and lobbed the open can of coke at Enders who caught it the wrong way up. Cola splattered out onto the table and into Enders' lap before he could turn the can upright. 'Any more lovey-dovey matey stuff and I'll say you tried to touch me. I am not opening my mouth again without an appropriate adult and a solicitor.'

She didn't. For the next twenty minutes Vanessa sat half-turned away from them and stayed silent. First Savage, then Enders, and then both of them tried to get through to her. Nothing. They adjourned to the corridor, Savage flicking her business card down on the table in front of the girl before she left the room.

'That worked well, ma'am.' Enders said.

'Very funny. I thought we were getting through to her for a moment.'

'The tears?'

'Bloody fools we are. I'll get her released and break the news to Hardin.'

Savage went back into the room and told Vanessa they were going to let her off with a verbal warning. The girl shrugged her shoulders and stared at the floor. Savage left her moping and went to find the custody officer. Afterwards, a call came through for her and ten minutes later when she returned to bid Vanessa goodbye the girl had already left. A pool of cola dribbling over the edge of the tabletop had yet to be cleared up, but Savage's business card was gone.

Chapter Seventeen

Riley had been dreaming of Julie Meadows. They'd spent the afternoon on the beach lazing around. A swim, a couple of drinks and then back to the hotel room to make love. He'd lain down on the bed and she'd climbed on top, easing him inside. Then she'd ridden him, the intensity increasing until she'd cried out. 'Darius!'

He stirred. The voice wasn't Julie's. The tone was gruff and low. Menacing. Whoever it was spoke again.

'Darius Riley my old mucker. Or should I say fucker, eh?'

Riley brushed the straw away from his face and sat up. A short, squat man stood in the doorway. Thick neck, bald, a scar running down past his right temple. Teeth grinning with a flash of gold. Pumpkin head.

'Ricky Budgeon.' Riley noted a piece of wood in Budgeon's hand. A pickaxe handle, sans axe. He inched backwards, bringing himself to his knees.

'That's right my lover. Sticky Ricky Budgeon. Just can't get rid of him, can you?' Budgeon moved into the room, the tall man now visible behind. 'Don't mind Stuey, he's in a good mood right now. Apologises for all that bad language earlier.'

'Ricky,' Riley said. 'It's been a while.'

'Yeah. A while. Not much longer to wait though. All be over soon.'

'Come on, Ricky. We can work something out.'

'Hey?' Budgeon moved into the room. 'Work something out? You screw my girl, shaft me up the backside and you think we can work something out? Bloody comedian. Only I'm not laughing.'

'Ricky, it wasn't—'

'Yes it fucking was!' Budgeon raised the piece of wood and jumped forwards. Riley put his arm up to defend himself as Budgeon swung, and the wood smacked into his forearm, knocking him off balance. The pain jabbed up to his shoulder and he collapsed in the straw.

'The thing is,' Budgeon said as he stood over him, the veins bulging from his neck. He put a finger to his forehead and tapped twice. 'I might be thick as a plank, but I'm like an elephant up here. I never, ever forget. And that means you're history, pal. Dead. Understand?'

'For God's sake, Ricky. Think about what you're doing. You kill a cop and they'll be all over you. You'll never get away with it.'

'What do you think, Stuey?' Budgeon half turned towards the door. 'You worried about a few country plods?'

'Never, Ricky. Not from what I've seen so far.'

'No, and neither am I.' Budgeon prodded Riley with the lump of wood. 'There's a few things we need to know from you, but I'm going to leave off until tomorrow. If I get involved right now I'll get too emotional. But don't worry, we'll have a chance to chat again later. And I can tell you I'm going to enjoy that very much.'

Budgeon moved away and brushed past Stuey.

'Be seeing ya, mate,' Stuey said, winking as he pulled the door closed. 'Soon. Very soon.'

At a little after nine Monday morning, Savage met Hardin in the car park at Crownhill for the journey to Exeter for Savage's Standards interview.

'Late is not a good idea,' he said, as Savage climbed into his car. 'Not for this appointment.'

Hardin's Jaguar ate up the miles between Plymouth and Exeter and all-too-soon they'd arrived at force HQ, Hardin entering the meeting first to present his evidence and personal recommendations. Savage sat in an anteroom staring at pictures of past Chief Constables and watching the clock on the wall tick its way through the minutes. After an hour or so a PA asked Savage to go in.

The room for the interview had been chosen with intimidation in mind, and Savage's footsteps echoed as she strode across a huge empty space towards her inquisitors at the far end. They sat on the long side of a large table, their papers spread across the glossy surface, jugs of water positioned within easy reach and a plate of biscuits too. A single chair stood a few feet in front of the main table, with a small side table alongside. A glass of water stood on the side table, but no biscuits. If a sword had been resting on the main table Savage wouldn't have been surprised because the scene resembled a military court martial, an event which Pete had once described to her.

Hardin sat at the far end of the table and he gave her a thin smile as she walked in. He wouldn't be involved any further and unless invited he would remain silent throughout the proceedings.

'DI Savage, please take a seat.' The woman in the centre

introduced herself as Assistant Chief Constable Maria Heldon and her two colleagues as Chief Superintendent Graham Downside and Detective Chief Inspector Ray Ford.

Heldon and Ford were with Devon and Cornwall police and based at force HQ in Exeter, Heldon being the Assistant Chief Constable with responsibility for the Professional Standards Department. Downside came from the neighbouring force: Avon and Somerset. He was present to ensure the other two didn't whitewash the tribunal. Savage didn't think he needed to have bothered coming because Heldon had a reputation as a very tough officer. Hatchet Heldon was a moniker which had stuck, partly because of her thin face with its billhook-like nose, but also because whenever she caught a sniff of trouble she would come down hard. Loyalty to fellow officers wouldn't stand in the way of the rulebook. The reference to her looks was unfair, because she was an attractive woman in her fifties, with high cheekbones and penetrating eyes. If you discounted the nose.

DCI Ford was cut from the same chunk of caveman rock as Davies, and Savage reckoned he'd be the only one on her side from the start. There would be a problem because she was a woman, but he'd put his prejudice to one side if he thought she was a good copper.

Downside was another matter. Clean-cut and immaculately turned out, he'd want to appear impartial to begin with, but in the end he'd go with the ACC so that news of his cooperation would filter back to his superiors in his own force.

'At the outset,' Heldon began, 'we want to say that your valued role in the detection and apprehension of the killer Matthew Harrison is not in doubt. Your quick thinking at Harrison's cottage saved a young girl's life and your work in tracking Harrison down may well have saved other girls from a similar fate as the one which befell Kelly Donal and Simone Ashton.'

'Thank you, ma'am.' Savage said. 'I only did my—'

'However, today we are concerning ourselves only with the incident which took place not far from your house at Bovisand, just outside Plymouth. I am sure you will agree we must judge your actions that night on their own merits, without regard to your earlier heroism.'

Savage nodded.

'Now, the PSD report found you left the scene of the car crash in which Harrison was killed before any other units arrived. That is a serious offence for a member of the public, but for a police officer it is grave.'

'My children. I had to get back to them. Harrison had been at my house and—'

'We are aware of the so-called extenuating circumstances you put forth in your defence, but you must surely had thought of the consequences of leaving the burning car. When the fire brigade arrived the vehicle had already exploded. Had any members of the public been around they might have been seriously injured or killed. And then there is the matter of Harrison. You said in your statement he was dead when you looked into the car, but did you check? Did you take his pulse? Did you consider removing him from the car so you could try resuscitation? You had a duty of care to him and you failed to deliver.'

'Duty of care?' Savage shook her head, not quite believing what she was hearing. 'For God's sake he was a bloody serial killer. He'd killed two young girls and brutally raped a third. If we hadn't turned up at his cottage he would have killed her too. After he escaped from the cottage he broke into my house and attempted to kidnap my daughter. If he'd succeeded he would have raped and murdered her as well.'

189

'As I said, we are aware of the extenuating circumstances and we—'

'Extenuating fucking circumstances?' Savage said, aware she was losing control of herself. 'You make them sound like something I need to put down in a form somewhere, tick a couple of boxes alongside and sign my name at the bottom. The case involved abduction, rape and serial murder. Real-world policing you don't appear to know a thing about.'

'Charlotte?' Hardin. Concerned. Right hand twitching on the table as if he needed his mouse. 'I think ACC Heldon is just trying to cover all the angles. To ensure there's nothing that has been left out. Do you understand what I am saying?'

'Thank you, Conrad,' Heldon said. 'We want to be positive the threads are all tied up, to make sure there are no issues which might come back to bite us in the future.'

'What could come back to bite us? Do you think anybody cares Harrison died in that car crash? Don't you remember the headlines afterwards?'

Heldon turned to Ford. 'Ray?'

'If I recall, the best one was the *Sun*'s "Better Fried Than Tried" banner,' Ford said, the beginning of a smile indicating he, at least, was being won over by Savage's performance. 'They were just echoing the public's reaction though. I think there was some concern that had Harrison lived he would have been able to get away with pleading diminished responsibility on account of the abuse he suffered as a child.'

'That's as maybe,' Heldon said, 'but we are not here to pander to the mores of the masses, we are here to uphold the law. If we followed the guidance of the popular press we would allow vigilantes to roam the streets. The consequence of which would be sex offenders swinging from every lamp post.'

'And that would be anarchy.' Downside spoke for the first time. 'Don't you agree, DI Savage?'

Before Savage had time to answer, Heldon was bringing up a previous incident, citing it to show this was not the first time she had acted irresponsibly.

'You arrived at a scene where DI Phillip Davies was in command. Armed officers were covering a property and you entered, despite DI Davies telling you not to.' A smile spread across Heldon's face, glee evident. 'I can only assume you like disregarding the rules, but I can tell you if you do so again I will kick you down the ranks so *fucking* fast you will wish you were wearing a parachute.' She turned to Downside. 'Anything else?'

'I think I would like to hear DI Savage tell us in a few words about the crash. Just so we can hear the account from her own mouth.'

'I submitted a written statement,' Savage said. 'I spent hours being interviewed. Everything is in—'

'Nevertheless . . .'

Savage sighed. 'OK. Harrison was at my house. He had overpowered Stefan – he is my childminder – and when I entered the house he overpowered me too. He tried to kidnap my daughter, but I was able to get free and he drove off. I followed him in my car. It was night-time and Harrison didn't know the roads around my place. After a few miles he came to the bottom of a hill where there was a humpback bridge. His vehicle flipped upside down. I went to see if I could get him out of the car but he was already dead. I assumed he had broken his neck. Part of the car was on fire and I saw he had a can of petrol in the back. I retreated to a safe distance and the car exploded. After that all I wanted to do was get back to my children.'

'But he might not have been dead,' Heldon said. 'The

pathologist didn't have much to go on because Harrison's body was so badly burnt, but the post-mortem concluded he hadn't broken his neck. In fact there were no broken bones at all. The airbag had protected him from serious skeletal injury. The pathologist said if it hadn't been for your statement there would be no way of concluding anything other than that Harrison burnt to death. If he *was* alive, then his death was something you should have tried to prevent.'

Savage said nothing. The three officers across the table stared at her. Hardin was looking at the ceiling.

'DI Savage, I want you to think carefully before you answer my next question.' Heldon leaned forwards and placed both hands flat on the table. 'Are you sure Matthew Harrison was dead when you left the scene of the crash?'

Hardin cleared his throat, as if about to say something, but a sideways glance from Heldon had him searching the tabletop instead of opening his mouth. Ford had cocked his head to one side and was scratching his chin. Downside wrote something on the pad in front of him. Heldon waited.

'Yes, ma'am.' Savage said. 'I'm sure.'

No one said anything. Downside scribbled another note and showed it to Ford, who nodded. Heldon continued to hold her gaze, looking down her pointed nose like a soldier sights down a gun barrel. Downside pushed the pad over in front of her and she glanced down and then shuffled her own papers.

'Good. We will be making our final report next week and I will be liaising with the HR department to see whether you would benefit from additional training. Apart from that, I can tell you we will be recommending that no further action be taken. The incident will, however, remain on your file.' Heldon smiled, bloodless lips pressing together. 'For future reference, you'll understand?'

*   *   *

Riley had expected them back soon, but most of Monday had passed with no sign. He spent the time looking for some way to break out of the stable, but other than the fact that the door frame was a bit rickety, the place seemed secure. There was nothing to use as a weapon either and the chance of being able to overpower anyone with the injuries he had was minimal.

Monday early evening and the door opened. Budgeon and the stick insect with the white face.

'Stuey an' me,' Budgeon said as they came into the stable. 'We've just got a couple of questions. Shouldn't take long and then you can get back to your beauty sleep.'

'Beauty sleep,' Stuey said. 'Funny, Ricky. Funny.'

'See?' Budgeon turned to Stuey. 'Stuey's in a good place right now. Be nice to keep it that way.'

Riley said nothing as Stuey lifted his hands and showed the pickaxe handle.

'Hope you're not going to make it too difficult,' Budgeon continued. 'Only we're not much in the mood for that, are we, Stuey?'

'No, Ricky. Not in the mood.'

'So you simply need to tell us the date, time and method and then everything will be fine.'

The two men moved into the stable and pulled the door shut behind them. Stuey patted the axe handle.

Riley wasn't a soldier, hadn't been trained in resisting interrogation, but he knew a couple of things: First, if he was going to lie he'd need to make them beat the lies out of him. He had to take some more pain to convince them he was telling the truth. Second, he'd have to tell the truth eventually, but once he had he was history. He needed to postpone that moment for as long as possible.

'Date, time and method of what?' Riley said.

'Now who's being funny?' Budgeon raised a hand to his head and rubbed a spot above his right eye. 'Stuey?'

'Nice one, Ricky,' Stuey said, grinning. 'Leave him to me.'

Stuey stumbled through the straw towards Riley. He held the pickaxe handle up as if it were a baseball bat. Riley backed up into a corner, figuring there'd be less room for Stuey to get a full swing at him.

Stuey shook his head and then the end of the handle was coming in fast, jabbed in like a sword rather than swung, avoiding Riley's arms which had been held at his sides. The blow caught Riley in the face, glancing off his left cheek. He raised his hands too late and then Stuey pulled the handle away, sweeping it down to crack Riley on the knee. He collapsed on the ground and groaned, hearing Stuey fling the bat away and move in closer.

'Darius,' Budgeon said. 'Before I get riled just tell me the truth.'

'I don't know,' Riley said. 'We didn't have the exact route or time. We were still waiting on the intelligence.'

'That's not what I wanted to hear.' Budgeon nodded at Stuey.

Riley could do no more than bring his arms up to protect his head as Stuey began to kick and then punch him. The pain from his collarbone was excruciating, and a flush of nausea swept over him as he fought to stay conscious. Then Stuey was moving out of the way and Budgeon took his place. Thick hands reached in and grasped his neck, squeezing hard and shaking at the same time. Spittle dripped from Budgeon's face as he shouted down at Riley.

'Tell me you bloody fucker! Tell me where the drugs are!'

Riley saw Budgeon's face revolve and distort as he struggled to breath. Chubby fingers pressed in on his windpipe and he gulped and tried to suck in air.

Nothing.

His lungs wouldn't fill, Budgeon's grip was too much. He closed his eyes, felt his body go limp. So much for the acting. This was it. Game over. A rushing sound filled his ears and then he had the sensation of falling. He opened his eyes to see Budgeon far in the distance, all grin and round face, chubby arms reaching down to snuff the final breath out of him.

'Ricky,' Stuey said from miles away. 'He's going. Let him talk.'

Budgeon gave Riley a final shake and then let go. Riley slumped in the straw. He sucked in air. Saw the stable resolve itself and Budgeon stand up and walk back to Stuey.

'Darius?' Budgeon said, panting hard. 'When you're ready.'

Riley didn't move. He let the oxygen revive him and then he waited as long as he dared. Stuey muttered something and retrieved the pickaxe handle.

'It's a boat,' Riley said, feeling the pain in his jaw as he spoke. 'Pretty sure next Monday's the day. Most likely the evening.'

'"Pretty sure" and "most likely" won't cut it,' Budgeon said. 'I like to back sure-fire winners.'

'That's the best I can fucking do, OK?' Riley shook his head and was about to say something when he felt the nausea return. He rolled onto his front and retched into the straw, hearing Budgeon and Stuey muttering to each other. The room span again, darkness sweeping in. When he came round a minute or so later the two men had gone.

Chapter Eighteen

Marsh Mills, Plymouth. Monday 21st January. 5.51 p.m.

The day could have been worse, Savage thought. Much worse. True, she had perjured herself in front of ACC Heldon, a woman who wouldn't hesitate to bring the axe down if she discovered the truth, but at least she *hadn't* discovered the truth.

Buoyed by the marginal victory, Savage went to the supermarket on the way home to get something special for a cosy night in with Pete. She was halfway down the wine aisle in Sainsburys, looking at an Argentinian Malbec and wondering if the 'special offer' label on the bottle meant it was crap or if the store were simply being generous, when her phone rang. She didn't recognise the number but the young voice sounded distinctive.

'Is that the cop woman?'

'Vanessa?'

'Don't try and make me tell you anything that I don't want to because I won't. No one else is to know about this either.'

'OK,' Savage said, at the same time wondering how she would be able to keep Vanessa out of her records should the girl come up with something useful. 'When and where do you want to meet?'

'Now. Why do you think I'm ringing?'

Savage heard Vanessa mutter a distant 'bloody hell, stupid thick bitch' and she smiled to herself at the girl's childhood logic. She had the same desire for instant gratification as Jamie. Then again, Jamie was only six years old. 'Now' didn't suit her though.

'Can we do this tomorrow, Vanessa?'

'It's now or we're done. Comprendez fucking vous?'

Savage wondered where Vanessa had picked up the phrase, certainly not at school. 'OK. Now. Where?'

'Meet me next to the giant prawn thing down in the Barbican in an hour. And don't bring anyone else or I'll scram.'

'OK, I'll—'

She'd gone. Savage sensed Vanessa had enjoyed the call. All of a sudden the girl was important, not just a cog in somebody else's big machine.

Savage dialled home to explain she'd be late, and when Pete protested she reminded him he had missed around fifteen years of evening meals and said she would be as quick as possible. Next she phoned Enders and told him to rustle up a couple of people and send them down to the Barbican. Finally, she finished the shopping, drove back into the centre of town and parked in a small car park on Vauxhall Street. From there it was a short walk to the Barbican.

Early evening in January and the quayside cafes and bars were quiet. Later, even with the cold and it being a Monday, people would be wandering the cobbled streets, searching for drink, sex, someone to fight with, or all three.

Savage walked past the bars and continued down towards the Mayflower Steps where the giant prawn stood atop its white tower. Silhouetted against the city glow, the thing resembled an alien life form descending to earth. Leaning against a wall nearby, a girl in a very short skirt gazed out across the inky water to where the Mountbatten ferry glided up to the Barbican landing stage. What a thing to be wearing in the middle of January, Savage thought. Then the girl turned round and Savage realised it was DC Calter.

Calter walked across the cobbles and peered down into the Barbican, checking her watch and muttering something under her breath. Then she took a mobile from her bag and started texting. The whole time she didn't catch Savage's eye once, even though she came within a few feet of her.

Savage's phone rang.

'Stay on the line and start walking up to the Hoe.' It was Vanessa. 'I am watching and if I spot anyone following or if you hang up I'm gone.'

Savage turned away from the prawn sculpture and began to walk up the gentle rise away from the bright lights of the Barbican, all the while keeping the phone to her ear. Plenty of people were walking along the road so she didn't think Vanessa would be able to spot Calter or anyone else present, as long as they were careful.

She'd gone a hundred yards or so when Vanessa began shouting in her ear.

'The ferry. Run for the ferry!'

To her left, a road led down to a car park. At the far end of the car park the Barbican landing stage jutted out into the water. The Mountbatten ferry she had noticed arriving earlier lay alongside the landing stage and now the skipper gave a 'parp' of his horn, signalling his intention to leave for the short journey across the Plym. The last of the passengers stepped off the boarding ramp and down into the boat. Savage sprinted down the road to the car park, waving her hands to attract the attention of the crew. He'd already cast off the warps but the helmsman was using the engine to hold the boat against the quay. Savage ran along the boarding ramp and the crew held out his hand.

'Steady, my lover,' he shouted to her. 'No need to run.'

Savage walked the last few paces and stepped down into the boat. She sat down and glanced up to see Calter staring over the car park wall talking into her phone. Now she met her eyes and the DC nodded and turned away. The boat went astern and then powered forwards, turning to aim for Mountbatten on the other side of the estuary. She dared not look back to discover what Calter was up to. Hopefully she would think of something, but the distance was three or four miles by land round to Mountbatten and it would be thirty minutes before the ferry returned and set off once again.

The ferry took only five minutes to reach the landing station on the other side and as always Savage marvelled at the boat-handling of the skipper as he pulled alongside the jetty and used the prop wash to move the vessel into position. The boat kissed the pontoon with a touch as light as a feather falling to the ground.

She still had the phone to her ear, but Vanessa didn't speak until Savage went up the walkway and stepped on to land proper.

'Turn right and head for the end of the breakwater,' Vanessa said.

In front of Savage the lights of the Mountbatten Hotel looked more inviting than the walk along the path which led to the breakwater. A few smokers sat outside, and inside, at a table next to a window, a family tucked into an evening meal. The smoke from the glowing cigarettes of the alfresco drinkers spiralled upwards into a sky where stars were beginning to twinkle. A number of people strolled back and forth on the path which led to the breakwater, their winding route lit by a handful of streetlights. On the breakwater itself – a three-hundred metre long by fifteen metre wide strip of concrete atop a mass of ballast – Savage spotted the lights of several fisherman. The seaward side was always a popular spot and the council had gone so far as to put stainless steel bait-cutting blocks atop the seawall. The presence of the fishermen reassured Savage; nothing much could happen out here with them around.

As she neared the end of the breakwater she searched around for Vanessa. Aside from the fishermen, a couple walking hand-in-hand back towards the landward end seemed to be the only people around. At the tip of the breakwater stood a small tower known as the Plymouth Yacht Club Start Box. On race days yacht club officials directed events from the room at the top. Stairs ran up and round both sides and Savage assumed that the girl was hiding somewhere behind the tower.

'Where are you?' she hissed into the phone.

Nothing.

She approached the stairs on one side of the box and climbed up. At the top, a man in a long raincoat stood holding a slim bag, his thin shape dark against the sky. There was no sign of Vanessa. Savage moved away and once more spoke into her phone. Still nothing. Then a click and dead air.

'DI Savage.'

Savage whirled round. The man had turned from the railings. Close-cropped grey hair framed a bony face. The slit of a smile forming as he moved forward. The face appeared familiar, but she couldn't quite place it.

'Something to show you.' The man put his bag down on the top step and unzipped it. Inside was a laptop. He flicked up the lid and the computer woke from its sleep. A finger on the trackpad and a video window sprung open.

Savage looked around. Two fishermen were chatting not more than thirty metres down the seawall, the dull glow of a torch as one showed another his collection of lures, the sparking of a match as cigarettes were shared.

'Who are you?' Savage said as she leant in towards the screen where shaky footage from a mobile or home video had begun to play.

'Never mind. Just watch.'

The screen showed a night-time scene, but the picture was poor. In the centre a flicker of flame came from the middle of something large, black and shiny. In the background, piercing beams from a car's headlights illuminated the area. The camera operator had steadied now and Savage gasped when she realised what it was she was watching; the black, shiny object was Matthew Harrison's upside down Shogun. And the figure standing next to the wreckage was her. Now she could hear the soundtrack too, the voices indistinct, but a two-way conversation was definitely going on. At one point Harrison's voice rang out, a plea for help. Savage watched herself in horror as she walked away from the wreckage and vanished behind the glare of the headlights.

A minute or so later the car was turning round, red tail-lights moving away and disappearing into the distance. Then the Shogun exploded. Everything went white as the camera's sensor overloaded before the exposure compensated and reds and oranges and yellows filled the screen. There was something else as well, something on the soundtrack for a few seconds. Matthew Harrison screaming as the flames consumed his body.

'Well?' The man pulled down the lid of the laptop and

201

zipped up the bag. 'In the light of your meeting with ACC Heldon earlier today, would the Inspector like to make a statement?'

'Who the fuck are you and what do you want?'

'I need some help. A favour or two.' He pulled a photograph from an outside pocket on the bag and then hefted the bag on to his shoulders. He snapped the photograph down on the seawall and started to walk down the steps. 'In case you forget. Bye now, I'll be in touch.'

'Where's Vanessa?' Savage shouted after him, snatching up the photo before it blew away.

'She's fine. Don't worry about her, she's smart and can take care of herself.' The man became a shadow as he walked by the fishermen with their lights. 'See you soon, Charlotte.'

Savage squinted at the photo, realising it was a still from the video showing her next to the wrecked car. She crumpled the paper, shoved it in a pocket and turned and grasped the railing in front of her with both hands, gripping tight to steady herself. She stared out across the Sound where the water swirled, moved by unseen forces, pinpricks of white starlight dancing on the black surface.

Fuck! Who the hell was the guy? And where had he got the footage from?

She turned around again and leant against the rail, looking back along the breakwater towards the lights in the car park at the end and the glow from the pub. Closer, the two fishermen turned to eye a woman passing them. She was dressed for the town centre with a halter top full of promise, a miniskirt cut close to the tops of her thighs, but the low-level lighting set into the seawall cast a yellow glow onto flat, sensible shoes.

'Ma'am?' A woman's voice hissed in the darkness. Calter. 'Is that you? Are you OK?'

* * *

202

They had drunk the bottle of Malbec and only the dregs remained in a cheaper bottle of nameless red sitting on the living room table. Savage leant on Pete's shoulder as he dozed on the sofa beside her. *Newsnight* flickered on the TV, the volume turned way down, Jeremy Paxman scowling out from the screen.

The incident with Vanessa and the man on Mountbatten Breakwater had scared her and when she arrived home Pete picked up on her mood straight away. Savage mumbled something about the Standards interview and said she was knackered, stressed, and overworked and needed some downtime. They put the kids to bed and ate late, Pete not asking her about opening another bottle of wine once the first had gone. After the meal they slouched in front of the TV watching some mindless crap and Pete massaged her shoulders before he drifted off.

On the television a politician squirmed in his seat as Paxo put the knife in and twisted. Savage knew how the poor man felt. The only difference being in her case the person twisting the blade into her was *themselves* a politician.

Councillor Alec Jackman. Deputy leader of Plymouth City Council and a prominent member of the Devon and Cornwall Police and Crime Panel.

Out on the breakwater the man had seemed familiar, but it was only when she'd arrived home and strode into the kitchen and saw his face staring out from the front page of the *Herald* – Jackman and a group of councillors touring the Drake Circus shopping centre – that she'd realised his identity. She'd dropped the carriers containing the shopping on top of the paper and grasped the back of a chair to steady herself. When Pete had asked if something was wrong she'd been tempted to say 'wrong' was the understatement of the year. Instead she'd pointed to the

203

bottle poking out from amongst the shopping and told him to find a corkscrew.

Now, as she lay curled up against Pete, she wondered what the hell Jackman wanted from her. Something to do with Redmond's death? The Tamar Yachts MD had, she remembered, been Jackman's brother-in-law. If that was the case why couldn't he just report his concerns in the usual way?

Savage didn't want to think of the possibilities or what might happen if she didn't do exactly as Jackman wanted, but try as she might she couldn't push the thought from her mind. The video footage clearly showed her leaving Harrison to burn to death in the car. Dismissal from the force could only follow from such a revelation and criminal charges would be more than likely.

She looked across at Pete. His eyes were closed but he had a smile on his face. Lost in a dream. How would he take the news if all should come out? Would he stand by her or would he feel betrayed? After all, she hadn't confided in him. He'd be protective of the children, but other than that Savage realised she had no idea how he would react. The thought brought a queasiness to her stomach, as if she was in their little boat at the top of a huge wave and about to crash down into the trough.

At that moment a buzzing came from the table. Her phone. An incoming text message.

Pete stirred, but his eyes only opened for a moment before fluttering shut again. Savage reached for the phone. The number was an unfamiliar one. She clicked to read the message.

Remember, remember that night in November.

A chill iced along her fingers and up her arms causing her to shiver. Only one person could have sent the message. Bastard. Jackman wasn't going to let this go and was using a classic blackmail technique: pile on the pressure before making any demands so that when they came, acceding to them would seem by far the easiest option. Savage untangled herself from Pete and went into the kitchen. Her fingers hovered over the phone. Her instinct was to call Jackman and scream at him, but that would only show he had unsettled her. Better to ignore the message. She took a number of deep breaths and then switched the phone off.

She went back into the living room. Pete had woken and was staring at the TV, where the credits rolled over Paxman's darkened studio. She held out her hand to him, sighing and feeling as if she was ready to drop.

'Come on old sailor,' she said. 'Let's go to bed.'

Back home in Mannamead, Jackman pulled back the sliding door in the living room and stepped out into the garden to have a cigarette. A breeze tingled against his face. Cold. Stars above the city glow. Way up high, something strobing against the black night. A plane, heading west, out of here.

His wife, Gill, was upstairs in bed trying to sleep, but mostly just crying. Jackman had been up there, put his arm around her, handed her tissue after tissue as she talked about her brother Gavin. Jackman wanted to shake her and tell her that Redmond had been a loser, that she'd scarcely had a good word to say about him when he was alive. Instead, he listened to her rabbiting on about how she wished she'd spent more time with him, helped him more, been more of a family. It was all too late now, she said, but they would have to make amends, see what they could do for Vanessa. She was family too, wasn't she?

'Yes,' Jackman had said, tucking his wife down and kissing her on the cheek. 'Of course she is.'

Jackman fired up, sucked in, breathed out. The smoke slipped away into the night air, his thoughts swirling round too. After the meeting with DI Savage he'd had an argument with Vanessa. She'd called him an old fogey and he'd slapped her. Wanted her after that too, but she'd buggered off to meet some friends, leaving him to return home. Never mind, she'd be sorry later, he was sure of it. Maybe he would need to be a little more understanding. She'd just lost her dad after all. Maybe Gill was right about needing to do more for Vanessa. If only the silly cow knew.

Somewhere a few streets off a police siren grew in tone and volume. Jackman smiled to himself, relishing the irony in the words that came to mind as the sound fell away and the unseen vehicle sped into the night.

Cop car.

Out on the breakwater things couldn't have gone better. The shock on the bitch's face, visible in the glare from the laptop, had been well worth waiting for. But the shock was the least of the woman's problems. Soon he'd follow up the meeting, turn the screw, get what they needed. Yes, they could still get out of this one, emerge on top. With a little help from their friends.

Chapter Nineteen

Nr Bovisand, Plymouth. Tuesday 22nd January. 7.10 a.m.

Savage hadn't slept well. The wine she had hoped would
send her off had instead kept her awake, her head buzzing
with the incident with Jackman. She must have caught a
couple of hours, but all too soon the window behind the
curtains began to lighten, the new day inescapable. She
heaved herself out of bed and stood in the shower for
much longer than usual, as if the water might wash
away the memory, the evidence or both. Breakfast and
readying the kids for school was accomplished on autopilot
and the drive to work seemed to take forever. On arrival
at the station she half-expected to be summoned to Hardin's
office, imagining her fellow detectives waiting there to
arrest her.

In the foyer, the desk sergeant nodded a greeting before
returning to his paperwork. A fresh-faced DC smiled as he
passed her in the corridor. As she entered the Major Crimes
suite, DCI Garrett asked her if she wanted a coffee. Obviously
'murderer' wasn't tattooed on her face, nor had a warrant
been issued; Councillor Jackman had kept quiet. Savage felt
relieved for a moment, but then the anxiety returned. If
Jackman wasn't taking the legal route – the route the

well-respected deputy leader might be expected to take – then he wanted something else.

She tried to erase the thought from her mind as she strolled across to Calter and Enders. Calter babbled into a phone while Enders sat at his desk, peering at his screen and running his finger down a list of registered and suspected sex offenders.

'DS Collier told me to carry on searching for an inter-mediate, um, node. Someone Owers may have associated with who knew Redmond. No chance the Liston girl might have known Owers is there? Make our life a bit easier if she had.'

'No,' Savage said, hoping Enders wouldn't ask what had happened last night. 'I got nothing useful from her. Anyone else?'

Enders brought up a pretty diagram on his screen. Collier's arcs of probability had increased to four, but the new one appeared as flimsy as the first three. Enders pointed to one of the lines and began to fill Savage in when Calter put her phone down, the clatter as she did so turning heads.

'We've fucking got him, ma'am!' she said, face beaming.

'Who have we . . . er, "fucking got"?' Savage asked.

'Stuart Chaffe. The guy you chased the other day. The one with the van seen over near Durnford Street the night Owers disappeared. The prat had a shunt on the Tamar Bridge. Starts a fight with another motorist and we get called. Response take a look at the bridge cameras and realise the van and Chaffe are on our to-do list. When the patrol turns up he is stuck in the jam with nowhere to go. So the nutter jumps.'

'No!'

'Yeah, right. Well the MOD Police picked him out of the water down near the docks. Gave him a cup of tea and a

208

pair of handcuffs. He's being taken to Charles Cross at this moment.' Calter grinned. 'Happy days, yes?'

When they entered the interview room at Charles Cross, Savage was not pleased to see a local solicitor called Amanda Bradley alongside Stuart Chaffe. Bradley was all heels, legs and teeth. Plus just the right amount of cleavage showing where the top three buttons of her shirt were undone. A whole lot of style but very little substance. Savage had often wondered how she'd managed to pass her law exams and even more amazingly how she'd gained a partnership in one of the most respected firms in the county.

Chaffe sat impassive, hair still wet, clothing looking like something the custody officer had dredged up from the lost property box: shell suit trousers and a baggy fleece several sizes too big for his gangly frame. As Savage and Enders entered he chuckled and then spat into his plastic beaker, plonking it down on a Formica table stained with coffee, tea and burn marks.

'Well I never, the Jehovah Duo. Spare me all that crap from the other day and absolve me of my sins, would you?'

'I don't think even the Pope could do that, Stuart,' Savage said as she took a seat. 'Not from the look of the list I've seen.'

'I understand my client has been arrested on suspicion of murder,' Bradley said, pointing a pink-nailed finger down at a printed sheet in front of her. 'The evidence, such as it is, being entirely circumstantial, I suggest we get on with the interview and then he can be released.'

They did just that, Enders preparing the tapes and pointing out the video camera, Chaffe shrugging and shaking his head, muttering about having 'done nothing' as Bradley made some notes.

Savage worked her way through their preliminary questions, building up a picture of what Chaffe had been up to in the time since he'd been released, and then moving onto establishing where Chaffe had been when Owers and Redmond had been killed. Chaffe claimed he had been at home over the weekend when Owers was killed and kipping in his van the night Redmond got cut open.

'Where, Stuart?' Savage said.

'Some lane on Dart-fucking-Moor. Freezing my nuts off because you tossers turfed me out of my flat.'

'We didn't turf you out, you did a runner when we asked you about Mr Owers, remember?'

'Same difference.'

'Look, your van was seen near where Owers disappeared. You told us you were just in the area. Well if you're as innocent as you say you are then why run? – and why the hell jump from the bridge? We all know Tom Daley's a Plymouth lad but I'm not sure it's a good idea for half the city to try and emulate his diving feats.'

'Emulate?' Chaffe curled his lip and looked blank.

'It means copy. Which brings me back to Gavin Redmond. He's killed in a manner displaying your handiwork. Face it, everything points in your direction.'

'Good as a confession, Stuart,' Enders said. 'I bet your mucky prints are all over the scene.'

'They're not.'

'Wear gloves, did you?' Savage said.

'Didn't do it, Inspector, that's why.'

'If either Owers or Redmond have been in your van, we'll find something.'

'Don't think so, but be my guest. Just don't scratch the paintwork.'

'I wouldn't worry about it. By the time you get out the whole

210

thing will have rusted to the ground. Your last stretch is going to seem like a mini-break compared to what you'll get this time. Unless you can explain yourself. For instance, I get Owers, nasty piece of work, but Redmond? Why do him? I've had a word with my boss and he's keen to see us strike a deal so we can sort this mess out. Help us, Stuart, and it can only benefit you.'

'Yeah, sure.'

'You can start by telling us who was the man with you in the van. A witness saw two people in the vehicle. You weren't alone, were you? Maybe it wasn't even you who killed Owers and Redmond, maybe it was this other guy. If that's the case then he'll be the one going down, won't he? Tell us what you know.'

'I don't know fuck all,' Chaffe said, leaning back and putting his hands behind his head, laughing. 'And neither do you.'

'And that,' Bradley said, speaking for the first time since the interview proper had started, 'is that. My client has co-operated fully with you and answered all your questions. I suggest you come up with something a little more substantive if you wish to continue to hold him.'

Chaffe turned and grinned at Bradley. She smiled back, showing her immaculate dental work.

'We're not done yet, Ms Bradley,' Savage said, glancing at the clock on the wall and then getting to her feet. 'I'll see that Mr Chaffe gets something to eat and we'll resume mid-afternoon.'

'Sausage and chips'd be nice,' Chaffe said. He gave Savage a wink and then laughed again. 'With plenty of ketchup, get my drift?'

Back in Major Crimes at Crownhill, Savage went over the interview with Enders. Chaffe was right, they had nothing on him other than a sighting of his van. She'd speak to Layton about giving it the once over, but wondered if they even had enough to make that worthwhile.

Enders began to outline an idea he had for the second round, trapping Chaffe by making him think they had more than they did. Savage was only half listening. She couldn't seem to concentrate, the affair with Jackman still uppermost in her mind. Enders stopped mid-sentence and she opened her mouth to apologise. Enders looked past her to a young DC hovering at the door. Savage told the DC to spit it out.

'A woman is down at the front desk, ma'am. Miss Julie Meadows from the kids' charity, NeatStreet. Wants a word with someone about DS Riley.'

'Never heard of her,' Savage said. 'Can you deal with whatever she wants?'

'Julie is Darius' girl,' Enders said. 'His new squeeze. He met her when we were over in North Prospect investigating the Kelly Donal killing, tail end of last year. I think the pair of them are infatuated. I am trying to find out exactly what's going on between them, but he keeps the details to himself.'

'Sensible. If he told you, the news would spread like wildfire.' Savage turned to the DC. 'Perhaps you'd better send her up here.'

A couple of minutes later Julie Meadows appeared at the entrance to the crime suite. The little visitor's badge was clipped to a big fluffy jumper which came down over curvy hips, and at first sight Savage didn't think the woman looked Riley's type. Short dark hair, little or no make-up, somehow too casual with no hint of glamour or style. But when she spoke to introduce herself the words came out like fizzing bubbles rising in a champagne glass and Savage wondered if the girl wasn't the perfect complement to Riley's neat, reserved character.

212

'DI Charlotte Savage,' Savage said. 'And this is DC Patrick Enders, he works with Darius.'

'For my sins,' Enders said.

'Thanks for seeing me,' Julie said. 'My concerns all seem a bit foolish now I am here.'

'Tell us about them then, Julie.'

'Well, as you will be aware, Darius is supposed to be on holiday.'

'Yes, he told me all about his little trip,' Enders said, shaking his head. 'Winter sun. The bloody Caribbean. He kept ribbing me about my own holiday. I've got a week booked at Easter. Disneyland. And that's Paris not Florida.'

'Ha, small coincidence there. His family on his grand-mother's side are French.'

'As are mine,' Savage said, 'but on my grandfather's side. Another coincidence.'

'Darius has gone to Martinique where the family were originally from. There are some nephews and cousins he has never met. He had planned to spend a week visiting them and then . . .' Julie stopped and smiled. 'Well, I am supposed to be joining him for the second week for a more relaxing beach holiday.'

'OK. I am with you so far. What's the problem?'

'The arrangements with his relations were pretty loose. Darius was going to stay in a hotel in Fort-De-France and visit them from there.'

'And?'

'I texted a couple of messages to Darius about my travel arrangements, but I didn't get any replies. I tried phoning but I couldn't get his mobile. Finally I rang the hotel.'

'And did you speak to Darius?'

'No. They confirmed he had a reservation but said that he hadn't turned up. I don't have any contact details for his family either here or abroad so I tried phoning the airline. He took a flight from Exeter to Paris and then to Martinique. Neither Flybe or Air France would give me any information about passengers or whether or not Darius had boarded the flight.'

'They wouldn't. Security. But they will to us.' Savage gestured to Enders and he moved back to his screen and picked up a phone.

The next few minutes were awkward as Savage tried to assuage Julie's fears. She suggested there could be any one of a number of explanations. Perhaps Darius had changed his mind and gone to stay with a relative after all and maybe his phone had broken or been stolen. Despite Savage's best efforts, Julie didn't appear to be reassured.

'Even if his phone was stolen surely he would find a way to call me, wouldn't he?'

'You would hope so but . . . Well, men can be complete tossers sometimes.'

'Ma'am?' Enders said, the expression on his face sombre. 'Not good, I'm afraid. I called someone at force HQ in Exeter, a guy I know who has contacts at the airport. He made a quick enquiry and Flybe confirmed Darius was booked on the eight forty-five a.m. flight to Charles de Gaulle. However, he never boarded the plane. In fact he never checked in at all.'

'But . . .' Julie's hand went to her mouth. 'He texted me a couple of times first thing in the morning. The first message said he was waiting for the taxi to arrive and that the week coming was . . . well . . . it was going to be the longest week of his life because he would miss me so much. The second message was some sort of pun I didn't understand. Just one word: Budgen.'

'Like the supermarket?' Savage said.

'I suppose so, yes. Darius liked word games, silly innuendo and stuff, but this I didn't get.'

'You've checked his flat?'

'Yes. I rang and I even went round although I couldn't get in.'

'OK. You were right to come and see us. I am going to make this official because things don't quite add up. The best thing you can do is go home and we will call you as soon as we know anything.'

Julie thanked them and left, the fizz all gone out of her.

'What do you think, ma'am?' Enders said.

'I am at a loss, Patrick. If Darius had been in an RTC, surely we'd know about the accident. You'd better get round to his flat right away. I'll get someone here to begin chasing taxi companies. I only hope there is some simple explanation to this.'

Two hours later and the simple explanation Savage hoped would be forthcoming was conspicuous by its absence. Enders called through from Riley's flat. He'd gained entrance and reported that the place seemed clean and tidy, fridge empty, everything looking exactly as one would expect if Riley had left the place to go on holiday. A card from a local taxi firm lay on the kitchen table and scribbled on the card a time: 5.30 a.m. Alongside the card there was a flyer offering a New Year, winter blues special: fifty per cent off pre-booked return trips to Exeter Airport. Savage called the firm – Moor to Shore Taxis – and spoke to a girl with a heavy Eastern-European accent. The girl confirmed a booking by a Mr D Riley and said the run had been made by one of their drivers, a Mrs Lynn Towner. Savage heard the clatter of keys and then the girl was saying there was nothing flagged up on the system to indicate any problems or complaints regarding the pickup.

Savage hung up, more confused than ever. Riley had somehow managed to go missing between the airport drop-off and check-in. Foul play seemed unlikely. He must have gone somewhere voluntarily. Had he got cold feet and decided to ditch Julie Meadows along with the holiday? Despite what Savage had said to Julie earlier, she thought it unlikely. Riley wasn't that kind of bloke. At least she hoped not.

'Ma'am?' Denton called across from a nearby terminal where he'd been checking traffic reports. 'Been looking through the accidents again. There was an RTC and a fatality occurred, but the accident involved a motorcyclist in collision with a milk tanker. The lorry had come down the slip road and onto the A38 at Chudleigh. The driver had neglected to use his mirrors and caused the motorcyclist to swerve into the outside lane where he had been hit by a car.'

'OK. So what's your point?'

'Well the eastbound carriageway was blocked for three hours from five in the morning while an investigation took place,' Denton said, rubbing the scar on his cheek with his hand. 'If the taxi got stuck in the jam then Riley would have missed his plane.'

'Yes,' Savage said. 'But maybe she didn't get stuck or managed to find an alternative route.'

'Possible,' Denton agreed. 'But we should ask her anyway.'

'This is more substantive, ma'am,' Calter said. 'I've been going through the incident log for that morning. Under "crimes reported" nothing. I then went back and examined all logged calls. Just come across this one: a pensioner called one-oh-one to report something suspicious taking place on a country lane near Ashburton. The caller, a Mr Ron Jeffreys, said he spotted a taxi parked in a lane near the A383 just off the main dual carriageway and close to his bungalow.

This was at six in the morning. The man reported a black guy getting out of the taxi and acting suspiciously. He phoned us immediately, the call was logged and the man told to call back if he saw anything else.'

'And did he?' Savage said.

'No, doesn't look like it.'

'Riley, got to be,' Denton said. 'Why would the taxi have stopped there?'

'This doesn't smell right,' Savage said. 'If you ask me it's beginning to appear as if the taxi never went to Exeter.'

Denton and Calter said nothing and Savage got up and returned to her own office, needing some space to think. Thankful DI Maynard – with whom she had recently been forced to share the small room – wasn't there, she sat in his chair, her own being stacked with files. She stared at a cup of cold coffee Maynard had left on his desk, her own concerns all but forgotten.

This was serious. If Riley had gone AWOL voluntarily his behaviour was out of character. Savage had only known him a year, but his diligence, intelligence and coolness had endeared him, not only to her, but to many other officers. She couldn't see him abandoning his usual values on a whim. Unless there was something he hadn't told them.

Savage reached out for the cup and touched the little plastic stirrer. A skin had formed on the surface of the coffee and as she moved the stirrer the skin slipped away, revealing the pale, cold liquid concealed beneath.

Riley had been undercover up in London. He was someone who was comfortable playing a role, hiding his real self away far beneath the surface. Who down here in Devon really knew him? Savage pushed against the thoughts bubbling up in her mind. She liked Riley and didn't want to imagine him being involved in any kind of deception; and yet beyond

217

some sort of sudden madness, it was difficult to come to any other conclusion.

She picked up the phone and called Hardin and began to explain the situation. Before she had got far into the story a whooshing sound came from the earpiece and then some mumbled swearwords.

'*Sternway*,' Hardin said. 'We are going down. Sinking.'

'What makes you think this has anything to do with *Sternway*, sir? Riley's on holiday. This could be some sort of misunderstanding.'

'Hey? Oh yes, of course, Charlotte. You are right, that's what it is. A misunderstanding.'

The phone went dead and Savage was left staring into space, wondering what the hell Hardin was talking about.

Chapter Twenty

Savage was still pondering Hardin's cryptic remarks at a little after noon when she drove into the pothole-strewn car park at the front of Moor to Shore Taxis. Office was too grand a word for their HQ, a Portakabin-like structure with a tarpaulin secured over one end.

To the left of the office was an open-sided shed where a green and blue car stood on a set of ramps. The buzz of an electric welder came from under the car and a shower of white stars bounced out onto the ground, reminding Savage of Bonfire Night sparklers.

Savage had seen the Moor to Shore vehicles around town, even taken one a couple of times. A cursory glance at their premises made her decide she would settle for paying a couple of quid more the next time. It was like a budget airline: you *really* didn't want to know what went on in the maintenance hangers.

The budget airline analogy made her think of Flybe. She'd flown with them a few years ago when she'd gone on a weekend away to Paris. The kids had gone to the grandparents and she and Pete had taken a taxi from Plymouth

219

to Exeter Airport the same way Riley had. She always had a few cards from local taxi firms in her wallet and had picked one at random and phoned and booked the cab. That was the way most people would do it. If Moor to Shore had been involved in any way with Riley's disappearance, how had they planned it?

'Alright sweetheart?' The voice came from a man who had lumbered out from behind the cabin. He was in his fifties, body gone to seed, face seen better days considering his nose was covered with some sort of splint and he had one black eye. He was pulling the fly on his trousers up with his left hand, the right one encased in white, a bandage wrapped around two of the fingers. He grimaced at Savage when her eyes dropped to his crotch for a moment. 'What you looking at?'

'Didn't your mother ever tell you to shake?' Savage nodded down at the man's jeans where a line of dark ran from mid-thigh to knee.

'I had a bit of an accident, OK, my lover? If you fancy rubbing some cream on I'm all yours.' The man began to unzip his jeans, reaching in with his hand.

'It's not lover, thank you.' Savage pulled out her ID. 'DI Charlotte Savage, Plymouth CID.'

'Shit.' The man stopped and zipped himself up. He stomped round to the office front, shaking his head as he opened the door. 'When I was up at the hospital I told your lads I wasn't going to press charges so what's your game, girl? Is this a fucking honeytrap?'

'Honey is for bees. I'd need something else round here wouldn't I, Mr . . .?'

'Sorry? Oh, name's Dowdney. But you can call me Dave.' Dowdney smiled. 'All my friends do.'

'Dowdney?' Savage recalled Enders larking around a few

days ago. Something about Dewdney pasties and a castration game gone wrong. 'As in you were at A&E last week?'

'Yes. I just said so.' Dowdney stared down at his feet, the bravado gone. 'I thought that's what you'd come about.'

'No, Mr Dowdney. I'm not interested in what happened. I wanted a word about a driver of yours, a Mrs Lynn Towner.'

'Fucking hell, what's she gone and done now? Another prang?'

'Is she prone to accidents?' Savage said, looking over to three parked taxis, one of which had a big dent in the near-side wing.

'Yeah.' Dowdney followed Savage's gaze and gritted his teeth. 'That's one she did a couple of weeks ago. Wouldn't have minded, except she lied about it. Told me somebody bumped her in the Marsh Mills Sainsbury's car park, but I checked the satnav and she'd been over in Cornwall to St Austell and beyond. Wasn't even on company business. She still owes me for one she had before Christmas too.'

'Why keep her on if she is such a bad driver?

'Oh, you know . . .'

'No, Mr Dowdney, I don't know. That's why I am asking.'

'Well, I feel sorry for her. Hard to find a job these days, especially when you are a fifty-something woman. Look, can you get to the point because I haven't got all day to stand around exchanging witty banter.'

'Pickups. Do you make a note of them?'

'Course I do. Otherwise I'd be getting ripped off by my drivers left, right and up the arse.'

'Last Friday. 5.30 a.m. early morning ride to Exeter Airport. I would imagine the customer booked the pickup.'

'Right.' Dowdney paused, flinched, and then raised a hand to scratch at the splint on his nose. 'You'd better come into the office.' Dowdney opened the door into the Portakabin, stepped up and went in. Savage followed.

Up one end a teenage girl with blonde hair, a bare midriff and painted-on-jeans sat at a workstation. She wore a headset with a swivel down microphone and was fiddling with a mobile.

'Don't overwork yourself will you, Elina,' Dowdney said.

The girl glanced up but didn't say anything. The screen in front of her flashed and she began speaking, Savage recognising the Eastern-European accent as the one she'd heard on the phone earlier.

'Moor to Shore, door to door, where to please?' Her fingers moved from the phone pad to the keyboard.

'All logged, see?' Dowdney said. 'Let's go into my office, we can access the data from my machine. If one of our drivers made the pickup it will be on the system.'

At the other end of the main area a door led into a small room. A table stood up against the window and a laptop sat in the centre surrounded by paper. Away from the window a leather sofa had a white duvet and pillow piled up one end. Savage wondered if one of the reasons Lynn Towner had been kept on could have anything to do with the cosy sleeping arrangements.

'Sometimes I work late,' Dowdney said, noticing Savage's interest. 'Easier to stay over than tramp back home in the early hours.' Dowdney turned back to the desk and began to access the logs. '5.30 a.m. Last Friday?'

Savage moved over and stood at Dowdney's shoulder. A calendar flashed back through the days as Dowdney clicked.

'No, nothing. You must be mistaken. Are you sure of the date?'

'Yes.' Savage nodded back towards the office. 'Elina, when I rang this morning she told me Lynn Towner did the pickup.

She got that information from somewhere. Now there's no record. Why's that?'

'No idea.' Dowdney followed Savage's gaze. Scowled. 'Maybe someone deleted the record accidentally.'

'I see.' Savage turned back to the screen. 'We found a business card alongside a promotional leaflet. Your company. Would the person who deleted the record by any chance be you, Mr Dowdney?'

Another pause, the only sound the clatter of the keyboard from the next room and then a nervous cough from Dowdney.

'Look, OK, I'll come clean.' Dowdney held his hands out and shrugged his shoulders. 'I thought there might be trouble. Elina said the police had called and, well, Lynn's always scraping her car. I just wanted to do her a favour.'

'Where is Lynn Towner now?'

'Hang on.' Dowdney reached for the mouse and clicked a couple of times. 'She's not working at the moment, but she comes on duty at one. That's about thirty minutes from now.'

'Wait there.' Savage moved out of the office and went outside where she phoned Calter. After a brief conversation she went back inside.

'Book her for me,' she said to Dowdney. 'Towner. Pickup at the main railway station, destination Exeter Airport. Two passengers. Name of Calter.'

'Hey?'

'Just do it. And I'm listening. One hint to her that anything is amiss and what happened to take you to the hospital last week will be the least of your worries.'

Lynn Towner's green and blue taxi swung into the waiting area in front of Plymouth's mainline station some thirty-five minutes later. Calter and Enders had been hanging around outside and they approached the car, opened the doors and got in, Calter in the front, Enders in the back.

'Exeter Airport?' Towner said and Calter nodded. Towner looked around at Enders. 'No luggage?'

'Travelling light,' Calter said and Towner shrugged and pulled away.

'What time is your flight? Could be a bit of traffic around.'

'We've allowed plenty of time,' Enders said.

Towner was a big woman, having strong features and a curvy figure. Given her age – early fifties Calter guessed – round suited her. Twenty or thirty years ago she would have been turning heads everywhere she went, but now the gloss had gone. It wasn't her age, there was something else, an edge in her voice and a certain inflection in her mannerisms which suggested a life turned sour.

Towner headed out of the station, through town and soon they were speeding up the slip onto the A38, Towner cutting out from behind a lorry and crossing the chevrons before the slip had joined the main road. As they sped along the dual carriageway Towner fiddled with the satnav, paying scant attention to lane discipline.

'You go to the airport often?' Enders said from the back. 'Only it's not hard to find.'

'Two or three times a week, so I know where it is right enough. Other routes I have trouble with. Short-term memory loss.' Towner chuckled to herself. 'Not great for a taxi driver, is it? Thing is, my usual car's off the road and I can't quite get to grips with the controls on this unit. Just wanted it on in case of traffic.'

'I think you took a mate of mine to the airport a few days ago. Black guy? You would have picked him up here in Plymouth. He was heading for the Caribbean. Lucky bugger.'

'Might have.' Towner turned to look back at Enders, taking a little too long for Calter's liking. 'Can't say I remember him though.'

'Can't remember a black guy?' Calter said. 'Strange, because I don't suppose you get too many round here.'

'Funny thing is,' Enders continued, 'I haven't heard a thing from him. Bastard's probably sunning himself amongst a load of babes and has completely forgotten about his mates back in rainy old Devon. What do you think?'

'No idea.' Towner stared straight ahead and the speed of the car increased, as if she was trying to get the journey over as quickly as possible.

'No rush, Mrs Towner,' Calter said. 'We've got plenty of time. As long as you can manage to remember the route.'

'What the hell is this about and how do you know my name?' Towner gripped the steering wheel, knuckles white. She swerved out into the outside lane to overtake a lorry, pulling in front of another car. The driver leant on his horn and shouted silent words through his windscreen at them.

'Take it easy, Lynn,' Calter said. 'We simply want to find out what happened to a mate of ours. You see, we know he isn't sunning himself on a beach in the Caribbean. We also know that you did give him a ride but that you never took him to the airport.'

'Fuck it!' Towner pushed her foot to the floor and the taxi increased its speed again.

'Steady!' The dial on the dashboard was nudging ninety. Calter reached into her jacket and pulled out her ID. 'Don't do anything stupid. Let's just pull over at the next lay-by and we can have a talk.'

Towner glanced at the ID and then wrenched the wheel to the left. The car swerved into the nearside lane, cutting up a Tesco lorry. An airhorn blared and the taxi hit the curb and lurched onto the verge. Calter's head smacked into the ceiling and she was aware of Enders bouncing across the back seat. They ploughed through a mass of saplings, Towner stamping on the brake. The car went sideways for a moment, slewing in some mud and slowing until it bumped back onto the road and jolted to a halt, facing the wrong way half across the nearside lane.

Towner opened the door as the taxi stopped and Calter reached across to try to grab her arm. The woman wrenched free from Calter's grip, leapt out and ran away from the car. There was the sound of rubber squealing on tarmac and then a thud. Calter saw something flying into the air and landing in the road as she heard the airhorn again, aware of a huge mass of jack-knifed truck swinging across the carriageway, the lorry sliding down towards the taxi.

The prospect of a late lunch at home with Pete faded when Hardin asked her to come to the Theatre Royal's Mezz restaurant. An odd place to meet, Savage thought, but Hardin had been insistent. He needed to be in town anyway, he said, wanted the latest on Riley, the lowdown on Fallon and where Savage had got to with Redmond's daughter. Oh, and he was bloody famished too.

Hardin sat over by a window, gazing out at the buses queuing on Royal Parade. He had a pint of bitter on the table in front of him and when he saw Savage approach he slid the glass to one side, hiding it behind the fold of a menu.

'Only the second this week, but don't tell my GP,' Hardin said. He looked around as if his doctor might be dining in the very room. 'And I've opted for the handmade beefburger with extra cheese and bacon. Plus chips.'

Savage smiled to herself and decided to only have a starter

of some soup and bread, but she joined Hardin in a drink and ordered a bottle of Stella.

'Riley,' Hardin said. 'Any news?'

Hardin's expression was downbeat, lacking the anxiety Savage would have expected. Almost as if he knew Riley's fate.

'Sir, is there something you should be telling me? You don't seem that bothered Riley's gone missing.'

'Hey?' Hardin had reached out for his beer, but now he stopped. 'Now look here, Charlotte, we don't all have to wear our hearts on our sleeves. In fact it might be better for everyone if some people kept their emotions in check a little more.'

'Sir, I only—'

'Fuck it, Charlotte,' Hardin raised a hand and wagged his finger. 'You haven't got a monopoly on feelings. You think the rest of us don't care? I wouldn't be in this job if I didn't care and the day I *do* stop caring I'll resign. All that feminine-intuition-different-way-of-doing-things rubbish. You're nothing special, understand? Bloody women.'

'I hardly think the fact that I'm—'

'Shut it.' Hardin glared at Savage and reached for his drink again. He took a long slurp of his beer and placed the glass back behind the menu. He paused, bit his lip and then looked off into the middle distance. 'Do you remember a lad by the name of Gareth Malms? He was a PC in Manchester when I was first on the beat up there. Not a mate, but I knew him. Went missing while on patrol one Saturday lunchtime. We pulled all the stops. Massive search. Dogs, helicopters, army. Nothing until the following Tuesday when we found him. No happy ending, he was dead. From his injuries it was apparent he'd been tortured for several hours before he died. We reckoned it was retaliation for a crackdown on dealing in the area, but no one ever went down for his murder.'

'I'm sorry, sir.'

The food arrived before Hardin could say anything, but as the waitress placed the plates down he smiled.

'Accepted,' he said as the waitress left them. 'But don't ever let me hear crap like that from you again, OK?'

'No, sir.'

'Believe me, I'm as vexed and upset about Riley as you are, but there's stuff going on you know nothing about. You do your job and I'll do mine.'

Savage wanted to ask Hardin what he meant, but given his outburst she decided not to. Instead she filled him in on Dave Dowdney and told him that Calter and Enders were currently on the way to Exeter in Lynn Towner's taxi. The interview would be conducted en route.

'What?' Hardin's fork stopped mid-air on the way to his mouth. 'Is that . . . wise? More importantly, did you do a risk assessment?'

Savage admitted she hadn't done a risk assessment. It hadn't entered her mind. She'd simply thought the ploy was a good way to catch Towner out, especially if Calter and Enders made her take the route she had driven after she picked Riley up.

Hardin shook his head, but moved on, segueing into a conversation about Vanessa Liston without explanation. Was the girl going to help? Did she know anything about her old man's activities? What chance she would be able to tell them about the time of the pickup so they could move on Fallon and bring *Sternway* to a conclusion?

'The girl is a no-go, I am afraid, sir.' Savage sighed and took a drink from her bottle. 'I am not sure she is going to come up with anything to help us as regards Fallon.'

'Damn.' Hardin continued eating for a couple of minutes. Then he wiped a finger across his lip and licked the tip. 'Can you give me anything? A glimmer of hope?'

Savage thought about the way Vanessa had set her up with Jackman. No way she could mention any of that to Hardin. The girl was off limits now. She shook her head and followed Hardin's gaze as he turned and stared out the window again. A double-decker bus threaded its way out from a bus stop, the beam from the headlights reflecting on the wet tarmac. Ahead, another bus was trying to turn into its own stop, but a delivery van was in the way, hazards flashing, not a soul inside to respond to the bus driver's thump on the horn. Behind, the traffic stretched nose-to-tail all the way down Royal Parade and around the Derry's Cross roundabout. Dozens of cars stuck in the queue, going nowhere.

'Gridlock,' Hardin said.

Then his phone rang.

Savage returned to Crownhill to await news. All Hardin had told her was that two officers from Plymouth had been involved in an RTC on the A38. He didn't have any names but said you didn't need to be a bloody detective to work it out. As she had got up to leave the restaurant Hardin took another call, his words of 'no bloody risk assessment' all too audible as she walked out.

Back at Crownhill she sat at her desk trying to sort out getting the records for Riley's mobile phone, but couldn't even begin to fill in the paperwork. What the hell was going on? Life appeared to be conspiring against her, events running out of control, bad news piling up. Her hand shook as she tried to put her signature to a document, so she gave up.

A few minutes later DC Denton came into her office, the

line of the scar on his face white against his flushed cheek. He blurted out confirmation that DC Calter and DC Enders had been in a car crash, along with a taxi driver from Moor to Shore Taxi. The A38 had been closed, he said. The Air Ambulance had attended. It was unclear if there had been any fatalities. The whole thing was a fucking nightmare.

Denton gazed down at his shoes, as if the shine might reveal something in the way a crystal ball does. Nothing doing, he looked up at Savage. 'God, I hope she's OK.'

Savage spent the next half hour trying to get the full picture from Derriford Hospital, failing in all the confusion to make sense of anything. An hour later though Enders breezed in, a plaster on the back of his right hand the only indication he had been in an accident.

'Luck of the Irish, Jane called it.' Enders said, hunching his shoulders and turning the palms of both hands upwards and looking to the ceiling. 'Doesn't explain why I haven't won the lottery yet, does it?'

Enders went on to say Calter had received a knock on the head, but the doctors had given her the 'all clear' and sent her home. Lynn Towner, though, could have done with some Irish luck. When the car had come to a rest she hadn't had a mark on her. At least at that point. Calter had tried to grab her, but Towner leapt out. She stumbled into the road and was hit by a car. She'd somersaulted over the bonnet and landed in the carriageway where a Tesco lorry ran over both her legs.

'Oh no,' Savage groaned. 'What are her chances?'

'She's in ICU, unconscious, intubated. Fifty-fifty she'll live. Even if she does we won't get anything out of her for at least a couple of days.'

'What kind of life if she does survive though?' Savage said.

'If you want my opinion she deserves all she gets, ma'am.

230

She was something to do with kidnapping DS Riley. Definitely. Plus she nearly killed me and Jane.'

'Well let's hope she lives so she can give us some answers.' Savage paused for a moment, not wanting to bring the next subject up. 'Hardin is not best pleased. He has been going on about health and safety. He wanted to find out if I carried out a risk assessment before letting you get into the taxi.'

'You're joking, right? "Excuse me Mrs Towner, may I examine your driving licence to check for endorsements? Are you a safe driver? Do you frequent with known crimos? Are you likely to want to put a police officer's life in danger? No! OK, great, please ignore what I just said and act as if nothing has happened. Oh and if you could wait half an hour while I fill this form in and return to the station to shove it up the Super's arse."'

'Well said and I am glad you and Jane are OK.' Savage patted Enders on the back. 'Although I suggest you rephrase the last bit of your statement if and when Hardin questions you.'

After the interrogation, Riley had nursed his bruises. His shoulder still hurt and through Monday night and Tuesday he found himself sweating, rivulets trickling down him, soaking his clothing and making him alternately hot and cold. He tried to drink as much as he could in order to prevent dehydration, but the fever brought a delirium which meant it was all he could do to remember to breathe. No one came all through the day, although he heard cars coming and going, voices raised once, Budgeon and someone with a Spanish accent.

Sometime late Tuesday afternoon his fever seemed to diminish, the weather changing too. Rain pattered down outside, forming puddles in the gravel drive, but the air was warmer, no longer quite so icy. With the clouds overhead, the day never really got started and the gloom in the stable didn't help Riley's mood.

Budgeon would be back for more information soon and even if Riley gave him everything he wanted it wouldn't be enough. As the man had said, he didn't forget. And he certainly wasn't going to forgive. Riley pondered his options and decided that at some time he'd have to try and jump Budgeon and Stuey. He'd probably fail and they'd probably kill him but it would be better to die trying.

As he began to work out how on earth he'd take them both on, the door rattled and opened. A beam of torchlight scythed its way across the room before settling on him. He held up his hands to try and block the light and see what was beyond. Shadows moved behind the light and he heard the bark of the dog again, the one which sounded big and very bad.

'Get the hell in there.' The voice belonged to Stuey and he sounded none too friendly either.

Something tumbled through the open door and fell to the floor with a groan and then the light swivelled away, a voice from the corridor shouting out.

'Look after him, Riley,' Stuey said. 'You wouldn't want another fuck-up on your hands, would you?'

The door crashed shut, the wooden frame jarring with a crack. The dog barked again, the yapping fading into the distance until there was nothing but the laboured breathing from the crumpled body lying in the straw.

Riley moved out from the corner and crawled across the floor towards the dark outline. The man – and it was a man, that much Riley could tell – breathed with a harsh rasp, wincing at each intake.

'Alright, mate?' Riley placed a hand on the man's shoulder and the man flinched. 'You're going to be OK.'

232

'London. South of the river. Got that right at least, didn't I?' The man let out a grunt which might have been a laugh and then groaned. 'They broke a couple of ribs, Darius, and they ain't finished yet.'

'Kemp. Marty Kemp. How the hell did you . . .?' Riley left the question hanging, knowing before the man spoke the answer Kemp was going to give.

'Circumstances, mate. Bloody circumstances.'

Chapter Twenty-One

Budgeon was at the window again, watching the light creep into the day. Waiting.

The waiting was the part he'd always found hardest. The boredom. Nothing to do but run things round in his mind, try and work out if everything was set up right.

This time he was pretty sure it was. True, Redmond hadn't squeaked as much as Budgeon would have liked and what Riley had come out with wasn't much better. In the end it wouldn't matter. Big K and Lexi were as good as history and the drugs his. He wondered if the pair of them had been as confident all those years back, when they'd sent him up off the motorway. Budgeon hadn't wanted to go that day. Couldn't be arsed. Big K and Lexi had insisted.

'Russian geezer,' Big K had said. 'Bristol way. You need to meet him.'

'Russian? What the fuck? Are we doing business with commies now?'

'They're not commies,' Lexi had said. 'Not any more. It's the future, bud. These guys have got money. Believe me. Get in with them and it could open up opportunities. Know what I mean?'

234

He hadn't, not really, but he'd gone anyway.

'Take Stuey,' Big K had said. 'Just in case.'

Stuey went everywhere with him those days. Fucking loon, but there wasn't a piece of yellow in him. In a scrape Stuey'd sooner end up with his head kicked in than give an inch.

'Russians,' Stuey says, grinning as he ducks into the passenger seat of the Beemer, bottle of vodka in hand. 'Monster drinkers, so I've heard.'

With Stuey along it's as well to keep within the speed limits. No need to draw unnecessary attention. Exeter, Taunton, Bridgewater. Stop for a slash and an early pint. Back at the car, whistle at some pussy walking past. Jeans like they'd grown on her, arse that could launch a thousand ships.

'Have a gander at that, Stuey. Imagine her bent over the bonnet.'

Stuey laughs, imagining her bent over the bonnet. All he can do, imagine. The way he looks, he wants action, he has to pay or blag a freebie off one of Big K's girls.

Off again, pushing onward. Somewhere after that a mirror full of blue lights and a cop car alongside too, the gesture from the officer in the passenger seat to pull over.

'Calm, Stuey, calm.'

Indicate. Move to nearside lane. Hard shoulder. One car in front, one behind. Doors opening, these officers not Traffic. Talking of traffic, where is it? The motorway has gone quiet in both directions. Not a car to be seen.

They are walking back now, one with a pistol, one with a semi. Behind, in the other car, the officers sit, waiting. No chance of a sneaky getaway.

'Calm, Stuey, calm.'

Shouting from a distance.

'Get out of the car.'

'What?' No words, just a mime, hand cupped to ear as if it is a struggle to hear the officer's instructions.

Closer. The guy with the pistol has a stance like the man has been watching too many US cop shows. To the side now. Standing in the centre of the carriageway. Flattened if they hadn't stopped the traffic.

Hands up. Surrender. Sort of – because one hand is sneaking down again, feeling beneath the seat for something cold, heavy, comforting. Then pulling the gun out and up and going for the door handle with the other hand.

The side window crazes like frosted glass. Bang comes later. Lying back in the seat. Head sticky. Lucid, but not moving. World going all funny, colours like taking an acid trip in a cinema.

Another officer approaching on Stuey's side, Stuey's hands held high.

'You're hit, Ricky,' Stuey says. 'Fuck, fuck, fuck.'

'Calm, Stuey, calm.' Still able to speak, but the words slurred. Not acid now, more like having done a bottle of Scotch.

Click.

Stuey has opened the door. He's getting out.

'Hands where I can see them,' the officer says.

Stuey obliges and thrusts them high. Stupidly high. He is so tall and thin that it looks almost comical, as if Stuey is one of those toy dolls you can pull to any length. Stretch Armstrong. Was that the name? Stretch-fucking-Stuey.

Laughing now. Is this the acid trip, the bottle of Scotch or real life? There's snot trickling out, blood flowing down over one eye, all the while Stuey getting longer and taller and thinner.

Stuey wiggles his fingers, like he is in some chorus line. He just needs a garter and stockings, some sort of ragtime fucking piano backing track. For a split second the officer looks up, distracted.

Funny thing, time. When a minute should last forever it's gone in a flash, when hours need to fly by, they drag like a weight pulled up a steepening hill.

Right now the few hundredths of a second the policeman takes are quite enough. Stuey's right arm moves down in a jerk, catches the knife that appears in thin air. Magic. Or possibly hidden up his sleeve. Stuey's right leg comes up. Something the lad learnt from watching too many Bruce Lee movies. Roundhouse kick. Snap. His foot connects with the officer's arm, the semi-automatic weapon flicking upwards. Now, in slow motion, Stuey's hand moves down and slices across, finds flesh beneath the stab vest.

The pair of them fall over together, Stuey slicing again and then reaching in with his other hand and pulling and pulling. Tug of war, except Stuey's definitely on the winning team.

Trouble is the other officer has come round to help his buddy. 'You're a fucking dead man!'

His pistol is right up against Stuey's head, but the bang doesn't come. The gun has jammed. Instead the officer smashes the weapon into Stuey's skull. Once, twice, three times.

Poor old Stuey is out for the count, lying next to the other officer, head resting on the man's guts. Soft, better than the hard concrete. Stands to reason doesn't it? The police are the good guys, considerate. Nothing too much for old Stuey and Ricky. Probably just pulled them over for a dodgy brake light. Even now things have gone a little sour they've found the time to give Stuey a nice comfy pillow.

Light is fading now, like the day just got speeded up somehow. Evening. Twilight. Sleep.

And sleep was the one thing that didn't come easy any more. Tossing and turning. Thinking back. Streaks of light shooting in the dark. A tracer bullet bringing searing pain.

What had the doctor said? Acu-bloody-puncture? Well they'd tried that on Redmond, Stuey-style. It hadn't helped much.

The sun pierced the horizon, rays like that bullet. Budgeon scrunched his eyes against the brightness, feeling sandpaper scrape across them. He clenched his fists and let out a growl of rage against the dawn, against the whole fucking world.

Lexi, Big K and Riley. The sooner they were dead the sooner he'd be free.

The drama of Tuesday – Riley going missing and the accident with Calter and Enders – meant Savage managed a good night's sleep, if only because she was worn out. The incident with Jackman had slipped from her consciousness, but alone in her office on Wednesday morning, the reality hit home again. She fired up her computer and spent some time trying to discover all she could on the councillor. After half an hour she realised the guy was a power junkie. The way he spread himself around the various council committees and appeared to work tirelessly for countless organisations spoke volumes. Frequent appearances in the papers and on local TV suggested he was a media tart too. Jackman was an interfering busybody, a little dictator with an agenda. Savage remembered him from the encounter on the breakwater, the way his long, bony fingers had moved across the laptop. Those fingers had found their way across the city, getting into all sorts of organisations. And that made him very dangerous.

She stared out of the window at nothing and wondered where Jackman was and what he was doing. He was in control and all she could do was wait and worry. She shivered and found herself breathing all-too-fast, gasps coming one after another, until a trilling noise in the background snapped her vision back into focus. She turned and looked at the phone for a moment before reaching for the handset.

The call was from the custody officer at Charles Cross. He wanted to know about Stuart Chaffe, what was the score? Savage cursed, she'd forgotten all about Chaffe and now his twenty-four hours were up. The sergeant sounded pissed off. He'd received an earful from Chaffe's solicitor, Amanda Bradley, talk of complaints and all sorts of trouble. They wouldn't be wanting to hold him any longer, would they?

'Release him,' Savage heard herself say, wondering at the same time how she was going to square the mess with Hardin.

She needn't have worried because Hardin had other things on his mind, and up in his office Savage, Davies and Garrett got to hear all about them.

'I've just got news that bloody Foxy's coming over on Saturday,' Hardin said, peering at his screen. 'He is concerned about Riley, wants to know what we are up to, feels if he is looking over our shoulders it will spur the troops on. He also thinks the presence of the Chief Constable will serve to reassure the good people of Plymouth that everything is being done to track down and catch Owers' and Redmond's killer. Between now and then I want you lot to reassure *me* that everything *is* being done to track down and catch Owers and Redmond's killer. And find Riley.'

'Sir?' DCI Garrett leant forward and cleared his throat. 'One piece of good news is the DNA evidence confirms the body discovered at Owers' place is that of Simza Ellis.'

'Huh?' Hardin looked up from his screen as if he had missed the gist of Garrett's sentence. The sneer beginning to creep across his face showed he hadn't. 'Good news? You call that *good* news?'

'At least her family will have clo—'

'Fucking hell!' Hardin slammed his fist down on the desk.

'Don't ever tell me it is good news when we have to inform some poor woman her little girl has been raped and murdered by a sicko paedophile.'

'We managed to get—'

'Forget it! The CC's not going to want to hear excuses, he wants *results*. Riley, Redmond, Owers. In that order.' Hardin raised a hand and waved it at Garrett, silencing him. 'Charlotte?'

'We've got a dozen bodies to blitz the stuff on Riley,' Savage said. 'They've been at it since seven this morning and with respect, sir, I think we need to come clean with them on the *Sternway* connection to the murders. Otherwise they're going to be working in the dark.'

'Agreed. I'll brief them myself. Soon as.'

'At first I thought Riley's disappearance was some sort of mix-up, but what happened in the taxi with Lynn Towner and DC Calter and DC Enders suggests otherwise. Since Riley was working on *Sternway* it's logical we start with that angle. The two killings are also bound up with the drugs op. Motive on the Owers killing at first sight appeared to be revenge or a vigilante attack. Then we get Redmond. On its own we'd be drawing the conclusion that his informer status had been discovered and Fallon had killed him. But why would Fallon do that, when the result would be to draw attention to Tamar Yachts and possibly scupper the coming delivery? Ditto why would he have anything to do with Riley's disappearance? We also have nothing to connect Redmond's killing with that of Owers.'

'Apart from the cocaine,' Davies said.

'Yes,' Savage said. 'Apart from the cocaine, the manner of the killings and those black and white markings, yes. Those facts tell us they're connected, but we don't know what the link is.'

'So then,' Hardin said. 'Who, why and how?'

'The "how" of Riley's disappearance is down to Lynn Towner and Dave Dowdney. Towner's still unconscious and at the moment there's no sign of Dowdney at his home or at Moor to Shore Taxis. The "who" and "why" remains—'

'Whoever did this the killings, Riley – they're in the business.' Davies leant back in his chair, balled his right hand and slammed the fist into his left palm. 'Bam! Bam! Bam! World War Three. Job done.'

'Phil, will you please stop talking in bloody riddles,' Hardin said. 'What do you mean?'

'They were highly professional in the planning and carrying out of the attacks and the message was explicit. Vice, I'd say. Some kind of move.'

'You mean the Bristol firm? The one we had intel on before Christmas?'

'Quite possible. Somebody muscling in on Fallon's little empire at any rate. Trying to scare him off. It could explain why they have taken Riley too.'

'Sounds a bit OTT to me. Why not just go direct to Fallon?'

'Eastern Europeans, the lot in Bristol, and they don't work like that. I remember hearing from a friend on the Met about this Russian guy who ran a couple of dozen Natashas. He started losing girls at the rate of one or two a week. They just disappeared. He didn't cotton on for ages, not until his girlfriend goes missing too. By then it was too late for him to get out. They found his body down in the river at Gravesend. He'd been in the water for best part of a month, but you could still tell it wasn't natural causes.'

'For God's sake, Phil, can you leave your hard-boiled stories on the bedside table where they belong?' Hardin shook his head. 'Quite frankly this is pathetic. The lot of you. We need the connection between Owers and Fallon and we need to understand Riley's place in all of this. Get the info, get the intel and get back to me. Preferably before the Chief Constable arrives. Or else we're all buggered.'

'Sir? One more thing,' Savage said. 'Marty Kemp? On Saturday you said he was planning to come down. Well we could really do with his input on this. When is he expected?'

'No idea. He said he'd be here on Monday or Tuesday, but as of yet I've not heard from him.'

'The facilitator at Exeter?'

'Bloody ditto. She's tried to make contact but nothing. Kemp's force can't raise him either.'

'But . . .' Savage looked at the others. Davies wore a grimace, Garrett just shook his head. She lowered her voice to a whisper. 'Shit.'

'Couldn't have put it better myself,' Hardin said.

His words wrapped up the meeting and the three of them left him staring at his screen and clicking with his mouse. Savage wondered if he was enjoying a relaxing game of Minesweeper.

Hardin was good as his word and gave a briefing in the Major Crimes suite mid-morning. After he'd left, morale seemed, if anything, a little lower. Savage figured that people didn't like being kept in the dark, even if the subterfuge was for good reason. She began to work the room, talking to individual officers about *Sternway* and trying to smooth the waters, but getting more exasperated by the minute. She'd just moved across to Enders and Denton when Calter appeared. She walked in to a big cheer, a round of applause and a number of officers shouting out 'every little helps'.

'Huh?' Enders said.

'The Tesco lorry, you numbskull,' Denton said. 'The company are considering moving into the criminal justice arena, didn't you know? You are going to have to spend two years minimum on the tills before you can move into CID.'

'They're not, are . . . you're winding me up, right?'

'People,' Savage said interrupting. 'Forget the jokes. We need to concentrate on Riley.'

'Sorry, ma'am,' Denton said. 'But we need to lighten up sometimes. We'd go mad otherwise.'

'I'm pretty close to going mad now, Carl. At every other moment you and Patrick are mucking around instead of focusing on the task in hand. Riley's missing, there's a little girl murdered by some sick paedophile and a guy knifed to death in a stairwell. If there's a joke in there then I'd sure like to know about it.'

Enders opened his mouth and almost looked as if he was about to deliver a witty put-down. Instead he closed it again and hunkered over his keyboard. Denton appeared shell-shocked and Savage felt bad for a moment, the same as if she'd shouted at her children. Her outburst had scratched the veneer of cheerfulness in the room and revealed despondency beneath. Officers shuffled to their desks and there were a few murmurs of discontent. You stupid idiot, she thought. Hardin had told her she didn't have a monopoly on emotion and he was right. Everyone had their own way of dealing with the situation and the jokes were just that.

'Listen up,' Savage said, trying to sound contrite. 'Feelings are running high. The Chief Constable is worried about the effects on morale if we can't find out what has happened to Riley quickly. I guess he's probably right. For once.'

There was a trickle of laughter, a slight thaw of the frostiness. Savage continued.

'Hardin is taking overall control of the investigation into Riley's disappearance on the direct instructions from the Chief. The DSupt wants to make sure everything is handled correctly. However, day-to-day, hour-by-hour, you're stuck with me breathing down your necks and cracking the whip.'

'Where are we at then?' Calter asked.

Savage brought Calter up to speed and outlined the *Sternway* connection and the theory that somebody was out to muscle in on Fallon's operation. Then Denton told her what she had missed regarding the search for Riley. It didn't amount to much.

'We've got some ANPR data which shows Lynn Towner's taxi on the A38 near Ivybridge,' Denton said. 'Cameras farther on towards Exeter registered nothing. It isn't conclusive proof she didn't go to Exeter, because the cameras can miss vehicles for various reasons, but it's another nail in her coffin. Sorry, you know what I mean.'

Denton began to recount Towner's history. She had three kids – two sons and a daughter – from a marriage which had ended soon after the third child had been born. The children were grown now, themselves married and with children.

'Mum's a bit of embarrassment, apparently,' Denton said. 'Several prosecutions for soliciting and as we know she's not exactly the world's best driver. Still, the children were pretty defensive when questioned, not exactly helpful from what I hear. But then again why Lynn Towner would be involved in anything to do with kidnapping DS Riley is a mystery.'

'Vice?' Calter said. 'Some pimp, maybe?'

Denton shook his head. Towner was a streetwalker, he explained. Latterly she'd used the taxi. A sort of mobile escort business. As far as the inquiry teams could make out she had no connections to organised gangs, pimps or dealers. The only victim in the crimes she committed was herself.

'OK,' Savage said. 'This afternoon Patrick and I are going to visit the old guy who saw Towner's taxi parked on the lane. Jane, sorry, HR have informed me you are on "light duties" for today at least, so you'll stay here and pull together some things to do with Riley, phone records and such. I'll clear it with the DSupt that you can have access to Darius' files in case there is something there.'

Calter looked crestfallen and as Savage left the room she came over for a word.

'Cheer up, Jane, it could be worse,' Savage said, winking at Calter. 'I might have asked Carl to help you.'

Chapter Twenty-Two

Enders wittered on about Denton's crush on Calter as he drove Savage east along the dual carriageway towards Ashburton.

'The poor lad,' he said as they turned off the main road into a narrow lane and parked up next to an isolated little bungalow with a small lawn and flowerbeds already full of daffodils. 'He'll be quivering stuck next to her back at the station. He's putty in her hands. Like watching a spider with a fly or a cat with a mouse. Cruel.'

'What about a female praying mantis?' Savage said, suppressing a laugh as they got out of the car.

'Oh, he'd love that.'

'Patrick?' Savage pointed up the concrete ribbon leading through the pretty little garden to the front door.

A man in what could only be described as a smoking jacket, stood on the porch, a pipe in his mouth and a copy of the *Racing Post* in one hand.

'Police or double glazing?' he said, laughing and waving the newspaper and inviting them in, eyes following Savage as she walked up the path. 'Police is my hunch. I've never seen such a good-looking double glazing saleswoman.'

'Mr Jeffreys?' Savage said. 'DI Charlotte Savage and DC Patrick Enders. It's about the incident you reported the other day.'

'Uh-huh.' Jeffreys nodded. 'Is this what you term victim support? Because I'd have preferred a response on the day rather than some sort of lefty hand patting now.'

'Not victim support, Mr Jeffreys. Just a few questions.'

'Well, if it helps catch the bastard I'm only too keen to help.' Jeffreys let them move past and into the house.

The hallway had a clear plastic runner down over the white carpet and in the living room the sofa and armchairs were adorned with little lacy mats on the backs and armrests. A table and bureau in a dark brown veneer were from an age when such styling would have been considered fashionable.

Jeffreys offered tea and while he busied himself in the kitchen Savage and Enders stood in the bay window. The little lane turned a dogleg just past their car and when Jeffreys came into the room with a tray of mugs he nodded.

'Parked on the corner it was. I saw the, er, black guy, standing by the taxi and thought, this isn't right. Not out here, not at this time of the morning.'

'Which was?' Savage said, moving to an armchair and accepting a mug.

'Six. I'm up with the birds these days. *Before* the birds at this time of year. It was still dark of course, but the interior light in the taxi was on. Well, when I saw what was happening I went to the front door sharpish and checked it was locked. Put the chain on too. Then I called you lot. I can tell you I was scared, thought he'd be coming in and murdering me in my bed.'

'You weren't in your bed, Mr Jeffreys.'

'No, but you know what I mean. The riots. That lot. Drugs, isn't it? Always drugs and guns. Rappers, they call them, I believe.'

'What happened then?' Savage put her tea down, beginning to find the liquid, which was the colour of the furniture, as bitter as the conversation.

'I spoke to someone on the phone and they were dismissive. Told me to call back if anything happens. Idiot. How am I going to be able to call back when some burglar is knifing me?' Jeffreys went over to the window. 'When I came back in here there is a white van out in the middle of the lane and the black guy is getting in the back.'

'White?' Enders said. 'What type?'

'Not sure, not a little one, more like a delivery van or the sort builders would use. Anyway, they had trouble turning in the road. Back and forwards, back and forwards they went before they drove off, the taxi following them.'

'Whoa, hold on,' Savage said. 'Rewind. The black guy got in the back?'

'I say "getting", more like being forced. Two other men dragged him in and then the doors closed and they did the turning thing.'

'For God's sake why didn't you call us again?'

'Well, I . . . I guess the black guy scared me. I was glad to see him gone. I thought he was probably up to no good and was simply getting his just desserts. Anyway, you lot weren't interested the first time, were you?'

'Mr Jeffreys, do you realise who the black man was?'

'No. Some druggie?'

'He was a police officer.'

'Never! I didn't know, how could I? I mean black. Down here in Devon. In the police of all—'

'For fuck's sake!' Savage stood, feeling herself shake, wanting to go across and smack the old guy in the face. 'I don't know what the hell we can charge you with, but if anything happens to our officer I promise you we'll find something. Get the rest of the details, Patrick, while I go and look outside. There's a stink in here and it is making me sick.'

She left the house and went down into the lane. The road was single track, but on the corner up from the bungalow a gateway allowed access to a field. The verge was a little wider next to the gate and it was an obvious point to turn around. Savage strode along until she found what she was looking for: some tyre marks had ridden the verge. She knelt to examine one of them. The width was wider than a car would have made and yet it didn't have the knobbly indentations which would indicate the track belonged to a 4x4; they could well have been from a transit van.

She took out her phone and called through to Charles Cross. When she managed to reach the custody officer he had a dose of dry humour for her.

'Long gone, ma'am. But he signed for the clothing we gave him to replace his wet stuff so I'm sure he'll be back with that.'

'Jesus!' Savage said, hanging up as Enders came down the path and joined her in the lane. 'That had to be Chaffe's van. It was there when Riley was taken and I let the bugger walk out this morning. I just phoned the custody centre to check and he's been released.'

'Oh shit.'

'Understatement of the year. We had Chaffe and . . .' Savage shook her head, once again feeling a rush of emotion and anger. Only this time the anger was directed at herself. 'We have failed Darius big time. There's me wittering on about you lot joking. I'm the joke. I should have realised that—'

'The van, ma'am,' Enders said. 'It will probably still be in the pound. Then there's his flat.'

'Of course.' Savage tapped her head. 'Well done. You get on to them and make sure they don't release it, get a team round to Chaffe's flat too. I'll call John Layton.'

An hour and a half later, Savage was back in her office at Crownhill, and Layton was on the line, telling her that the van represented a veritable feast for someone like him.

'Got a big handprint on the rear bumper, inside, some dried blood, loads of fingerprints and a few pieces of silver plastic which I couldn't place at first. Turns out to be from a phone. Nokia, one of the latest models. You know where this is leading?'

'Riley.'

'Yup. Riley's mobile contract specifies the same type.'

'So he was definitely in the van?'

'His *phone* was in the van. You'll have to wait on the prints and blood. There's something else though.'

'Go on.'

'I found a scrap of pink material snagged on a rough edge on the floor. It's from a dress. Not just any dress, mind you. The fibres match the material found in the plastic crate alongside Simza Ellis.'

'*What?*'

'Yes. There are also some curly hairs which look very similar to ones I found down in the caravan. I'll need to match them too, but I'd say it is a cast-iron cert that the girl was in the van sometime. I should be able to confirm it later.'

Savage hung up and placed her own phone on the desk, giving it a spin. Then she sighed, watching the whirl of black and silver until the phone stopped revolving.

Somebody had snatched Riley. The same person had been involved with taking Simza. The question was, who? Owers surely had something to do with the girl, but he was dead before Riley went missing. Stuart Chaffe? It appeared to be his van which had been used in the kidnapping, but Savage didn't think he had the brains, certainly not brains enough to deal with the complexities of the *Sternway* case. Which tended to suggest there was somebody else, somebody they knew absolutely nothing about.

Lateral thinking, Savage thought. They had the connections from Riley and Redmond to Fallon and *Sternway*. What wasn't apparent was any sort of connection between Owers and Fallon. Find that link – another of Collier's nodes – and they'd be one step nearer to what was going on.

A close look at Owers' previous conviction revealed nothing, nor did a trawl through old crime reports and a keyword search across the national database. There were plenty of entries relating to Fallon and to Owers but none correlated.

Frustrated, she went and grabbed a coffee from the machine down the hall and returned to her office, sitting in Maynard's chair once again. She looked for a piece of visible desk to rest her cup on, but the surface was covered with documents. Maynard was working on some fraud case involving dodgy housing benefit applications and it certainly looked to be generating a lot of paperwork. She moved a piece of paper and put her cup down, glancing at the sheet and noting it was a list of letting agencies Maynard had selected for visits. Four from the top was a name she recognised

Dream Lets.

She took a gulp of coffee. Owers' letting agency had been Dream Lets. In life, such a coincidence might be shrugged off as just chance, the same way two people might be amused to find they shared the same birthday. In police work a coincidence like that raised a red flag. The fact the company had been flagged as potentially involved in criminal activity gave her an idea. She picked up the phone and called through to the Hi-Tech Crime Unit to ask about progress with the USB memory stick she had found at Owers' flat. Doug Hamil, the chief technician, was apologetic.

'Layton gave me the stick last week but I only got around to processing it yesterday. Sorry about the delay, we're swamped over here.'

Savage could well understand. Just about every case these days involved computers and mobiles and all the data needed to be extracted, catalogued and stored as potential evidence.

'No problem. What was on the stick?'

'An encrypted and compressed backup file which contained bloody hundreds of spreadsheets,' Hamil said. 'Accounts for a number of local businesses going back several years. Cashflows, P and L, duplicate sets for private and tax use which the Inland Revenue would be interested in I am sure. There were also a few pictures. Pretty tame really, considering. Stuff you could find on the web in thirty seconds. Innocent, except when you consider the bloke who was downloading them. I'll send everything through.'

Savage thanked Hamil and hung up. Seconds later an email arrived, dozens of files attached. She saved the files to a folder and then searched through. There it was: Dream Lets. A number of spreadsheets dating back several years. Owers had been doing accounts for the very agency he had rented his house and flat from.

Savage didn't bother opening the spreadsheets, instead she made a list of the other businesses and fired off an email to a contact in Economic Crimes. Ten minutes later and the information came back: the majority of the businesses Owers did accounts for were owned by one particular holding company, in turn owned by a name all too familiar to her.

Kenny Fallon.

'Charlotte. Your job I think,' Hardin had said when she'd come to him with the Owers connection.

The job being to interview Kenny Fallon.

'He knows that we know that he knows. See what I mean?'

Savage had. If they ignored the links they'd uncovered Fallon would wonder why. With his suspicion raised he'd reschedule any delivery and *Sternway* wouldn't stand a chance.

Fallon lived in Saltash, meaning Savage had to drive over the Tamar Bridge into Cornwall. The little town clung to the hillside, the bridge spanning the river and piercing the very heart of the place. Few people stopped though, as they sped down the A38, drove across the bridge and went through the twin tunnels which ran under part of the town.

After crossing the bridge, Savage left the main road and headed out on a country lane to North Pill where Fallon's house sat on the banks of the estuary. A long drive curled down towards the river through neat lawns, a number of marble statues punctuating her progress as she drove along. At the front of the property the drive swept past the columned front door on its way to a detached garage which had some sort of accommodation over the top. Behind the house, the land sloped away in another expanse of immaculate lawn all the way to the estuary, where gulls wheeled in the air above the incoming tide.

As Savage brought the car to a halt, the front door opened, one of Fallon's goons standing there on the step. Fallon appeared from behind the muscle and shook his head as she got out.

'Can't even spare a proper cop for good old Kenny Fallon? You know, a bloke? Tut, tut, tut, what is the world coming to?'

Fallon ran a hand through his greying shoulder-length hair. With his scraggy Van Dyke beard and sideburns, he looked more like the member of an ageing rock band than a gangster. Drugs though were the only common theme. And Savage didn't think Fallon was foolish enough to ever dabble himself.

'DI Charlotte Savage,' Savage said. 'Got a problem with that have you, Mr Fallon?'

'With a nice bit of eye candy? Not at all. 'Cept they don't usually look as good as you, do they? Boilers, most of the rest.'

'I've no idea. Can I come in?'

'Be my guest, Charlotte. I was thinking I might be due a visit from you lot.' Fallon waved an arm at the man on the step. 'Let Detective Inspector Savage through, Kev, then go and check out the grounds.'

'Expecting trouble, Mr Fallon?' Savage said as she followed him in to the house.

'Nothing out of the ordinary. Man like me makes enemies. Kev's my driver, but he's handy too.' Fallon didn't elaborate further, just swept his arm in the direction of the hallway and then led her in and through to the kitchen. 'In here. It's down to me to make you a coffee or tea, today being the maid's day off and all.'

Inside, the decor was subtle, but expensive. The kitchen had come straight out of *Grand Designs*, with a long breakfast bar in front of a huge glass window which looked out over the garden to the estuary. A golden retriever lay sleeping in a

254

dog bed by the window. The dog's eyes opened as they entered, the tail thumping a couple of times. Fallon went over to a coffee machine the size of a small car and reeled off the names of a string of hot drinks, face dropping for a moment when Savage said she would be fine with a cup of tea.

'Suit yourself,' he said, then rummaged in a cupboard for a couple of mugs and some teabags and then pressed a button on the coffee machine.

The machine gurgled away and while Fallon made the teas Savage began to ask him about Franklin Owers and Gavin Redmond.

'You see Mr Fallon, they both had connections to you. Franklin Owers was your accountant and you have a substantial shareholding in Redmond's business. Now they are both dead.'

'Coincidence.'

'Really?' Savage smiled. 'I thought lightning didn't strike twice.'

'Can do, if you run out of luck.'

'And is that what happened to Owers and Redmond? They ran out of luck? Look, I don't know what Owers was up to, but I'd hazard a guess he was involved in helping you with tax evasion, something dodgy. Redmond I don't know much about, although I understand the business has had financial difficulties in the past.'

'Tax *avoidance* is the word. Totally legal. As for Redmond, since I invested in Tamar I think you'll find the business has done well. And I resent your implication that there is something dodgy going on. All my business interests are above board. Legit.'

'If they're above board then why did you employ a shit like Owers as your accountant? The only answer is you knew you could persuade him to fiddle the books.'

255

'The accountants I use are Hemming and Sons in Liskeard.' Fallon squeezed the teabags with a spoon and dumped them in the sink. 'Owers helped me with some bookkeeping, that's all. I knew him from way back, years ago. I was giving him a second chance. For old times' sake.'

'I don't believe you for a moment. If he hadn't been of some use to you he wouldn't have been allowed within a mile of your place.'

'He had strict instructions. I told him if he ever went near any little girls again I'd . . .' Fallon passed the teas across and smiled. 'Well, after our little chat I figured he wouldn't dare.'

'He did though, didn't he? We know that now. Did you discover something and decide to carry out your threat?'

'No. You've got it wrong there, love. I never killed either of them.'

Savage paused and took a sip of her tea. She turned to the window. Down near a small pagoda in the centre of the lawn another heavyset man in a leather jacket stood smoking.

'Let me guess,' Savage said, nodding through the window. 'Your gardener?'

'You must be psychic, Charlotte,' Fallon said with a grimace.

'Say I believe your claim that you didn't kill Owers or Redmond. That means somebody else did. Somebody who is out to get you. Unfortunately for Owers and Redmond, whoever they are decided to enact their plan via third parties.'

'Bloody cowards.' Fallon went to the sink and pushed the teabags into the large central plughole, pushing a button to one side. A high-pitched sound whirred for a second. 'Why don't they come knocking on my front door? Then I'd show 'em.'

'Who are "they", Mr Fallon?'

'Look, love, why don't you let me deal with things?'

'I'm afraid the police don't work like that. Besides, if you were managing to deal with things Redmond and Owers would still be alive.' Savage took a drink of her tea. 'You are approaching fifty now aren't you? Isn't it time you stepped back? From what I understand the young guns from the East are coming and they don't play by the old rules. It would be much better if you let us deal with them.'

'"Young guns from the East"?' Fallon shook his head. 'Who told you that crap? You lot don't know what the fuck you're talking about.'

'Well, perhaps you would like to enlighten me?'

Fallon said nothing for a moment. He scratched his beard. Savage could see some crumbs in amongst the silver hairs; the remains of Fallon's lunch. He turned to the window and stared down at the estuary.

'That river,' he said, pointing with the teaspoon. 'The tide's been coming in and out for centuries. Millennia. Beyond that, even. Nothing you or I do can change a thing.'

'Very philosophical, but I don't see what—'

'History. We all make it, but not in the way we choose. Know who said that?' Savage shook her head. 'Karl fucking Marx. He wasn't right about much, but the prat was right about that.'

'I'm surprised you're so well read, but can we get back to the point?'

'Like I said, history. Things happen and they can come back to haunt you.' Fallon turned back from the window and jabbed the teaspoon at Savage. 'Like with you and that pervert. The one you killed.'

'If you're talking about Matthew Harrison, he died in a car accident.'

257

'You might not know it, but I've got a mate on the council. Alec Jackman.'

'What the . . .?' Savage clunked her cup down on a nearby work surface. She tried to compose herself. 'Jackman, your friend?'

'Video evidence.' Fallon chuckled. 'Alec showed me. Tasty.'

'I don't . . .' Savage felt something catch at the back of her throat, a spasm which constricted her airways. The kitchen began to blur and for a moment she thought she would faint. She put her arm out for balance and gripped the edge of the worktop. Then Fallon moved up close and grabbed her arm. He leaned in close and sniffed.

'I can smell something, Charlotte,' he whispered. 'And it's not your perfume. It's the stink of corruption and illegality.'

'No way,' Savage said. 'Forget it.'

'But that's the problem, I can't. Seeing you next to that car, making the decision to sentence Harrison to death, that turned me on, I can tell you. You've got guts. More guts than Alec for sure. You can help me and maybe I can help you in return.'

Savage shrugged off Fallon and moved across to the French windows. The tide was still coming in, sweeping across the mudflats, and engulfing what had only minutes ago been solid land. She turned back to Fallon.

'Like you, Charlotte,' he continued, 'it's not the future I need to be worried about, it's the past.' Fallon moved back over to the coffee machine and scraped a stool out from beneath the work surface. He sat on the stool and then ran both hands through his hair, shaking the greying mane loose. 'For now, let me tell you a story. Once upon a time there were three little boys, princes, waiting to ascend to the throne. They were friends. They played together, laughed together, did everything together. Until one of them did something

258

they shouldn't and the other two decided to punish him for it. The naughty prince was banished from the kingdom and all was well and good. And that should have been the end of it. Happy ever after, nighty-night, sleep tight, and all that bollocks.'

'Only the prince came back?'

'In one.' Fallon had picked up his cup and now he swirled the remains of his tea around and stared down at the dregs. 'And now the returning prince wants to be king.'

'Name?'

'When I want your help I'll let you know.' Fallon spat into his cup and put it down. 'Never been one for grassing, see? Let's just say you were correct back in what you said earlier. Take a peek in your records. Last century. History. Ancient history.'

Chapter Twenty-Three

By the time she returned to Crownhill the sun hung low in the sky, silhouetting the big tower blocks to the south-west. Any heat the ball of orange had provided was fast radiating heavenward. Savage stayed in her car, engine running, heater on and sod the global warming debate.

Fallon and Jackman. In cahoots. How on earth was she going to handle the situation? She couldn't walk into the Crime Suite and announce Fallon's revelation because the two of them were working a pincer movement, with her in the middle. As the car fugged up around her she tried to think. She needed information and she needed it off the record. That way she could manage the evidence and filter anything dangerous which could threaten Fallon and thus lead him to shop her.

She decided to take a punt. She picked up her phone and called Dan Phillips at the *Herald*. He sounded surprised to hear from her and she could almost hear his ears prick up when she asked him what he knew about Kenny Fallon. 'Let's meet' was all he would say, and named the Eastern Eye on Notte Street.

An hour later she entered the restaurant and found Phillips sitting at a window seat.

'Fallon is a regular here,' he said as Savage came over. 'Loves the place.'

Savage sat down and looked around. Usual Indian it wasn't; no sign of white tablecloths, dodgy prints on the walls and no stained carpet. The place was very much in the twenty-first century with black leather chairs, smart tables and fancy lighting. If the waiter had brought over some item of nouveau cuisine on a square plate with a zig-zag of sauce she wouldn't have been surprised. She was glad to note the extensive menu contained traditional dishes along with some exotic house specialities. Phillips recommended the chicken Kalam's Delight, so she went with his choice.

Once a beer had been set in front of each of them along with some poppadums and condiments she asked about Fallon again.

'Ah, the lovely Kenny Fallon. Plymouth's very own born and bred mini-gangster. Hard man turned property tycoon. Friend of people and politicians alike. Sponsors kids' footie teams, helps old ladies across the street, kneecaps local bad boys who get too out of line. Which part of all that you want to believe is up to you.'

'I want to find out about his roots. Specifically friends and acquaintances from those early days.'

'Is this about Alec Jackman?'

'I . . .' Savage reached for her beer. Took a gulp before continuing, aware her voice had a quaver to it. She feigned ignorance. 'Who's he? The name sounds familiar.'

'Deputy Leader of the council. Sits on the Police and Crime Panel too. If you're looking to link Jackman and Fallon, I wouldn't bother. I've been down that route several times and I can't find a thing to pin on him. Jackman and Fallon grew up on the same street and you'll catch them occasionally having a curry here together, but Jackman is so clean his arse cheeks squeak when he walks. At least he appears that way.'

'And you suspect he isn't?' She put the beer down with a little extra care, heart thumping.

'Look, if you ask Jackman about his relationship with Fallon, he says the two of them were in and out of one another's houses when they were kids. Their mothers were best friends. He says you can't choose social bonds and you don't break chains like that simply to get on in life. It's all good stuff, but I am positive the friendship goes deeper.'

'In what way?'

'Like the development on the other side of Sutton Harbour, for instance. Planning was turned down five years ago and then Fallon buys the land from the original developer cheap. Now there is a swanky block of flats on the plot. The official line is that the design changed and priorities altered. The economy needed stimulus and it wasn't the time to be fussing over technicalities.'

'You think Jackman got a backhander from Fallon for getting the planning through?'

'Can't prove it. Anyway, the payback might not have been so crude. Even if Jackman earned beans from the deal he can stash them away and plant them later.'

'And you can't find them to dig them up?'

'No. The only piece of mud I can find to sling at Jackman is his predilection for girls. Young girls.'

'You mean . . .?' Savage wondered if Jackman might in any way be connected to Owers. Phillips disabused her of the notion when he answered.

'Not like that. Over sixteen but under eighteen. Last I opened a law book, sex with a sixteen-year-old was legal. Unfortunately for my scoop. I want to go with the story, but my editor doesn't. No public interest he says, which is rubbish. Middle-aged councillors having sex with young girls is *exactly* what the public are interested in. Trouble is my boss doesn't want things stirred up, not unless I can discover something illegal.'

'OK,' Savage said, cracking a poppadum in half and dipping a piece in some raita. 'But the person I am interested in isn't Jackman.'

'Who then?'

'It's somebody else from Fallon's past. Somebody who may have been away for a time. Possibly the person got on the wrong side of Fallon at some point. Maybe they fell out over something. Whatever, they bore a grudge.'

'And they're back?' Phillips' eyes lit up and Savage could almost see his brain working overtime, putting two and two together. He took a swig of beer from his bottle and leaned forward. 'Now I *am* interested.'

'Well?'

'Would I be right if I linked Fallon with that paedophile who was killed and Gavin Redmond? Who, coincidentally, was Alec Jackman's brother-in-law and ran a business which Fallon has a fifty per cent stake in.'

Savage said nothing. She pushed the plate of popadums to one side as the waiter brought over the main courses, the steam carrying a wonderful aroma of spices.

'I knew it!' Phillips said, putting his bottle down. 'How did I miss that?' He chuckled to himself and began shovelling forkfuls of food into his mouth, mumbling through rice and korma. 'Do you remember a man named Ricky Budgeon?'

'Say that again: Budgen? As in the shop?'

'No, e-o-n. Budgeon.'

'Shit,' Savage said, thinking on the text Julie Meadows had received from Riley. 'Tell me.'

'This is way back now, getting on for twenty years I'd

guess. Well, Mr Budgeon is driving up the M5 to Bristol, and he is pulled over by armed officers keen to check the boot of his car. Ricky goes for a gun but he's not fast enough. He takes one in the head, critical, but he lives to tell the tale. He's got a mate in the car and the nutter pulls a hidden blade and slices open one of the officers and pulls his—'

'Guts out with his bare hands.'

'You know Stuart Chaffe then?'

Savage nodded. 'Seems I do. Go on.'

'At first it appears that apart from the gun the car is clean, but later the SOCOs lever off the tyre from the spare in the boot and discover five kilograms of coke inside. Both men go down for a long time, Chaffe for longer, if I recall. They'd be out now, though.'

'So, where does Fallon fit in with this?'

'When Budgeon was a kid he lived on a street in North Prospect, three doors up from Fallon. Became known as Geordie on account of his dad coming from Newcastle to work in Devonport dockyard. In his teens Budgeon affected a North-East accent and the nickname stuck. When Fallon went down for possession years ago word on the street was he'd carried the can for Budgeon. Did the time because he wouldn't shop his mate. He earned a lot of respect for doing so too. Back when they were in their twenties they became notorious in North Prospect. Nothing went down without their permission. The two of them built a business, riding a wave of misery to financial success.'

'Until Budgeon copped it.'

'In one. With Budgeon out of the picture, Fallon took over. Since that day he's hardly put a foot wrong. Now many of his businesses are legit, helped by the fact Jackman is always around to smooth things along. As you'll be aware, Fallon keeps any vice at arm's length. He gets commission, favours and things like that, but never anything to link him in directly. Sweet, no?'

Savage scraped the last of her food from the plate and sat back in her chair.

'You know more though, don't you?'

'Perhaps.' Phillips smiled, the smile vanishing as he continued. 'I want an exclusive and I want to be on the spot when anything happens. Got it?'

'OK.' Savage nodded. 'I'll see what I can do. Promise.'

'Right. So way back when Budgeon and Chaffe got nicked the word was Fallon and Budgeon had fallen out over a woman. Some high-class escort. Working name of Lynnette, I think. She was a little older than them and they both became infatuated. That was the germ of it anyway. From there the dispute burgeoned, became much more. It hurt Fallon. Remember he'd taken the rap for Budgeon, done time for him. Seemed like Budgeon wouldn't return the favour.'

'Are you saying . . .?'

'Supposition.' Phillips leant forwards, dropping his voice to a whisper. 'How did you guys know to stop Budgeon? How come he was stopped by *armed* police? The take wasn't a routine bust by any means.'

'Intel?'

'No. Back then it was all so primitive and anyway, their little network was sewn up tight, held together by a combination of reward and punishment. Listen, I heard a story once about a lad who grassed up a small-time dealer – the dealer was one of the little men at the end of the supply chain – apparently the lad got taken to a remote spot up the Tamar at low tide. Budgeon and Chaffe took one of those U-shaped bike locks and clamped the lad's neck to a block of concrete with a ring bolt set in the top. They took him out on the mud and dropped the block. Then they went back and sat on the bank, cracked open a couple of tinnies and waited for the tide to come in. They go home and come back at the next low tide to remove the body.'

'Sounds like something dreamt up to scare people.'

'Yeah. Except for the before and after pictures which circulated in the local pubs for weeks afterwards.'

'Jesus.'

'Doesn't save. I know.' Phillips necked some more of his beer. 'So it wasn't down to good policing that Budgeon got caught. No, Budgeon and Chaffe walked into a trap. Maybe they didn't even realise the cocaine was in the boot, but the charlie was in such a large quantity that even if Chaffe hadn't gone mental it would have ensured they both went away for a long time.'

'So Fallon grassed them up?'

'I doubt it was as clear-cut and he certainly wouldn't have done it himself. Probably just a got a mate to drop a few words here and there. A warning about the gun.'

'And the cocaine? That was a lot of money to throw away.'

'I shouldn't think Fallon thought like that. He would have called it something different. An investment in his future perhaps?'

'Do you have any evidence for this hypothesis?'

'No, but a paper trail must exist. Someone in the force set up the take and can only have planned the operation on the word of someone else. The rumour is they did very well out of it too. Then again there always seems to be a rumour or two flying around when it comes to the police and organised crime. You'll need to do some digging your end to find out who. Mean time – if I am reading you right about Owers and Redmond – I'd say Fallon's original investment has just gone deep into the red.'

* * *

266

Savage had meant to go straight home after the meeting with Phillips, but instead she decided to return to the station. The reporter had intimated that Ricky Budgeon and Stuart Chaffe had been dumped in it by Fallon and that the intel for the bust came through a police officer on the force. She had a pretty good idea who might have been the police conduit for the information and a ten-minute search through the old records relating to the motorway bust proved her right. The informant had been one Dave Dowdney, now the owner of Moor to Shore Taxis, and the detective who had elicited the information from Dowdney and passed across the date and time of the car trip was a young DC called Philip Davies.

Savage drove back from town feeling a touch queasy on account of the beer, the curry and the confirmation of her suspicions concerning Davies. When she got in she found Pete and Stefan in the kitchen nursing a couple of beers too. Pete looked unimpressed when she opined the virtues of the Eastern Eye.

'You might have got a takeaway for us,' he said, pointing to the remains of their own dinner. 'We had pasta and pesto plus some old garlic bread we found in the bottom of the freezer. Best before May 1872.'

'The trouble with you,' she said, as she went over and put an arm around her husband, 'is that you spent too many years having what amounts to a personal chef on hand twenty-four seven.'

'True, but there's nobody to cuddle at night.'

'So you say. I have my doubts though. I am sure last year you were bunk-hopping all the way from Devonport to Tierra de Fuego and back again. What say you Stefan?'

'Don't involve me,' Stefan said, holding up his hands. 'I only work here, but speaking from personal experience, when I'm on a yacht I never mix business with pleasure.'

'I don't blame you,' Savage said. 'I've seen the guys you race with. Big, hairy and their personal hygiene consists of a wipe down with a J-cloth every few days. Talking of which, I am going to go upstairs and have a soak in the bath while you two talk shipboard romance.'

Savage left them arguing over the merits of allowing women on boats and went upstairs. While she ran the bath she pondered over what Phillips had told her and the discovery of Davies as the lynchpin in the action which had resulted in the arrest of Budgeon and Chaffe. She slipped out of her clothes and into the mass of white bubbles.

Davies had moved up a couple of ranks since the incident, all the time becoming more and more notorious as the man who had his finger on the pulse of the Plymouth underworld. During the intervening period he had spent a couple of years on the Met before returning to Devon and flirting with SOCIT – the Serious and Organised Crime Investigation Team. Savage knew he'd never got on well when on assignment with them. The reasoning was he wasn't a team player and couldn't knuckle down to the painstakingly detailed work required. Another theory occurred to Savage: Davies was still in league with Fallon. It would explain the relative failure of operation after operation to catch the big fish behind the small-scale dealers.

If Davies had had a part in helping Fallon to build his drug empire then Jackman had too. Jackman had served on the old Police Authority and now he was a member of the Police and Crime Panel, the body which held the Police and Crime Commissioner to account. The position gave Jackman access to privileged information. Between the two of them Davies and Jackman probably knew – or could find out – everything there was to know about police operations. And that included operation *Sternway*. Which meant Fallon had likely known about Redmond's role as an informer from the beginning. Any intelligence Redmond had supplied was tainted.

And Riley?

Now the nonsense text message he'd sent made sense and from what Dan Phillips had told her Budgeon and Chaffe could well be involved in his abduction. The reason had to be to do with *Sternway*. The two of them had tortured and killed Owers, probably for whatever financial information he had on Fallon. Redmond had met a similar end. What fate might befall Riley Savage tried to put from her mind.

What she couldn't put from her mind, no matter how hard she tried, was the video Jackman possessed. She felt ashamed that instead of concentrating on Riley's predicament she was focusing on her own, but Jackman could end her career, put her behind bars, maybe even break up her family. Somehow she had to stop him.

Savage let herself slip down into the water so only her eyes, nose and mouth were exposed. She closed her eyes and let the warmth cocoon her, relishing the sense of isolation at the same time as she heard the pulse, pulse, pulse of the blood in her ears.

Kemp hadn't slept easy for the first few hours, the man coughing his guts up. Not blood though. Riley thought that was, if not a good sign, then better than it might have been. Later Riley heard snoring, Kemp far away in the land of nod. Somewhere nicer than a freezing cold stable anyway. Riley spread a layer of straw over the man's prone form and wondered what would be left of him come tomorrow.

He needn't have worried because Kemp slept most of the next day too, occasionally coughing and then muttering something in his half-sleep. The rest appeared to do him good, because hours after the light had gone he woke, the cough back, but Kemp cheery. All things considered.

'Drink?' Kemp said. Riley helped him over to the water trough. 'Prefer red, mate, but if white is all you've got . . .'

Kemp spluttered as he drank, coughing phlegm into the trough.

'Sorry about that. I've contaminated your fine cellar.'

Riley wondered how the man could keep up the good spirits. Maybe he'd just spent too much time undercover. It could get to you in the end. Or maybe, like Riley, he was losing it.

Riley wanted to know what had happened, how Kemp had got here. Kemp settled back in the straw and made himself comfortable.

'I'm back up north, couple of days off, sitting watching the lunchtime news and there is Redmond, face beaming from the TV – only from what the reporter is saying he's not going to be doing that again.'

'He's dead?'

'Yup. I call Hardin and he tells me the latest. Redmond's been cut open. "Eviscerated", according to the pathologist. Hardin wants to know if we're secure and I want to know too. If we've been blown then there is no way I want to come back down to Devon. Cream teas, lovely coastline, Dartmoor? You can bloody forget it. You had no idea about Redmond being our man so it is down to the Chief Constable, Hardin, a DI at Exeter and DI Davies. No way is it the CC and I think we can discount Hardin, which leaves the facilitator at Exeter and Davies. I sat in a room with Davies once; too much aftershave. Lynx, I think. Whatever, it didn't disguise the smell. You might not have pies down this end of the world, but you've got pasties and I reckon Davies has his fingers in a load of them.'

'So Fallon finds out about Redmond from Davies and then takes him out? Makes sense.'

'Sort of. Except Hardin says they aren't convinced Fallon is in the frame. He reckons the murder is connected to another killing and most likely nothing to do with *Sternway*. He spins me a story about Redmond being an innocent caught up in some vigilante business, something to do with some paedophile. I don't buy that, but what-the-hell, if I don't come back down here then *Sternway* ends with Redmond's death. So I pack Marty Kemp into a suitcase and whizz down the motorway.'

'Got it.' Riley pulled some more straw over himself. 'But I don't—'

'Wait. This is the bit where I cock up. Big time.'

'OK. Go on.'

'I check into my usual place, the Premier Inn at Marsh Mills. It's not the Hilton, but the place is inconspicuous and I can turn up and sit in the car park, make a booking on my laptop and then stroll in.'

'And that was a mistake?'

'Total fuck-up to return there. I just wasn't thinking right.'

'Redmond.'

'Yes.' Kemp half sat up, propping himself on an elbow. 'Redmond had my mobile number and my name. The only other thing he knew about me was that I stayed at the hotel because I met him twice in the pub next door. When he was being sliced up he must have come out with the one thing he thought might save him.'

'You.'

'Yeah. Little fucking me.'

Chapter Twenty-Four

Crownhill Police Station, Plymouth. Thursday 24th January. 9.15 a.m.

Thursday morning and Savage went to find DS Gareth Collier to brief him on the Budgeon angle. She told him about the relationship with Fallon and explained that Budgeon may well have returned to Plymouth with vengeance on his mind. Collier listened but by the time she had finished he looked as if he was about to have kittens.

'This lot,' he said with a sweep of his arms; Savage not knowing if he meant the people in the room or the array of whiteboards and other incident room paraphernalia. 'All in one huge melting pot. Riley as a misper plopped in as well. Plus now you're telling me there's a new guy, Budgeon. Know what I'm going to call it?'

'No,' Savage said.

'Operation *ByTheSeatOfOurPants*. Because it's a joke, right? All this.' Another wave of his arms. '*Corulus, Brougham, Sternway*. Finding Riley. Budgeon. Forget any semblance of organisation, forget trying to process actions in a meaningful way. No, shove everything in a pile and that sucker Collier will sort it out.'

Savage listened as Collier went to outline the problems.

His arcs of probability had been distorted, he said. New nodes were springing up left, right and centre. It was total evidential overload. Savage smiled and tried to appear sympathetic. Collier's standard procedure was to moan about things for a minute or two and then get on and do the impossible.

'You know,' he said. 'I'm thinking you should just let me have the policy book and I'll crap on a couple of pages and give it to Hardin with my resignation.'

'Will you reconsider if I get you a coffee?' Savage said.

'Will I . . .?' Collier reached up and smoothed the fuzz on top of his head. 'Oh bloody hell. Alright then.'

Collier began barking out orders while Savage went to get him a coffee. By the time she returned she was pleased to see officers bent to keyboards and working hard, a photo of Stuart Chaffe now up on one of the whiteboards.

'Chaffe's the initial target,' Collier said. 'The evidence Layton found in the van puts him at the centre. He had something to do with the little girl and Owers, Riley was in his van and Ricky Budgeon is his mate. We've got nothing much on Budgeon so action point two is research on him, but find Chaffe, and I reckon we find Budgeon and Riley.'

Collier left an unsaid question hanging in the air. Savage could see by the expressions in the room that other officers were thinking along the same lines: why the hell had she let Chaffe go? She didn't say anything and saw faces turn back to screens. She'd mucked up and she knew it was because she had been distracted. She could blame the crash Calter and Enders had been involved in, sure, but what had really made her take her eyes off the ball was Alec bloody Jackman and the damned video of her and Matthew Harrison.

She left the team to it, returned to her office and sat staring out of the window, sipping bitter coffee from a paper cup.

The video was dynamite and Jackman knew it. He'd want to extract the maximum value from blackmailing Savage. Given his involvement with Fallon that could only mean *Sternway*. Which indirectly meant Riley. And that meant she had to bite the bullet.

Jackman answered after a couple of rings, interrupting her attempt to say anything. He had space in his diary for a ten-thirty a.m. meeting. The cafe on the Hoe. He'd see her there.

An hour later, as she got out of her car and walked to the cafe, she wondered if the venue was Jackman's idea of a bad joke. Not a stone's throw from the toilets where Owers' body had been discovered crammed into a cubicle.

She approached the cafe and spotted Jackman sitting at a table outside. He was wearing the same raincoat as the other night, but now it was light she could see his features: short hair, dark eyes and a wide mouth which in the picture on the front of the *Herald* had been a slimy smile. Now it was more like a grimace.

Jackman noticed her approaching, but did nothing to greet her. Instead he tore the corner off a sachet of sugar and poured the contents into his cappuccino, stirring it with a wooden spatula and then taking a scoop of foam and sucking it in between his lips.

Savage scraped back the chair opposite him and sat down. Jackman said nothing for a few seconds, merely took another sachet of sugar and repeated the actions of emptying, stirring and slurping.

'Sweet,' he said at last, looking up at Savage for the first time. 'Very sweet.'

'OK. Point made. Now what the hell do you want?'

'I want what anyone wants who involves the police. Help.' Jackman glanced down at his phone, moved his hand over

274

the number nine on the keypad and pretended to press down three times. 'Think of this as a personally delivered distress call.'

'999 is for emergencies only.'

'And you don't think this is one, you stupid cow? A psycho on the loose and me as a potential victim? For God's sake woman, this *is* an emergency.'

At first sight Jackman had appeared calm and in control. His face wore a white pallor Savage had taken for the natural coolness of a man who didn't need to raise his temper. Now she could see the blood had drained from his cheeks, the lack of colour down to fear.

'What am I supposed to do?'

'Catch the bastard.'

'And who is "the bastard"?'

'Come on, I *know* you know. You're not stupid. You've been to see Kenny so you know the story. I bet he told you in his own inimitable way, but you'll have worked it out.'

'Look, what do you expect me to do? We are looking for the killer, I don't see how you think I could help you further.'

'Ricky Budgeon is a psycho. Not right in the head. He's going to come after me next.'

'Budgeon.'

'Of course. The black and white stripes. Newcastle United. The cocaine. Budgeon wanted us to know from the start so we'd be scared.'

'You'd every right to be. You and Fallon set up Budgeon so Fallon could take over. Budgeon went to prison while you and Fallon made a mint. Fallon built a string of dodgy businesses on the back of the money and you went legit and made a fortune too. Now it is payback time. You can't really blame Budgeon for wanting what he regards as his.'

'Budgeon scares me, but that's not all. What he's done has stirred things up over at Tamar Yachts.'

'I'm sorry about your brother-in-law. He got caught in the crossfire.'

'Rubbish and you know it.' Jackman picked up his cup and took a gulp. 'He was up to his neck in trouble. The thing is, now he's dead it would be very handy if Gavin's connection to me could be swept under the carpet.'

'How exactly can I do that? You were related for God's sake.'

'Don't be flippant with me, detective.' The cup went down heavy on the table and brown-grey liquid slopped out, a puddle sliding towards Jackman's phone. He moved the phone out of the way and looked across the table at Savage, eyes narrowing. 'I realise I can't hide the fact that my brother-in-law is a loser whose enterprise needed regular doses of cash to keep afloat. What I want to conceal is my direct involvement in anything – how shall I put it? – untoward? Gavin was a prick. He was starting to get uneasy and his loyalty was about as thin as the layer of wax he shone his boats with. I wouldn't be surprised if he left a little insurance policy somewhere. Which is where you come in.'

'Look, your family problems are your business. Redmond got out of his depth. Now you'll just have to weather the storm.'

'It's not as simple as that.' Jackman leant forward, lowered his voice. 'I need you to help me hide certain emails I've sent him.'

'What emails?'

'Doesn't matter. Just get rid of everything I've sent him.'

'You've . . .' The realisation struck home and Savage was unable to complete the sentence for a few seconds. She shook her head. 'You've been passing stuff directly to Fallon and Redmond, Redmond in turn feeding the wrong info back to us.'

'Gavin was a loser, but he wasn't stupid. Do you think he'd risk crossing Kenny? Now, those emails will be on Redmond's office machine, probably linked to their server which luckily is on site. I want them deleted, removed, ignored, I really don't care what. As long as they never see the light of day. With the emails gone, the only evidence linking me with Tamar and Kenny is circumstantial. You'll tell your superiors it is precisely because of this circumstantial evidence that Budgeon believes I am part of Fallon's network and thus need police protection.'

'Why not simply ask Fallon to get rid of the emails? He owns part of the company, presumably he could get access.'

'I don't trust him. Plus there's all that computer forensic stuff. I know your guys can get to deleted emails, even retrieve things from disks which have been formatted. You'll find a way of making the problem disappear for good.'

'And what about Fallon? Where does he come in?'

'Kenny's got his own ideas, wants something too. He's going to call you and when he does you'll do what he says. If you know what's good for you.'

'Shit!' Savage put her head in her hands and ruffled her hair. The situation was surreal. The deputy leader of the council, a member of the Devon and Cornwall Police and Crime Panel, had just admitted to her that he was involved in the murkiest aspects of Plymouth's underworld and she couldn't do anything about it. Worse, she was going to have to help him. She looked up and shook her head.

'What exactly am I supposed to do? I'm a single detective on a large team, what if I don't get to those emails first? What if I can't find them, fail to delete them or can't remove the evidence? What if there are backups somewhere? What if Fallon wants more than I can deliver?'

'Then ACC Maria Heldon gets a private viewing of the main feature. The one where you're the star.' Jackman took his phone from the table and shoved it inside his coat pocket. He pushed his chair back and stood up. 'She's a sour-faced, humourless bitch, but even she will enjoy the show, don't you think?'

Savage watched Jackman walk out of the cafe grounds and off along the Hoe, his raincoat disappearing behind a gaggle of foreign students in their brightly coloured identikit yellow waterproofs. They crowded round the Drake Memorial, taking it in turns to have their picture taken with Devon's most famous son and pointing and laughing at his tights and frilly culottes. When they moved on over towards the red and white lighthouse Jackman had gone.

'You think you can cross me and get away with it?' Budgeon swung the pickaxe handle once more and the wood thudded into flesh. The man uttered a guttural cry, but the response was not much more than a physical reaction; he was losing consciousness fast. 'Answer me, fucking answer me!'

Budgeon chucked the handle away and bent to the body. The yellow straw all around the man glistened with red and a stench of urine overpowered the smell of horse shit.

'I'd thought about letting you off,' Budgeon whispered. 'But I changed my mind, so this is it. Bye-bye time. Anyone be shedding a tear once you've gone? I don't think so. Never trust a woman, hey?'

'Never, boss.' The voice came from Stuey. He stood over near the door, cradling Budgeon's shotgun. 'Find 'em, fuck 'em, forget 'em.'

'Give me the gun.' Budgeon pulled himself up from the

straw. He was getting fed up of this. The beating had gone on for long enough. At first he'd let his rage carry him along, but he'd soon tired. Now he just needed resolution; one more piece of the jigsaw to be fitted.

'Fucking hey, Ricky,' Stuey said, waving the barrels in Budgeon's direction. 'You're really going to do it? Rock and fucking roll!'

'Stop mucking around and give me the gun and then go and get some petrol and some rags and stuff. I've got an idea that'll kill two birds at once. Something to throw those piggy-pigs off the scent.'

'Sure thing, Ricky.' Stuey handed Budgeon the gun. 'This is going to be great. Payback time at last.'

Budgeon cracked the gun open and checked both barrels were chambered. He snapped it shut again and walked over to the body slumped near one wall.

'Look up you fucking coward,' Budgeon said bringing the gun to bear.

The head turned slightly, the eyes rolling open for a moment. Utter despair. A movement of the lips bringing forth a whimper which maybe was a last plea for mercy.

Budgeon placed the barrels up against the man's forehead. A stab of pain stung him in an identical position on his own head and a white light flared somewhere deep inside his skull. Itching. Burning. Boring through his brain. He shook his head. Blinked. Pulled both triggers.

Chapter Twenty-Five

Crownhill Police Station, Plymouth. Thursday 24th January.
11.07 a.m.

Calter was disappointed to still be confined to desk work. While other detectives were off doing the legwork involved in tracking down Stuart Chaffe, Collier had tasked her with getting more background information on Ricky Budgeon.

Calter soon discovered Budgeon was costing the taxpayer in disk space if nothing else, because his name brought up dozens of references on the Police National Computer. Each reference was accompanied by the same mug shot which revealed Budgeon to be a thickset man with broad shoulders, round face, bald or close-shaven head and not much neck. He looked like a bouncer or a rugby player, or maybe a wrestler, and everything about his appearance said 'thug'. The most recent entry showed he'd done nine months on remand in a case connected with cocaine dealing up in London. The case had collapsed due to mistakes made in the operation to snare him and Budgeon had been acquitted at the end of May last year.

She drilled deeper and discovered the operation had taken place under the auspices of SCD7, a unit within the Specialist Crime Directorate of the Metropolitan Police which dealt with organised crime. Half-an-hour's more research and three phone calls later she was talking to DCI Tom Bryant, an officer within SCD7 who had been involved with the case. Bryant had a soft, low voice – a whisper Calter found soporific – and sounded more like an East End gangster from the sixties than a modern policeman. She asked him about the operation to catch Budgeon.

'It was part of the Middle Market Drugs Partnership,' he said.

'Sorry?'

'You and me both, sweetheart,' Bryant said, a sigh coming down the line. 'Things were a whole lot easier back when we simply went and kicked down a few doors and arrested the buggers.'

Sure, Calter thought. Back when you could get away with calling women colleagues 'sweetheart' or planting a packet of drugs under a suspect's bed and neither word nor action would raise an eyebrow. She asked Bryant to explain.

'The partnership involves a number of agencies working together, the idea being to disrupt class A drug supply in the capital. We're not talking about targeting the guys pushing wraps, we go after the big boys.'

'Budgeon?'

'Right. When we first encountered him it was a few years after he had been released from a long stretch inside somewhere up north. We knew you lot had busted him over drugs so we weren't too surprised to find him running with some Colombians. In a neat reversal of roles Budgeon acted as a middleman between the spics and a number of different smuggling operations. Budgeon never went near the drugs himself, he was a facilitator, arranging the deals and creaming a percentage off the top. In addition he provided muscle in the form of hired yardies – or rather ex-yardies. The muscle made sure the deals stayed sweet and nobody pulled any funny business. Rumour is, if they did, Budgeon liked to get personal. Do you remember the sack of body parts pulled out of the Thames at Teddington Lock a few years back?'

'Vaguely.'

'Budgeon's handiwork. Allegedly.'

'So how come Budgeon isn't inside?'

'Evidence. We caught three of the Colombian's foot soldiers receiving twenty kilos of cocaine from two of Budgeon's men. Bang to. At the trial the judge hands out sentences totalling forty years.'

'And Budgeon?'

'Like I need reminding, love. Back to pretrial and our main witness against Budgeon is a South American woman, a beauty who had come to the UK with one of the Colombians, but is now Budgeon's young squeeze. None of the spics will testify against Budgeon, but the CPS reckon the girl will. She's got a little nipper see? Wants to protect the kid. We know the girl was at a number of meetings with the Colombians and Budgeon where they discussed terms. Sorted, we think. She'll give evidence in return for immunity from prosecution and a citizenship deal which we can get her, because if she is deported to Columbia she's dead in a week, right?'

'Yes, but I don't get it, what went wrong?'

'I'm just getting to that, love. Everything is looking good until two weeks before the trial starts the bloody CPS tells us they are dropping the case against Budgeon. Turns out our undercover officer, the guy who'd sniffed half of all this detail out, has been sleeping with the girl and the CPS say if we use her as a witness her evidence will be viewed as un-re-fucking-liable. We might end up losing the lot of them so we have to drop Budgeon from the case. We never got a chance to go after the head honchos either. Talk about cock-up.'

'So where's Budgeon now?'

'Now you're asking. Sitting in the sun drinking sangria, I expect.'

'In January?'

'In Spain. He's got property out there, assets laid down in the good times. Last we heard he was putting his feet up and counting his losses from the recent slump in the market. Whether his stay is for good or just a sabbatical, I have no idea. As long as he keeps out of the country he is off our agenda. SOCA are trying to recover assets, but cooperation across borders is tricky. So much for the E-fucking-U arrest warrant.'

'And if I told you he might be back in the UK, down here in the West Country?'

'How did you . . .?' Bryant paused, Calter sensing she had wrong-footed him. The moment passed, and any hint that the DCI had been flustered vanished as his voice came back on the line. 'I'd not be surprised. The intelligence unit informed me that he took some trips across from Spain to Devon a while before we arrested him. Flew into Exeter, according to the immigration data. Didn't seem to relate to our case so I didn't waste resources on investigating further.'

'Nobody thought fit to tell us though?'

'We like to keep things tight up here, love. Intel is best shared on a need-to-know basis. You country bumpkins don't . . . I mean didn't need to know. However, if he's turned up on your patch I'd be interested in keeping tabs. Anything comes up then keep me informed. Perhaps I might even need to take a trip down your way. If I do, I'll buy you a drink, take you out for dinner. Old copper like me, I'd love to teach a young lass like you a few tricks. Get my drift?'

283

Calter bit her tongue and said she'd be delighted and then asked Bryant if he would send her some more info on the case and on Budgeon too. She'd be very grateful.

Bryant took the bait and said he would, telling Calter not to forget about their date as he hung up. True to his word, twenty minutes later an email pinged in along with several documents attached and links to dozens more.

Calter went to get herself a cup of tea and then began to digest the information. The documents went into more depth about the recent case, but didn't offer much new. Calter was not happy to discover that in several places they'd been redacted, rows of Xs filling line after line. The missing information obviously referred to the undercover parts of the operation which the Met had decided should not be released beyond SCD7.

Next she went through the links Bryant had sent. Most were to public documents, but several were to items on internal networks and she found she didn't have the authorisation to access them. So much for Bryant's help.

The final document Bryant had included was a copy of an email from the Commissioner of the Met to members of the SCD7 team who had been involved in the Colombians/ Budgeon operation. Calter couldn't understand why Bryant had included it until she saw his name mentioned a couple of times. The head of the Met was gushing in his praise for the DCI, saying he was directly responsible for the success of the operation. Crafty bugger, Calter thought. He wanted to show her how good he was, that he was the star of the show, as if it might help him get into her knickers.

Loser.

She was about to close the document when she spotted something near the end. Commiserations about missing out on sending Budgeon down, the Commissioner was saying, but we'll get him and the South Americans next time. Rumour suggested Budgeon was planning something out west, down in the slimepit he had crawled out of. An ongoing operation to be run by SCD, with the agreement of Devon and Cornwall Police, would ensure that when he did so he and the Colombians would get their comeuppance. Once arrested, the Met would get first dibs. And this time they'd make it stick.

Huh? Calter thought. What was that about? What ongoing operation? If there was one it was nothing she knew about. She wrinkled her nose, thinking there was something odd, something not quite right. She'd have to get back in touch with Bryant and ask him about it, if he'd tell her. A little niggle in her head told her she had missed something else too, an obvious clue. Didn't Bryant say Budgeon had turned up in London after a long stretch inside up north? She stood up and went over to one of the whiteboards. On one side there was a timeline showing what Franklin Owers had been up to. It spanned twenty-five years, detailing jobs he'd held and places he'd lived. There was a big gap a few years back where Owers had been in prison, the name of the establishment being HMP Full Sutton.

She returned to her computer and spent five minutes putting Budgeon's name into a couple of searches before she found what she was looking for.

'Fuck, fuck, fuck!' Calter clapped her hands in front of her. 'This is it! Yes!'

'Result by any chance, Jane?' Denton said from the next desk, tone flat, eyes fixed on his own screen.

'Full Sutton. Ricky Budgeon was at Full Sutton prison. Same time as Owers.' Calter grinned. 'How does Chief Constable Jane Calter sound to you, Carl?'

'Scary,' Denton said, shaking his head. 'Very scary.'

* * *

When Savage returned to the station she found Calter and Denton on cloud nine. It was all she could do to bring them down to earth. Calter had printed off a picture of Budgeon and the three of them stared at it as Calter went through the information she had found on the PNC and explained about the connection with Owers.

'So Owers may well have met Budgeon in prison,' Savage said. 'Then Owers comes back here and returns to work for Fallon.'

'Yes, ma'am,' Calter said. 'It isn't too far-fetched to think he was told to do so by Budgeon in order to glean information about Fallon's affairs.'

'Maybe told at first, then later blackmailed.'

'Ma'am?'

'Simza Ellis. John Layton says the forensics point to her being in Stuart Chaffe's van. Chaffe and Budgeon were mates years ago before they were busted and we know the man who instructed Peter Serling, the builder, to dig up the patio at Owers' old residence was short and stocky with little or no hair and Serling's e-fit is a ringer for Budgeon. He somehow knew the girl was buried there and he used that knowledge to blackmail Owers into cooperating. From Owers, Budgeon gained all the details he needed about Fallon's business and the amount of money washing through Tamar. When he was done with Owers he killed him to tidy things up. To scare Fallon too probably.'

'So Chaffe and Budgeon had something to do with Simza's disappearance?'

'Maybe. Maybe they simply lent Owers the van. As to the stuff up in London . . .'

'It all makes sense, ma'am. Sounds as if Budgeon was into some major deals up there. Perhaps he got wind of Fallon and what was going on in Devon. He renewed his contact with Owers and learnt of the delivery Fallon had planned, decided he wanted to grab it for himself. DCI Bryant told me Budgeon had moved permanently to Spain, but I think SCD know more than they're telling. I wouldn't mind betting they have a pretty good idea where Budgeon is and it's not lying on a sunlounger on the Costa del Crime.'

'So have you checked the Spanish angle?'

'I managed to speak to an officer in Malaga, but his English was crap and my Spanish worse. As far as I can gather Budgeon owned a little holiday villa complex in Torremolinos. It was sold for way below market value around the time Budgeon was arrested up in London. It sounds to me as if he did that to avoid sequestration of his assets. The officer said Budgeon used to live between Torremolinos and London, flitting in and out. The police over there were well aware of him and kept an eye on his movements and those of his wife.'

'*Wife*?'

'South American. The woman who was to give evidence at the trial I reckon. Anyway, Budgeon no longer owns anything out in Spain and according to the Border Agency's records he's in the UK. Bryant was pulling a fast one when he told me Budgeon was abroad. He's here, and Bryant knows it.'

'Good work, Jane,' Savage said. 'Now we just have to decide how to use the information and how to persuade SCD to help us.'

Calter started to protest. There weren't any decisions to make. They needed to go to Hardin with what they had and he could then press SCD, maybe involving the Chief Constable too. SCD couldn't plead ignorance then, could they? There was also the supposed ongoing operation with Devon and Cornwall Police.

'Last time I looked, ma'am,' Calter said, 'we *were* Devon

and Cornwall Police, so we need to ask DSupt Hardin what the fuck is going on?'

Savage held up her hand. Calter's overriding virtue was also her main vice: she said it as it was. Right now Savage needed a little subtlety, if only because it was the only approach which might save her skin. She began to explain that a cautious approach would be best, only to be interrupted by the trilling of her mobile.

'Charlotte? I've got a job for you.' The tone was gruff and low, barely audible against the noise in the incident room, but Savage recognised the voice at once.

Fallon.

She stepped away from Calter and Denton and pushed through the double doors into the corridor.

'Jesus! Are you crazy?'

'Many people have said so, Charlotte. But Uncle Kenny always has the last laugh. It's the other folks who end up raving and chewing on chair legs, not me.'

'Calling me when I'm at the station, it—'

'I'm a concerned citizen, simply alerting you to the possibility that there might be a drugs shipment coming in tomorrow night. I want you to prepare for a surveillance operation. You'll need your marine boys on standby as well. You'll get a text message with the location tomorrow.'

'If you think I'm going to be your puppet you're mistaken.'

'Blackmail may be Alec Jackman's way, but it's a last resort for me, Charlotte. I find people respond better with some sort of inducement.'

'You can forget it. I'm not taking your money and—'

'Who said anything about money? I hear on the grapevine that you have an officer missing. If you show willing I'll see what I can do my end.'

'I still can't—'

288

'Yes you can. Remember the video. Goodbye.'

The line went dead as Calter came out of the Crime Suite.

'Bad news, ma'am?' Calter said. 'Your face sort of gives it away.'

'Personal, Jane,' Savage said, trying to compose herself. 'Nothing for you to worry about.'

'Sure? I mean if I can help in any way . . .'

Savage moved to re-enter the incident room, but paused at the entrance. For a second she considered unburdening herself of everything. It would be a relief to confide in someone about Harrison and the way she had left him to die, about Jackman and the video, about the way she was becoming embroiled with Fallon. The young detective flicked her fringe with one hand and smiled across the corridor. Savage knew she was genuine, that she would listen, maybe even break the rules to help.

'Thanks for the offer.' Savage held the door open for Calter. 'But I'll be OK.'

Chapter Twenty-Six

Nr Bovisand, Plymouth. Friday 25th January. 4.35 a.m.

Savage was floating in a warm blue sea next to an ice-white beach fringed with palms somewhere in the Pacific. A small yacht lay anchored in the lagoon. Somehow, impossibly, she had managed to sail from Plymouth to Micronesia non-stop and now was enjoying the feeling of freedom from all responsibility which came from being thousands of miles from anywhere. Then the phone rang and Pete was moaning about the time and she was trying to find the handset as Enders' voice crackled down the line.

'Bloody hell, Patrick. Couldn't it wait?'

'Tamar Yachts is on fire.'

'Shit!' Tamar Yachts. Gavin Redmond's business. 'Where are you?'

'Er, outside your place, ma'am. Hardin told me to come over and get you.'

'Why didn't you ring to warn me?' Savage groaned and began to clamber from the bed. 'Sit tight, I'll be out in a few minutes.'

A few minutes didn't give much time to do anything much except get dressed, brush her teeth to wake herself up, and grab a banana from the fruit bowl in the kitchen. As she opened the door to Enders' car he eyed the banana.

'Oh, bloody hell, have the thing then.' She got in and handed him the piece of fruit. 'You look like a moping dog and you know I don't like dogs at the best of times.'

'Thanks, ma'am.' Enders peeled the banana and stuffed it in his mouth, handing Savage back the skin when he had finished. 'Lovely! These little Caribbean bananas are so much nicer than the bland South American ones. You know I always make a point of buying—'

'Well? I hope you didn't wake me up so we can sit in the car and discuss the merits of banana growing regimes. Get a bloody move on!'

Enders started the car and drove off, navigating the little roads through the countryside back to Plymouth. At a little after five a.m. the streets were deserted and Enders ran red light after red light without encountering anything. Soon they were through the centre of town and arriving at the Stonehouse Bridge Roundabout, with Princess Yachts' main office on their left. They drove on to the bridge and into a chaotic scene lit by the blue strobing lights of fire appliances, police cars and ambulances and the inferno of the Tamar Yachts' building. From their vantage point on the bridge they could see million pound motor yachts floating free in Stonehouse Pool, the shiny white hulls reflecting the orange glow from the fire. Several ribs were darting in and out amongst the yachts, trying to attach lines, while further out the fireboat nosed past several loose day boats and came into the bottom reaches of the pool, giving a blast of a siren for good measure. Over on the Princess Yachts side things seemed more organised and boats were being moved down river under their own power by staff.

Richmond Walk, the road where Tamar Yachts was, had been cordoned off, so Enders pulled the car onto the pavement on the bridge and they got out and walked. She asked an officer on the perimeter as to the whereabouts of Hardin and he pointed down to a fire engine. Hardin stood alongside DI Davies, the two of them deep in conversation with a fire officer. Every now and then Hardin turned to glance at the scene of devastation behind him and shook his head.

Davies, Savage thought, what sort of stake did he have in all of this? If he was still deep in with Fallon then he'd be doing his own brand of firefighting. He'd be trying to cover up anything which might lead the *Sternway* team in Fallon's direction. And he'd probably know about the video too.

Savage and Enders went across. An intense heat from the burning buildings warmed Savage's face as they approached Hardin, his own face incandescent; whether from heat radiation or anger, Savage didn't know. An inner cordon had been set up and no one but fire officers were being let through. Presumably that was what Hardin was arguing about. The cordon appeared to be a sensible move on the part of the fire brigade since huge flames were licking their way out of the roof of the building and every minute or so a popping noise echoed out as some canister or other exploded inside.

'Too dangerous,' Savage heard the man say and as she approached he turned to her to explain.

'There are a lot of hazardous materials inside, ma'am. Fibreglass, resin, paint, thinners, diesel, petrol, gas for welding, propane and butane on the yachts. The place is a bloody fireball waiting to happen.'

'Evidence,' Hardin said. 'We need the evidence.'

'Don't worry, we'll investigate fully once the fire is out and dampened down. We'll find out how the blaze started.'

'Not evidence of arson, we've got evidence for an ongoing case in there. We need to get in and seize computers and paperwork.'

Davies looked as if he wanted to say something, but all he did was shift his stance and glance across at Savage.

'Sir?' Savage took Davies' cue and decided to draw the conversation away from the building. 'The boats?'

'Yes, the boats,' Hardin echoed. 'What idiot released them? We need them impounded immediately.'

'*I* ordered the boats be cast off,' the fire officer said. 'It seemed better they float free than become part of the blaze. I am sure the lads across at Princess will help recover them when they have finished with their own boats. The RNLI are standing by, but their role is to protect life first. They've got a rib down at the far end of the pool checking for anybody aboard any of the boats. Your guys are down there too, I believe?'

'D Section?'

'Yes, Inspector Frey and his men.'

Hardin huffed and muttered something about trigger-happy cowboys, a jibe Savage thought entirely unfair. Time and time again D Section had proved themselves just about the most professional bunch of police officers you might expect to come across. But then Hardin had never been one for running around and getting all hot and sweaty.

Hardin had started off on some other rant when he was interrupted by a loud bang as a huge explosion roared out and a section of the roof gave way sending sparks, smoke and dust into the dark sky, followed by a plume of black smoke billowing up from the building. The fireman made his excuses and moved off to direct things. Davies stepped away too, muttering something about checking in with a couple of contacts.

'Won't be anything left for us at this rate,' Hardin said, eyes tracing the plume of smoke heavenward. He removed a handkerchief from his pocket and wiped his brow. 'The whole of operation *Sternway's* budget blown sky-high. Literally.'

'Closed him down though, sir. Fallon isn't going to be running any drugs through Tamar for a long time.'

'It didn't bring any busts though and I don't think a little local difficulty like this is going to put paid to Fallon's games. He'll find a way to bounce back.'

'Ma'am?' Enders had approached with another guy he introduced as Steve Geet, the deputy yard manager. 'Mr Geet, tell DI Savage what you just told me.'

'It's one of the boats. She's missing.'

'Are you sure?'

'She's a fifty-footer worth half a million, of course I'm sure.'

'And she was tied up at the wharf?'

'Yeah. She's a boat we took in part exchange last year so she's on brokerage, but in the books as being owned by us. We've been using her to demonstrate a load of new kit and to entertain clients.'

'Couldn't she have drifted off?' Enders asked. 'Got swept out to sea?'

'No, lad.' Geet stared at Enders like the DC had gone bonkers. 'We're on spring tides, see?'

'No, I don't.'

'Springs are always morning and evening this part of the world. The tide won't turn for a while yet. When the fire brigade arrived there was method in their madness at releasing the boats. The chief officer didn't know the exact time of high tide, but he told me he'd noticed the full moon a couple of days ago. From that he knew we must be near springs and that high tide would be breakfast time or close to. Since it was three o'clock when they arrived he knew if he released the boats they wouldn't go anywhere.'

'Sorry?' Enders still wore a blank face.

'The tide was coming into the pool and the boats would merely drift around hereabouts. The worse that could happen is they might drift into the river and be swept upstream.'

'And could that have happened to the missing boat?'

'I doubt it. We'd have had reports or one of the MOD boats patrolling the navy yards would have spotted her.'

'So she's been taken.' Savage said. A statement, not a question. 'Was she locked up?'

'You betcha. She had some fancy security too. Like I said, demo stuff.'

'So who could have got acccss?'

'Well the keys were kept in the office and that was locked up at night, but theoretically anyone could go in there and get them. In an emergency we might need to move her quick, see?'

'And do you think that is what happened?'

'Well if that was the case then where the bloody hell is she now?'

The question was a good one and as Geet went back to trying to save the business and thus his job, Hardin wanted to explore the issue of the missing boat some more.

'So where might it end up?' he said to Savage.

'I'm no expert on motorboats,' she said, 'but she'll probably do twenty-five knots. In a few hours she could be anywhere.'

'Please, Charlotte, "anywhere" is not helpful, be more specific.'

'The Channel Islands, France, on route to Southern Ireland or Spain.'

'Across the Atlantic?'

'No. These type of motorboats don't have the range for that.'

'So, what do we reckon? This new man, Ricky Budgeon, he sets the fire and then takes the boat. Another strike at Fallon?'

'He kills Owers and Redmond, which disrupts Fallon's drugs business. Doing this,' Savage waved her hand in the direction of the burning buildings, 'removes it altogether.'

'Bugger.' Hardin followed Savage's gaze. 'We've got nothing.'

A vibration in Savage's pocket came a moment before a brief warble and she reached for her phone. The screen glowed in the darkness, Vanessa Liston's number at the top of the list of messages. She pressed a key to access the text.

drug boat in cawsand bay tonight be there

'Anything for us?' Hardin said, moving closer to peer at the display.

'No,' Savage said, deleting the message. 'Junk.'

It was two hours later when the chief fire officer revealed that they'd found a body over in the loading bay.

'Not pretty,' he said. 'You'll be glad you've not had breakfast.'

Within thirty minutes Savage had been joined by Layton and a very bleary-eyed Nesbit and together with Enders they suited up and then picked their way through the remains of the main building. A firefighter led them over a section of collapsed roof, the warped metal straining underfoot and steam rising all around. As they clambered down from the wreckage into the loading bay area Savage smelt the unmistakable whiff of burnt flesh. The stench was like bad meat grilled on a barbecue. Savage wore a face mask, as did the others, but the thin material did nothing to lessen the awful smell. On the far side of the bay a forty-five gallon oil drum lay on its side, wisps of smoke still curling out from the open end. The thing inside, burnt to a crisp, could just be seen.

'Thing' was the wrong word, Savage knew. The blackened mass of flesh and bone had once been somebody, but she was finding it hard to equate the horror in front of her eyes with anything which had ever been living. There was no hair, no patch of skin which hadn't been burnt, no eyes and just stumps of raw flesh where the ears had once been. The lips had gone too and the shiny enamel of the teeth shone out against the soot like a smile in an advert for a whitening toothpaste.

Two fire officers stood next to the drum. In their protective clothing they looked more like astronauts or divers. Savage was envying them their filtered breathing system. They bent and began to pull the corpse from the drum, easing it out onto a large tarpaulin which had been spread on the ground. The body came out head first, the skin scorched all over and the colour of charcoal. The arms had been pulled up, as if the person was trying to protect themselves from the fire, the fists clenched. Likewise, the knees had been raised.

'Were they alive when the fire started?' Savage said, thinking the position of the limbs must indicate some last-ditch attempt at survival.

'Not necessarily,' Nesbit said. 'The body tends to assume that stance as a result of the heat. Which by the look of things was extreme.'

Nesbit moved closer and pointed down to the abdomen and then to the thighs where the skin had split in great gashes, well-cooked muscle visible beneath.

'Note the clothing,' he continued. 'Any artificial fabrics have melted away and the natural ones are almost completely carbonised.'

As the fire officers completed the removal a photographer took pictures. Nesbit indicated that she should take some close-ups of the head, where Savage could see part of the top of the skull was missing.

'Andrew?' she asked.

'The calvarium – the skull cap – is absent.' Nesbit knelt on the tarpaulin and put his face down close to the head. 'Again, that could well have occurred because of the fire. The pieces might be inside the drum. However, look at the nasal bone. Parts of the frontal bone remain above it and I can see certain characteristic markings, a splintering if you like, which indicate that this person didn't die from fire-related injuries.'

'You're talking in riddles, Andrew. Give it to me straight.'

'He – and from the size of the body we can say it's a "he" – had the top of his head blown away by something. Best guess would be a shotgun fired from point-blank range.'

'Shit,' Savage said. Rather than take a closer look she turned away, taking in the surroundings of the loading bay. The area was strewn with debris from the collapsed roof. 'Here?'

'John?' Nesbit nodded at Layton.

'Impossible to say at the moment,' Layton said. 'We'll need to scour the area for pellets. If we don't find any, then unless we find another crime scene, we'll probably never know.'

'Ma'am?' The voice at her shoulder belonged to Enders. He'd been talking to a firefighter at the edge of the bay and now he strolled over and gazed down at the body. 'Fuck!'

'Not pretty,' Savage said. 'Let's move away for a moment.'

'No, ma'am, the shoes, the bloody shoes!'

'What are you talking about?' Savage turned to the body and followed the blackened legs down to the feet. There *was* a pair of shoes, the soles melted, but the leather above dried

298

and still with a distinctive cut-out pattern on. She still didn't understand what Enders was trying to tell her. 'And?'

'They're . . . oh my God . . . they belong to . . .' Enders put his hands up to his face and something like a wail came out. Then he was sobbing.

'DC Enders, pull yourself together. Tell me what you think you've seen.'

'The shoes, ma'am,' Enders said, tears now streaking down his cheeks. 'They're DS Riley's.'

Jackman strode into his kitchen for breakfast to find his wife staring at the flip-down television. Her mouth hung open, shock on her face, as she looked at the orange glow on the screen.

'Jesus,' Jackman said. 'Is that . . .?'

'What's going on, Alec? Just what the hell was Gavin involved in?'

Jackman didn't reply. Instead, he left the kitchen and went down the hall to his study. Flicked on the little TV in there and watched a reporter interview a fire officer. 'Arson,' the officer said when asked about the probable cause. Jackman switched the TV off and wondered if the cop woman had come good. She'd set the fire to destroy the evidence. For a moment he felt a frisson from the realisation of the power he must hold over her, but then he was worrying. She'd gone too far, mucked things up. Fallon would go apeshit. He stood at the window, shaking his head as he dialled. Fallon answered in a couple of rings.

'You watching this, Alec?' Fallon said. 'Budgeon's work.'

'Budgeon?' As Jackman said the name he felt a moment's relief before his head filled with new worries. 'Shit. The business, the pickup, everything. What the hell are we going to do?'

'Forget that, pal. I was there last night. I'm down on the pontoons when the alarm goes off. I'm thinking about investigating when the bloody place goes up. I was an inch from getting fried. All that talk about your supposed influence with the police, all that poncing around and fancy words. Done nothing, has it? Budgeon's running around doing as he pleases. We don't do something we're fucked.'

'We're fucked anyway, Kenny. Tamar Yachts has gone.'

'That's what I thought at first, but I've been thinking on it. Apart from scaring me witless Budgeon's actually done us a favour in torching the place.'

'But—'

'But nothing. The pigs ain't going to be interested any more. The business will get a payout from the insurance and we're off the hook.'

'The delivery, you idiot. No Redmond, no Tamar, no boat. What are you going to do?'

'The word is *we*, Alec. And I've got us a boat. That's what I was doing there last night.'

'What?' Jackman shook his head. Crazy. Clearly Fallon had no idea. 'The pickup is ten miles offshore, it will be dark and we've got to locate and grab a small bundle in a two metre swell. Who the fuck is going to be able to do that? Ellen bloody MacArthur?'

'You're not far wrong there, mate.' Fallon chuckled. 'Who do you think helped me last night?'

'I've no . . .' Jackman got it then and turned from the window, smacked the desk with his free hand and sat down hard in his chair. 'You are joking, right?'

'Nah, mate. She's a good little girl. Must be in her genes because she knew her way around that boat as well as her old man. The only thing I don't understand about the girl is why she is letting you pork her, but each to their own.'

'So we . . .?'

'Yes. Tonight. We head out there, retrieve the goods and we're quids in. Five million profit, minimum. That and the insurance money funds my new development. A luxury waterside collection of apartments on the Tamar Yachts site. Gold dust, Alec, gold dust. And I've thought of a name too: Phoenix Heights.'

'You're mad, Kenny.'

'You better believe it, because I am going to need your help to push through the planning.'

'And Budgeon?' Jackman put a finger to his mouth, started to worry at a fingernail. 'What about him?'

'Forget about Budgeon. We concentrate on this. After tonight we'll sort Budgeon. Once and for fucking all.'

Jackman hung up and chucked the phone on the desk. He could hear Gill sobbing now, a sound almost like a wail echoing down the hall. He reached across and pushed the door hard so it slammed shut. Bit his fingernail again.

Chapter Twenty-Seven

Crownhill Police Station, Plymouth. Friday 25th January.
11.27 a.m.

Bodies pressed against walls, people sat on desks, a few had spilled out into the corridor. Savage had never seen the Crime Suite so packed. And yet the voices didn't rise beyond a whisper. When DSupt Hardin entered the room even the whispering stopped. Hardin had put on his uniform, an ill-fitting affair which had seen better days. Still, Savage thought, it was a nice gesture.

'This is a sad day,' Hardin said. 'DS Riley was a capable and intelligent cop and a fine man. He only arrived here a year or so ago and yet in that time he managed to make many friends and to impress all his colleagues with his hard-working attitude. He was instrumental in the conclusion of a number of significant cases. He will be greatly missed.'

A chorus of 'hear-hear' rang out and Savage noted as well that several officers were openly crying.

'It goes without saying,' Hardin continued, 'that we are going to catch the bastards who did this. However long it takes, whatever resources are required, we're going to get them.'

This time voices were raised higher, anger and aggression

evident in the responses and as Hardin continued with his eulogy-cum-briefing Savage sneaked from the room and returned to her office. She felt overcome by tiredness and simply didn't want to hear any more. For once she would have been glad to see DI Maynard, but as usual he was nowhere to be seen.

Savage sat at her desk and wrapped her arms around herself. Until now she'd kept herself together, tried to act with professionalism. Riley had deserved no less, she'd thought. Now a wave of bleakness washed over her. She'd liked Riley. A lot. In fact, when Julie Meadows had turned up she'd felt a tinge of jealousy. In a different life Savage could have imagined herself with Riley. Now though he'd gone forever, taken away before she'd had a chance to express her feelings.

Savage reached for the phone as the tears began to flow. She'd call Pete now, tell him what had happened, tell him how much she loved and needed him.

The door burst open before Savage had dialled the outside line.

Layton. Standing there with a wide smile on his face. Laughing. Drunk on something much stronger than alcohol.

Savage scowled at him and wiped at her face.

'What the fuck do you think you're playing at?'

'It's not Riley!' Layton shouted. 'Nesbit just called from the hospital. When they were transferring the body to the morgue drawer he took a look. The body had to be straightened to get it in and when they did so he could see the man wasn't tall enough to be Riley. Nesbit decided to do a preliminary examination there and then. There was a patch of unburnt skin on the man's back. White skin. He's a Caucasian! IC bloody one!'

'But the shoes? Several people confirmed they were Riley's. They were the correct size too.'

'Who cares? The body isn't Darius'. One hundred per cent confirmed.'

Savage felt the tears come faster as she stood up, but this time she was smiling, laughing too, Layton's happiness infectious. Through the door behind Layton, bodies surged in the corridor, a single euphoric voice shouting above the growing crescendo. The shouting ceased as Enders barged past Layton and fell through the doorway and into Savage's arms.

'Darius, ma'am,' Enders said, all inhibitions forgotten as he held her for a moment. 'He's alive!'

'Begs the question though,' Layton said flatly, as he tried to ignore Enders' overt display of affection, 'exactly whose body is it?'

The answer to Layton's question, Savage thought, lay in the fact that although the body wasn't Riley's, the shoes were. When the news came back from the inquiry teams that all seventeen employees from Tamar had been accounted for she knew the corpse must be another of Budgeon's targets. Somebody from the past, somebody who had crossed him and had now paid the ultimate price.

After Enders had calmed down she pointed him in the direction of the car park. Half an hour later they were parked on the front lot at Moor to Shore Taxis in Cattedown. They got out and Enders opened the door of the shabby Portakabin office. Elina sat at the desk wearing the phone headset over the top of iPod earphones. She looked up and plucked the earphones out.

'Is Dave around, love?' Enders asked, climbing the step and going in, Savage following. 'And if he isn't, do you know where we can find him?'

'No he isn't,' the girl said. 'And I'd bloody well like to know where he is too. I had to open up this morning and then deal with a load of customers from last night. They'd booked pickups but it turns out nobody was here to assign the jobs. Plus he usually pays me Fridays. Owes me for a couple of weeks he does. Stingy bastard.'

'That his car?' Savage pointed through the window over to a battered Nissan parked between a pair of taxis.

'Yes.' The girl squinted and her forehead creased, as if she'd just noticed the car for the first time. 'Don't know what it's doing here. He usually walks to work and if he drove then where the hell is he?'

She picked up a nail file from the desk and began to work on one of her fingers, the varnish blood red. Then she stopped, bit her lip and stared up at Enders as if he might have the answer.

'You got petty cash here?' Savage said. 'Some sort of float?'

'Yes. A few hundred in the safe. Nothing more.'

'I suggest you go and get your wages from there, plus a bit extra. I doubt Moor to Shore's going to be opening tomorrow.'

'You're telling me to . . . You *are* police, aren't you?'

'Can't be any harm in taking what Dowdney owes you,' Savage said. 'After that give us the keys and get off home. There'll be lots more police round here soon and they are going to want ID and all sorts. Understand?'

The girl's face appeared blank for a moment and then she was standing up, smoothing down her skirt as if in a vain attempt to make it a little less revealing, and tottering on her tiny heels into the next room.

'Ma'am, what are you doing?' Enders said. 'She's probably a part-time tom, maybe an illegal. We should be bringing her in, not letting her nick a load of Dowdney's dosh.'

'The girl could do with the money and Dowdney isn't

going to miss it since he is, to use an unfortunate expression, toast.'

'Bloody hell, ma'am. Are you saying the body at Tamar is Dowdney?'

'Lynn Towner. Do you know who she is?' Enders shook his head. 'Budgeon's old squeeze from way back. I reckon Dowdney's been shacking up with her on and off over the years. That will have pissed Budgeon off, but worse, Dowdney was the guy who shopped Budgeon to us. Undoubtedly he was under Fallon's orders, but I don't suppose that would cut much ice.'

'What made you suspect?'

'Budgeon's acting like a psycho, but everything he's doing is calculated. As soon as we had the confirmation that nobody from the Tamar workforce was missing then I knew the body had to be part of Budgeon's plan. His anger isn't random, it's unleashed against certain targets.'

'That includes Riley,' Enders said, raising a hand to his head and rubbing. 'Whatever he's done.'

'That's the point: whatever Riley's done. I don't think he was taken because of his knowledge of operation *Sternway*. That might be useful to Budgeon, but it's incidental. Riley worked UC up in London and Budgeon was there too. I bet there's a connection.'

'Riley never talked about anything he did in his time on the Met.'

'No, he wouldn't have done. He's not a show-off and he follows the rules to the letter. You don't blab about undercover work, you keep operational details to yourself. Even when it's all over.'

'The ironic thing is, ma'am, if he *had* said something we might be in a better position to help him.'

Savage couldn't argue with that. Instead she nodded over

306

to where the girl was coming out of the office, a big smile on her face, tempered when she realised she was being watched. Then she shrugged and was across the room and out the door. The last sight Savage had of her was through the office window, the girl dodging puddles on the forecourt, still teetering on the heels, but a definite spring in her step nonetheless.

Savage moved into the inner office, noted the small safe secured to the floor had been left open, and pointed out the sofa and duvet to Enders.

'Doesn't look too comfy,' Enders said. 'But then again, neither does Lynn Towner.'

'When you get to Dowdney's age, Patrick, you'll realise that Lynn Towner's still got something men want.'

'Some men.'

'Putting that aside, Budgeon got Dowdney and Towner to get Riley in the taxi. Dowdney was really only peripheral, and once he'd served his purpose Budgeon kills him. That leaves Towner.'

'He's going to kill her too?'

'He hardly needs to, does he? She's unconscious in the ICU at Derriford. Even if she wasn't I doubt he'd harm her, there's too much history between them.' Savage knelt in front of the safe and peered in. 'Which is good news for us, because she's Budgeon's Achilles heel.'

'She is?'

Savage nodded and then began to go through the contents of the safe. On the top shelf a cash box was open, only coins rattling around in the bottom, and there were various documents, car registration papers, and forms from the council. Enders moved up behind her and leaned over.

'What you looking for, ma'am?'

'I was hoping for a satnav unit. When I was here on

Tuesday Dowdney pointed out a car Towner had trashed a couple of weeks ago. He said she'd crashed it down in Cornwall but lied about it. He knew she was lying because he'd seen the route on the satnav. It's a bit of a long shot, but Chaffe was heading across the bridge into Cornwall when he was caught.'

'You reckon Towner's met Budgeon down there somewhere?'

'I reckon she'd have needed to in order to plan Riley's kidnapping. I don't think Dowdney had a clue where Budgeon was, hence he didn't realise he could have been revealing Budgeon's location when he told me about Towner's bump.'

'And wherever she went the route will be in the satnav?'

'Yes. Even if she cleared it there could still be evidence the boys in Hi-Tech Crimes might be able to get at.'

'Bloody hell, ma'am!' Enders beamed at Savage. 'If you're correct, the satnav could take us straight to Riley.'

'Except,' Savage said, pointing back at the safe, 'the wretched thing's not here, is it?'

The bang had started Riley out of his sleep. A gunshot, close at hand. The retort echoing through the building. For a second he'd raised his hands in defence. As if it would have made any difference.

Afterwards, he and Kemp had worked their way through the possibilities. An unlucky rabbit? Or Budgeon?

'Maybe he's had an accident,' Kemp had said. 'Blown his bloody head off.'

Fat chance, Riley thought. Life didn't go like that. Kemp seemed to be able to draw on an infinite well of humour and good spirits, but his own was running dry.

Sometime mid-morning Stuey brought in more food. Two

loaves of white Hovis and three litres of milk. Stuey pushed the food in with his foot while pointing a shotgun at them, taking no chances now he had two prisoners to deal with. He muttered an 'enjoy' as he slammed the door shut, the padlock and chain clinking on the outside and then a whistle echoing in a corridor as he walked away.

Riley went to retrieve the food. As he picked up the milk pain shot up his shoulder. He leant against the door and cursed. As he shook his head and straightened he noticed something odd about the doorframe: a large crack had appeared, running from close to the middle right up to where the frame met the lintel. The whole thing was set into the stonework in an amateur fashion. Bodgit and Scarper had clearly been at work because a couple of large coachscrews had been driven into the ancient mortar between the large stones. The mortar didn't provide much of a grip and the wood had splintered around one of the screws and the split passed close by the other. A good shove on the door and the frame might well give way completely. The door would still be locked with the bolts, but it wouldn't take much to force the whole lot – door, frame and all – out of the way, especially if he spent a few hours working away at the mortar.

He didn't say anything to Kemp, just took the food over and plonked it down.

'We get out of this, Darius, I'll treat you to Sunday lunch at Gidleigh Park.' Kemp tore open one of the packets of bread. 'You know, the Michelin place over near Chagford?'

'You're on.' Riley said as he unscrewed the cap on the milk carton and took a long draught. 'As long as it's something better than a swilly roast.'

'Hey?'

'Plymouth slang for beans on toast. In certain parts of the city it's what passes for Sunday lunch.'

'Been a revelation working down here I can tell you, mate,' Kemp said through a mouthful of bread. 'Coming, as I do, from the refined environs of Manchester.'

'Manchester?' Riley had started on the bread too, mumbling his words out. 'Must have pained you playing a Liverpudlian then?'

'Not really. Chance to act like a right dickhead.'

'But Redmond knew the truth?' he asked, passing Kemp the milk carton.

'He knew most of it, yes,' Kemp said, nodding towards the door. 'And it seems like he told that to this lot.'

'To Budgeon.'

'The way you said that, sounds like Budgeon is your bête noire. Not sure if the phrase is appropriate, you being black. But there you go.'

'It's spot on.'

'Well, your Mr Budgeon wanted to know all about operation *Sternway*.'

'And you told him?'

'Of course I did. Everything I knew.' Kemp moved a hand to his chest. Winced. 'Not that it helped much. I think he thought I'd give him details of the pickup. I told him I didn't know. Which was when he got a little mad. From what I've seen of the man so far, neither of us have got a hope.'

'There is that,' Riley said.

Riley wondered how Budgeon saw the world. If he allowed for degrees of betrayal or if every act was elevated to the same level. With Budgeon, Riley knew it was quite possible for a red mist to descend, clouding all judgement and leaving him pursuing only one avenue. He looked at Kemp.

'What do you reckon?'

'I think we're hostages. He's after Fallon and his business

and should anything go wrong he can use us in some way. Must be the only reason we're still alive.'

'Not with me,' Riley shook his head. 'I busted him up in London. I was UC and Budgeon walked right into a trap. We set him up. That's why I am here. He's tried to get some information out of me, but in the end it's nothing to do with *Sternway*.'

'Shit. If you busted him then how come he's out?'

'We couldn't make it stick,' Riley said. 'One witness couldn't give evidence and then others retracted their statements. He had a bloody good solicitor too.'

'Well, sounds like that solicitor signed our execution warrants, didn't he?'

'She,' Riley said, remembering the confident woman who had managed to sniff out the true story and thus destroy any chance of securing a conviction.

'Bitch,' Kemp said, spitting into the straw and letting himself slump down.

'Yeah,' Riley said, thinking not of the solicitor but of the South American girl he hadn't been able to resist. Her light brown skin, dark hair, curvy figure. Those bewitching eyes. His total and utter stupidity. 'Bitch.'

By midday Savage had briefed Hardin on the missing satnav. He'd agreed the unit was vital evidence and authorised a search of both Dowdney's and Towner's places. Dowdney had lived in a flat above a hydraulic hose shop not far from the taxi business. Towner rented a council house in Devonport. An hour in, and the police search adviser was reporting a blank and recommending that Towner's children's places should be searched as well.

The officer could recommend all she wanted, Hardin had told Savage, but there was no legal grounds for rooting through relatives' properties. Where would it end? Second cousins twice removed? In the end he'd placated the PolSA by dispatching inquiry teams to interview the children to see if they could shed any light on the missing unit. If any of them appeared to be lying then they could go from there.

Dead on her feet and starving too, Savage returned home. In the kitchen Pete was eating lunch, a bacon butty dripping with ketchup. The kids had been taken to school by Stefan and, according to Pete, were wondering where their mother was. Savage said sorry and explained about the fire at Tamar Yachts and the confusion over the body. About how much she loved him too.

'I'm glad,' Pete said, grinning. 'Because if I didn't know better I'd assume you were having an affair. Leaving the house in the middle of the night in the company of a young man.'

'DC Enders?' Savage moved over to the table and grabbed half of the sandwich. 'No way. And, as you said, you do know better.'

'Lucky that.' Pete smiled, touched her on the arm and gestured at the remaining bacon in the frying pan. 'You can have the rest of that, I'm off. Got some cadets to deal with this afternoon.'

'OK.' She smiled back. 'See you later.'

Except, she thought, she might not.

drug boat in cawsand bay tonight be there

The message from Fallon relayed via Vanessa Liston.

If she ignored the message would Fallon and Jackman really expose her? If they did then Jackman would be in trouble himself, the relationship between him and Fallon out in the open and the pair of them facing trial for corruption. If the evidence from *Sternway* came out as well, then there'd be drugs charges too.

On the other hand Fallon had hinted he might be able to help find Riley. If that was true then it put the issue in an entirely different perspective. She owed it to Riley to go along with whatever Fallon was up to.

She got up and went over to the cooker. The bacon had gone cold so she turned on the gas and shook the pan as the fat started to sizzle. Then she rang Inspector Nigel Frey, head of the marine section.

Frey answered after a couple of rings. He was pleased to hear from her and after talking about the chaos out on the water at Tamar that morning, he wanted to know about Pete. They should get together soon, he said, have a few drinks. Now Pete was home they'd be racing this year, yes?

Savage interrupted him and asked how he was placed for tonight. Only, she needed a favour.

Chapter Twenty-Eight

Plymouth Yacht Haven. Friday 25th January. 4.25 p.m.

'Are you sure Pete is happy about this?' Frey said, pulling a fender in over the side of the boat and carrying it aft.

'Nigel,' Savage said. 'How many times do I need to tell you? Puffin is *our* boat. We own her jointly. And don't tease me about her name like you did the last time we beat you in a race; Samantha came up with it and you argue with her at your peril.'

They were heading out of Plymouth Yacht Haven on Savage's yacht, a little Westerly the family had owned for several years. The boat had taken Savage and Pete to ports along the Devon and Cornish coasts as well as to the Channel Islands, the trips something of a busman's holiday for Pete, although a world away from commanding thousands of tons of steel frigate across oceans. Savage stood at the helm as Frey and Bob Stephens – one of Frey's officers – pulled in the fenders and coiled the docklines. Frey opened a cockpit locker and shoved a couple of fenders in. Stephens plonked several coils of rope on top.

'As long as the boss-man is cool with it,' Frey said. He dropped the lid of the locker, clicked the catch shut and then pointed ahead to where a sailing dinghy was crossing their track, bobbing on the waves left over from the passing Mountbatten ferry.

'Got them.' Savage turned the boat to pass behind the dinghy and the crew waved a 'thank you'. 'About thirty minutes from the end of the Mountbatten breakwater, OK?'

'Thirty minutes! We'd do the trip in five in the RIB.'

'Yeah, well you can't brew a cup of tea on the RIB can you? And if you want to have a comfort break you have to do it in your drysuit.'

They rounded the breakwater and at once felt the long, loping swell coming from the south-west. Savage turned the boat and then flicked the switch on the autopilot. The wheel in front of her began to move left and right as the unseen computer took control and steered a course towards Cawsand Bay, where the sun had already set, leaving a pale sky above the dark Cornish coastline.

Frey came aft again and sat in the cockpit along with Stephens. Savage remained standing and the three of them went over the plan once more.

Before they reached the bay Stephens would go below and remain out of sight. Savage and Frey would pilot the boat in and find an anchorage to the south of the bay. In the summer the place would be rammed with yachts, but even in the winter one or two hardy locals would brave the cold for a night at anchor, so their yacht wouldn't look suspicious. They would then cook a meal and retire early, not out of the ordinary for a couple. With the only light on the boat, the anchor light, high on the top of the mast, they would be able to use the night-vision binoculars Frey had brought along to keep watch on their target.

As Frey and Stephens went further into the details Savage wondered exactly what Fallon had planned, what kind of set-up he would lead them into. She didn't think they were

315

in any danger; Fallon wouldn't be so stupid. Likely it was some kind of diversion. She tried to convince herself she was only going along with his plans because of Riley. At least Hardin had seized on the idea when she'd told him she had received an anonymous tip-off from a reliable source.

'Could be the last throw of the dice for *Sternway*,' he'd said, looking grim. 'Quite possibly for Riley too. The Liston girl has turned out worse than useless. Intel is as thin as a piece of bog paper. Everything at Tamar has turned to ash. The Chief Constable is coming tomorrow. We need something. Anything.'

Hardin had even suggested she liaise with Frey over the set-up and timing of the operation, which had made Savage happier over his involvement. At least she wasn't asking him to step out of line for her.

'And the target is already there?' Stephens asked.

'Yes,' Savage said, pulling herself from her own thoughts. 'The boat anchored up in the centre of the bay about an hour ago. It looks as if it's the missing cruiser from Tamar Yachts.'

'You got people over there watching? I can just see DC Calter walking into a pub in Cawsand on a cold January night. They'd probably print a story in the parish magazine.'

'No. You can see the bay from my house. We've got a big spotting scope in the living room so I put Jamie on the job.'

'I knew the force was having to cut back, but employing a six-year-old?'

Savage smiled and then pulled the hood on her waterproof up and zipped the front up tight. A crepuscular glow from behind the low Cornish hills was all that remained of the day and the temperature was dropping fast. There was a breeze coming from the west and the wind raised a myriad of cat's paws which danced this way and that on top of the swell. Out in the Sound a naval auxiliary vessel was tied up to one of the huge buoys and its deck lamps glowed orange, becoming ever brighter as night fell.

'At this rate we will be anchoring in the dark,' Frey said, a little smile forming on his lips.

Savage knocked the throttle lever forward, adding a knot to their speed and the boat ploughed on through the now-inky sea.

By the time they reached Cawsand Bay the lights in the village were bright, their reflections sparkling in the water. At least the wind had died now they were in the shelter of the Rame Peninsula. One other yacht lay tucked away close to the wooded hillside and in the centre of the bay sat a large white motorboat surrounded by a strange blue glow from a number of underwater lights.

'That must be her,' Frey said. 'Not exactly keeping a low profile are they? Quite a sight. Probably cost more than your boat is worth just to fill her fuel tanks.'

'Call me a snob, but I know which I'd rather be on,' Savage said.

'All that white leather not your thing then?' Frey laughed and moved out of the cockpit and up to the bow and began to ready the anchor. Savage circled the boat and picked out a suitable spot. A couple of bursts of throttle in astern slowed and then stopped the boat. Frey dropped the anchor and Savage gave the engine some more power in astern until they began to glide backwards. The anchor chain rattled out and after they had backed down enough Frey snubbed the anchor and Savage put some more power on to dig it in. The chain stretched out in front of the boat, bar taut, and Frey indicated the anchor was holding. Savage cut the engine.

Silence.

A car in a lane somewhere revving up a hill. A dog barking. The rhythmic sound of the swell surging onto the beach.

'OK, so what do we do now?' Frey had come aft.

'We do what couples do when anchored in a remote spot.' Savage smiled as Frey raised his eyebrows. 'Put the curry on and get out our image intensifiers.'

Budgeon stared down at the headline on the front page of the paper.

Police Fear Body May Be Missing Officer.

Today's news, already out of date.

'They were never going to fall for it, Ricky,' Stuey said. 'Thick they may be, but they're not idiots.'

'And I am, is that what you mean?' Budgeon scrunched the paper and threw it across the workshop. 'We were so close to getting Kenny. If he hadn't sped off in that boat of his he'd have been barbecued like Dowdney. I've had it, Stuey, fucking had it.'

'I was just saying, that's all.'

'Well quit. In fact fuck off out of here before I lose my rag and thump you.'

'Careful, Ricky. You wouldn't want to do that.'

For a moment Stuey rose up. He was lanky, but he could move fast. Budgeon thought he'd probably be able to take the lad, but it wasn't worth the risk.

'Sorry.' Budgeon held his hands up in surrender. 'The head, Stuey. Getting to me. The pain.'

'Well take some fucking aspirin.' Stuey turned and stomped out of the workshop, cursing as he went.

Budgeon clenched his fists, gritted his teeth and sucked in air, feeling the chill of the night cool his insides and calm him. He relaxed. Stuey was right. The police were never going to think Dowdney's corpse was Riley. Not with DNA and all that. But the diversion had been worth a try and the fact that the body had been discovered at Tamar Yachts would only serve to increase Fallon's unease. He'd have realised he'd escaped the same fate through sheer luck.

When he'd blown the top half of Dowdney's head away, Budgeon had felt a few seconds blissful release, the like of which he hadn't felt when he'd killed Owers or Redmond. Those two men had been incidental to him, but Dowdney had blabbed to the police and he'd screwed Lynn Towner too. Just like Fallon had.

Budgeon walked across to the workbench and began gathering some things together. His hands shook as he piled tools into a bag. He picked up a hammer and held it for a second, his hand clenched hard around the handle.

Jackman, Fallon, Riley.

The feeling when they were all gone would be heaven. The nirvana he'd long been seeking. And Riley was only a few metres away. Ten steps across the yard. How easy it would be to go to him now. Bring the hammer down on the man's kneecaps. Smash his fingers. Swing the lump of metal into his skull over and over again until his brain was nothing but mush.

Budgeon raised the hammer high into the air and looked at his arm shaking above him. The lump end glinted in the light from the overhead tubes and a beam flashed across his eyes like a laser. The effect was instant and he raised his other arm to cover his face as he felt the rage boil and bubble inside. He let out a roar of pain. The cop had to die and right now seemed like a good time. He lowered the hammer, placed it on the workbench and let his eyes scan the rows of chisels, the screwdrivers, the billhook, an axe, a hacksaw. So many ways to kill . . .

No. Not yet.

He had to keep Riley and Kemp alive in case things went wrong. Collateral. Budgeon lowered the hammer and placed it in the bag. Jackman and Fallon needed to come first. And tomorrow he'd go after them.

The curry had come from a couple of tins and was supplemented by some sachets of dried rice and vegetables which looked as if they had been packed for astronauts. Despite appearances the meal had tasted delicious, helped by the cold chill that had descended on the bay.

Now they sat in the dark, Savage and Stephens cradling mugs of tea while Frey pressed his night-vision binoculars against the glass of a porthole. The slight current in the bay caused the boat to swing around on its anchor and every so often Frey had to move from the port side of the yacht to starboard or vice versa in order to get a good view of the motorboat.

At eleven-thirty he alerted them to the fact that a dinghy had launched from the beach and was heading for the motorboat. The whine of the outboard echoed off the waterside buildings and cut through the silence in the bay.

'Who's onboard?' Savage said.

'Two people. Well wrapped up. Can't see if it is Fallon. Now they are circling their boat. Checking her out.'

'No worries,' Savage said. 'It is the sort of thing I might do.'

'They're not boarding,' Frey said. 'One of them just tapped the side of the boat and now the dinghy is coming this way.'

'Do you think we should simulate sex?' Stephens said, a chortle piercing the gloom.

'They are definitely heading for our boat.'

'Call the lads?' Stephens spoke again, serious this time.

'No,' Frey said. 'We need to sit tight. Hang on, someone is moving about on the . . . what the fuck?'

320

Frey jerked back from the port as a flash shone through the glass, which for a moment lit up the interior of the boat with an eerie glow.

'Parachute flare,' Frey said, moving towards the companionway steps. A second later the VHF radio in the cabin crackled, a woman's voice coming from the speaker, the transmission overloaded and distorted.

Mayday, Mayday, Mayday. This is motor yacht Sea Mist, Sea Mist, Sea Mist. Mayday, Sea Mist. We are in the centre of Cawsand Bay. We are taking on water and sinking. We—

The call ended before the mayday had been completed.

Savage followed Frey up into the cockpit. The parachute flare floated high above them, the burning phosphorus illuminating everything with a harsh, orange light.

'Anchor!' Savage yelled, but Frey was already running forward. 'Let all the chain out and release the end. We haven't got time to bring the whole lot in.' She turned the key in the ignition and felt the little engine chug into life beneath her feet.

Frey released the locking mechanism and the chain rattled out, coming up with a snatch when it was all gone. He bent down and cut the rope securing the bitter end of the chain to a ring in the anchor locker. The chain gave a final rattle as the end slid overboard.

Savage could hear Stephens down in the cabin calling in the police RIB on his own radio. At the same time the VHF squawked out again. This time the message was from Brixham coastguard replying to the distress call. Sea Mist didn't answer. Savage slipped the throttle lever forward, spun the wheel and the yacht surged into the turn, swinging round to point towards the motorboat.

'She's listing,' Frey shouted. 'Look!'

Sure enough the fifty-foot hulk was down at the bow and

321

leaning hard over on her port side, indicating a mass of water somewhere in the hull.

They were already approaching the boat and now Savage had the job of slowing her own craft and manoeuvring alongside. She weighed up the options. She didn't fancy approaching on the port side of the boat since the whole thing might roll down on them. The starboard side would offer only an expanse of hull, way higher than the gunwale of her boat. She decided to come across the stern where a bathing platform offered a chance to get aboard. As they came alongside she shoved the throttle back hard into reverse. The boat slowed and touched the motorboat. Frey leapt from the yacht and landed on the sloping surface of the bathing platform, scrabbling to grab a cleat. Savage pushed the throttle to neutral and yelled at Stephens to take the helm. Then she clambered onto the cockpit seating and jumped across.

'I won't tell Pete,' Frey said, holding out a hand to steady her.

'What?'

'That you abandoned your vessel.'

Savage turned and saw her yacht gliding away into the darkness, Stephens at the wheel. Frey clambered across the teak deck to the steps which led up to the boat proper and Savage followed. The boat was leaning at an angle of nearly forty-five degrees, but didn't seem to be going over any more and since she was anchored there was no motion. They edged over the sloping aft deck to the glass doors which led into the saloon.

'Anyone onboard?' Frey shouted through the open door before he turned to Savage. 'I don't fancy going inside. Once the water gets to one of those open hatches on the foredeck she'll go down in seconds.'

Savage listened at the door. A splashing sound came from outside the boat and a machinery whine from somewhere deep down inside; that would be the automatic bilge pumps struggling to cope with the influx of water. Apart from the pump, there was nothing. And yet . . .

'Somebody sent the Mayday, where the hell are they?' She cocked her head. Down below something crashed over. Then there was another noise. Bang, bang, bang. A muffled voice calling out.

'Oh my God, somebody *is* onboard.' Savage began to move into the saloon but Frey blocked her.

'No, Charlotte. This is my job.' He began to unfasten his life-jacket.

'What are you doing?'

'Don't want it auto-inflating if I am down below. It might trap me.'

Frey dropped the life-jacket and scrambled into the saloon. Savage moved back and crossed to the starboard side of the boat – the side that was uppermost – and began to edge along the side deck towards the bow to find out if she could close the hatches on the foredeck. She scrambled past the smoked glass windows until she reached the expanse of white deck at the bow. Right next to her feet was the first hatch, a small one only open a hand's breadth. She pushed on the smoked perspex, banging the hatch shut. In the centre of the deck a larger opening lay well out of reach. Although the deck had an anti-slip surface it wouldn't help much when tilted at such an extreme angle. She searched around for a piece of rope but everything had been stowed away. Shit! The black water was creeping ever higher. Only a couple more feet and the sea would reach the hatch and the boat would downflood and sink like a stone.

She took a breath, let go of the stainless steel rail and slid down to the hatch using her feet to brace herself when she reached it. She had started to push the hatch shut when she heard the banging again, clearer this time. There was someone in the cabin below!

She grabbed the hatch, wrenched it up and stuck her head down. A splintering sound came from somewhere to her right and a beam of light flashed round the cabin. Frey stumbled through the forepeak door, his torch picking out a young woman in Musto waterproofs. The list of the boat had tumbled her to the lower side of the cabin where she lay amid a jumble of duvet, pillows and a mess of blonde hair.

Vanessa Liston.

'Jesus!' Frey crawled across the cabin to the girl, stretching his arms out to reach for her. The girl tried to back away from him.

'It's OK, Vanessa,' Savage shouted from above. 'Police!'

'Come on,' Frey said, yelling at the girl and pointing to the cabin door.

'No time!' Savage shouted. The water had reached the edge of the hatch and was beginning to cascade into the cabin. 'Pass her up.'

Frey grabbed Vanessa around the waist and staggered to his feet, trying to balance in the lopsided cabin. He hefted the girl up through the hatch and Savage grabbed her under the arms, leaning backwards and pulling her out. The two of them rolled away from the hatch and into the sea.

'Oh God!' Savage cried out as the shock of the cold water hit her and then came a 'bang-whumph' from her life jacket as the CO_2 canister went off. The life jacket inflated and rolled her onto her back and for a moment she struggled to hold Vanessa round the waist. Then she had her and she pushed off from the boat using her feet. The sea was pouring in through the hatch now, the boat lying very low in the water.

Behind her, perhaps thirty metres away, the white hull of her own boat materialised out of the gloom like some sort of ghost ship. Stephens was circling, trying to bring the yacht nearer to pick up Savage and the girl. Then Stephens pointed away to the east where a low rumble began to grow in intensity. In the distance, across the black sea, a blinding light pierced the night. D Section's RIB.

Savage looked back at the motorboat. A horrible sound came from the hatch as the opening went below the surface and a vortex of water slurped around the escaping air.

'She's going down!' She shouted at Stephens to keep clear and kicked out to move even further away from the sinking boat. 'Nigel!'

There was no sign of Frey as the smoked glass of the saloon slid into the black water. The bridge deck with its array of aerials and the big white radar dome was last to go, leaving nothing but a scattering of blue and white cockpit cushions floating free amidst a slick of oil.

The roar of the RIB's engine filled Savage's ears and the boat's searchlight swept across the scene. Stephens was shouting into his radio, directing the RIB. And then, twenty metres away on the other side of where the boat had been, the beam from the searchlight picked out a cockpit cushion which bobbed low in the water, as an arm emerged from the sea and wrapped itself around it.

When the boat had gone down they'd aimed the dinghy for the shore and beached on some rocks. Jackman had slipped in the surf and cut his knee, his clothes were soaking, his nerves shot. As they clambered up the rocks into the woods surrounding the bay Fallon was laughing.

'Rock and roll, hey, mate? Rock and fucking roll.'

'What on earth are you on, Kenny?' Jackman collapsed in the dark beyond the tree line. 'You're a half a million down on the boat, God knows how much down on the sweet stuff, and the bay is swarming with the bloody Royal Navy.'

'We've sold 'em one, Alec. You, me and Ness. Not to mention that bitch cop. Played a blinder. Hole in one, last-minute winner, taken the tit-heads on the final straight. Not being immodest, but sinking the boat was absolute genius.'

'Sinking the boat?' Jackman shook his head. Now he knew for sure Fallon was crazy. 'I don't see how this result is a victory. There's a bundle of cocaine worth several million pounds floating somewhere beyond Edison Rocks. It's either going to sink or get washed up on some beach where an honest citizen is going to find the stuff and call it in.'

'Not going to happen.'

'You're off your fucking head.' Jackman struggled to his feet, aware of a searchlight sweeping the shore below them. 'Let's get out of here.'

'You're right about that. The last bit. We'll walk down into Cawsand and find some old banger I can TWOC. Interesting to see if I've still got the knack.'

'Interesting? If the police catch us we are both going away for a long time. Me especially. As soon as they find the drugs we've had it. We may as well come clean and try to plead mitigating circumstances.'

'What?' Fallon's face loomed closer in the dark, his hands grabbing Jackman by the shoulders and spinning him round. 'You going to 'fess? Grass Kenny up? You do and you're out of here. Off this planet. Understand?'

'Easy, Kenny.' Jackman lifted Fallon's hands away and started walking along the track. 'I'm just being realistic.

326

When they get their hands on the cocaine they'll be able to join the dots. Even this lot of jokers can do that.'

'As I said before, that's not going to happen.'

'Why not?'

'Simple,' Fallon said, waving an arm back down to the sea. 'Because there is nothing out there. The powder's here already. Took a road trip from Rotterdam to Esbjerg.'

'Where the hell is Esbjerg?'

'Denmark. From there across to Harwich and along the motorway. One time they'd have been checking for hardcore videos on that ferry route. Now they don't bother much about anything. A risk, sure, but worth it.'

'What the fuck was all this about then? Your little jaunt to Cawsand has ended with us nearly getting arrested.'

'You think I was going to let the drugs come in the same way after Redmond got hit? Either Budgeon got the full details from him or the pigs will have wised up to what's going on. I figured it was time for a change of plan.'

'So?'

'Listen, Alec.' Fallon tapped his head with a finger. 'We had to get a bit cute. There's strategy and there's tactics. Strategy has remained the same. The tactics just got a bit diversionary, the diversionary part being the sinking of the boat. Seems to have worked, doesn't it?'

They'd reached a break in the trees now and could see the bay. The Plymouth lifeboat sat in the centre, along with a police RIB alongside a small yacht. Farther away in the deeper water a naval cutter inched forwards, a bright search-light sweeping the coastline.

'I'm not sure about that,' Jackman said. 'And anyway, how does this sort Budgeon?'

'Nothing for him either. Not now. He'll catch the scent of what's happening and decide he is better off out of it.

327

He's not going to risk getting caught just to have a pop at us.'

'What about Ness? She's only a girl, she could have been drowned in that stunt.'

'Only a girl? You know, Alec, that's exactly what I thought until you started convincing me she was all grown up. Now quit moaning and let's get the hell out of here.'

Chapter Twenty-Nine

In the end the RNLI had sent a lifeboat, the Navy a Coastguard cutter, and a helicopter had been scrambled to search for the men in the dinghy. The dinghy had been found floating empty off Rame Head, but there was no sign of the men. The sea hadn't been rough, but in January the temperature was low enough to mean they wouldn't have survived long if they'd gone overboard. Savage had taken her yacht back to the marina with Stephens, Frey had returned with his men on the RIB, and Vanessa Liston had gone to the lifeboat station and in the confusion ended up being moved from there to the custody centre at Charles Cross.

It was from the custody centre that Calter rang Savage at six-thirty the next morning to tell her the girl was saying nothing and was demanding to leave forthwith. Savage told Calter to stop her from leaving and then she rolled over and tried to get back to sleep.

Three hours later she turned up at Major Crimes to find Calter arguing with Enders. The only way Calter had been able to prevent Vanessa Liston from doing a runner was to arrest her on a charge of theft and criminal damage. Enders seemed to be finding the whole thing hilarious.

'Correct me if I am wrong, ma'am,' Enders said, laughing, 'but I thought we were hoping to get her on our side.'

'Arresting her was the only thing I could think of,' Calter said. 'I didn't know the full facts of the situation since I had been dragged from my bed at six o'clock.'

'Children!' Savage said. 'Calm down. I'm sorry, Jane. You were put in an invidious position, which was partly my fault. The scene became confused very quickly and there were so many people and agencies involved that we lost track of Vanessa. To be honest, by the time I got my boat back to the marina I was suffering from mild hypothermia. Bob Stephens took me home and I collapsed into bed. Pete made me a cocoa but one sip was enough to send me to sleep.'

'Not to worry, ma'am. Sorry I boobed.'

'You did fine. Now, I want the girl brought from the custody centre to Crownhill. We'll conduct the interview in a more informal setting and see if we can't get back into her good books.'

'Ha!' Enders said. 'She was trapped on the boat, nearly drowns and is then arrested. This I have to see!'

'No, I've got a job for you.' Savage glanced out of the window at the drizzle. 'You are going to take a trip around the Rame Peninsula. I want to find out what happened to the two guys in the dinghy and the best way to do that is to knock on a few doors and find out if somebody heard something. Rame is a quiet part of the world, so a car coming down a lane late at night would be remembered. Off you go.'

'Wrap up warm,' Calter said and blew him a kiss as Enders groaned and loped off.

By the time Vanessa Liston had been fetched from the

main station and brought to Major Crimes things hadn't become much clearer. Kenny Fallon's solicitor had called the police to say he'd heard some of Mr Fallon's property had been recovered and then subsequently damaged by the police. A claim for damages was being drawn up and would be with them later.

Hardin, luckily, was absent due to the visit of the Chief Constable. He was accompanying him on various duties around the city so he'd not had a chance to comment on the debacle.

Savage elected to interview the girl in her office, thinking an informal setting would work best. Calter brought her in.

'I suppose I ought to thank you,' Vanessa said, running her fingers through her matted blonde hair. 'For last night.'

'Yes, but Inspector Nigel Frey is the one you really need to thank.' Savage poured a cup of coffee and pushed a tray of cherry bakewells across at the girl. 'He risked his life to get you out of there.'

'Thanks. Mr Kipling. My favourite.' Vanessa took a cake and mumbled through crumbling pastry and white icing. 'I mean thanks for what you did, not the cake.'

'That's OK,' Savage said, laughing. 'It's our job. Providing cakes too.'

Vanessa smiled and then carried on eating before taking a slurp of coffee. 'It was so cold in the water last night. When they took me to the lifeboat place they had to put a fan heater on me to stop the shivering.'

'You're OK now. So take your time and tell me what happened. From the top.'

'Everything?' Vanessa reached out again and took the cake.

'Yes.'

'Only . . .' The girl moved the cake to her mouth and then

331

paused. She turned to look at Calter and then back at Savage. 'Some of it's private. I'd prefer to speak to you alone.'

Savage waved at Calter to leave and the DC got up and left the room, glancing back over her shoulder as she closed the door, scepticism written all over her face.

'So?' Savage said.

'I messaged you, didn't I? But you never turned up. They'd been to the pub in Cawsand and when I saw them coming back I didn't know what the fuck to do so I pulled a hose off one of the seacocks and opened it. Then I sent a Mayday, only I didn't realise how fast the water was coming in so I abandoned the message halfway through.'

'What were you doing in the cabin?'

'Looking for my mobile to try and phone you.' Vanessa laughed. 'As if that bloody mattered. Something must have fallen against the door when the boat lurched over and I couldn't get it open.'

'OK. Let's go back a bit. Why did you sink the boat?'

'You know why.'

'I don't, Vanessa. You'll need to explain it to me.'

'Because of Kenny Fallon and Alec Jackman. You were supposed to bloody catch them. You told me Fallon killed my dad. That's why I did it. For my mum too. You know, the drugs and everything.'

'Vanessa, I didn't say they killed your dad. I said they were bad people.'

'You said I had to help you undercover, sort of like Jason Bourne. You told me you'd arrest them. But you never arrived, so I had to sink the boat to stop them getting away.'

'Shit, I . . .' Savage shook her head. 'And the pickup?'

'What pickup?'

'You were there to pilot the boat out into the Channel, weren't you? Fallon and Jackman know nothing about boats, but you do. You were going to take them offshore so they could find a package dropped overboard from a ship.'

'Huh?'

'Look, Vanessa, don't muck around. You are in serious trouble. Just tell me the truth. Fallon asked you to send the message to me earlier. This whole lark was some sort of set-up wasn't it?'

'You know what? I feel bad about this because I like you and well . . . you did rescue me.'

'Then please tell me truthfully what happened tonight. What was *supposed* to happen tonight.'

'I've no idea what you're talking about, but I've got a message from Kenny. He said you were his friend and were looking out for him. That you'd make sure whatever story I told you would be believed.' Vanessa took another bite of the cake and smiled. 'That's true, isn't it?'

Jackman had arrived home in the small hours. He climbed out of his wet clothes and collapsed into bed alongside his wife. Slept in the next morning. Knackered.

He woke to a noise from downstairs. The dog howling, a cry Jackman sometimes heard in the night when the animal wanted to go outside. He reached out an arm for Gill, realising as he found the bed empty that she'd have long gone. Off to a friend, no doubt. Or a spot of retail therapy followed by a session at a nail bar. When your brother had died a violent death, getting your nails done by a brainless girl who'd be rabbiting on about the latest *X Factor* boy band would be all you'd need to cheer you up.

Jackman shook his head and wished he was at the flat with Vanessa. Imagined her body beneath him. Then he rolled over and got out of bed, padded naked out of the room and went to find the dog. If the thing had shat on the carpet he'd give it a right bollocking. Not that the task would be easy: Maxi was fifty kilograms of Pyrenean Mountain dog. The type of animal nobody would argue with. Not if they knew what was good for them. The dog had taken down a burglar once, mauling the young lad in the kitchen. Jackman had spent five minutes persuading the dog to let go of the boy's leg.

When he reached the top of the stairs and peered down he saw that the fucker *had* made a mess. There was something down on the half landing, something red-brown.

Bugger. Gill would go apeshit. New nails or not.

Still naked, Jackman descended, stopping a couple of stairs above the landing. A smear of red swirled across the white carpet to a pile of something like sausages.

Intestines.

Jackman frowned, wondering if the dog had somehow got hold of a rabbit or a cat.

'Stuey's got a way with a knife. But you'd remember that, of course.'

A squat man with a fat round head beamed up from the floor below. The smile revealed a gold tooth front centre. He pointed down to a massive bundle of fur lying at his feet. A puddle of red oozed across the parquet and around the man's feet.

'Ricky, no!' Jackman stepped back and then slipped over, scrabbling on the stairs before managing to get to his feet and run up them, to where a tall, thin man with a face which had the complexion of fresh feta cheese stood on the top landing.

Jackman looked down to his stomach where the silver of a blade flashed, a tiny nick drawing a globule of blood. The blade moved down and caressed the top of his groin, the tip twisting in among his pubic hair.

'He's got some nice tackle, Ricky. Tasty. Look good on a plate with a couple of tatties.'

'Not now, Stuey,' Budgeon said, wiping the sole of his foot on the dog and picking up an Adidas holdall at his feet. 'We don't want Alec to get the wrong idea. We're all friends now. No bad feelings.'

'Look, Ricky,' Jackman said. 'Back then it was Kenny's idea. He set you up. You know that. I was against it, but Kenny insisted, wouldn't listen to reason.'

'Yeah, sure, Mr Sneaky Sneak.' Budgeon came up the stairs and looked at Chaffe. 'Get him in the bedroom, Stuart. We'll sort it out in there.'

Chaffe gestured with the knife, making a flicking motion. Jackman shrugged and walked down the corridor to the master bedroom. When he got there he reached out for his dressing gown which lay on a chair.

'No need for that,' Chaffe said. 'Like Ricky said, we're all friends now. No need to cover up.'

'Lie on the bed,' Budgeon said, dropping the holdall down and unzipping it. He took something from the bag and threw it across to Chaffe. 'Para cord, Stuey. Lovely bit of kit. Should do to keep Alec still while we have a little talk.'

Chaffe pushed Jackman towards the bed, a final shove sending him sprawling on top of the duvet. Then Chaffe was unwinding the cord and wrapping some of it round Jackman's legs, pulling it tight and fastening it somewhere beneath the bedframe.

'Arms now, Stuey,' Budgeon said. 'One each side.'

Chaffe pulled off a length of cord and flicked the knife a couple of times. He pointed the knife at Jackman and made him lie flat. Then he tied a loop around each wrist, binding tight and yanking Jackman's arms in turn so that one was tied to each side at the head of the bed.

Budgeon took a couple of things from the bag and they clumped to the floor. He removed his leather jacket and put it on a chair. Faded tattoos rippled on exposed biceps, and a grubby white t-shirt strained over a muscled torso.

'Now then, Alec.' Budgeon's squat face sneered as he came close, looking as if it had been distorted by a funfair mirror. 'We just need the answer to a simple question. There's no phone-a-friend, no fifty-fifty, so think carefully before you reply.'

'Ricky, I told you—'

'Shut it. Just listen.' Budgeon moved away again and bent over something on the floor as he spoke. 'Where are the drugs, Alec?'

'Don't you watch the news? The boat sank. We never got to make the pickup. They're in the middle of the English Channel.'

'Wrong answer.'

'Ricky! Didn't you hear me? We didn't get the drugs. Honest.'

'Honest?' Budgeon laughed. 'The same type of honest that sent me up to Bristol to get a bullet in my head? I know Kenny, he ain't going to leave several million quids' worth of charlie to the seagulls. The whole thing was a ploy. Kenny's little joke to fool the cops.'

'No, Rick, it's the truth.'

'Ricky?' Chaffe said, waving the knife and grinning. 'Can I have a go at his meat and two veg now?'

'No,' Budgeon said. 'Go downstairs and keep watch. Things might be about to get a little noisy up here.'

'Fuck it!' Chaffe spat at Jackman and then stomped out of the room.

Budgeon was rustling inside a large plastic bag, pulling something out, placing it on the dressing table and then fiddling with some packaging. Then he began to whistle a flat, tuneless song that Jackman vaguely recognised.

'Orange, Alec, orange.'

'Sorry?'

'Companies like the colour orange.' The packaging was orange. An orange cardboard box with a picture on the front, the product obscured by a big yellow sales sticker promising fifty per cent off. 'Sainsbury's, Orange phones, easyJet, B&Q, Nickelodeon. Hell, I saw an advert for Amazon the other day. Do you have any idea what colour their logo is?'

'No.' Jackman tilted his head, trying to make out what Budgeon was unpacking from the box. Something with a cable and a plug.

'Fucking orange!' Budgeon undid a couple of ties and discarded a piece of cardboard.

The tuneless whistling had become more melodic. Jackman tried to place it. Some piece of music from a film he'd seen. An old film with gangsters and a robbery gone wrong. What the hell was the movie called?

'Anyway, as long as something works I don't give a shit what the colour is. Colours are for women and poofs. Know what I am saying?' The grin again as Budgeon pulled out an extension lead from the holdall and began to uncoil it, plugging one end into a socket near the dressing table and bringing the other end over to the bed. The whistle had gained in intensity, the tune becoming more familiar.

'What are you . . . doing?' Jackman squirmed, felt his bowels loosen, a piece of crap slip out, the excrement moving beneath him as he struggled. He shivered as some weird spasm went up through his body, ending with a quiver of his lips.

'OK, one more time. I'll say the words slowly so you can understand. Where . . . are . . . the . . . drugs?'

'I . . .' Jackman closed his eyes for a moment. Heard Budgeon whistle again. The tune, he had the name now: 'Stuck in the Middle with You'. The film: *Reservoir Dogs*. Jesus! Jackman opened his eyes and screamed. 'Esbjerg! Esbjerg! That's where the drugs have gone.'

'Where the hell is that then?'

'Sweden. Norway. Fuck, I don't know, but they're coming into Harwich and then down here.'

'Where?'

'I don't know. Kenny never told me. One of his lock-ups or rental properties probably. You're right, the whole boat thing was a set-up to fool you and the pigs.'

'You sure?'

'Yes!' Warmth spread across Jackman's stomach and the top of his thighs as his bladder lost control.

'Good boy. You know what?' Budgeon stared down at the trickle of urine which had accumulated in Jackman's belly button. 'I believe you, Alec, I really do.'

'Then for God's sake, please let me go!' Jackman struggled against his bonds, but his movement only served to cut the cord deeper into his wrist and ankles.

'No can do, Alec. Not after what happened back then. Took one in the head, didn't I? Been killing me ever since. Doing you is the best form of pain relief I've got.'

'Ricky, please, I—'

'Now back to what I was saying about colours. It's not only the box, is it? Look, they even made the product orange too.' Budgeon plugged something into the roving socket and held up the item, all orange plastic and flashing metal. Next came a click, a deafening high-pitched whine and the blur of the spinning disc. 'Works though, doesn't it?'

Jackman screamed and then began to blubber and beg, his eyes unable to focus on anything but the words on the side of the tool. Budgeon followed his gaze and smiled.

'Black and fucking Decker. Bloody awesome piece of kit, hey lad?'

Chapter Thirty

Savage spent most of Saturday morning trying to concoct a statement out of the story Vanessa Liston had spun her. The best she could come up with was something along the lines of what Vanessa had already told her: the girl had got confused and blamed Fallon – as the owner of Tamar Yachts – for her father's death. After the earlier interview with Savage she'd mistakenly believed she was helping the police in an official capacity. When Fallon and Jackman asked her to come out on the boat she'd complied, thinking there was something dodgy going on. When she saw them returning to the boat she deliberately sank it, issuing the Mayday to alert the authorities.

Savage sat at her desk and stared at the words on the screen. God knows what Hardin was going to make of the account. She fired off an email summary and then decided to get off home before Hardin picked up the message. In the end she only got as far as the car park. She thought about ignoring the desk sergeant's shout as she opened the door to her car, but then wheeled round to face the music.

'Seymour Drive, Mannamead, ma'am,' he shouted across.

'The bloody deputy leader of the council's been attacked. All hell apparently.'

Jackman.

Savage jumped in her car and headed into town, battling the Saturday traffic. It was thirty minutes before she reached the wide, tree-lined streets of Mannamead. As she turned into Seymour Drive she spotted Dan Phillips and his photographer, and beyond them were three patrol cars, two CSI vans and several other vehicles disgorging various officers. Phillips raised a fist at her as she drove past, but he wore a big smile and as the photographer swung his camera to take a shot of Savage getting out of her car the reporter put a hand out and pushed the lens down.

Savage suited up and went along the street to the front of Jackman's house. A sweep of tarmac led in from a pair of wrought-iron gates and several of Layton's CSIs, dressed in their coveralls, were inspecting the surrounding lawn and flowerbeds. The house itself was a grand Edwardian affair which sat on a good-sized plot. She hesitated for a moment at the gates as she spotted a 'Beware of the Dog' sign on one of the brick gateposts.

'It's alright,' Layton said, emerging from the front door and shouting across. 'The dog is inside and it is very much dead.'

'How did it die?'

'Piece of steak covered in what I guess might be rat poison. The meat was posted through the letterbox. Dog went for the steak, choked on the poison, killer gained entry and slit the dog's throat and then . . .' Layton pointed at the driveway. 'We've done that so you can come in.'

Savage padded across the drive and approached the door.

'Forced entry?'

'Yes.' Layton pointed to splintering around the Yale lock. 'Sledgehammer. A single blow would have been enough if the deadlocks and bolts weren't on. Which they weren't. Jackman and his wife probably didn't think they were necessary. The dog, see? Anyone trying to make it into the house would think twice when confronted.'

'Big was it?'

'Massive.' Layton smiled. 'Not like that thing you were scared of on Durnford Street. This thing was Baskerville territory.'

'Thanks, John. I'm going to have nightmares now.'

'Don't worry, you won't be thinking of the dog once you've seen inside.'

Layton was right.

The animal's body lay at the foot of the stairs, a line of Layton's stepping plates forging through a lake of red as if they were stones crossing the corner of a pond.

Up in the master bedroom the crimson spray across the wall wasn't part of the interior design. The coloured stain was more blood. A line ran down the wall and over the padded headboard. On the king-sized divan a pool had soaked into the duvet and cascaded over the edge of the bed onto the carpet. A mini Niagara. More stepping plates led into the room and a CSI stood on a pair next to the bed. She dipped a pair of tweezers into the coagulated liquid and pulled out a piece of white, dropping it into a plastic container.

'See what I mean?' Layton stood behind Savage. 'The blood would have hosed out for the first few seconds as Jackman flung his arm around. His blood pressure would have dropped fast though and since he was tied up he couldn't do much to stem the flow. He had the sense to place his arm underneath his body and that helped.'

'Jesus.'

'Luckily the ambulance arrived within fifteen minutes.'

'How the hell did he call it?'

'Didn't. A neighbour heard screaming, saw an unknown vehicle outside – some kind of sports car she reckoned – noted the busted door and called us. After making the call she came back. Two guys were coming out of the house and when they saw the neighbour they just got into the car and drove off. The neighbour went inside and made another triple nine for an ambulance from the bedside phone while Jackman was screaming. She put a tourniquet around Jackman's arm. Probably saved his life. Cool lady.'

'What happened to Jackman's hand?'

'Beats me. The paramedics searched for a couple of minutes but Jackman was in a serious way so they didn't hang around.' Layton reached up, tipped the top of his Tilley hat and smiled. 'If I come across a stray limb I'll let you know.'

'And the weapon?'

'Hard to say what it was.' Layton nodded at the CSI. 'There are some shards of bone in amongst the blood and some specks of bone dust so I reckon the weapon was a powered cutting device like with Owers. Let's hope they took some pictures up at the hospital before they cleaned him up.'

'OK, I've seen enough.' More than enough, she thought. The scene was an abomination, the blood on the bed a visceral reminder of the terror Jackman had gone through. Layton had been right, she wouldn't be thinking about the dog as she fell asleep tonight. Correction: *if* she fell asleep.

Savage left Jackman's place by early afternoon. Door-to-door enquiries hadn't produced much, other than a confirmation of the make of car which had sat on the drive for half-an-hour while Jackman had undergone some DIY surgery courtesy of Ricky Budgeon.

'A Porsche?' Calter said as the two of them drove westwards

over the Tamar Bridge on their way to visit Fallon again. 'Have we got an index?'

They hadn't. While several witnesses had recalled the car, only one had remembered anything to do with the registration number.

'A white rear plate,' Savage said. 'Which means a foreign vehicle. I'm thinking Spanish.'

'Works for me, ma'am. Budgeon could have bought the car in Spain and come over on the Santander ferry. You think the ANPR cameras can deal with a foreign index?'

'I guess, but since we don't know what it is they're not going to be much help. There're enough foreign cars around that just looking for any non-UK reg is going to involve an awful lot of screen time. And time is what we don't have.'

Calter nodded and turned to look out at the view from the span. Just to the south was Brunel's innovative railway bridge, to the north the Tamar Valley where a line of trot moorings hugged the western bank of the river. Somewhere beyond them stood Fallon's house, but in the drizzle and murk Savage couldn't make out which one it was.

Five minutes later and they turned into Fallon's place, Calter commenting on the statues at the side of the drive.

'Money and power, but not much style or class,' she said.

'That's Kenny Fallon for you, but when you possess the first two you don't have to bother about the others do you?'

'Wouldn't know, ma'am. Never had much of any of them.'

The house lights were blazing and as they got out of the car Savage looked around. A grey mist seemed to be slithering up from the river, almost as if the mudflats of the estuary had become ethereal. A figure moved in the shadows at the top of the stairs to the accommodation over the garage: Kev the driver, keeping an eye on things. The other one would be around somewhere too and Savage reckoned they'd be tooled up. Not knuckle dusters or a billiard ball in a sock; they'd be armed. She raised an arm and Kev acknowledged her and then disappeared back into the flat.

Calter rang the bell and a minute later the door swung wide, Fallon standing silhouetted in the glare from within.

'Cagney and Lacey this time, is it?' Fallon uttered something like a laugh and then shook his head, his expression turning downcast in an instant. 'You'd better come in. The wife's in the living room with a couple of chums so we'll use the kitchen again if you don't mind.'

Fallon trudged to the back of the house. This time the dog didn't even bother to open its eyes to acknowledge them.

'Alec Jackman,' Savage said once they were in the kitchen. 'Your mate on the council. The guy you took on your little jaunt last night. I guess you already know what happened?'

'Alec let me down.' Fallon's eyes flicked over to the door, to the sound of laughter which floated in from the hallway. 'Couldn't deal with the pressure.'

'It wasn't pressure he had to deal with. It was Ricky Budgeon and his mate, Stuart Chaffe, armed with a knife and an angle grinder. They broke in, killed the dog and then did a spot of redecorating in the bedroom. Jackman is fortunate to be alive.'

'Jesus!' Fallon thumped the top of the coffee machine and let out a sound almost like a growl. Then he reached up and retrieved a glass from a rack over the breakfast bar and a bottle of gin from a cupboard. 'He's going to pay. Big time.'

'You're the one who's paying. Twenty years away and now he is back to claim what he believes is his. What you and Jackman took away from him when you set him up.'

'It was fucking business!' Fallon shouted and then shook his head, sighed and moved across to a large refrigerator, lowered his voice to a whisper. 'You don't take it personally.'

'Maybe *you* don't, but Budgeon has. What's more this bloody nonsense has affected *me* personally too. Budgeon's got one of our officers. God knows what he is going to do to him.'

'I told you I'd help.' Fallon had opened the freezer compartment and was fiddling with a tray of ice, Savage surprised to see his hands shaking. 'So far I've drawn a blank.'

'Is that all you can say? Pathetic. No wonder Budgeon thought he could breeze in here and take over.'

'What do you expect me to say? If I knew where to find Ricky I wouldn't be chatting to you now. I'd have it sorted. I've got people out on the streets all over. Every little slimeball I can find has been offered a wad of cash or a good kicking. Nobody knows a bloody thing.' Fallon put the tray of ice back into the freezer and took out a large bag which contained meat or bones for the dog. The dog opened its eyes, raised its head and got up from the bed and waddled over, sniffing the air. Fallon brought the bag over to the breakfast bar and tipped the contents onto the tiles. The bones fell out amid a cluster of ice flakes and the dog yapped several times and tried to jump up.

'Oh fuck, ma'am.' Calter. Hand to mouth, trying to control the retching.

The bag didn't contain food for the dog at all. Savage stared at the frost-covered flesh, the white bones poking out, the curled fingers, the nails painted in an alternating pattern of black, white, black, white.

'The hands, ma'am. The missing hands.' Calter gulped air, groaned, and then moved to the sink, where she vomited.

'They've been coming in the post,' Fallon said, as if talking about utility bills, all the while using a bread knife to separate the chunks of flesh into three. 'The latest one came by courier half an hour ago. Didn't quite know what to do with them.'

*   *   *

346

Savage had been at a loss to know what to do with the hands as well. The situation didn't appear in the manual. In the end she had called John Layton and he'd turned up with a cool box, a cylinder of dry ice and a smile that promised a joke or two. She told him not to even think about cracking any gags as he packed up the hands and headed off for the mortuary.

Calter cleaned herself up in one of Fallon's plush bathrooms and then sat in the car, embarrassed at having been sick, door open in case she was again. After Layton had gone, Savage went over and stood by the car.

'Sorry, I'm not usually like this, ma'am. Must have been the bang on the head. That and what happened to Lynn Towner. Her legs. Somehow all just got to me in there.'

'Don't worry about it,' Savage said. 'If there had been room alongside you at the sink I might easily have joined you.'

'What on earth was he doing with them?'

'While you were upstairs he told me he'd kept them as a reminder of what he was going to do to Budgeon when he caught up with him. World War Three, Davies said. It is beginning to look as if he was right.'

'Darius, ma'am.'

'Yes. Not looking good. I'm beginning to wonder . . .' Savage didn't want to finish the sentence and simply shook her head.

She was saved from thinking any more on the matter by a call from Hardin, the DSupt out of breath chasing the Chief Constable as he pressed the flesh in the city centre. Vanessa's verbal evidence was a complete dog's dinner and wasn't going to cut it, he said. Fallon would be able to claim the girl was a lovesick child. Distraught from the death of her father, she was living in a fantasy world. Where were the drugs? The supply boat? Evidence of some sort of plan? Jackman becoming a victim put Fallon out of reach. Political

347

expediency. Bad form to kick a man when he's down.

'Marty Kemp?' Savage said. Hardin muttered something about the bloody idiot going AWOL and told Savage to get someone else to clean up the investigative mess from last night and this morning and then concentrate on finding Riley.

The conversation over, Savage stood for a moment, trying to focus on what to do next. When her phone rang again she jumped, half-expecting it to be Jackman until she realised Jackman wasn't going to be ringing her any time soon. The call did concern another patient at the hospital though. One of Crownhill's PCs had been summoned by doctors on account of the fact that Lynn Towner, the taxi driver, had been moved from intensive care to the high-dependency unit. She was conscious and talking and demanding to know what the hell was going on. The officer said Towner had asked him whether she was being held against her will.

'Got to be joking, right?' he said to Savage. 'What's she going to do, crawl out of here?'

'Jackman?' Calter said. 'Are we going to visit him while we're up here?'

Savage concentrated on reversing the car into a space in the hospital car park and then cut the ignition.

'No,' she said, thinking even if Jackman was conscious he wasn't going to be best pleased to see them. Especially since he'd asked for police protection. 'We'll leave him for another day. I don't think there's much he can help us with. It's Lynn Towner who will have the answers.'

In the HDU, Towner occupied a bed by a window, a slit of sunlight sneaking through the blinds and shining on a 'Get Well Gran' card sat on a side table. Towner didn't look as bad as Savage had feared, with just a patch across the right-hand side of her face, a neck brace and a cast which covered her right shoulder and arm. But then again there were her legs. Or rather the remains of them. The right leg bulged with a cast and bandages, while the other lay under a white sheet which covered some sort of cage which held the material clear. According to the ward sister the left leg had been amputated above the knee and the doctors weren't holding out much hope for the other one ever being of much use either.

When Towner spotted Savage and Calter approaching she tried to turn her head, but the neck brace prevented her from moving more than an inch or two.

'You've got a nerve,' Towner's voice rasped out, something between a whisper and a Dalek, as her eyes focused on Calter. 'Look at me, look what you did!'

'Shut up,' Savage said, surprising herself with the tone of her voice. 'You're lucky we don't arrest you on a charge of attempted murder. It's a miracle you were the only one badly hurt. You could have caused a pile-up.'

'Miracle?' Towner's eyes flicked down to her bedclothes. 'They never fucking happen to me. It's always the other buggers that win in life's lottery.'

'Half the time you make your own luck. You didn't do yourself any favours by getting involved with Ricky Budgeon again. Helping him kidnap DS Riley. Why, Lynn? Or should I say Lynnette? That was your name back then, wasn't it? Back when you hooked up with Ricky.'

'I helped him as a favour. I loved him, the fucking tosser.'

'You were kidding yourself. He was never going to come back to you.'

'I did it for the old times, not for now.' Towner laughed, the sound more like the bark of an old dog. 'Now is too bloody late, isn't it? That's life for you.'

'What old times?'

'You don't understand. Your kind never do.'

'What's that supposed to mean?'

'It means you've never craved love because someone has always been there for you. Not for me. Never. Not until Ricky came along. You might not believe it but Ricky was always a gentleman, he couldn't do enough for me.'

'And Kenny Fallon and Alec Jackman didn't like that did they?'

'No.' Towner's eyes closed and she sighed. 'To them I was something to be purchased, unwrapped, used and discarded. With Ricky it wasn't like that. He loved me.'

'They all wanted you, but Budgeon was there first. So Kenny decided Ricky had to go. Next thing and Ricky is stopped on the M5 near Bristol, and when police check the spare wheel they find five kilos of cocaine in the boot. My boss would probably call that bloody good policing. I'd say it sounds too good to be true. What do you think?'

'Ricky was set up.' Towner opened her eyes and she sniffed. 'I know that now, but at the time Kenny said Ricky was unlucky, that the bust was simply one of those things.'

'Fortuitous for Kenny though, wasn't it? I mean he got to fill Ricky's shoes. At least for a time.'

'He dumped me after six months.'

'And things went downhill from there, didn't they? At least for you. Kenny Fallon is doing alright though, isn't he?'

'Bastard.'

'You and Dowdney, you're an item, aren't you?'

'It's not like that.'

'No? What is it like then? Dowdney fucks you on that grotty sofa and slips an extra twenty quid into your wage packet? True love.'

'How dare you! What right have you to speak to me—'

'Every right. You are an accessory to the kidnapping of Sergeant Riley. You've probably sentenced him to death.

You're scum, the sort of thing I might scrape off the bottom of my shoe.'

'Ma'am?' Calter put an arm out and touched Savage on the shoulder. 'Shall we all calm down a little?'

Savage ignored Calter and moved up the bed, closer to Towner.

'Budgeon comes back and he needs a favour. You and Dowdney go along with it. Make a plan to pick up Sergeant Riley and hand him over to Budgeon. What you don't realise is that your current squeeze, lover boy Dave, was the very person who passed the information to the police back when Budgeon was busted. He was the one who did Fallon's dirty work.'

'No!' Towner moved a hand up to her face, flinched as she did it. Her eyes filled with tears. 'Dave?'

'They're all the same, Lynn.'

'Not Ricky. He loved me.'

'Ricky has killed at least three people. He's a murderer.'

'Oh God!' The tears flowed now, twin rivers streaming down Towner's face. 'My life, it's gone.'

'Lynn,' Savage lowered her voice, softened the tone. 'We need your help. You did the wrong thing the other day in the taxi and you did the wrong thing when you agreed to help Ricky Budgeon. However, in view of what happened I think a judge would be lenient with you. Especially if you help us. All you need to do is tell us where we can find Ricky. Come on, Lynn. Think of your children.' Savage glanced at the card on the table. 'Think of your grandchildren.'

'Fuck off!'

'Where is Ricky Budgeon?'

'Fuck off.'

'You've met him recently, haven't you? All I'm asking is that you tell us where that was.'

'Didn't you hear me the first time?'

'Your satnav,' Savage said, calming things down again and

changing tack. 'The one you had in the taxi when you had a bump the other week. Who'd you give it to?'

'I . . .' The initial bemusement which spread on Towner's face changed to a sly grin. 'What sat nav?'

'Lynn, I know you visited Budgeon and I know he's somewhere down in Cornwall. You just need to give us a hint.'

'Go away, I'm not telling you anything.'

'It would be better if you did.' Savage moved forwards and placed a hand on Towner's right leg, pushing down ever so slightly.

'You wouldn't bloody dare!'

'Thanks to you, Budgeon has got DS Riley. He's probably going to torture him and kill him. I will do whatever I need to in order to get him back. Whatever, understand?' Savage pressed on Towner's leg and the woman squirmed and let out a gasp. Her right hand moved up to her pillow and twitched around a small black object, something like a remote control. A bleep sounded way off down the ward.

'Ma'am?' Calter flicked her head to indicate the nurse rising from the nursing station and moving towards them.

'Everything OK?' The nurse's voice floated across the ward and her pace quickened, shoes clicking on the hard floor.

'Fine.' Savage turned away from the bed and tapped Calter on the shoulder. 'We were just leaving.'

Chapter Thirty-One

Back at Crownhill and Davies was waiting for Savage in the Crime Suite.

'You and me, Savage,' Davies said. 'Hardin wants us in the briefing room for a *Sternway* meeting. Can't understand why his office wouldn't have done.'

Neither could Savage until they walked into the room to find Simon Fox, the Chief Constable, sitting behind the table alongside Hardin. Both men wore full uniform, the silver buttons gleaming beneath the spotlights and reflecting in the polished table top. Behind her Davies had a coughing fit, spluttering into a handkerchief and muttering an apology. Savage could only move forward, shake Fox's outstretched hand and hope he didn't notice the sweat on her palms.

'DI Savage,' Fox said. 'Good to meet you again. DCI Hardin tells me you are working hard as usual.'

'Trying my best, sir.'

Fox gestured for them to sit and when they'd done so Hardin began to outline the progress *Sternway* had made so far. That didn't take long, so then he moved into the facts from the other operations, detailing the confluences with

Sternway and explaining the issue with Redmond and what they knew about Budgeon.

Savage didn't know why Hardin was bothering; Fox knew all this already and from the gleam in his eyes he knew something else too. Hardin finished and handed over to Fox who smiled and then leant forward in a conspiratorial fashion.

'Nothing, and I mean nothing, goes beyond this room. Understood?' Savage nodded, Davies grunted a 'yes, sir' and Fox continued. 'I am very distressed to hear about the disappearance of DS Darius Riley. Riley is a good copper. Did some fine work on sorting out the mess on the Harrison case and on *Sternway* he has been invaluable in liaising with the UC officer.'

Savage listened, wished Fox would hurry up and get to the point. Beside her Davies shifted in his seat.

'Riley's from London,' Fox said. 'He was undercover for a while, instrumental in the detection and arrest of a number of big players. Things got hot for Riley so he transferred down here.'

'We're glad he made the move, sir,' Savage said. 'He's a good officer. Clever too.'

'Well, the heat up in London was real enough. Riley was involved in an operation which netted a number of Colombians. There was another man as well: Ricky Budgeon, whom I believe you're fingering for the murders and the attack on Councillor Jackman. Due to certain difficulties Budgeon managed to escape justice up in London and the case against him was dropped. DS Riley was obliged to transfer away from the Met, but the transfer to this *particular* force was somewhat artificial. SCD11 – the Specialist Crime Directorate intelligence unit – had become aware of plans Budgeon had in place to move back down here. He wanted an easier life away from the gangs up in London, he wanted to get back at Fallon for shopping him all those years ago and he saw an opportunity to develop the import side of things.'

'So Riley came down here to get Budgeon?' Savage said.

'Not exactly. Riley came down here because we believed previous operations against organised crime had been compromised. From inside. We needed a competent officer guaranteed to be free from corruption. However, around the time of Riley's transfer SCD11 discovered Budgeon had been back in the West Country before he was arrested in London. DS Riley wasn't aware of that. Budgeon had a particular reason to dislike Riley, something to do with a woman of his and the fact that Riley was the UC officer who sprung the trap which led to Budgeon's arrest. SCD decided they could use that to their advantage. The trouble is Budgeon moved before they were ready.'

'What?' Savage said, as a wash of anger rose within her. Hardin moved his hands out from under the table and made a gentle downward motion with them. Savage ignored him. 'You fuckers set Riley up? Bastards!'

'Charlotte,' Hardin said. 'Riley came here to cover the Fallon angle, to work as a normal DS, yes, but at the same time find out why Fallon had managed to keep one step ahead of us. Which is why when he first went missing I immediately thought "*Sternway*." Turns out I was wrong.'

'Yes, because it was Budgeon. You knew he was coming, with all the consequences that might have, but you never told Riley.'

'To be fair to DCI Hardin,' Fox said, 'nobody was aware of the full facts but myself and one other senior person. Even Riley's contact at force HQ didn't know. This was about getting *Sternway* up and running and ensuring if it was compromised we would be on to the mole immediately. Budgeon was a bonus.'

'A bonus! For fuck's sake! Are you going to say that when DS Riley turns up missing one hand, tortured to death? You lot are a bunch of pen-pushing tossers and I—'

'DI Savage!' Hardin stood up and shouted, face red, fists clenched. 'You'll retract your remark immediately.'

'It's OK,' Fox said, waving Hardin to sit down. 'I understand DI Savage is angry because she is concerned about her officer. I respect that, but getting hot under the collar is not going to find DS Riley.'

'What is?' Davies said, speaking for the first time, his voice still gravelly from his coughing fit. 'And who's to say he'll be alive when we find him?'

Savage turned to Davies. She had forgotten he was there. His thin lips pressed together in what Fox and Hardin would be interpreting as a grimace. She thought it more likely Davies was smiling. The chickens had been coming home to roost but now they were heading for the pot instead.

'Phil,' she said, 'do you have any information? From your . . . um . . . contacts?' Savage stressed the word 'contacts' a little too hard and Davies opened his mouth and then bit his bottom lip. 'I mean you're pretty clued-up on the more shadowy figures in this city, aren't you?'

'Is this true, DI Davies?' Fox asked. 'Have you got some insider information that can help us to find DS Riley?'

'Huh?' Davies seemed confused, as if unsure for a moment as to whether he was being accused of something. He stuttered out a couple of words which Savage couldn't make out and then mumbled something about 'informants' and 'seeing what he could do'.

'What about SCD?' Savage asked. 'Don't they know where Budgeon is?'

'All they are saying to me,' Fox said, 'is that he is in the area, meaning Devon and Cornwall. Members of the team

356

are down here at the moment trying to track him down, but his precise location is unknown.'

'And you believe them?'

'Why not?' Fox shook his head. 'You think there's some sort of conspiracy? DI Savage, this is the Met we are talking about, not a force in some third-world country.'

The CC waved his hand, dismissing any further objections, and then began to outline a plan of action which involved a fresh search of the whole force area. Isolated properties would be visited by local police, and soldiers from 42 Commando would be involved in scouting Dartmoor, Bodmin Moor and parts of the coast path. There would be an aerial search using the coastguard and police helicopters and all the data from numerous ANPR units would be deployed to try and track down the routes Chaffe's white van had taken. In addition, known criminals were to be targeted in dawn raids and questioned about Riley. Radio and television appeals would be broadcast, but only after the searches had been carried out so as not to alert Riley's captors as to what was going on. In short, the counties of Devon and Cornwall wouldn't know what had hit them.

It sounded impressive, as it was supposed to, but Savage didn't hold out much hope for Riley. She nearly found herself spitting out the word 'tickboxes' but managed to restrain herself. The Chief Constable was right: getting angry wasn't going to help Riley now.

The meeting wrapped up and Savage and Davies left the Chief with Hardin. Savage stopped in the corridor and blocked Davies' way.

'Where is he?' Savage said.

'I have no idea where DS Riley is.'

'And if you did?'

'I'd tell you. On my word.' Davies sneered. 'For what it's worth.'

'Look, Phil, I know you're up to your neck in Fallon's shit, but if you can find Darius I'll keep schtum.'

'I don't know what you are talking about. I do know we've got a mutual friend on the council.'

'Alec Jackman can shop me for all I care, although I doubt he's much bothered now. If you and your crimo mates don't help me find Budgeon, then I'll ensure you go away for a very long time.'

'And you? ACC Heldon will have you lynched.' Even as he said the words Davies looked worried, as if he hadn't considered Savage would drop herself in it.

'I'll get dismissed, maybe even charged with something, but I'll survive because I did the right thing. You'll spend your time inside prison in segregation, never knowing who to trust. If you ever get there. I don't think Fallon will want to risk you spilling the beans.'

'You stupid cow!' Davies stepped forwards and went to push her, but someone appeared at the end of the corridor and he moved his hand and slapped the wall instead. The woman paused for a moment before entering a room down on the right.

'For God's sake, Phil, get a grip.' Savage told herself she had to calm down too. Davies was canny and she knew he was trying as hard as her to find a way out of the situation. 'We are both heading for code brown, as Hardin might say, and personally I'd like nothing better than to see you slip under. I know you feel the same way about me. However, we can both save each other and rescue Riley too.'

'And how the hell are we going to do that?' Davies said, stepping back and leaning against the wall.

'If you are instrumental in rescuing Riley then, unless Riley himself brings up some compelling evidence to prove otherwise, you're in the clear.'

'Fucking hell, Savage,' Davies said, his usual grimace broadening into a fully-fledged smile. 'You're one clever bitch, I'll give you that. Still doesn't help us find Riley though, does it?'

'I've got an idea. I want you to get a message to Fallon. You and I will rendezvous tomorrow.'

'Going on a date are we? Didn't know you cared.'

'Yes, and I don't.' The same DC re-emerged from the room at the end of the corridor and glanced up again, before turning her head and scuttling away. 'Now, I'll tell you the message I want you to pass to Fallon and then let's get the hell out of this corridor before people start spreading unhealthy rumours about me.'

A scream jerked Riley awake. He blinked, trying to resolve an image in the almost pitch black. Was that Kemp? Then he heard the noise again. Not a scream, a *screech*. An owl outside somewhere.

Kemp lay on the other side of the room, snoring and wheezing. Riley wondered whether he'd be a hindrance. No matter, he couldn't leave him. He sat upright. Nothing to hear now, not even the owl. The silence probably didn't mean much out here in the country. He put his right hand to his left wrist, touching the skin where his watch had been. Knowing the time would have been handy, but he'd simply have to rely on his instinct. And now felt right.

He pushed himself up and stood, feeling the cold beneath his bare feet. He moved to the door and examined the surround. All through the day, while Kemp had slept, he'd used a sharp stone he'd found on the floor of the stable to chip at the mortar around the coachscrews. Now he was sure a good strong shove would either crack the frame or dislodge it from the wall.

Riley stood and listened again. Was it quiet enough outside to allow them a fair chance of getting away? Him? – yes, but

Kemp? The man was knackered, broken in body if not in spirit and he didn't look as if he was going anywhere soon. Riley moved back over to where Kemp lay sleeping.

'Mate.' Riley touched Kemp's arm. 'Wake up. Time to go.'

'Huh? What?' Kemp rolled over and flinched. 'Shit! That hurt.'

'You alright?'

'Yeah. OK. Sort of.'

'Think you can run?'

'Nah, mate. Not with this rib.'

'Walk?'

'Stagger, maybe. Will that do?'

'It will have to,' Riley said, turning away so Kemp wouldn't catch the grim expression on his face. 'Come on.'

Riley helped Kemp to his feet and then moved over to the door. Light streamed through the cracks and Riley put his eye against one. An empty corridor stretched away to a door at the end which had a glass panel in the centre and through the glass, nothing but black. On the ceiling a fluorescent tube flickered on and off, but other than a moth trying to make sense of the intermittent light, nothing appeared to be moving in the corridor. True, if someone was sitting or standing to one side of the door they wouldn't have a chance, but he suspected they didn't have a chance anyway so there was nothing to lose.

'We good to go?' Kemp coughed from behind Riley. 'Because I fancy a full English for breakfast and all we got yesterday was a few slices of bread and no tea. Hospitable these guys ain't.'

'We're good.' He pulled back from the door and turned to Kemp. 'When I break the door we have to move fast. I am hoping the door at the end isn't locked. We get through and go to the right. That takes us away from the house and the other buildings. Beyond that, fuck knows.'

'Let's hope for something better than a Little Chef,' Kemp said. 'And I'm buying.'

Riley nodded and put his hand up and fingered the crack in the door frame. He placed his shoulder below the crack, moved back half a step and took a couple of practice shoves. Then he stepped back a good two paces, took a breath and lunged at the door. A sharp retort rang out as the crack opened and the right-hand part of the door frame came away from the wall. Riley grasped the frame and pushed forward. There was the sound of splintering wood and the frame fell outward, dangling from the left hand side where a coachscrew held fast. Riley stepped through the gap into the corridor and beckoned Kemp.

The corridor was empty. On the left there were a couple of doors, both closed, and down at the end, the exit. Riley moved down the corridor, hearing Kemp stumbling behind him, and reached the door at the end. He tried the handle and pulled the door inward. Unlocked.

Kemp raised a hand, thumb pointing up, smiled at Riley, and collapsed. Riley ran back and helped him to his feet, supporting him under the arms. Together they staggered to the door.

Outside, the lights from the house blazed out. From one window came the characteristic flicker from a television. A halogen security light fixed to one corner brought daylight to a section of the driveway in front of the house, leaving shadows where the beam didn't penetrate. Riley helped Kemp away from the building and they crossed a patch of gravel and headed towards a hedge where the darkness appeared absolute. As Riley stepped from the gravel onto the strip of grass in front of the hedge, a blinding light flooded his vision. The entire area was now lit up and they stood bathed in a white glare which came from another security light high on a steel pole.

Then the dogs started barking.

'Come on!' Riley pulled Kemp and dived for the hedge. It was some sort of evergreen, soft leaves but dense within. Riley pushed through, feeling twigs scratch across his face as he dragged Kemp after him. On the other side a stock fence ran parallel to the hedge. Riley started to straddle the fence, too late realising it was topped with barbed wire. His trousers ripped and a barb caught him halfway up his thigh, digging into his flesh. He threw himself up and over and rolled into the pasture. Kemp lurched up to the fence and simply folded himself over, screaming as the barbs caught him across the stomach. He fell down beside Riley.

'Shit,' Kemp said. 'I'm fucked.'

'Come on, you can make it.'

'No, mate.' Kemp spluttered the words out. 'Here, I want you to have this.'

Kemp scrabbled in the back pocket of his jeans, pulled out a small square of card and handed it to Riley.

'What—'

'Her real name's Ellie, not Elsie,' Kemp said as shouts echoed in the night air behind them. 'My only chance is if you can get help. Now go!'

'Breakfast,' Riley said and clambered to his feet. 'Full English, right?' He didn't wait for Kemp's answer but began running away from the fence and down the field towards what appeared to be a copse at the bottom. When he reached the woodland he turned back. A beam from a powerful torch swept the hedge and two large black shapes shot along the path of white light. A moment later the shapes collided with something and a frenzied barking and growling filled the air. Kemp screamed for perhaps five seconds, before his voice changed to a low, wailing moan which seemed to go on and on and on.

Riley slunk back deeper into the shadows at the edge of the copse and moved along its boundary. The torch flicked this way and that, the light approaching the dogs. Voices floated down to Riley: Budgeon, Chaffe and the Columbian. When the torch reached the dogs someone said something in Spanish, 'Hijo de puta!' the only words he could make out.

Next came a bang.

Riley didn't wait any longer. He ran along the edge of the woodland, past an old caravan, until he reached a place where the rickety fence had fallen over. He trampled across the wire, feeling a barb scrape across his soles, and into the wood. Now the land fell away at a much steeper angle and the ground underfoot was uneven. Twigs cracked and brambles pulled at his clothing as he headed downward. He stumbled forward, tripping over a root and fell against a tree trunk, knocking his head. Disorientated, he glanced upwards and glimpsed torchlight overhead, the beam waving back and forth, picking out the skeletal shapes of the bare branches. Now the sound of panting and whining floated amongst the trees and when he looked up the hill he saw two men entering the wood. The dogs were on leads now, but lunging forward, eager to be free.

He rolled away from the tree and onto a path which ran across the hill. It was wide and grassy, possibly for forestry vehicles. He stood up and started to run. Up above him a yell rang out followed by a crashing as the men lumbered their way down the hillside. The path ran parallel to the contours, weaving this way and that as the hillside curved round, but the ground was easy and soft under his bare feet and he sprinted along, heart pounding. Behind, the noise from the chase diminished. By the sound of things the dogs were still on their leads which meant his pursuers wouldn't be able to move as fast as him. The path began to climb and after another quarter of a mile or so it ended in a five-bar gate. He vaulted over and landed in a narrow lane. The barking became a frenzy of yapping and snarling.

The dogs were loose again.

Riley headed right, his shredded feet pounding on the tarmac. He just had to reach a larger road, one with traffic, one where someone could help him or at least see what was going on and report it. The road began to climb, at first only gently, but after a short distance the hill became steeper. He took in great gulps of air, but he was tired now. No way would he be able to outrun the dogs.

He turned and looked back the way he had come.

Headlights!

A car was coming up the hill, the engine slipping into a lower gear as it hit the steeper part. Riley held up his hands as the light dazzled him. He waved at the vehicle as the car slowed, a door opening as it stopped alongside.

'Get in, I'll give you a lift.' Gruff. Hint of a Geordie accent from the plush white leather interior.

Riley bent to peer inside and found himself looking down the barrel of a sawn-off shotgun, Budgeon grinning at him.

'Darius,' Budgeon said. 'Going somewhere?'

'Ricky,' Riley said.

'Of course! Who were you expecting, your fairy bloody Godmother?'

Chapter Thirty-Two

Calter dialled the mobile number she had for Tom Bryant, the detective with the Met's Specialist Crime Directorate she'd spoken to a few days ago. Getting the number from the over-officious administrative assistant at New Scotland Yard hadn't been easy, so she was relieved when an answer came in three rings.

'DCI Bryant.' The low whisper sounded cautious. 'Who's that?'

'DC Jane Calter. Devon and Cornwall. Remember.'

'How could I forget a beautiful voice like yours? What can I do for you, love?'

'I heard a rumour some of your boys were down this way. I wondered if that included you and if it does would you like to buy me Sunday lunch?'

'Who told you that?'

'Well, do you?'

'Hang on a moment.' Calter heard muffled words and then a bang like a door slamming. 'Be my pleasure, sweetheart. Could be in Plymouth by one-ish.'

'Not Plymouth. Wouldn't want my boyfriend finding out. Can I come to you?'

'Look love . . .' Bryant paused, made a huffing sound and then a low whistle. 'Yeah, I reckon you could. I'm in a hotel in Truro. They've got a nice little restaurant and who knows, maybe we can have a drink in my room afterwards.'

'Sounds great. Text me the address on this number and I'll see you in a couple of hours.'

Calter ended the call.

'Brilliant,' Savage said. 'When the Chief Constable told me some of SCD were in the area I figured your DCI Bryant might well be along for the ride. Make sure you call me if you get anything. And be careful.'

'I don't even want to think about not being careful, ma'am.'

Bryant turned out not to be as bad-looking as Calter feared. Fifty-something, neat grey hair, reasonably trim and wearing an expensive suit, he'd be a catch. If you were fifty-something yourself.

He was sitting in a bay window in the hotel bar, briefcase open on the table, his head turning as she approached. A smile spread across his face as he looked her up and down. No shame when he stared down at her legs again and repeated the process.

'You're a bit of a looker, DC Calter.' Bryant laughed. 'If you don't mind me saying. Ever considered undercover work?'

'No, I haven't.' She sat down, crossing her legs. 'But I am always open to offers. If that's what that was.'

'Of a type.' Bryant winked, closed the briefcase and put it on the floor. 'If you know what I mean.'

Bryant continued to flirt as they chose and ordered food; Bryant having a steak and chips, Calter plaice with new potatoes. The Met officer went for a pint and Calter followed suit, Bryant raising an eyebrow as if he'd never encountered a woman who drank anything but Babycham. Calter wondered which primeval swamp the DCI had crawled from.

Easy chit-chat followed, Calter letting Bryant take the lead but teasing him every now and then, making sure he knew she was a bit of a feisty character. The chase would excite him and he wouldn't want her served on a plate. Not that he was going to get her.

After they'd finished the meal, Calter steered the conversation towards Ricky Budgeon. Was that why Bryant was down in Cornwall?

'That would be telling,' Bryant said, tapping the side of his nose. 'Let's just say you'll be reading about it in the papers before long.'

'You know where he is?'

'Know where he'll be going. Back inside, where he belongs.'

'That means you must have some fresh evidence.'

'We are awaiting developments, alright? What you don't realise is that this thing is not just about Budgeon. There's much more to it than that. Some very big fish. Now, why don't we change the subject? I'll cut you a deal. No more Budgeon talk if I promise to let you know the minute I've got anything. OK?'

'Look,' Calter reached across the table and touched Bryant's hand. 'You probably know we've got an officer missing.'

'Careless.'

'We think Budgeon's got him. Budgeon's down for three murders in Plymouth already and we—'

'You're worried about this officer?'

'Yes.'

'Understandable, but it's under control, so relax. Budgeon

is not getting away this time and I promised to tell you didn't I? Soon as.'

'Sure, Tom. Thanks.' Calter smiled, half-pouted, trying hard not to overdo it. 'That would be good of you.'

'Right, I need a slash. Another drink? Only I'll go to the bar on my way back.'

Calter said she'd love another and then watched Bryant weave his way through the dining room to the toilets.

Shit. Bryant wasn't giving much away. He'd want to get inside her knickers before he gave her anything. And that was definitely not going to happen.

She stretched out her legs, realising all her silly posing had given her cramp, and in doing so kicked something under the table. She looked down. Bryant's case. Brown, smart, executive. The kind which usually had 'tosser' engraved on the nameplate. She bit her lip, turned around. A group of five businessmen stood at the bar. No sign of Bryant.

She reached down and tried one of the latches. It flicked up. Click. The other flicked up too. She laid the case flat and opened the lid. The thing was crammed with documents, dozens of them. Bedtime reading for a cop who couldn't get his hands on anything more interesting.

Fuck it! She could hardly start to sort through them now. For a second she thought of taking the case and doing a runner, but that would be curtains for her career. Then she saw the *A–Z of Cornwall*, a Post-it sticking out a few pages in. She opened the *A–Z* at the note and saw some pencil lines, an arrow and a circle. The Post-it had an address on it.

She glanced up. Bryant was at the bar, paying for the drinks. A couple of pints and a chaser, Bryant struggling to pick up and hold the three glasses.

Calter peeled the Post-it away from the map, closed the

lid of the case and flicked the catches down. One catch wouldn't stay shut. She pushed it down again. Click. Yes!

'Alright?' Bryant put the drinks down on the table, head cocked.

Calter slid the Post-it into her shoe and then ran her hand up her leg as she straightened. She let her fingers spread out as they reached her thigh and touched the hem of her skirt, moving it a little higher.

'Fine. Just a bit of an ache. Need a massage.'

'Lovely.' Bryant grinned and leered down at Calter's legs. 'Got a meet later, but I reckon I could spare an hour right now if you are up for it. Big comfy bed in my room.'

'Yes, OK.' Calter said, watching Bryant's mouth drop open. 'Finish your drink while I go and freshen up.'

Bryant started to say something, asking if she was serious, but Calter was already away and moving across the room. She walked straight past the toilets and through the hotel lobby, stopping for a moment at the entrance to wait for the young man who had been sitting alone at the bar.

Bloody hell,' DC Denton said as he caught up with Calter. 'What the hell were you doing with his case? Talk about a close-run thing.'

'Tell me about it.' She smiled at Denton, feeling a surge of adrenaline rising within her. 'Let's get the hell out of here.'

Riley awoke with a fresh set of bruises, not remembering much more than Ricky Budgeon glaring out of the Porsche. Seconds later Chaffe and the Colombian had turned up with the dogs and given him a good hiding, and the memories of what had happened afterwards had gone.

Kemp.

Riley remembered him at least. The man passing over the photo of his daughter, next the screams, finally the gunshot.

They'd executed Kemp in cold blood and it didn't take much working out who was going to be next.

Riley pushed himself up from the straw into a sitting position and rubbed himself. Chaffe had landed a couple of blows on the already fractured shoulder and Riley had slipped into unconsciousness as the pale face had grinned down at him, Budgeon's words of 'easy, Stuey, easy' the last thing he'd heard before the black closed in.

'Sweet dreams, Darius?' The same voice now, gruff and low.

Riley swivelled round towards the sound, flinching in pain as he did so. Budgeon sat in one corner of the stable atop an upturned beer crate, his shotgun cradled in his lap.

'You know, Riley,' Budgeon said, 'I'd call you a thick black cunt except as you'll be aware some of my associates are black and I quite like cunt. Just thick will have to do.'

'Ricky.'

'Yeah, Ricky. Now I wish I could say I've been having sweet dreams too.' Budgeon stood and pointed the gun at Riley. 'But ever since that fuck-me-around up in London I've had a bit of a headache. Tends to keep me awake at night, thinking on things. Like, how I could be so stupid as to get shafted by somebody I thought was a mate.'

'It's just a job,' Riley said. 'You're a crook and I am a cop. Nothing personal.'

'Nothing personal? So what do you call screwing Ana Maria Lozada behind my back? My girl.'

'I was trying to get information, Ricky. That's what UC officers do, isn't it?'

'Tell me, Darius, do undercover cops usually carry condoms as part of their kit?'

'Hey?' Riley blinked, swallowed and shook his head, not understanding what Budgeon was on about. The gun

370

twitched in Budgeon's hand, a tremble visible on the trigger finger. 'Sorry, I don't—'

'You fucking joker. The kid. He's not mine, is he? He's bloody well yours!'

'What?' Riley took a sharp intake of breath as he saw Budgeon's whole frame shake. 'You're crazy.'

'He's too dark. Even with a South American as his mother he shouldn't look like that. Coal-black, plain chocolate, not like his mum at all. I didn't want to believe it, but it all makes sense. You're pumping her every bloody chance you get, not surprising she gets pregnant, is it?'

'No, Ricky, you're mistaken. The timing's all wrong. He can't be mine.'

'Timing? Stuff the timing. You fucked my woman and she's had your kid. You say it's nothing personal? I'd call that personal. If it hadn't been for her I might have let things lie. But disrespect like that? *¿El ladron que roba a otro ladron tiene cien años de perdon?* No, not for you. In my book you broke the rules. I spent a dozen years inside thanks to Fallon. Then I get out and work hard up in London. Do some deals, make a little money. I begin to think about making my comeback down here, put all the plans in place and everything, and you come along. Of course, I think you are kosher at the time because you're in with us doing lines, shifting the gear and sniffing pussy. In the end *my* pussy. I didn't realise you were Brad fucking Pitt blacked up until way too late and you are ramming your bloody Oscar up my arse. All the time on remand I'm thinking how I'm going to find you. Until I spot your face in the paper. The nice cop helping out with a group of kids. I didn't even need to go looking for you, did I?'

'We're on to you, Ricky. It's a set-up.'

'Rubbish.' Budgeon shook his head. 'You're so far behind

the times I'm surprised you haven't got a history degree. Your lot don't have a clue.'

'We've got all the intel. There's a whole operation dealing with you and your kind. We're about to close the entire Plymouth drug supply network down for good.'

'*Sternway*?' Budgeon laughed. 'Do me a fucking favour! Redmond told me nearly everything, Kemp the remainder, so the only place *Sternway* is going is backwards. Fast. Backwards, geddit?'

'You won't get away with this. Get out while you can.'

'Thanks for the advice, mate.' Budgeon stood up and moved to the door. 'I'm bricking myself, can't you tell? Now I'll give you some advice in return. If you let people get away with pulling stunts like the one you pulled up in London you'll be taken for a fool every time you step out your front door. You have to make them pay, leave a message, something people will remember for a long time. A very long time.'

Budgeon rapped on the door with the butt of his gun. The door opened and Budgeon stepped through.

'Just so you know,' Budgeon paused and looked back, the thin man and the Colombian appearing behind him. 'It's nothing personal, hey? Now, Stuey's got some more questions for you.'

Chapter Thirty-Three

Davies struck up a match and it flared in the fast descending gloom. The light cast dancing shadows around the car's interior before he put the flame to the tip of a cigarette, inhaled, and then flicked the match through the gap at the top of the window.

'That's against regulations,' Savage said. 'I'll have to sue you for forcing me to breath your second-hand smoke.'

'The price of fags these days, you're lucky I don't bill you for your share.'

The cigarette was Davies' third in the last hour and Savage had noticed he had a couple of packs of twenty stuffed in the glove compartment. She had a bottle of coke, a jumbo bag of nachos and three Snickers. In the health department she didn't know which were worse.

They were parked a way farther on from the entrance to Fallon's place, pulled into a gateway where a break in the hedgerow gave them a view down to the house

'Bloody hell. How much longer?' Davies said.

'Patience. You told him, he'll either phone me or more likely move without us.'

'I don't know. Fallon's losing it. Not sure if he has the bottle any more.'

'Well, you know him better than I do.'

'What's that supposed to mean?'

'Come on, you're on Fallon's payroll. You have been for years. You must know him as well as anyone.'

'You wouldn't understand, it's not as simple as it seems, never has been.'

'Yeah, right!' Savage shook her head and then reached for the bag of nachos. She ripped them open and took a couple. 'Anyway, ignoring all that, let's hope Fallon *has* got the bottle. Else we're stuffed.'

'I sent a message to Fallon, told him about your thoughts re: Towner's satnav and that she knows where Budgeon is. I don't see how it helps, there's not much he can do to her.'

'Not to her. She's not going to give anything away,' Savage replied. 'But I think she stashed the satnav somewhere for safe keeping. The search teams came up empty on her property, on Dowdney's too. Her children denied all knowledge when questioned, but that was a given. What Fallon can do is find the satnav. If the children have it, he'll get it. Remember, Towner's offspring have kids themselves. Fallon sends his thugs round and they say "give us the satnav or else . . ."'

'Bloody hell, I thought you had children? You really are an uncaring b—'

'Fallon doesn't do that type of violence. He's old-school, like you. He'll use threats, but they'll be enough.'

'I hope you are right, because I *am* old-school. I'd hate to think any kiddies might get hurt. Or women for that matter.'

Savage smiled and offered the bag of nachos to Davies. 'You weren't thinking that earlier.'

'No, I wasn't, but we're on the same side now. At least for the moment.' Davies took a couple of nachos, munched them and peered out of the windscreen.

The lights were blazing, and earlier they'd seen Fallon and

his wife and kids sit down in the dining room for tea and cakes before the maid drew the curtains. Home sweet home, Savage had thought, thinking of her own children stuck without their mother yet again.

Now lights went on upstairs and Savage imagined the children protesting at having to complete last-minute homework or have a bath before dinner and bed. Things were a little more lax in her household and she knew Pete and Stefan would be watching the afternoon Premiership match, Pete hoping Jamie might bath himself, get his own dinner and put himself to bed. Samantha would be on Twitter, Facebook, Skype or possibly all three. Doing her homework at the same time, most likely.

Savage leant back in the seat and closed her eyes for a moment. It would be nice to be home, she thought, cuddling on the sofa with Pete while Stefan joked around and—

'We're on!'

Savage snapped her eyes open, startled by Davies' voice. Headlights swept the interior of the car as a vehicle came along the lane and turned right into the gateway to Fallon's house. It was Fallon's Range Rover, Kev – Fallon's driver – at the wheel. Another car, some sort of BMW, followed the Range Rover down the drive.

'Three up each vehicle,' Davies said. 'He means business alright.'

Before the cars had reached the bottom of the drive the front door to the house opened and out came Fallon. He had a long, thin bag under his arm.

'Bloody hell,' Savage said. 'That's a shotgun.'

'Shit.' Davies' hand moved toward the ignition. 'You still on for this?'

'Of course. Riley is depending on us and I know how much you love him.'

'Fuck off!'

Davies waited until Fallon had clambered into the back of the first car and then he turned the ignition. He'd kept the lights off and they both slumped low in their seats as the two vehicles turned around, came up the drive and out onto the lane. They immediately speeded up and headed into Saltash, turned right onto the A38 and went through the Saltash tunnel. Davies followed some distance behind. Plenty of cars were streaming across the bridge into Cornwall, late shoppers heading back home, and Davies tucked in a few cars back behind an empty flatbed truck.

'How the fuck are we going to explain this to Hardin?' Davies said. 'He's going to want to know how we knew where to go.'

Savage didn't answer, just stared ahead, trying to keep track of the tail lights of the two cars as they left the town and headed into the countryside.

Denton hadn't been keen on Calter's plan to go it alone. As they turned off the main road and headed towards Constantine, he argued they should tell Savage the address immediately.

'Suppose we need backup or something unexpected happens?' he said.

'The boss has got her own bit of surveillance to worry about, Carl. All we've got is a cross on a map. First sign it has anything to do with Budgeon we'll call her, OK?'

'OK.' Denton switched from sidelights to headlights and swerved to avoid a large pothole. 'If you say so.'

They drove on, Denton slowing when they reached Constantine, Calter reading from the satnav and peering down at the Ordnance Survey map she had open on her lap.

'Right in the village and a mile or so farther on we need to turn off. Down a track and then find some place to park.'

Ten minutes later, and they were plunging down a tiny lane which led to a terrace of cottages next to a farm. Denton pulled the car onto a muddy verge and glanced across at Calter, who was pointing down at the map.

'Got to walk across a couple of fields, Carl,' she said. 'We'll be able to see the place on the other side of the creek. If this was summer and we had a picnic it might be fun.' She peered out of the windscreen at the dark clouds overhead.

'Jane?' Denton said, pulling a Mars Bar from his pocket. 'I brought this. I'll share it with you if you like.'

Sweet boy, Calter thought, but a total pushover.

The farmyard appeared deserted, although smoke rose from a chimney on one of the farm cottages in the terrace. They headed out of the yard around the edge of a ploughed field which fell away down to a hedgerow. Beyond was a small area of pasture and some woodland and farther on, a line of mud marked the creek. The landscape ahead was greying in the coming twilight, the perspective flattening out the distance. The scene looked like a charcoal drawing.

They reached a gate and went through into the pasture, crossing the field and finding a stile into the woodland. Now the land fell away to the creek and the path zig-zagged down beneath the bare trees. Despite the lack of leaf cover, in amongst the trunks night seemed almost upon them. Halfway down Calter paused next to a large oak and motioned Denton over.

'Let's stop.' She moved past the oak and stood behind a pile of logs. She gestured down at the creek. 'We can watch the property from here.'

'What do you mean watch?' Denton said. 'I thought we were just going to check it and then call it in?'

'Did you now?' Calter smiled, lifted her binoculars and squinted through. 'We've no idea if this has anything to do with Budgeon yet.'

Denton snorted and pulled out the Mars Bar, muttering something about a dinghy on the far shore.

Calter adjusted the focus ring and swept the binos around until she spotted the white shape at the high-tide line, a rope leading from a small rowing boat to a tree on the bank.

'Must belong to the house.' Denton tapped her arm and pointed at the grassy slope which ran up from the shore.

Calter lowered the binoculars. A large barn conversion sat in extensive grounds. Lights twinkled from the windows. To one side stood a tennis course and, attached to the house, a conservatory with a pool. To the other side a patch of ancient woodland and, to the front, a gravel drive swept past a barn and a long, stone building. The place was magnificent, a house fit for a lottery winner or a movie star, and the position was a bonus. Away from near neighbours, the closest habitation appeared to be a farm at the top of the hill. The only blot on the landscape was a shabby caravan in an adjoining field at the edge of the woodland.

'Priceless,' Calter said. 'Sure beats my flat.'

'Never,' Denton said, handing her half the Mars Bar. 'Your place is cosy. I like it.'

Bloody hell, Calter thought, the boy has lost it. She wondered who was worse: Denton or Bryant. Bryant was a dinosaur, but Denton dripped like a faulty tap.

'Hang on,' Calter said, looking at the caravan again. 'Are we missing something bloody obvious here? I didn't recognise the address I nicked from Bryant, but that caravan seems awfully familiar. I swear it's the same one stuck on the board back in the incident room. This is the place where Patrick and DI Savage came to. You were right, Carl, I should've called it in. I'll phone—'

'Jane!' Denton hissed. 'Look at that!'

The sight caused Calter's blood to run cold. The damp

378

feeling in her neck sent icy fingers down her back and she shivered. The sudden harsh wash of a security light had come on and in the patch of white a man stumbled from the door of the long stone building and fell to the floor. Two other men strode into the lit up area and began to kick the first man where he lay. Then they picked him up and dragged him across the yard towards a different building. Calter raised the binoculars to her eyes and rammed the zoom lever to maximum. She twiddled the focus ring until the tableaux snapped clear. The men disappeared into the building, the door swinging shut. Calter blinked. It had happened in a flash, but one thing was unmistakable. The guy being manhandled was black.

'Jesus, it's Riley, come on!' Calter dropped the binoculars and moved back from the pile of logs, grabbing Denton by one arm. They scrabbled back up the slope and behind the oak tree. She took her phone from her pocket and jabbed at the keyboard, putting it to her ear and taking deep breaths. Nothing. She looked at the phone. No bars. Shit!

'You got one?' she asked Denton, but he was already staring down at the display on his phone and shaking his head. 'OK. You stay here. We need to know if they go anywhere. I'll go back up the hill and see if I can get a signal there. If not I'll go to the farm.'

'But . . .' Denton looked at her for a moment.

'Which of us did the Plymouth half-marathon in under one forty?'

Calter placed her hands on her hips for a moment, took a deep breath and started to run up the hill. By the time she got to the top she was feeling the pain. She checked her phone again. Still nothing. Bugger. She climbed the stile and ran across the pasture to the gate that led into the big ploughed field. She fumbled with the latch, trying to work out how the hell you opened it, before the bolt came free and she wrenched the gate open. She started across the field, falling almost straightaway and rolling in the soft furrows, before staggering to her feet and lumbering on.

Five minutes later she reached the first of the farm cottages and stomped up the path and rapped on the door. Nothing. She leapt the little hedge to the adjoining cottage. This time she caught a movement behind the front room window, the twitch of a curtain and a shadow moving back. She pressed her face up against the window and saw an old lady raise her hands to her face and cower. Calter fumbled in her pocket and took out her warrant card, pressing it against the window.

'Police! DC Calter. I need to use your phone.'

The woman disappeared from view and Calter cursed. A few seconds later though she heard the front door click and it swung open, the old woman standing in the doorway, holding out a shaking hand, in which was a cordless phone.

For the first few miles they were both jumpy, thinking at any moment Fallon would turn off somewhere. After that though they settled down for a long drive. There was less traffic now and they reached Bodmin in thirty minutes. Fallon's convoy swung onto the A30 dual carriageway and speeded up. Keeping tabs on them and staying a reasonable distance behind became more difficult and Davies kept shouting at Savage, concerned they were losing them. After less than a quarter of an hour they turned off the A30, heading for Truro and Falmouth.

'Where the fuck?' Davies said, smacking the indicator stick down as he took the sliproad. He tapped the dash behind the wheel. 'Lucky I filled up before we left.'

Savage was about to answer and say something about there not being much of the country left, when her mobile chirped out.

Calter.

The DC's words came out of the phone in a torrent, but Savage had the gist in the first five seconds.

'Constantine,' she said to Davies, thinking the name sounded familiar as she hung up and then realising why. 'Of course, the bloody farm where Owers stayed! I'll give you directions, you concentrate on the road.'

Directions weren't necessary since Fallon led the way, his convoy anticipating the route as fast as Savage could call it out. They rattled round the outskirts of Truro, the two cars ahead paying scant regard to the speed limit, Davies struggling to keep up. Then Fallon skipped off the main road and dived down a country lane. They shot through a small village with a few streetlights and then they were in darkness.

Up ahead, the two vehicles turned right at a crossroads. Davies slowed to take the turn. As he pulled out into the road a loud honking came from their left as a patrol car shot into view. Davies braked hard and Savage felt the seatbelt dig into her chest.

'What the hell?' Their car had stopped in the centre of the road and Davies slammed into reverse, backing out the way. The patrol car came roaring past, blue lights flashing and siren blaring, closely followed by a police van and another car. Davies smashed the gearstick forward again and turned to follow.

Up ahead, the convoy Fallon was in had pulled to the side of the narrow road, the nearside wheels of the vehicles riding the verge. The police cars slowed down and eased past before accelerating off again.

'It's not them they are after!' Savage said. 'Get moving!'

Davies floored the accelerator and the back end swung round. The wheels screeched and they surged forward. A quarter of a mile farther on Fallon had got out of his car and walked back to the second vehicle. He looked up. Savage lowered the window as they approached and Davies slowed the car.

'Going somewhere, Kenny?' she said. 'Only you said you'd call me, remember?'

'Charlotte, Phil. What the hell are you playing at?'

'Drive on,' she said to Davies, flicked the switch and the window slid up. She turned in her seat to see Fallon thump the roof of the car and start bellowing something to the driver. 'Jesus, he's not happy.'

'Saved him a stretch,' Davies said. 'On reflection he'll thank us.'

Davies put his foot to the floor and they sped away, Savage hoping to God Davies was right.

Chapter Thirty-Four

'Wakey wakey, it's show time!'

Riley blinked, Budgeon's voice was on the edge of his consciousness, but the bright light was real enough, drilling into his eyes and causing his head to pound. He made to move his hand to his right cheek where a sharp pain throbbed, but couldn't. Either his limbs weren't working or . . . he was tied up.

'Now Darius,' Budgeon continued. 'Stuey said you put up a bit of a struggle, that you didn't answer his questions.'

Riley screwed his eyes shut, before opening them and blinking several times. A shadow loomed over him for a moment and then moved back so the light fell on his face again.

He was in some kind of vast barn or workshop. Off to one side was a workbench with tools hung on a pegboard, a large vice fixed to the edge. Strip lights floated above him, suspended from the ceiling. He lay on some sort of table, the hard surface doing nothing to ease the pain from the bruises. He tried to move again, feeling cold chains against his bare arms and hearing them rattle down on the table as he gave up any further exertion as pointless.

'Questions,' Riley said looking up at Budgeon's face, remembering only the pickaxe handle blurring as Stuey swung the weapon over and over again.

'Stuey gets a bit carried away sometimes.' Budgeon shook his head as he fiddled with some orange rubber tubing which had brass connections at either end. 'I told him to take it easy, but then again, you didn't give him what he wanted, did you?'

'I . . .' Stuey had been screaming, frothing at the mouth, ranting something about Fallon's drugs. 'I told him I didn't know. I don't know.'

'Strange, that. Up in London you always seemed to know a great deal more information than me. I was hoping the same applied down here.' Budgeon stopped what he was doing and lowered his voice. 'Seems I was wrong though. Never mind. Least it means you don't need to worry about Stuey hitting you any more. It's just me now.'

'I . . .' Riley tried to think fast, to find something he could use to bargain with. 'I can help you locate the drugs. They'll be ashore somewhere. A lock-up or in one of his properties. I don't know where, but I can find out for you.'

'I'll just untie you then shall I? Give you a phone? Maybe let you go?'

'I can get the info, Ricky. Honestly.'

'But you don't know *now*, Darius, and that my friend is a real shame.' Budgeon reached down, screwing the connections on to two gas bottles which sat on a trolley beneath the bench. He dropped the rest of the tubing and came across to Riley, bending over and putting his face up close. 'You're a fucking joker. I'd laugh except that you cost me a whole lot of money and all that time on remand. There's the opportunity cost too. Know what that is? I do, because I did a fucking A level in economics when I was inside the first time. I'll explain in terms you'll appreciate: it means while I was lying on the bunk in my cell tossing myself off I was missing fucking a whole lot of cute pussy on the outside. Understand?'

'Girls are in short supply in prison, so your right arm's going to be getting a lot more exercise.'

'Well, yours isn't, mate, thieving bastard.' Budgeon went back to the bench and pulled up the tubing again, attaching the free ends to something Riley couldn't see. He turned and showed Riley. 'Oxy torch. Do you know, I learnt how to use one in the nick the first time I was inside? How stupid is that? Talk about university of crime. Anyway, this is a lovely bit of kit. Produces a flame which burns at several thousand degrees. Cuts through metal like butter.' Budgeon put his hand in a pocket and pulled out a lighter.

'Now, Ricky. Come on.' Riley began to breathe harder. 'We can work something out. There must be something—'

'NO THERE FUCKING ISN'T!' Budgeon flicked the lighter and pulled the trigger on the torch. He waved the lighter near the nozzle and the torch whooshed into life, making a sort of roaring, growling sound, the yellow flame turning blue as Budgeon adjusted something on the handle. 'Well, now it's payback.'

'Like I said before, Ricky, I was only—'

'SHUT UP!' Budgeon took a pair of pliers from the workbench and used them to pick up a short length of iron rod. He held the torch in front of the rod and the iron began to glow a dull red, brightening within seconds to a vivid orange colour. He smiled and dropped the rod in a bucket of water to one side of the bench. Riley heard a hiss and a cloud of steam exploded from the bucket and rose into the air, dissipating as it reached the overhead lights.

'Ricky, please. You don't want to do this.'

'That's where you're wrong.' Budgeon sneered and raised the torch. 'I've been looking forward to this for days.'

Riley tried to roll sideways to put leverage on the chain binding his wrists to the table, but it was hopeless. Budgeon came towards him, a grin on his face. Riley worked up a globule of phlegm and spat in Budgeon's direction. Budgeon merely moved to one side.

'Now, this will hurt,' Budgeon said, grinning and adjusting something on the torch. 'Quite a bit. Although I doubt you'll be conscious for long.'

Riley opened his mouth to shout, but nothing came out but a rasp. He screwed his eyes shut, the fuzzy grey and white squares floating in front of him resolving into an image of his grandfather, a soft Caribbean lilt telling him he'd messed up big time.

You ain't got shit under that cup, Darius. Nothing, I reckon, but a bag of bones.

The roar of the torch increased in intensity, sounding something like a jet plane on take-off. Riley opened his eyes. Budgeon was moving closer, scanning Riley's body before he settled on his right hand. His tongue lolled out, hanging over his bottom lip, and his face screwed up in concentration as he made a final adjustment to the flame.

Then he lowered the torch.

Davies caught up with the police convoy as the lead vehicle pulled over at the entrance to a farm and let the van drive past. Savage recognised the farm as the one she had visited the week before, the one where Owers had stayed in the caravan and killed Simza Ellis. A little farther on and they arrived at the luxury house. The van smacked into the fancy gates, crashing through and taking down one of the brick pillars to the side, then careered down the drive, slewing round by the steps leading to the front door. The rear doors opened as it stopped, half-a-dozen armed officers leaping down, two of them carrying a battering ram. Within seconds the door of the house lay flattened and the response team ran in.

386

Davies pulled their car on to an expanse of mud to the side of the lane and they both jumped out. One of the patrol cars blocked the drive entrance, two armed officers standing alongside, weapons pointing towards the house where a rectangle of yellow cast a glow out into the yard. Even from the top of the drive Savage could hear the shouts from inside, the tearful screams of a child too. The officer nearest to them wheeled round, sighting down the barrel of her weapon and shouting out a warning. Savage already had her warrant card out, held high.

'DI Savage and DI Davies, Plymouth,' she said, moving forwards as the officer lowered the gun.

'Serious Crime Directive,' the young woman said.

'What's up?' Savage asked, thinking the girl didn't appear old enough to hold a driving licence, let alone a Heckler and Koch sub-machine gun.

'We've been waiting to move on this place for days, but one of your lot phoned in on a triple nine so we had to go now.' The girl nodded down the driveway. 'My Governor – DCI Bryant – he's in there. He'll want a word when this is over. As you can imagine, he's not best pleased.'

Savage spotted movement from over near one of the barns as a figure walked out of the shadows into the beam of a halogen security light. He stood silhouetted, the light from behind him casting a tall, thin shadow across the yard.

Stuart Chaffe.

'Down!' the girl yelled as Chaffe raised his pump-action shotgun and pointed the weapon in their direction. Savage dived behind the car alongside the girl, hearing the bang and the sound of the pellets spattering into the side of the vehicle as she fell to the floor. Davies was sprawled on the ground in the open, face down in the dirt, hands over his head.

Clikclak. Chaffe cycled the gun and fired again, the retort

combining with the sound of shattering glass as he took out one of the police van's windows.

Clikclak.

'Fucking dead, the lot of you!' Chaffe yelled, his footsteps padding out a rhythm as he ran into the yard.

Beside Savage the two armed officers crouched with their backs against the car. The male officer made a signal to the girl. Spoke in a whisper.

'Take him, Chrissy. No need for a warning.'

The girl moved faster than Savage would have believed possible, swinging round and up, two shots echoing in the night. Bang-bang. Double tap. Something out in the yard fell and brushed the gravel.

'He's down,' the girl said. 'Not moving.'

Savage pulled herself up and peeked over the top of the car. Chaffe lay prone on his side, steam from his final breath floating up in the glare of the light. The girl moved from behind the car and ran forward. The male officer followed, covering Chaffe as the girl approached, knelt and put her fingers to the man's neck.

She made a quick shake of her head and then stood. Her colleague walked up and patted her on the back.

A man with a flak jacket over a suit came out of the house and jogged up towards the cars.

'Tom Bryant,' Davies said, pulling himself up from the mud. 'Well I never.'

'You fucking sheepheads,' Bryant said, raising his hand as he approached, thumb and forefinger held together. 'We were this close to the South Americans and now that little bitch of yours has blown it.'

'You've got Budgeon?' Savage said.

'No. There's only his wife and kid in the house. Looks like he's flown along with the spics.'

'But Chaffe . . .?'

Savage looked across at the two armed officers standing over the dead man and then swivelled her head towards a shiplap barn. One of a pair of full-height doors, high and wide enough to take a tractor, stood a few feet ajar. Harsh white light flooded out.

And then came the high-pitched whine of a machine tool.

'Riley!' Savage began to move across the gravel, but Chrissy and the other armed officer moved faster, arriving at the barn door just before her.

This time the male officer went first, rotating in through the entrance, Chrissy behind. Savage looked round the edge of the door.

Inside, fluorescent tubes floated high overhead, suspended from the ceiling by wire. They illuminated some sort of workshop: a bench with a heavy vice and an array of tools hanging on the wall behind to one side and, in the centre, a table, DS Riley lying tied to the thing with a mess of rope and chain. A short, stocky man in a sleeveless t-shirt stood to one side, some sort of electrical tool in his hand, a spinning disc whirling in a blur, the noise deafening.

'Armed police! Put that down!'

Budgeon smiled over at the door and then brought the tool down onto Riley's arm.

A shower of sparks flew up as Riley wriggled, forcing one of the binding chains into the disc. Then Budgeon was reeling backwards with a gasp, the bang from the gun seeming to come afterwards as he fell to the floor. Chrissy ran forward and covered Budgeon as he lay on his back, breathing hard, winded. The shock on his face turning to a grin as he stared at the angle grinder, where the works had been destroyed by the bullet.

Savage ran in, almost dancing across the space to Riley. She looked down at his arm, which appeared untouched.

'Are you hurt?'

'Yes, ma'am, pretty battered, but I'll live. I'd appreciate if you could untie me.' As Savage began to remove the rope and chains Riley continued. 'Nick of time and all that. He was going to use a cutting torch on me, but he forgot to check the gas. He ran out of oxygen for the torch and while he was setting up the grinder you lot arrived.'

The chains were off now and Riley swivelled himself off the bench. He rubbed his wrists and nodded down at Budgeon, face down on the floor now, being patted down, cuffs clicking into place.

'The odd thing was that he'd heard the shots, knew you were coming. He could have done a runner.'

'Well thank God you're OK, Darius.' Savage moved forward, wrapped her arms around Riley and kissed him on the cheek. 'You don't know how worried we were.'

Savage heard a cough from the doorway, turned her head to see Bryant grinning.

'Glad somebody is happy. Princess rescuing the prince is this? Fairy-tale ending?'

'Not at all,' Savage said. 'I was just telling . . . I . . . fuck, I was letting him know how much we missed him, alright?'

'DI Davies says you'll want a word with Budgeon before we take him. Would that be right?'

A shadow moved at the doorway and Davies materialised at Bryant's shoulder, pale face bleached even whiter by the fluorescent light.

'DI Savage is old-school,' Davies said in a low voice. 'Like you and me, Tom. I think she might want to ask Ricky about a little girl.'

'Huh?' Bryant cocked his head, raised an eyebrow and nodded. 'OK, Phil, just for you. Five minutes, Savage, and then you come to me and explain why that DC Calter of yours wouldn't look a hell of a lot tastier in a uniform.'

Bryant strolled across to his two officers as they hauled Budgeon to his feet. Said a few words. The male officer looked over at Savage and Riley and opened his mouth to say something, but Bryant raised a finger to his lips and made a shush sound before using the same finger to point to the door. The three of them left, the officer who had been starting to protest shouldering Davies aside as he passed. Davies spat on the floor and turned and stared out into the dark.

'Going to be a nice night with the weather clearing through. I think I'll take a peek at the stars. Be out here if you need me.'

It was just the three of them now. Budgeon stood impassive, hands cuffed behind his back, breathing slowly.

'Close, Darius,' Budgeon said. 'Very close. Next time there'll be no margin for error. I'll double-check the gas. Next time you are going to burn.'

'There won't be a next time, Ricky,' Savage said. 'You'll be getting a whole life term for what you've done. You'll be going back to meet your old mates in Full Sutton.'

'There's always a next time, always a way. And I'll make sure you get your share of what's coming too. Bitch.'

'You're lucky we turned up,' Savage indicated the table and the acetylene bottles. 'If Fallon had got here first you'd be getting a taste of your own medicine and the only thing burning would be you.'

'I'd have sorted him. No problem.'

'Well, you certainly sorted Owers, Redmond, Dowdney and Jackman. Not to mention Simza Ellis.'

'I never touched her. That was the paedo.'

'You knew Franklin Owers had Simza. She was alive in the caravan and you did nothing to save her.'

'It was business, that's all.'

'You met Owers years ago up in Full Sutton prison. He'd have been on the numbers, rule forty-five, but somehow you got to him. What did you do? Threaten him? Or maybe you were more canny and offered to protect him. Made sure he didn't slip in the showers or get a bowl full of Weetabix and razor blades for breakfast.'

'Me? Associate with the likes of him?'

'Not usually, no. But you knew Owers from when you were in Plymouth and you were banking something for the future. Owers had cooked the books for you and Fallon all those years ago and you guessed, correctly as it turned out, that Owers would continue to be of use to Fallon after he'd done his time.

'When you returned to Plymouth last summer you got in touch with Owers and told him he owed you. Just to be sure you invited him down to stay in the caravan. Once down here you pointed him in the direction of the Lizard knowing he'd find what was on offer too hard to resist. Did you just lend him the van or did you and Chaffe actually help with kidnapping the girl? Whatever, once you knew he had Simza you let her die so you'd have something to really scare him with, so he'd go along with your plans. You had options: you could spread rumours back in Plymouth so Owers would get lynched, you could ensure Fallon found out or you could tell us lot. I bet Owers was only too keen to help you.'

'Steaming bullshit. Besides, Owers would have killed again anyway. He couldn't help himself.'

'But he helped you, big time. You got the lowdown on Fallon's secret accounts, realised he was washing a fortune in drug money through Tamar. Your Columbian friends wanted in on that and you had the means to help them.

Poor old Fallon thought he had Owers by the short and curlies, that Owers wouldn't dare cross him. He didn't realise you had the fucker by the bollocks as well. As for the others, you simply wanted Fallon to feel some fear before you came for him.'

'Ma'am?' Riley. 'There's Marty Kemp as well.'

'He's here?'

'He's dead. We tried to escape and the dogs got him. They executed him.' Riley put a hand to his back pocket, pulled out a scrap of paper. 'He gave me this.'

Savage took the piece of paper. A photograph of a girl. Older than a toddler, younger than a teen.

'Who is she?'

'Her name is Ellie. She's Kemp's daughter.'

'Fuck.' Savage turned away from Budgeon and put her hands up to her eyes and rubbed. Thought of Vanessa Liston, another child who'd lost her dad. Then she remembered Layton pointing down to the body of Simza lying against the housebrick. Thought, inevitably, of her own daughter, Clarissa. She turned back to Budgeon. 'Just business is it?'

Savage looked at Riley and met his eyes, sensing something pass between them. Then she flicked her thumb in Budgeon's direction and started to move towards the door.

'Ma'am?'

'I didn't see anything, Detective Sergeant Riley. And if I did, it was self-defence, wasn't it?'

Riley leapt at Budgeon and punched him in the face, Budgeon reeled back and Riley grabbed the man's head and propelled him forwards, slamming his face down into the workbench where it glanced off the vice. Budgeon staggered, overbalanced and fell to the floor, blood pouring from his nose.

'Enough, ma'am?'

Savage nodded and turned and walked out into the darkness. Riley followed, pushing past Davies.

'Like I told you,' Davies said, glancing back into the building and spitting on the floor again. 'It's turning into a beautiful night.'

Afterwards

Sunday lunch two weeks later and Detective Superintendent Hardin was buying. Savage, Hardin and Davies sat at a table at one end of the Hotel Mountbatten bar, a big room filled with people. Families, loads of screaming kids and plenty of noise. Savage had opted for the lasagne, Hardin was tucking into a jacket potato piled high with chilli con carne and Davies had ham, eggs and chips.

'Now,' Hardin said, taking a slurp of his bitter and a mouthful of food before continuing. 'We've been over everything and I think I am clear on most of the events. However, there are a few . . . how should I put this . . . issues? Which is why we are meeting here. Off the record. Unofficial.'

Davies speared a chip into the centre of one of his eggs, eyes moving to meet Savage's for a moment before he concentrated on mopping up the yolk. Savage decided avoidance wasn't going to cut any ice with Hardin.

'Sir? I think I can ex—'

'Shut up.' Hardin laid his cutlery down and put both hands on the table either side of his plate. Finding that the pub hadn't provided him with a mouse to click he turned instead to his pint, took another slurp and stared across the room to where a little girl was bawling her eyes out because her brother had knocked her coke over. After a minute or so he shifted his attention back to Savage and Davies. 'The interviews are going well and Budgeon's not hiding anything. He'll cough for the murders and we might be able to get him on an accessory charge for the Simza Ellis killing too. On the other hand what have we got out of *Sternway*? Bugger all. Fallon is home free and unless a bundle of cocaine falls into our hands we won't get anything to stick.'

'No sign then?' Davies said, casting a half-glance at Savage and then biting the yokey end of a chip.

'Not a whiff,' Hardin said. 'In addition, SCD are furious that the Columbians got away, say we've blown the entire operation. God knows how much money wasted. They caught up with one of the little men – the guy at Budgeon's place – but the others never showed. Bryant said they were waiting for Budgeon to get the drugs.'

Davies didn't say anything else and Savage changed her plan; silence would be better. Hardin took up his cutlery again and sliced deep into his spud.

'There are many things I don't understand. Not only about *Sternway* and Budgeon, but about you two. Like, for instance, how you arrived at Budgeon's place at the same time as the SCD team. Why Lynn Towner is shouting about police brutality. Why two of her children's places get turned over. Then there's that boat of Fallon's going glug, glug, glug in Cawsand Bay. You might say it's my business to find the answers to these things, but at the moment I don't want to know.' Hardin cut again, splitting the potato and pushing one half to one side. He ran the knife back and forth, clearing a section of plate of food and then clinking the knife three times in the gap. 'There's a line. On one side the good guys go about their business, everything is above board, everything is kosher. I can write our actions up in the policy book and explain everything to the Chief Constable. I can go home after a day's work, kiss the wife, drink a glass of sherry and sleep easy. On the other side of the line . . .'

Hardin dropped his cutlery on the plate with a clatter and pushed the half-finished meal away. He took a final gulp from his pint and stood up.

'For once I've lost my appetite. I'm going, and I suggest you bugger off home too.' Hardin took his jacket from the back of his chair and put it on. Then he leant over the table, a flush of colour coming to his face. 'If I ever find out either of you has strayed over that line I'll string you up and hang you out to dry. Understand?'

Savage watched Hardin stride out of the pub and then she got up to leave as well. She touched Davies on the shoulder.

'Quits, Phil, OK?'

'I never gave up Marty Kemp to Fallon, you know?' Davies said. 'Redmond did. Hardin is right about lines you don't cross. There are rules, understand?'

'Jackman told me Redmond never went over to our side, that he was stringing us along. I wasn't sure if I believed him at the time. Doesn't matter anyway, it's all history now.'

'Sure, darling. History.' Davies reached out for his glass and raised it as Savage walked away. 'Cheers!'

That evening the kids insisted on fish and chips. A three-way paper and scissors game between Savage, Pete and Stefan led to Savage having to make the trip into Plymstock to get them. She decided to take the MG. The car hadn't had a run for a few weeks and could do with one. The night was clear and the chill as she stepped out the door made her have second thoughts for a moment. The heater in the car was crap and the ten minute drive wouldn't be enough to warm the interior.

It took three attempts to start the car, but once running the engine sounded sweet enough. When the weather was a little warmer and spring had properly arrived Pete had said he wanted to do a top-end overhaul. She was glad he had time to spare on odd jobs because the garden was a mess and the boat needed to come out of the water for a coat of antifoul and some much-needed maintenance. They already had plans for the summer and, despite the protestations of Samantha, who would have preferred to either remain at home or go on a package somewhere, a cruise to the Isles of Scilly was in the offing.

She flicked the headlights on and pulled out into the lane. Moonlight bathed the hedges either side with a pale white-wash and she put her foot down to climb the hill away from the house. The car accelerated with a growl and raced between the converging lines of the hedges as if in some video game. The kick in the back wasn't even as powerful as a modern family hatchback, but there was something about sitting low down with the old car rattling around her that was exciting.

The car climbed the hill and bounced over the undulations, eating up the road like an eager puppy scampering across a field after a rabbit. She slowed as she neared the top, bringing the car to a stop at the junction.

Right, nothing. Left . . .

The dark hulk seemed to come from nowhere, screeching as the wheels skidded on the tarmac and it stopped in front of her. The vehicle's headlights were off, but she recognised the distinctive shape of a Range Rover. The driver's door opened and the interior light flashed on for a moment as a figure got out.

Fallon.

The door clunked shut and Fallon strode round. He came to her door, tapped on the roof and crouched, face beaming with a wide grin. Savage wound the window down.

'Been waiting for you, Charlotte. Another hour and I would have called. But things are better this way. No records, get my drift?'

'What the fuck do you want?'

'That's no way to speak to Uncle Kenny, is it?' Fallon stood up and ran a hand down the front wing. 'This is a nice motor you've got Ten-a-penny but still a classic. Bet she wouldn't fare too good in those NCAP tests though. Something like my Range Rover would go right over the top and leave not much more than a pancake of metal behind.'

'Are you threatening me?'

'I'm saying if I had wanted to I could have smashed you to nothing a minute ago. If.'

'OK. So what *do* you want?'

'You've been a good girl, Charlotte. Very good. Davies and all that. Keeping quiet. Was a shame I never got to catch up with Ricky, but in hindsight maybe that was no bad thing. Would have turned out very messy.' Fallon looked at her, a sneer forming on thin lips, teeth flashing as the lips parted into a fully-fledged grin. He chuckled, a throaty noise which gurgled into a cough. 'You'll be pleased to know you needn't worry about that slimeball Jackman either.'

'I thought you two were friends?'

'Yeah, but sometimes it's nice to see even your friends get taken down a peg or two. Anyway, you can forget about the stuff he has on you. The Liston girl erased the video, every copy she could find. Told me she owed you. Alec was furious, but it's his word against yours now.'

'Get on with it. I'll be missed.'

'You've got a nice little family back at home.' Fallon gestured down the road. 'That's what life's all about, isn't it? The kids?'

'You can leave—'

'That's where you're wrong. I've got a little secret for you I picked up recently. Something you don't know, but should. A piece of information you'll want to act on. If you understand what I mean?'

'No I don't. What are you talking about?'

'You see I want to help you with your daughter, I—'

'Don't you *ever* go anywhere near my daughter. I swear I'll kill you if you do.'

'You've got the wrong end of the stick, Charlotte.' Fallon shook his head. 'Not Samantha. This is about Clarissa. I heard about that. Sad. An accident wasn't it? Up on the moor?'

Savage felt her heart flutter and a rushing sound come out of the dark and fill her ears. Fallon's words faded behind white noise as she struggled to focus. What was he up to? Why bring this up now? Realising he was probably trying to lay some sort of trap, she tried to remain calm and scrub all emotion from her voice.

'She was knocked off her bike,' she said, trying to keep the tone matter-of-fact, but hearing the quiver despite her best efforts.

'And they never caught the driver. No fucking justice in this world, is there?'

'Hit-and-run. The plates on the car were muddied up and I couldn't read them, didn't have time either.'

'Accident,' Fallon said the word again and spat a glob of saliva down to his right where it lay on the road and glistened in the moonlight. 'Apparently.'

'Get to the point will you? It is not a subject I like to dwell on.'

'Understandable. Got a daughter myself, you know? Anything happened to her . . .' Fallon moved his foot over the spit and scraped it into the ground.

'Look, if this is some sort of game then you can forget it. I'm not falling for—'

'Thing is, Charlotte, it wasn't as clear-cut as you think. Not the way the story came to me, anyhow.'

'What?' Her heart began to race again. 'You're just trying to get me wound up.'

'Not at all. This isn't business any more. Young girl like that, shouldn't be caught in the crossfire. Bad form. Not the way I do things. Not the way anybody should do things. Maybe it is the thought of the little gypsy kid, Simza. If I had known Owers had touched her . . . anyway as I said, I am doing you a favour.'

'Some favour!'

'If that's the way you feel then I'll—'

'No. Sorry.' Savage paused. She could almost visualise the noose Fallon was holding out, the crack marking the trapdoor in the floor. Still, she had to know. 'Go on, tell me.'

'I've got someone working on a name.' Fallon turned and strolled back to his vehicle. He paused before he got in. 'When I get an inkling, you'll be the first person I call. Goodnight, Charlotte.'

The door to the Range Rover clunked shut, the engine turned over and the lights went full beam, the glare so intense it caused Savage's eyes to water. She scrunched them shut and heard Fallon roar away. When she opened her eyes again the dark had closed in, a cool breeze slipping in through the open window and making her shiver as she turned the key in the ignition, the dashboard lights blurring in her tears as the car started and she pulled away.

Read on for an extract from

Mark Sennen's next novel,

Cut Dead, due in 2014

Prologue

Back then

The song ends and Mummy and Daddy clap. The candles on the cake flicker in the draught and Mummy tells you to blow them out. You lean forward and purse your lips, your baby brother moving alongside you to help, and you both puff for all your might. One, two, three, four, five, six. All out. The room plunges into darkness and you feel a sudden fear.

'Lights on!', Mummy says and Daddy switches the lights on and marches forward, the big knife in his hand, the blade shiny, sharp, ready for cutting.

The big knife lives in the kitchen, stuck to the wall above the cooker by magic. At least that's what Daddy calls it. The knife winks at you every time you pass by, a flash of light reflecting off the stainless steel, the glare mesmerising. You don't like being in the kitchen alone with the knife, especially not at night.

Because that's when the big knife talks to you.

'I am temptation,' it says. 'I am the explorer. I am the light.'

You've heard someone else speak like that too, in the cold of the church, but although the words are similar you don't think they can mean the same thing.

'OK, so who's going to have the first piece?' Daddy says and

for a moment you forget about the knife and instead concentrate on Daddy's words, knowing he is trying to trick you. You mustn't be greedy, must always be polite, if you aren't you'll get hit. You point to your brother. He smiles and claps his hands.

'Can I, Daddy, can I?'

'Of course you can, here, let's see.'

Daddy takes the knife and rests it on the white icing, using his other hand to push the blade down into the cake. He cuts again and then slides the knife under the cake and withdraws the slice. He stops. Doesn't give the piece to your brother after all. Daddy frowns. The inside doesn't look right, the yellow sponge is soft and mushy, not cooked properly. Daddy doesn't like that. He turns to Mummy and sneers at her.

'What's this?' Daddy's face reddens. 'I'm out working all day and you can't prepare a cake on this, of all days. Our special day. What do you think, boys?'

'Naughty Mummy, bad Mummy, naughty Mummy, bad Mummy.' You and your brother start the chant, the chant your Daddy has taught you. You hate singing the words, but if you don't there'll be trouble. There's been a lot of trouble in recent months because Daddy's changed in some way. You don't understand why, but you wonder if it's your fault, something you've done.

'Yes, boys. Naughty Mummy.'

Daddy steps forwards and slaps Mummy in the face. She raises her hands but it's too late. The blow catches her and knocks her sideways. Then Daddy has her by the hair. He is dragging her out of the room into the hall, pulling her up the stairs. Mummy is screaming and Daddy is shouting. They are upstairs now, the door to their bedroom slamming shut. You know what's going on up there because once you peeked through the keyhole. Daddy is doing something to Mummy and she doesn't like it. Afterwards Daddy will be sorry and Mummy will say everything is going to be alright, but this time you wonder if Mummy's words will come true because the big knife has gone. Daddy has taken it with him. You wonder how you will be able to cut the cake without it, but then you remember the cake is bad.

Your baby brother is crying and you tell him to pull himself together. You whisper the words Mummy says about everything being OK, but even as you say them you know they are lies. Parents lie to their children all the time. They tell them things called white lies. But there are other types of lies as well, other colours. You've learnt that.

'It's OK.' You repeat the words to your brother as you touch him on the shoulder, but you know something has changed today and nothing is ever going to be OK again.

Now

'Evening, Charlotte,' someone says as she climbs from the car. Another person nods. Not a greeting, just a simple recognition that she's here to share the load. The dirty work.

She walks across the field. Except it isn't a field, the mud is more sludge than earth, pools of water in footprints showing her the way from the gate to the tent. Not a tent for camping. Not a gas stove and plastic plates and mugs, squashed bread and sausages spitting in a frying pan. Not sleeping bags to slip into at night, snuggle down, cool air on face, stars above visible through the opening of the tent.

No, there are no stars tonight, only cloud from which rain tumbles in streams, as if from a million hosepipes. There are bags, yes, although these ones are black, the tent white, vertical sides flapping in the breeze, and inside the light comes not from a weak torch but from halogens. The people here aren't on holiday, not smiling, not laughing apart from one joke about the weather, the incessant rain, the lack of a decent bloody summer. Even then the laughter is nervous, not genuine, as if the banter which proceeded the joke was merely to take minds off the task in hand, away from the hole in the ground which the tent covers. But words can't do that, can't take her thoughts away from the horror down in the pit where a pump thrums, slurping water up a hose to discharge it a few metres away. A generator chugs somewhere in the background, and every now and then the halogens dim for a moment as the engine misses a beat.

She wonders who set this all up, who coordinated everything, who the hell is in charge of this nightmare. But really those details don't matter at the moment. The only thing that matters is that she doesn't throw up, doesn't cry, that she keeps her mind on the job.

Job, what a laugh. They don't pay her enough for this, couldn't. Nothing is worth this. Staring down into the hole, seeing the pitiful sight within, smelling the adipocere, thinking about her own little girl, dead years now. Thinking about her other children too, knowing she loves them more than anything. Knowing that nothing can be worse than this for a mother, for a parent, for anyone with an ounce of humanity inside them.

And while the others are talking, making comments, offering suggestions, she's letting her mind go blank, allowing just one thought in: a promise to the three souls dissolving down there in the clay that she will find who did this. A promise that she will do more than just find them.

Chapter One

Joanne Black had managed the farm for ten years, ever since her husband had run off and left her for a younger model. At first it had been a real struggle, a steep learning curve for a woman who had never even liked gardening and who used to get squeamish if the cat brought in a mouse. Needs must though, and within a few years she was looking after the five hundred acres as if she had been born to the task. Help had come from a neighbouring farmer and from her two workers, and if they had been sceptical at first they'd never showed it beyond a raised eyebrow or a 'are you sure about that Mrs Black?'

Ms Black.

She'd reverted to her maiden name when her husband had left and now she wondered why she had ever abandoned it in the first place. Why she had ever married Mr William Tosspot Granger as well.

The farm had come to them by way of an uncle who had no other relatives, and all those years ago the initial plan had been to sell it and do something with the money. But somewhere down inside, Joanne had felt that was wrong. She had visited Uncle Johnny as a child and remembered helping him bottle-feed an orphan lamb. 'He needs you, he does,' her uncle had said and Joanne felt a warmth in knowing that. Back home her mother said Joanne's eyes had sparkled when the lamb nuzzled the bottle and sucked down the milk. Somehow the uncle had seen that sparkle and years later, when writing his will, he'd taken a gamble. Right at the moment William and her had been going to see the land agent about selling the farm, Joanne had changed her mind. Taken a gamble too. Uncle Johnny may have thought Joanne was a long-shot, but hell, she was going to see to it that his bet paid off.

William had thought she was crazy. What did they know about farming? Wouldn't a couple of million in the bank be better than feeding lambs on a cold, frosty January morning?

No, it wouldn't.

Joanne chuckled to herself now as she opened the post. Bills, yes, but a letter from Tesco confirming a contract to supply them with organic lamb and two bookings for the holiday cottages. There was also a large cardboard tube. Joanne pulled off the end caps and extracted a roll of paper which turned out to be a poster. There was a note too: 'Hope you like this, sis. Happy Birthday, love Hal.' Hal was her brother and he lived in the US and worked for a large software company. Joanne unrolled the poster and gasped when she saw it was an aerial photograph of the entire farm. She had looked at maps on the web where you could load up such an image, but this was much better quality and at poster-size the detail was amazing.

Spreading the picture out on the kitchen table, Joanne spent a good ten minutes examining every last nook and cranny on the farm. It was while she was looking at one edge of the poster, where a corner of a field had been left to seed because the combine harvester couldn't turn in the odd little space, that she spotted a strange marking on the ground. She remembered how archaeologists used aerial pictures to find and map the extent of prehistoric monuments and wondered if the markings could be something similar. If it had been in the middle of the field she would have been worried about preservation orders and all sorts, but this was in a useless patch of muddy scrub.

Interesting.

She'd finish her coffee and then head out there on the quad bike, see what the ground looked like up close. Maybe there'd even be something worth finding there, like Saxon gold?

Two hours later, and if it *was* Saxon gold then Joanne was wondering whether somebody had got there before her.

'Here, Joanne?'

Jody, her farm worker, was manoeuvring the little mini-excavator into position at one end of the patch of earth. The excavator had a bucket claw on the end of an arm, the machine most often in use for digging drainage channels, and Jody had placed the claw above an area of disturbed ground.

Earlier, Joanne had zoomed down to the corner of the field on the quad bike and found the odd little piece of ground easily enough. She was surprised she had never seen it before, since the outline of a rectangle was visible where the dock and nettle and seedlings grew at a different density from the rest of the scrub. At one end of the rectangle the seedlings were this year's, the grass and weeds not so well established. Somebody had dug the muddy earth within the last twelve months or so. It was then she had decided to get Jody down with the digger.

Joanne nodded at Jody and the mechanical arm creaked as the claw hit the ground, the digger lifting for a moment before the shiny steel blades penetrated the top soil and Jody scooped up a bucketful of earth, swinging the digger round and dumping the spoil to one side.

Twenty minutes later the hole was a metre deep and about the same square and still they could tell they hadn't reached the bottom of the disturbance. Joanne began to think the exercise was futile, not the best use of Jody's time nor hers. She looked at the heavy clouds: imminent rain. Time to give up and head for a cup of tea. Even as she thought it little specks started to fall from the sky. 'Pittering' her uncle used to say. Next it would be pattering and then the heavens would open.

'Joanne?'

She turned to where Jody had deposited the last bucket of soil. Amongst the earth and stones a piece of fabric stood out, the shiny red incongruous against the grey-brown sludge. She moved over to the spoil heap and peered at the scrap of material. Saxon? Unlikely, she thought, not in nylon. And not with a Topshop label either.

'Fuck!'

Jody didn't often swear. Maybe when he thwacked his thumb with a hammer when fencing or if a cow trod on his foot, but otherwise never. Joanne looked back into the hole to see what had caused him to utter the obscenity.

The arm had pushed up through the mud, as if reaching out and upwards, trying to escape from entombment or maybe trying to cling onto the piece of clothing, the last vestiges of their dignity. Slimy water sloshed around the limb and nearby the round curve of a breast stuck out like an island on an ocean of grey. Joanne stared into the abyss, for all of a sudden that was what the hole was, and at the same time her hand groped in her coat pocket for her mobile. She pulled the phone out, a finger going to the keypad and pressing the number nine three times, and when a man with a calm voice answered she was surprised to find she responded in the same manner.

'Police,' she said.

And then she began to scream.

DI Charlotte Savage carried yet another plastic crate from the car into the house and through to the kitchen where her husband, Pete, was unpacking. She dumped the crate on the floor, and he looked over at her and shook his head.

'One more and that's it,' Savage said, before turning and going back to the car.

The summer half-term holiday had turned into an ordeal after the weather had delivered nearly a week of blustery conditions. Sunshine and showers would have been OK had they remained at home, but instead they'd opted to have a week sailing. Their little boat was cosy with two, but cramped with four, and if you added in a good measure of rain, a moody teenager and a bored six-year-old the situation became untenable.

Pete had insisted on sailing east from Plymouth rather than begin the holiday with a beat into the wind, saying the weather was forecast to change, giving them an easy run home. On the way east they had stopped overnight at Salcombe and Dartmouth, ending their journey at Brixham. The rain had come then and the weather worsened as two lows in quick succession came from out of the west, the latter developing into a nasty gale. Because of time constraints they'd set out from Brixham as soon as the second low passed, intending to do the journey back to Plymouth in one hop. Once they had rounded Berry Head though the weather deteriorated and they put into Dartmouth again. A phone call home and Stefan came out in their car and swapped places with Savage and the kids, the idea being that

Pete and him would bring the boat back whatever the conditions while Savage took the kids home. Stefan was the family's unofficial au pair and a semi-professional sailor. With Pete having been twenty years in the Royal Navy – the last five as commander of a frigate – the two of them thought nothing of bringing the boat back to Plymouth in a near gale.

She'd waited for two hours down at the marina for them to arrive and eventually a call came through from Pete saying they were at the breakwater at the edge of Plymouth Sound. Twenty minutes later, Savage stood on the pontoon and took their lines, Jamie, her son, shouting to his dad that he didn't look so clever. Stefan was grinning.

'Remind me never to go to sea with him again.' Pete pointed at Stefan. 'He's crazy.'

'The trouble with you, you old softy,' Stefan said, 'is that you are used to wearing your carpet slippers when you helm a boat.'

'The forecast said seven decreasing five or six,' Pete said, as he repositioned a fender. 'But it was a full gale force eight and the waves came up from the south out of nowhere.'

'They look a bit bigger when you are looking up at them instead of down, don't they?' Stefan said, still smiling as he threw Savage another rope.

The call came at around seven that evening as she was clearing the last of the enormous spaghetti bolognese from her plate. The brusque tone of Detective Superintendent Conrad Hardin rumbled down the line, his voice breaking up as he tried to find a signal for his mobile.

'Three of them, Charlotte,' he said. 'Three. Understand? Never seen anything like . . . don't know how . . . need to try and . . .'

'Sir?'

'Bere Peninsula, Charlotte.' The signal strong for a moment, Hardin's voice clear. 'Tavy View Farm. Nesbit is there, John Layton too, a whole contingent descending on the place, media as well. Bloody nightmare. Meet you in an hour, OK?'

Savage eased the car down the lane past a BBC outside-broadcast vehicle and a white van, nudged into a space behind the familiar shape of Layton's Volvo, and killed the engine. The car settled into the soft verge, the rain glittering in the headlights before she switched them off too. A bang on the roof startled her and she looked through her window to see the bulky figure of DSupt Hardin standing alongside. He tapped on the glass and she lowered the window, Hardin bending to the opening and apologising for calling her out.

'You know how it is, Charlotte,' he said. 'Thing like this needs quality officers on board. Can't afford to muck this one up because it's going to be something big. And I don't mean in a good way, get my drift?'

'Sir?'

'Best see for yourself. Across the field. Hope you brought your wellies.'

Hardin stood and walked away, disappearing into the dark for a moment before he reached a circle of light where a uniformed officer in a yellow waterproof was arguing with a woman. Savage noted the little black on white letters on the woman's jacket: BBC. Seemed like even the Beeb didn't respect the right for privacy these days.

Savage got out of the car and put on waterproofs and then a white coverall. A pair of boots completed the outfit and she trudged down the lane to Hardin. Just next to the lights the rear doors on a police transit stood open. Inside, the interior resembled a mini-office and John Layton, their senior Crime Scene Investigator, sat at a desk with another officer. On a laptop in front of them a schematic drawing of some kind overlaid a large scale map of the area. Layton was shaking his head, fussing over some minuscule detail in his characteristic manner.

'Charlotte,' he said, noticing her for the first time. 'Go and take a look.'

'You sure?'

'Sure I'm sure. The place is a complete mess already, nothing left to preserve. Besides, we've established a safe entry route. The field is too wet for my stepping plates, stupid little things are sinking right down into the mud, but we nicked a load of pallets from up in the farmyard and laid them down. Looks bloody stupid, but it was all I could think of. Got some proper walkways coming later, if we need them, but doing any type of fingertip search in this quagmire is going to be nigh on impossible. Here, sign yourself in. You'll need this too.'

Layton handed her a torch and an electronic pad and she scrawled her name before turning away and walking past the van to a gateway. Another uniformed officer in bright waterproofs stood in the gateway, water running down off the peak of his hood and dripping onto his nose.

'Evening, ma'am,' he sniffed. 'Nearly mid summer, so I heard. Reckon my calendar must have been printed wrong.'

Savage nodded and continued past, switching on the torch and finding and following a line of tape leading into the darkness. Several sets of footprints had filled with water and the torchlight picked out their muddied surface. In the distance something glowed white, almost welcoming in the way it provided a beacon to aim for.

Savage squelched on until she came to Layton's makeshift stepping plates: a number of pallets laid in a line which curled away from the edge of the field and towards the white glow. Closer now, and Savage could see what she already knew: the glow came from a forensic shelter. White nylon with blue mudflaps at the base. The chug, chug, chug of a small generator didn't blot out the noise of the pitter-patter of rain on the shelter's fabric nor the low hum of conversation coming from within the tent.

A figure in a white coverall stood at the entrance and Savage recognised the wisp of blonde hair coming from beneath the hood as belonging to DC Jane Calter. She tapped the detective on the shoulder. Calter turned.

'Hello, ma'am.' Calter pointed to the centre of the tent. 'Not my idea of a Friday night out to be honest.'

Savage peered in, shielding her eyes against the glare from the halogens, painful after the darkness. You could only call the excavation a pit, hole didn't do the yawning void justice. One of Layton's CSIs stood up to her neck in the pit, her PPE suit splattered grey-brown with gunge. Savage moved closer, realising as she did so that somebody else was down there. A face looked up at her, mud caked thick on grey eyebrows above little round glasses.

'Charlotte.' Andrew Nesbit, the pathologist, knelt at the bottom of the shaft. No jokes today. Face as grim as the weather. 'Never a nice time, but this . . .'

Savage moved to the edge of the hole where scaffold boards had been placed around the top to stop the edges giving way. Nesbit's arm gestured across the sludge and Savage breathed in hard at what she saw.

Three of them, Hardin had said. But the 'them' implied something you could recognise as human. Whatever was down there in the mud looked a long, long way from that.

'Bodies only,' Nesbit said. 'No heads. And by the look of things on this first one, no genitals either.'

'Christ,' Savage heard herself mutter under her breath, not really knowing why. The reference to a higher being was futile. No God could exist in a world alongside this sort of horror. 'Male? Female?'

'All females I think and they're . . .'

'What?'

'Markings, I guess. On one of them at least.' Nesbit moved a hand down and wiped sludge away from one of the grey forms. 'Cut lines. Dozens of the things.'

'That killed them?'

'No idea, not here. We'll need to get them out to discover that, only . . .'

'Only what?'

'Nothing. I can't be sure, not yet.' Nesbit stood, shook his head and then moved to the aluminium ladder and began to clamber from the hole. 'I do know one thing though.

'Andrew?' Savage cursed Nesbit, hoped he wasn't playing games with her. 'What is it?'

Nesbit stared down in to the mud, shook his head once more and then looked at Savage, something like desperation in his eyes. Then he seemed to get hold of himself. Smiled.

'I'm getting too old for this, Charlotte. Much too old.'

Chapter Two

Today the big knife is safe at home. You never take it with you on your missions. That would be much too dangerous. The knife has a mind of its own and can only be allowed to come out on one day a year. The Special Day. Not far off now. Not long to wait. There's just the small matter of selecting your victim. Truth be told though this one, like all the others, selected herself. Free will. A wonderful thing. But people should use it wisely, make their choices with care. And accept the consequences of their decisions.

You watch as she steps out of her house, the blue gloss door swinging shut, closing on the life she led before. She turns to lock the deadlock. Click. Can't be too careful these days. You like that. A sensible girl. Not that it makes any difference. Sensible or not, she's yours and nothing anyone can do or say will make any difference.

At the curb she looks up the street and waves at a neighbour. Exchanges a greeting. An au revoir, she'd call it, being a French teacher. You'd call it a goodbye.

The little blue Toyota she gets into matches the colour of the front door. It's a Yaris. 1.2 sixteen valve. List price nine five four nine. But you'd get it for a touch under seven K if you were prepared to haggle. The colour match is a nice touch, intentional or not. It's little things like that which catch your attention. Simple things. Serendipity. Chance. These days so much else is too complicated to understand.

Like your dishwasher.

The thought comes to your mind even as you know you should be concentrating on the girl. Only you can't now. Not when you are considering the dishwasher problem.

This morning you came down to breakfast to find the machine had gone wrong. You took a screwdriver to the rear and pulled the cover off, expecting to find a few tubes and a motor, something easy to fix.

No.

Microchips. And wire. Little incy wincy threads of blue and gold and red and black and green and yellow and purple weaving amongst white plastic actuator switches and shut-off valves. Pumps and control units, fuses and God-knows-what.

Except God doesn't know. Not any more. That's the problem.

Once he knew everything. Then man came along and took over God's throne, claimed to know everything. Now nobody knows everything.

You called the dishwasher repair guy out to take a look. He knows dishwashers. What about TVs?

You asked him as he worked on the machine and he said 'no, not TVs.'

His words worried you, but then you remembered you don't have a TV. You never liked the way the bits of the picture fly through the air into the set. That means pieces of people's bodies are passing through you. Not just their teeth and hair – the nice bits you see on the screen – but their shit and piss, their stomach contents. All of it has to come from the studio to your house and the thought of the stuff floating around your living room makes you gag.

'Fridges?' you said, swallowing a mouthful of spit.

'Yes, fridges. Can find my way around a fridge. At least to grab a tinny or two.'

The way he smiled and then laughed you weren't sure if he was joking or not. Hope not. You don't like jokes. At least not ones like that.

'Microwave ovens? Specifically a Zanussi nine hundred watt with browning control. The turntable doesn't work.'

'Not really, no.'

'What about chainsaws? I've got a Stihl MS241. Eighteen inch blade. Runs but there is a lack of power when cutting through anything thicker than your arm.'

The dishwasher man didn't answer, just gave you an odd look and put his tools away. Drew up an invoice which you paid in cash.

You looked at the invoice and noted the man's address in case the machine went wrong again. The man left the house and got in a van with the registration WL63 DMR. Drove off.

The girl!

Now she's driving off too, the blue Toyota disappearing round the corner.

That's OK. Cars run on roads the way the electricity flows in wires inside the dishwasher. Each wire goes to the correct place and each road does too. The road you are interested in goes left at the end, then straight on through three sets of traffic lights. Third exit on the roundabout. First right, second left and pull up in the car park. Usually she takes the first bay next to the big metal bin unless the headmaster has decided to bring in something heavy in which case he parks there so he can unload. Then she'll have a dilemma and might park in any one of the other forty-seven spaces. But you really don't need to worry about that now.

No, you'll see her again in a few days. Up close. And personal. Very personal.